WHITE WITCH
A NOVEL

BY LARRY D. THOMPSON

STORY MERCHANT BOOKS
LOS ANGELES
2018

STORY MERCHANT BOOKS

Copyright © 2018 by Larry D. Thompson. All rights reserved.

No part of this book may be reproduced or transmitted in any form or by any means, electronic or mechanical, including photocopying, recording, or by any information storage and retrieval system, without the express written permission of the author.

www.larrydthompson.com

ISBN: 978-0-9991621-5-6

Story Merchant Books
400 S. Burnside Avenue #11B
Los Angeles, CA 90036

www.storymerchantbooks.com

Cover & interior formatting by IndieDesignz.com

This is a work of fiction. Names, characters, organizations, places, events and incidents are either products of the author's imagination or are used fictitiously.

ALSO BY LARRY D. THOMPSON

DEAD PEASANTS – THE JACK BRYANT SERIES
THE TRIAL
SO HELP ME GOD
THE INSANITY PLEA
DARK MONEY – BOOK 2 IN *THE JACK BRYANT SERIES*

This is for my son, Kel, who introduced me to the *White Witch*

THE BALLAD OF ANNIE PALMER

(1973)

By Johnny Cash

On the Island of Jamaica quite a long, long time ago
At Rose Hall Plantation where the ocean breezes blow
Lived a girl named Annie Palmer the mistress of the place
And the slaves all lived in fear to see a frown on Annie's face

Where's your husband Annie where's number two and three
Are they sleeping 'neath the palms beside the Caribbean Sea
At night I hear you ridin' and I hear your lovers call
And still can feel your presence round the great house at Rose Hall

Well if you should ever go to see the great house at Rose Hall
There's expensive chairs and china and great paintings on the wall
They'll show you Annie's sitting room and the whipping post outside
But they won't let you see the room where Annie's husbands died
Where's your husband Annie...

PROLOGUE

ROSE HALL PLANTATION, JAMAICA (1812)

The sun seemed to burn its way through the Jamaican sky, stopping only when it hit the several hundred slaves working this part of the plantation. The male slaves were dressed in filthy, gray pants with no shirts. The women wore tattered gingham dresses with patch pockets, equally dirty. So far on this day, five slaves had passed out from heat exhaustion. The other slaves knew they must leave them where they collapsed. No time was allowed for dragging them to the stream for water or finding the shade of a tree at the edge of the field. Only if they were still alive at the next break were the others permitted to assist the fallen. The younger female slaves fashioned slings to carry their babies. None had shoes. Rudyard, the overseer—a large black man who was fortunate to have a wide brimmed hat—rode a brown mare that appeared to receive much better care than the slaves. He allowed a ten-minute break in the morning and the afternoon and twenty minutes for lunch. Otherwise the slaves, male and female, worked at cutting the sugar cane from early morning until the sun began to set over the Caribbean Sea. Since it was approaching midday, Rudyard periodically glanced at the sun and finally shouted, "Break, twenty-minute break. Leave your tools and machetes where they are. If you have any biscuits or bread crusts you can eat them. You know Miss Annie don't feed you any lunch. I know you want water. You can go up to the stream. Be back to work in twenty minutes. Hear?"

Some of the younger slaves hurried to the creek, which wound its way through the forest and the plantation before flowing into the ocean. They chose to walk to the edge of the forest where the trees shaded the stream and lowered the temperature of the water several degrees. They dropped to their bellies with their hands directing the water into their mouths. Once their thirst was quenched, they lay in the shade beside the stream. Some had a crust of bread in their pocket, which they ate, savoring each bite. The older ones—a few around thirty years of age, maybe one or two close to forty with sunburned, creased faces—shuffled toward the stream and waited for a place to open. Several stayed behind to check on the ones who had collapsed in the heat.

JaDon, one of the young males, waited for his mate, Ruth, who carried their baby in a sling, to drink as much as she could hold. He helped her to her feet and motioned his head toward the forest. Ruth nodded as they stepped across the stream. Others saw what they were doing and knew that if they did not call out, they would be put to death. As JaDon, Ruth, and the baby slipped behind the undergrowth, one of the men shouted, "Rudyard, JaDon and Ruth are trying to escape. They're probably headed for the Maroon Trail."

Rudyard wheeled his horse around and galloped to the plantation house. He jerked the horse to a stop behind the mansion and shouted, "Miss Annie, Miss Annie, escape, escape!"

Annie Palmer, a petite young white woman dressed in a long sleeved white shirt, an ankle length brown skirt, and riding boots, stepped onto a small balcony on the second level. She yelled to a slave in the house, "Manford, get Rudyard a musket. If they're on the Maroon Trail they will come to that opening in the forest any time now."

Behind the mansion the house slaves had heard the noise and were milling around in the yard below, some pointing off in the direction of the rain forest and occasionally casting sideways glances at the balcony. A gallows sat prominently in the center of the yard, the message clear: *Disobedience will be met with swift punishment.*

A gray-haired slave dressed in a white shirt buttoned to the neck, black pants, and black shoes, ran from the house and handed the musket to Rudyard, who turned and galloped up the hill toward the clearing. Before he could get there, the runaways burst from the forest. Knowing he could not get to the trail before they disappeared into the forest on the other side, he stopped the horse, took a deep breath, and aimed for the male slave. He said a prayer that he would be accurate, knowing that failing in this task could bring the ire of the White Witch down on him, and pulled the trigger. The man crumpled just at the edge of the forest.

JaDon forced himself to his feet. "Ruth, you and the baby need to keep going. Follow the trail. I hear it's a steep climb but well-marked. If you can get to Accompong, you'll be safe."

"I'm not going to leave you."

"You must. If you don't, both of us will die." He pulled a knife that he had hidden in his pants pocket. "I can hold them off for a few minutes. I love you."

Ruth sighed as she kissed him. After a lingering hug, she made sure the baby was secure and disappeared into the forest. As she did so, Rudyard dismounted. By then, other slaves were arriving. JaDon was bleeding from a wound in his side. He tried to maintain his balance as he waved the knife in the direction of Rudyard.

"Drop it, JaDon," Rudyard ordered.

JaDon looked down the hill to the mansion and gallows. "I'd rather you shoot me right here than be hanged. I'll lower my knife if you'll re-load your gun and put a bullet in my heart."

While Rudyard was an overseer, he was a slave himself and knew that JaDon was only asking for a quick and painless death. He nodded and pulled a paper cartridge from his shirt pocket. He half-cocked the musket, bit off the end of the cartridge paper, and poured some of the gunpowder into the pan. Next, he poured the remainder of the powder down the muzzle and pushed the paper cartridge behind it. Last came the bullet. Then he took the rod from its place alongside the barrel and pushed it into the barrel. While he was loading the musket, JaDon bent at the waist, managing to stay on his feet by putting his hands on his knees.

The other slaves stopped a few feet from Rudyard and watched his preparations. When he was done, he asked, "Any last words, JaDon?"

"Only that Ruth and our baby girl make it to the safety of the Cockpit Country." He forced himself upright and stood at attention, facing Rudyard with his eyes wide open.

Rudyard raised the musket and fired, knocking the young slave back several feet. The other slaves surrounded him. "Bring him down to the yard beside the gallows." Rudyard mounted his horse and rode back to the mansion.

The other field slaves had joined the house slaves below the balcony where Annie Palmer stood. When Rudyard dismounted, he handed the musket to Manford. Annie Palmer stared at him, anger filling her face. "I saw what you did. You showed him mercy and killed him up there instead of letting me watch him die here. I should have you hung in his place."

Rudyard said nothing.

"But I'm not. Instead, you will receive one hundred lashes. Justin, get the whip from the dungeon." She pointed to two others. "You get a rope and tie him to the gallows. When Justin returns, I'll at least get the satisfaction of watching his punishment."

Rudyard took off his shirt and leaned against the gallows while his wrists were tied to the boards. "Justin, can you count to one hundred?"

"No, Miss Annie."

"Then, I'll do it." She looked over the yard now full of slaves. "Watch this carefully. My punishment is swift and without mercy. Go ahead, Justin. And if I think you let up at any time, you'll be taking Rudyard's place."

Justin started flogging Rudyard as the witch counted in a loud voice.

"One hundred," Annie Palmer shouted with a smile on her face. "You can untie him and take him back to his hut in the slave quarters." Then she glanced around at the slaves below until her gaze stopped. She pointed to a handsome male slave and motioned him to go into the back of the mansion. The slave trembled when he saw she was pointing him out, having heard stories of what was to come.

The second floor of the great house was filled with bedrooms. Only one, the largest, was occupied. Annie Palmer's room faced the Caribbean Sea that lapped ashore about a quarter of a mile down the mountain from Rose Hall. The deep blue of the water was reflected by a lighter blue sky, dotted with white clouds that floated above the ocean. The open windows always provided a pleasant breeze to cool her boudoir and the four-poster bed that occupied the center of the room.

A graying house slave pushed the young male in front of him to Annie Palmer's bedroom, shoved him inside, and shut the door. Annie Palmer was standing at the foot of the bed. The slave glanced around the bedroom, eyed the open windows, and backed into a corner.

"What's your name, boy?" Annie asked with a smile on her face.

"Ah, Alwon, Miss Annie."

"Don't be frightened, Alwon. You'll enjoy this. I'm always aroused by watching torture. It is disappointing that Rudyard didn't die."

Annie started with the top button of her shirt and slowly, sensuously removed it, revealing a pink corset. The corset came next, exposing full breasts with aroused nipples. Alwon looked for somewhere to run, rushed to the windows, and realized the drop could kill him. Instead, he dived under the bed.

"Alwon, out here right now. Help me with my boots."

Alwon extracted himself from his hiding place. Annie sat on the bed as Alwon kneeled at her feet and unlaced her boots, never glancing above Annie's knees. As the second boot was removed, Annie directed him to sit on the bed. She rose, unfastened the buttons on the side of her skirt and slid it and a petticoat to the floor. Next, she put a hand behind her head and pulled on a comb, releasing her long, black hair to cascade over her breasts. She stood naked beside the bed.

"Now, Alwon, let me remove your pants." As she unbuttoned them, she caressed the young slave who became more frightened when he realized he could not control his erection.

Afterward, Annie lay on the bed beside Alwon who had fallen asleep, snoring quietly. She studied him for a moment, then rose and walked to a small glass topped table where she retrieved a dagger. A carving of a serpent wound itself around the handle with the snake's head at the top. The eyes of the snake were two rubies. She returned to the bed and stared once more at Alwon's sleeping form. Then, as if in a trance, she raised the dagger with both hands and plunged it into Alwon's heart. When she turned to put on her clothes, the sun came through the window, causing the serpent's eyes to flash in the afternoon light as if they were alive.

***

Ruth had climbed only thirty or forty yards up the trail when she heard voices below. She stopped to listen, and her baby started crying. She pulled the girl around to her chest and exposed her breast. The baby became quiet as she suckled the milk from her mother. Then she heard the shot. Tears filled her eyes, and she said a quiet prayer for her mate. When the baby was finished, she rose from the trail and started the climb once again. She had no idea where she was going or how long it might take to get there. At each stream she drank and chewed a crust of bread. As night fell, she was first cold, and then frightened. She found a tree close to a stream and lowered herself beside it, hoping that the stream might camouflage her scent and the sounds from her baby. After she wrapped the infant with the sling, she wrapped her arms around the child and shivered throughout the night, dozing only occasionally and very briefly. At the first light of dawn, she fed her child and once more started the climb. As the day wore on, she continued to climb, hoping at every turn in the trail she would see a village. Soon, she was stopping more often and longer. Still she refused to quit. The light was beginning to fade from her second day on the trail when she pushed through underbrush and saw the village. It must be Accompong, she thought. She walked timidly toward the huts until an old woman saw her. The woman rushed to Ruth and took the baby.

"You and your child are now safe. You are among the Maroons. I'll take you to my home and warm some broth for you. Once you are rested, we'll help you build a hut. You are now a Maroon."

Ruth smiled briefly before she fainted and fell to the ground. The old woman called for help and was soon surrounded by other Maroons who picked Ruth up and followed the woman.

****

Rudyard was barely conscious when he was dragged to the sleeping mat in his hut. His mate and family laid him on his stomach. He pointed to a box he had built that contained several shelves filled with leaves, roots, dried flowers, and an assortment of berries and nuts. "Heat those leaves in boiling water and put them across my back. If I cry out in pain from the heat, so much the better. Then, when it is dark, go into the forest and bring back as many of those leaves as you can find. I may sleep for two or three days. Just keep heating the leaves and apply them to the cuts. When I awaken, I'll be better."

Rudyard's wife, daughter and two sons did as he directed. When he awoke briefly on the second day, he pointed to some dark berries on the shelf. "Make a tea from those and give it to me every time I wake up."

Rudyard was an *Obeah* priest who knew and understood the ways of the mystical. He was also a bush doctor, capable of treating many sicknesses of his people. Now he applied that knowledge to heal himself. In a week he was able to sit up; in two he could stand and walk a few steps around the slave quarters. When he could sit, he called Mariah, his daughter, to sit with him. "Where is Alwon? Has he been here while I was sleeping?"

Alwon was Mariah's mate. She carried his child. "I haven't seen him since the day you were beaten. Some of the others saw the witch summon him into her house."

Rudyard slammed his fists on the mat beside him. "Dammit. We know what she does when she takes a young slave into the house. I've talked with Manford. She forces him to have sex, and when she tires of the sex she kills him or orders him taken to the dungeon where she watches as other slaves torture him to death. I'm sorry, Mariah, but this has been going on for too long. Once or twice a month one of our strong, muscular men disappears. Manford told me in confidence that the house slaves are forbidden to talk. Everyone else is terrified of her. I am not, and I'm going to put a stop to it."

"How can you do that?"

"Annie Palmer learned the ways of *Obeah* when she lived in Haiti. Only another person skilled in the occult can kill her. You know I possess those powers. You also have them. Up until now I have used such power only for good. But times have changed. When I am sufficiently well, I will kill her. And one more thing—before I do, I want you to leave in the dead of night, only when there is a full moon, and make your way to the Maroon Trail. We will prepare a pack with food and water sufficient for three days. Ruth climbed that trail with a baby and a few crusts of bread. Hopefully, she is now safe. You can make it. You must make it if you want a life other than that of a slave. Understood?"

Mariah grimaced at the thought of the journey, but knew she must do it. "I understand."

Two weeks later when the moon was full, Rudyard walked Mariah to the edge of the forest. He handed her a pack with a sling. A woolen shawl covered her shoulders. "Take this trail for about a hundred yards and you will meet the Maroon Trail. It's larger and wider. You should be in Accompong by tomorrow night. And you must know that tomorrow night the moon will still be full. I am going to kill the witch. We won't see each other again."

Mariah had held back her tears. Now they flowed like one of the mountain streams. "I won't see you or my brothers or mom again?"

Rudyard pulled his daughter to his chest. "No, but you will be giving a better life to your baby. And remember that as an *Obeah* woman, you must teach the *Obeah* ways to your child. They have been handed down through generations since our ancestors were kidnapped from their homes in Africa. You and your child and your children's children must carry on that tradition."

***

The full moon shown on the slave quarters that were now dark and quiet except for a small fire in front of Rudyard's hut, where he and four muscular young men talked quietly.

"No, Jackson, you need not be frightened. All the four of you are to do is dig a grave," Rudyard said as he pointed to four white crosses. "I have prepared the crosses. Once the grave is ready, I will go into the house and kill the White Witch. Since she is an *Obeah* priestess, once she is in the grave and her body covered with dirt we will plant these four crosses at each corner of her grave. That's the *Obeah* way. Once the crosses are in place, her soul cannot escape."

"Won't there be guards and house slaves around the mansion tonight?"

Rudyard shook his head. "She sends them away at night. She likes her privacy and is confident that no one would risk certain death by trying to kill an *Obeah* priestess. I have no such fear." He glanced up to the sky and studied the moon. "The time is now. Each of you take a shovel from that pile beside my hut."

They walked the two hundred yards on a path that was trod daily by the slaves. When they approached the gallows, Rudyard pointed to a light glowing from the second floor. "She's there. Manford says she reads in bed every night. We're going over here to the side of the mansion to dig her grave."

He pointed to an area at the side and walked two strides. "Two strides long and one wide. Six feet deep. Get to digging. I'm putting the white crosses here. Now, I must put myself in a trance to summon mystical powers. When I see you are finished, I will enter the mansion. Wait by the gallows until you see me appear on the balcony."

When the grave was complete, Rudyard walked to the back of the mansion and tried the door which he knew would be unlocked. He crept up the back stairs to the second floor, pleased that only one board creaked. He stepped across the hall, took a deep breath, and threw open the door to the White Witch's bedroom.

"Rudyard, what are you doing in my bedroom?" Annie Palmer demanded. When she saw his eyes, she realized he was in a trance. She closed her book and stared at it. The book rose and flew across the room, directly at Rudyard's head. He stepped aside, and it slammed into the wall behind him. He spied a pitcher on a table by the window and commanded it to hurtle through the air at the witch. Annie Palmer realized she was at a disadvantage as she lay in the bed. She threw the covers off and they landed like a drape over Rudyard, covering him from head to toe. He tossed them aside and turned his eyes to a portrait on the wall which flew at Annie. She ducked and it clattered against the bed's headboard. As it did so, she spotted her snake dagger on the nightstand. Before Rudyard could move, she commanded it to rise and fly into his heart. Rudyard cried out in pain and anger as he charged the White Witch. He wrapped his big hands around her neck and squeezed until she breathed no more. Knowing he was dying, he stumbled with her in his arms to the balcony and threw her over. As he did so, he said, "Remember to bury her the way I told you."

Then Rudyard died and tumbled over the balcony rail to the ground below. Three slaves started to run, but were stopped by Jackson. "We must bury her."

"I don't want to touch her," a second slave said.

"Look, she's dead. So is Rudyard." Jackson went to the witch and picked the tiny woman up in his arms, carried her to the grave, and unceremoniously dropped her into it. "Now, you don't have to touch her. Get your shovels."

The four young men did as they were told, quickly covering the witch with dirt. Then, one of them stopped. "What about her dagger? It's in Rudyard's chest. I hear it has its own magic powers."

"I'll get it," Jackson said. He walked over to Rudyard's body, extracted the dagger and returned to the grave where he dropped it beside the witch's body. The slaves shoveled for five more minutes when one said, "That's enough. I'm getting out of here. I want to be in my hut when she's found."

The other three looked at him and dropped their shovels. Jackson looked at the grave and the mound of dirt that was now piled above the surrounding earth. He nodded, dropped his shovel and ran with the others back to the slave quarters.

The four white crosses lay on the ground where Rudyard had left them.

CHAPTER 1

A white pickup pulled off a narrow blacktop highway in rural Arkansas, crossed a gravel parking lot, and stopped in front of a doublewide trailer. The pickup had a Global American Metals logo on the doors. Will Taylor was driving. He completed a cell phone conversation as he pulled the key from the ignition. Rodney Gore fidgeted on the seat beside him.

"Yeah," Will spoke into the cell phone, "he said the serial numbers matched. We're in the parking lot. I'll bring it over after Rodney checks it out." Will clicked the phone off and nodded to Rodney. Both left the pickup.

Will was in his mid-thirties, standing slightly over six feet. Brown hair, close cropped, outlined a face with blue eyes, a prominent yet handsome nose, and a mouth with the beginnings of laugh lines on either side. Anyone looking at his chest and biceps would know that he hit the gym hard three or four times a week.

Rodney was a computer geek who fit the definition to a tee. As tall as Will, he had stooped shoulders, probably from years of bending over a computer screen. Black horn-rimmed glasses matched his black hair. His body hadn't seen the inside of a gym since high school physical education class.

They glanced at a hand-scrawled sign above the door announcing the *Jolly Hocker Pawn Shop*. Upon entering, the men encountered what appeared to be a junk shop. Boxes filled with books, plates, kitchen utensils, and shop tools littered the floor. They were joined by microwave ovens, old golf clubs, tarnished musical instruments, televisions of assorted sizes, and floor lamps. Clock radios covered with dust filled three shelves. Guitars lined the walls. A glass case contained computers, pistols, rings, bracelets, and a few old GPS devices. On the wall behind the counter were an assortment of shotguns and rifles.

A bell rang when Will and Rodney stepped inside. At the same time a gap-toothed man with flaming red hair, wearing a white T-shirt labeled *Jolly Hocker,* came through a curtain behind the counter. A toothpick hung from the side of his mouth.

"You the Jolly Hocker?" Will asked.

"That's me. Name's Jeff. What can I do for y'all?"

"I called about the laptop."

Jeff looked puzzled, like he never got a call about a computer.

"I just called an hour ago," Will continued, not trying to hide his exasperation.

"The Dell Inspirion, serial number 6547895."

Jeff reached into the glass case and pulled out a computer. "Oh, yeah, man. Got it right here. Cost you $400."

Will glanced at the small tag hanging from the laptop and saw $100 marked on it. "Then why the hell does the tag say a hundred bucks?"

"Price went up."

Rodney was beginning to get nervous as he witnessed the confrontation escalating. "Will, just pay him. It's company money anyway."

Will's eyes flashed as he stared at the man behind the counter. "That laptop is stolen property."

"Near everything in here is stolen," Jeff laughed. "Hell, I done stole most of it myself. This is a pawn shop, man. It's $400."

Will reached for his wallet, extracted a hundred-dollar bill, and dropped it on the counter, then picked up the laptop.

"Hey, dude, you pay the $400 or you'll be the one who's stealing. If you leave with the laptop, I'll shoot your sorry ass. My brother-in-law's a deputy in these parts. He'll stand up for me."

Ignoring the owner, Will put the laptop under his arm and turned to walk away. Rodney's eyes bounced back and forth between the two as he took a step backwards.

The Jolly Hocker was no longer jolly. He reached into the case, pulled out a pistol, and pointed it at Will. "One last time. It's four hundred bucks!"

"Holy shit," Rodney yelled.

Will appeared to relent. "Okay, okay. Just let me get the rest out of my wallet." Will put the laptop back on the counter and reached for his wallet. Jeff relaxed and lowered his gun slightly as Will took out three one hundred-dollar bills. Jeff grabbed for the money, and Will let one of the bills slip. When it fluttered to the counter, Jeff looked down. That was the only opening Will needed. He twisted the gun out of the Jolly Hocker's grip with one hand and used the other to grab Jeff's hair and smash his face into the counter. He picked up the laptop and the money, then shoved the pistol into Jeff's mouth.

"Now you just lost the hundred bucks as well as this pistol. You try anything or contact your brother-in-law, and I'll be back. Then, you'll lose your life too. You understand?"

Jeff used his T-shirt to wipe blood from his nose and face, but nodded his understanding.

"Come on, Rodney. We got what we came for. Let's get out of here."

The Jolly Hocker followed them to the door and studied their license plate as they drove away. Then, he punched in a number on his cell phone.

CHAPTER 2

Will drove past a sign that said *Global American Metals Bauxite Mine 28.* Behind it was a modern construction trailer outfitted with satellite dishes on the roof. Beyond the trailer were miles of barren, red tinged earth. On the edges of the strip mine a thick forest of oaks and pines continued to grow…a reminder of what the mine once looked like. In the distance, giant front-end loaders were scooping up dirt and dropping it into even larger dump trucks.

When they turned to park in front of the construction trailer, Rodney asked, "Isn't there a way we could mine this bauxite and still not tear up the place like this?"

"Yeah," Will replied. "There probably is, but it would get too expensive and drive the price of beer cans out of sight. Alexa's only interested in the bottom line, not the loss of trees, animal habitat, and spotted owls. When we're finished here, she'll have someone smooth out the land, toss out some seeds, and claim that in about five hundred years the owls will be back."

Will and Rodney left the pickup, walked up two wooden steps, and entered the trailer. Sam Serano, the mine supervisor, sat behind a large desk at one end, comparing satellite images on a computer with a map of the mine on the wall. As they entered, he looked up. "You get it?"

Will tossed the laptop on Sam's desk, took a seat on one of the chairs facing Sam, and propped his boots on the corner of the desk.

"Will, take it easy with that laptop," Rodney exclaimed.

"Hell, Rodney, isn't this one of those I've seen on television that they drop out of a building and it keeps on ticking? Sam, there's your laptop. When Alexa made me head of global security for this company and said I was now a vice-president, I figured I'd be doing something a little more exciting than rummaging around dusty pawn shops for a week."

Sam picked up the laptop, checked the surface on both sides, and verified the serial number. "Yeah, this is my laptop. It can access the statistics on every one of our mines, worldwide. It can retrieve information on reserves in each of them, how much has been produced and how much remains. Our competitors would love to use this laptop to get into our servers. We're just lucky that the people who broke into my house were probably druggies looking for something to pawn. You find my golf clubs, by the way?"

"Sorry, that wasn't my assignment. As to the stuff in the computer, it's all password protected, right?"

"Yeah," Rodney interjected. "But, hackers crack these just for fun before breakfast.

"Still, isn't all of that crap in our quarterly financials anyway?"

Sam rose, went to a small table, and poured himself a cup of coffee. "Anyone?"

Will and Rodney shook their heads.

"Some of that crap, as you call it, is in our quarterly reports, but Alexa believes she has the right to spin the numbers as she sees fit to drive the price of our stock up," Serano said. "If she needs an extra penny per share to meet Wall Street expectations, you can bet she'll find that penny. Rodney, anyone hack into this?"

"Doesn't look like it, at least based on what I could check with that laptop. When we get back to Baltimore, I'll probe the servers just to be sure."

Will took his boots off Sam's desk and pushed back his chair. "Speaking of Baltimore, we have a plane to catch. The Jamaican team has a command performance before her royal highness."

5

CHAPTER 3

The executive suite of Global American Metals occupied the penthouse of the company's building in Baltimore. When visitors were given the privilege of being invited to the penthouse, they were expected to be impressed. The elevators opened to a reception area with paneled walls, indirect lighting, antique furnishings, and oriental rugs. The receptionist was blonde, beautiful, and professional. Behind her desk were double doors that led to the private offices of Alexa Pritchard. On the other side of the room were doors that opened to the office of the CEO and the board room, used only once a quarter when the board was invited to rubber stamp the decisions of Alexa and the CEO. Alfred St. John, the CEO, was rarely in the office since he essentially turned the company over to Alexa a year before when he was diagnosed with lung cancer. While he still showed up for quarterly board meetings. the other members of the board knew it was only a matter of time before he resigned and Pritchard assumed the role of CEO as well as president.

Will, dressed in grey slacks, a blue Global logo golf shirt, and black loafers, left his office on the sixteenth floor and rode up eight floors whistling "Hail to the Chief" as he did. When the elevator doors opened, he found Rodney, Manny Rodriquez, and Kaven Tillman seated on a couch. Manny was short, but well-built, with Hispanic features and complexion. He took a job with Global after graduating from the Colorado School of Mines and was project engineer for the newest Jamaican bauxite mine. Kaven was born and raised in Jamaica. Alexa hired him five years before and had carefully groomed him to be the face of Global there.

"High time you got here, Will Taylor," the receptionist said.

Will walked to her desk, put both hands on it, and leaned close to the receptionist, a grin on his face. "Tell the president that I saw another damn pawn shop on the way over here and couldn't resist one more look at ancient televisions, microwaves, and other important junk. Hell, I may set up my own eBay account."

The receptionist smiled and picked up her phone to announce that all four men were now present. She rose, turned, and ushered the visitors through the double doors into the palatial forty by forty-foot office of Alexa Pritchard. She was on the phone and directed them to guest chairs lined up in front of her desk. Will twirled his chair around with the back facing Pritchard and sat, straddling it. Will thought the timing of her phone call was nothing more than an act to impress visitors. After all, seconds before she was talking to her receptionist. Just then Pritchard hung up her phone, took a drag on the Marlboro cigarette that was constantly rotating from her mouth to her hand to an overflowing ash tray, and blew the smoke directly at the men in front of her. She smashed the cigarette out and reached in a jar for a Tootsie Pop, which she unwrapped and stuck in her mouth. "Figure every one of these is one less cigarette." She coughed and shoved the jar across the desk. "Anyone?"

Will took one, unwrapped it, and popped it in his mouth. The others shook their heads.

"Will, why can't you be on time once in a while? I allowed thirty minutes for this meeting, and now we're down to fifteen."

"Sorry, Alexa," Will replied. "I stopped to help a little old lady cross the street."

"Yeah, right. Old as in twenty-two."

"Close, Alexa. She did have four-inch heels, and I was worried she would topple over in the middle of traffic." Will smiled.

"Enough! You did find that laptop?"

"Took a week and almost being shot by a redneck pawnshop owner."

"Yeah, but you did get it, right?"

"Back safely in Sam's hands," Will nodded.

"Whose hands?"

"Sam Serano. You know, the foreman in charge of that mine." He shook his head. "A mine foreman must not be very high on your Christmas card list."

Alexa ignored the barb and turned. "Gore, any sign of a problem?"

"No, ma'am. I checked it out and checked the servers when I got back to headquarters. No problem. At least, none that I could detect."

Alexa stepped from her desk, turned her back on her visitors, and gazed out the window as if to signal that the discussion topic was changing. "You gentlemen know we're launching a new mine in Jamaica. What you haven't been told is that this is the biggest bauxite mine in the hemisphere. Our tests show it will supply our aluminum plants for forty years. Right, Rodriquez?"

"She's right, guys. It's gigantic."

Alexa circled around her desk and stopped in front of Kaven. "It's time for you to go home. You've been well coached. You know the company story. I want you on the front page of the newspapers doing media interviews, television, radio, you name it. I expect you to spin our story just like you've been trained. You ready for it?"

"Yes, Ms. Pritchard. I'm looking forward to it. My only concern is the Maroons up in the Cockpit Country. They've controlled that rainforest since 1739. They don't take well to intrusion in their lives or on their land."

Alexa's features hardened. "That's why we brought you on board. You know the locals and I fully expect you to handle any problems, including your damn Maroons. Clear?"

"Yes, ma'am. Just letting you know that there may be a few bumps along the way."

Rodney had been silent but finally interrupted. "Ms. Pritchard, why do you need me down there? I'm a computer geek and know nothing about Jamaica."

"Good question, Gore. Rodriquez has designed this mine using computer generated satellite images. He's only spent a few days on Jamaican soil. Delays in opening this mine will not be tolerated. I want you there just in case the computers start acting up. And that's one thing that I've learned over the years; computers can go haywire for no damn reason. If that happens, I want you right at the table with him."

"And that leaves me, Alexa," Will said. "I specialize in searching pawn shops. That my job in Jamaica?"

Pritchard twirled to face Will, who now rested his head on his crossed arms, obviously not intimidated. "Dammit, Will, quit being such a smart ass. I don't expect any problems. I just want you to confirm that all our security measures are in place at the cockpit mine. And while you're down there, you might as well check out our other operations. It's been a while since you've been to Jamaica." She glanced at a grandfather clock against the wall to her right. "You need to be heading to the airport. And Will, next time I call you to my office for a meeting, I want you in the waiting area fifteen minutes early."

"Roger that, Alexa. Tell you what, I'll just sleep on your couch the night before. I'll even bring my own pillow."

Alexa looked at Will with disgust as they left her office. If his dad wasn't the CEO's best friend, she would send him packing.

When the four men entered the elevator, Will selected the sixteenth floor.

"Will, don't we have to get to the airport?"

"We don't leave for three more hours. My folks are in the area. My dad has been working in D. C. for a couple of days. They should be waiting in my office right about now. I'm taking them to lunch in that restaurant downstairs. They'll drop me at the airport." The elevator doors opened on sixteen. "Tell the pilot to hold the plane if I'm a few minutes late." He smiled as the doors closed.

Will walked down the hall and opened the door to his office. "Your parents are already here," his secretary said.

Will nodded and opened the inner door to see his parents trying to identify buildings and monuments in Washington off in the distance. "I've got a pair of binoculars if you like."

Janice and Bill Taylor turned at the sound of their son's voice. Will walked to give his mother a big hug and gave a similar one to his dad. Will sized up his parents. Both now in their early sixties, his father was a graying image of his son. Janice could easily have passed for around forty-five.

"Sorry we couldn't get together last night. I had a late flight from Little Rock."

"No need to apologize," Bill said. "So, you're on your way to Jamaica. You taking your sticks?"

"Yep," Will replied. "Playing a course called *The White Witch* tomorrow. You ever heard of it?"

His dad shook his head. "Sounds interesting, though."

"I hate to rush you, but we only have time for a quick lunch downstairs. Then I need a ride to the airport. If you parked in the garage, my bag and clubs are in my truck. We can pick them up on the way out."

After they ordered, they sipped their iced tea. "What were you doing in Washington, Dad?"

"As you know, the defense business is booming since the new administration took over. We're bidding on a couple of good-sized defense contracts. I met with two congressmen and a senator from North Carolina along with a couple of generals, just the usual lobbying to maximize our position."

"What's going on in Jamaica?" Will's mother asked.

"We've got a new bauxite mine about to be launched; big one. Pritchard wants me to check out security at the new mine and the rest of our operations on the island. Nothing very exciting."

The waitress brought their food and refilled their drinks. Between bites of salad and club sandwiches, the conversation continued.

"How's Alfred doing, Dad?"

Bill Taylor wiped his mouth. "Actually, better than expected. Cancer's in remission, at least for the moment. He and I are back to playing golf a couple of times a month. What's your assessment of Pritchard?"

"Hard-nosed, give-no-quarter businesswoman. She was raised in the foster system, bounced from family to family. I hear she never knew her parents. She managed to get a college degree from some small school in Oklahoma, then clawed her way up the ladder at Global. Doesn't seem to mind who she steps on or over to get to the top. She's got something to prove. I presume it's to herself. Well, she does have a brother that she has mentioned once or twice. Maybe she's competing with him. Who knows? Most of the employees don't like her and her decisions but are too scared to say anything. So, they just keep their heads down and hope not to be noticed."

"You get along with her"?

"About as well as anyone, but that doesn't mean I respect her. I don't. You two didn't want me to join the Navy and become a SEAL. Still, when we rescued some of our troops in Afghanistan or blocked ISIS from taking over a village, in maybe a small way, I thought I was making the world just a little better place. Then, when I became a trial lawyer, our firm represented people that were injured because of a defective product or because of the negligence of a trucking company. I felt good about what I did. This job is nothing like I expected. I'm ready to move on when there's an opportunity."

"Why don't you just quit now, give your two weeks' notice? You put your resume out on the street, you'll have a job you can be proud of in no time," Will's dad said.

"Come on, Dad, you and mom instilled certain values in me. I committed to getting this Jamaican project off the ground. I just can't walk away from it now. It ought to be up and running in a month or so. Then, I'll go home for a few days and we can discuss my options." He paused and grinned. "I've always wanted to give politics a try. I hear we could use a few more honest congressmen. Maybe your company could throw a few dollars toward my campaign."

A pleased look cropped up on his dad's face. "You have no idea how many defense contractors I know. You say the word and I'll take you around to meet all of them. You've got an impressive resume. Decorated SEAL, undergraduate and law degrees from Duke with honors."

"Now, if we could just get you a pretty, wholesome wife, you'd be hard to beat," Janice said.

Will shook his head as he leaned over to kiss his mother on the cheek. "In due time, Mom, in due time. We'll continue this discussion when I return from Jamaica."

He put his napkin on the table. "One last question before we head to the airport. How's Emily liking being a full-time mom? Must be quite a change from the life of an obstetrician?"

"She's really enjoying taking care of your niece and nephew and not having to get up in the middle of the night to deliver a baby," Will's Janice replied. "When they get into middle school, she can re-evaluate."

Will glanced at his watch. "I'm sorry to rush you, but we better get going. I've got a date with the *White Witch*. I'm buying."

CHAPTER 4

The United Airlines Boeing 757 had been in the air for an hour. The first-class passengers had already been served their meal. Will was drinking his second glass of Merlot as he and Kaven watched a travelogue about Jamaica. Across the aisle, the food and wine had already put Manny and Rodney to sleep. The monitor showed a satellite view of the Caribbean islands while the announcer explained that they were divided into two groups, the Greater Antilles and the Lesser Antilles. On the northern end of the semi-circle of islands were the four largest: Cuba, Hispaniola, Puerto Rico and Jamaica.

The camera zoomed to Jamaica, displaying a lush tropical island with mountains dotting the center. The announcer explained that Jamaica was ninety miles south of Cuba and one hundred miles west of Hispaniola. Jamaica measured one hundred and forty-six miles from east to west and fifty-one miles at its maximum width.

As they watched, the camera switched to a montage of scenes from Jamaica—crystal white beaches with bikini clad women, a group of swimmers with snorkels and fins diving in an ocean as blue as a baby's eyes, cruise ships anchored off shore, the front of the Ritz Carlton Hotel.

"That's where we're staying. You know anything about it?" Will asked.

"Nope. Construction was finished after I moved to the states. Has the reputation as the best hotel on the island. We can thank your friend, Ms. Pritchard, for putting us there."

"Alexa's one tough woman, but she likes to travel first class and insists that her management does likewise."

The conversation was interrupted by the captain advising that they were entering their final descent. Manny and Rodney stirred in response to the announcement.

"Boy, that was one fast trip," Manny yawned as he stretched his arms.

"Yeah," Will responded, "particularly when you sleep most of the way."

After retrieving their baggage and golf clubs, they left the airport and found themselves in a blinding tropical sun.

Kaven pointed to a man dressed in a Global shirt and holding a sign with his name on it. "There he is. Hey, it's Orlando."

Orlando walked up to the group. Kaven introduced him to his friends, and Orlando directed them to a Land Rover with a Global logo. While they walked, Kaven and Orlando caught up on old times. After they loaded their luggage, Orlando handed the keys to Kaven and, offering to be of assistance, gave Kaven his cell number.

"Will, you want to drive?" Kaven asked.

"After you, sir. I've driven on the left side a few times around the world, but I'm a little rusty. I'll ride shotgun and watch you until we get to the Ritz."

As they left the airport Rodney said, "You think we'll get to use these golf clubs, or did we just pay extra to ship them for nothing?"

"We'll use them at least once. I've got us a tee time for eleven in the morning at the Ritz golf course. I hear it's a tough one. Take plenty of balls."

Kaven made his way around construction barriers on the road to the Ritz. In the distance were shacks where people lived without running water and children ran naked in the streets. Groups of men could be seen standing under trees and passing a spliff.

"Hey, they didn't show that on the United video," Will said.

"You're driving through a small part of the real Jamaica," Kaven said. "Along the coast here are fancy hotels, great restaurants, tourist activities to take American money. Get a couple of miles from the coast and I guarantee that you wouldn't want to drive those roads at night. Jamaica gained her independence from Great Britain in 1962, but we haven't made the progress we should have since that time."

"Yeah, but what about the Jamaican bobsled team?" Manny asked.

"Not our finest hour on the world stage, but a pretty funny movie. Now, if you want to talk about our Olympic sprinters, that's a different story."

The conversation drifted to the Olympics as Kaven stopped at the guardhouse fronting the Ritz, conversed in some kind of patois or creole English

13

with the guard, and the gate opened. The driveway was lined with Crotons, Daylilies, Heliconias, Ixoa, Jacaranda, Jasmine, Oleanders, and in the center of the circular drive at the entrance was a giant Poinciana tree overflowing with red blooms.

"What's that language you spoke with the guard? Wasn't Jamaica originally a British colony?" Rodney asked.

"You're right. Nearly everyone on the island speaks English well, but among the locals, we speak a dialect. It's based on English. If you listen carefully, you can understand most of it. You'd have to be here a while to speak it."

Global had arranged for their rooms; so, all they had to do was show their passports and pick up key cards. The bellman said he would send their golf clubs up the hill to the clubhouse. The only glitch was that the hotel was booked so that Rodney and Manny had to share a two-bedroom suite overlooking the ocean. Neither complained.

"Okay, men," Will directed, "let's meet in the lobby bar for a drink and then hit the restaurant. We don't go on the clock until day after tomorrow. That means a full day of golf, leaving here about ten in the morning. A good night's sleep and big breakfast should help our games."

After dinner, Will had settled into his room with a cup of decaffeinated coffee and was flipping channels on the widescreen television when his cell chimed. "Taylor."

"Will, it's Kaven. Sorry to bother you."

"No problem. What's up?"

"Ms. Pritchard just called. In her words, there's some goddam celebration up in Accompong tomorrow. She wants me there. Accompong is the town in the middle of the Cockpit Country, not far from our mine. It's Cudjoe Day, the anniversary of the day that the Maroon chief signed the treaty with the British. I should have remembered. It's usually just a peaceful holiday, something like a much smaller version of your July 4th. Still, she wants me to be there."

Will turned off the television and walked to his balcony overlooking the ocean as he talked. "You okay with that?"

"Should be no problem. Only, my mother has been telling me that the Maroons are really getting stirred up about the mine. So, yeah, I'm a little nervous. Alexa wants me to say a few words about the benefits of our mine. My only complaint is that she wants me to fly up there in a Global helicopter; said something about a show of force. I had to convince her not to send three."

"You want me to go up there with you?"

"No, I think that would only make any problem worse. At least I was born here.""Typical Alexa. She has all the diplomacy of Adolf Hitler. I agree there's no use in me attending and adding to the show of force. Call me if you get into trouble."

Will clicked off the phone and stared at the moon reflecting on the ocean. He could not bury the thought that this project was not going to be the cakewalk Alexa expected.

CHAPTER 5

Will, Manny, and Rodney met at the front of the Ritz promptly at ten the next morning and were met by a green hotel shuttle. When the driver opened the door, he said, "Morning, gentlemen. Looks like a beautiful day for golf. You ready to take on the White Witch?"

"White Witch, what White Witch?" Rodney asked.

"That's the name of our golf course. Named after Miss Annie Palmer. Folks around here used to call her the White Witch."

"I saw some attractive young ladies drinking a White Witch cocktail in the bar last night. She have her own brand of liquor, too?" Manny asked.

"No, suh. She's been dead for about two hundred years. If you don't mind, I really prefer not to talk about her. Let's just say she's just a legendary figure in these parts. Ask around. Someone will tell her tale, just not me."

Manny stared at the driver, a puzzled look crossing his face when the driver refused to talk more about Annie Palmer.

When they arrived at the golf shop, Will put the round on his room while Manny and Rodney perused the merchandise. Rodney picked up a red golf cap.

"Hey, get a look at this. All these caps have the White Witch name on the front and the "t" in Witch is a dagger. They even have a dagger on the back."

"And, the club logo balls have the same thing," Manny replied. "I'm going to buy these and use the dagger to line up my puts."

"Just so you'll know, gentlemen," the man behind the counter interrupted, "a sleeve of logo balls comes with the round."

"That's great," Rodney said. "Three balls may get me through the first hole."

Will headed out the door. "Come on, you two. The range awaits and then the mysterious pleasures of the White Witch."

The first tee was at the level of the clubhouse with the fairway winding through the jungle and down the mountain to a green that appeared to be suspended over the Caribbean. Will was given honors, teed his ball, and pulled a Callaway driver—8.5-degree loft—from his bag. After a couple of practice swings, he sent the ball two hundred and seventy-five yards right down the middle.

"Wow, where did you pull that from?" Manny asked.

"Took up golf back in my SEAL days. Our base had a golf course and I spent most of my spare time there. Had a six handicap before I took off my uniform and dived into the books at Duke."

Rodney stepped up to the tee and carefully lined up his ball so that the dagger faced directly down the fairway, adjusted his cap, and took an off-balance, awkward swing that sliced the ball into the jungle to the right. "Son of a bitch."

"Hey, dude," Manny grinned, "I warned you about coming on too strong with that waitress at the Ritz bar last night. She got pissed, man. Told you she would put a spell on you that would screw with your mind until you left Jamaica."

"Screw you, too, Manny. See if you can do any better. Ten bucks says you can't get within fifty yards of Will's ball."

Manny accepted the challenge and pulled a Taylor Made driver from his bag. He took a few practice swings, stood behind the ball visualizing his shot, and stepped up. Manny's swing was short, fast, and compact. His ball soared down the fairway and stopped about twenty-five yards behind Will's ball. "That'll cost you ten," Manny beamed.

Will and Manny climbed into one cart and Rodney drove the other one to the far side of the fairway in search of his ball. "Too bad about Kaven having to cancel on us. You're the all mighty vice-president of security for this little forty-billion-dollar company. Kaven going to run into any trouble up in Accompong?"

Will finished off a bottle of water, tossed it in a trash can, and started down the cart path. "If I thought there would be a problem, I'd be up there with him. Just a few of the locals celebrating Cudjoe's peace treaty. Some of them are a little stirred up about our bauxite mine gearing up in the Cockpit Country. Not unusual. Happens all over the world when we start a new strip mining operation. The locals get upset. Environmentalists and tree huggers march in front of our headquarters in Baltimore. The locals will settle down when they start getting paychecks."

"Yeah," Manny replied sarcastically. "Got to keep opening new mines if we're going to keep up with the world's demand for aluminum. A few trees aren't near as important as beer cans anyway. Hey, look over there. Rodney's disappeared into the jungle. This island have any snakes?"

"Damned if I know. I hope not. I have no problem facing a man with a gun, but for some reason I'm petrified of snakes, even little grass snakes in my yard. You'll have to ask Kaven when he gets back."

Just then they saw Rodney's club up in the air. Rodney drove it hard into the underbrush and his ball, along with a few vines, flew onto the fairway. Rodney walked from the jungle, saw his two friends looking at him, and did a Chi Chi Rodriquez imitation. He jousted with an imaginary opponent and then pretended to holster his club like a saber as Will and Manny applauded.

By the fourth green Rodney's game was warming up. He hit a bunker shot to within four feet of the hole. After raking the sand, he picked up his putter and a Red Stripe beer that he had discovered in the ice chest at the back of the cart. He walked to his ball and used his putter as a pool cue, sinking it for a par.

"We need to get these Red Stripes imported to America. Couple of them are good for the old game, even at eleven in the morning. Must be good for casting off spells, too, Manny."

As the three golfers walked from the green, Manny returned the conversation to Cudjoe. "Will, who is this guy and what's so damn important about what he did?"

"He was the leader of the Maroons two or three hundred years ago."

"Okay, I'll bite," Rodney interrupted. "Who the hell are the Maroons?"

"You got a Jamaican five hundred bill in your pocket?"

Rodney retrieved his wallet from the golf cart and extracted the requested bill. On the front was a picture of "Nanny of the Maroons."

"So now you'll want to know who Nanny was, too. The Maroons were originally slaves. They fought the Spaniards for a hundred and fifty years. Then when the Brits tried to take over the island, the Spanish freed the Maroons to fight the British. The Spaniards gave up and fled to Cuba and the British took control of the island. The Maroons fought the British for eighty more years.

They were masters of guerrilla warfare. They'd come down from their mountain retreat in the jungle, attack, and hightail it back up to their villages. After eighty years, the English decided it was easier to make peace than to continue a war they couldn't win. Cudjoe was the leader of the Maroons at the time. He's the one that signed the peace treaty that deeded the mountains and the rainforest, now called the Cockpit Country, to the Maroons."

"Wait a minute, Will. That's thousands and thousands of acres."

"Right you are, Manny. Brits really didn't care. It was a jungle up in the mountains. They couldn't grow anything up there. They wanted the land down by the sea where they could grow sugar cane and bananas. For nearly three hundred years the Maroons lived peacefully. Oh, they grew a little ganja, but generally just wanted to be left alone. Then we discovered bauxite up in their country and everything changed."

"You forgot about Nanny, Will."

"Sorry. She was Cudjoe's sister. She was leader of the Maroons on the east side of the island. They even named a town after her."

"How do you know so much about these morons, Will?" Rodney asked.

"Maroons, Rodney, not morons. Information is part of my job."

"Sounds like they were damn good fighters."

"Probably still are. Now they claim they'll stop our mine."

"Hold on," Manny said indignantly. "I'm the mining engineer in charge of this operation. We have a valid permit from the Jamaican Ministry of Mining. A few morons can't stop us. Let 'em celebrate old Cudjoe all they want. You just do your job and keep them away from my mine, so I can do my job."

"Maroons, Manny, Maroons. Not morons." Will again corrected his associate. "And, I don't want to rain on your parade, but if you didn't even know about the Maroon Treaty with the Brits, how do you know that our mine doesn't infringe on their territory?"

Manny thought a minute. "Like I said, we have a permit from the Ministry of Mining. I understand Ms. Pritchard paid a small fortune to get that permit. I just have to assume that the Ministry wouldn't give us the permit if they thought it would cause trouble."

"And what do you mean it's your mine," Rodney asked. "I heard you have just hiked around up there a couple of times. Don't you need to at least shovel a little dirt?"

"Don't need to," Manny replied. "With satellite photos and a computer, I can plan it from anywhere on earth. Still, I'm going to get my boots on the bauxite while we're here." He hesitated and turned to Will. "Someone needs to tell the Maroons who's in charge."

As they continued to talk, a course marshal drove up in a golf cart. "Pardon me, gentlemen, but you're holding up play." He pointed to four golfers on the fairway who were waiting to hit onto the green.

"Sorry, sir," Will said. "And please apologize to the foursome behind us." He got into the cart with Manny. "That's the reason Kaven's up there...to win over the Maroons. He's the local guy. Why do you think Alexa hired him five years ago? She may be a cold-hearted corporate executive, but she plans every move like a chess master."

CHAPTER 6

When they drove to the next tee, storm clouds were gathering over the Caribbean off in the distance. Rodney studied them warily and was about to say something when Will's cell phone rang. He glanced at the caller ID and saw it was Kaven. "Taylor."

Kaven was strapped into the passenger seat of a Global helicopter circling around a group of people in the center of Accompong, high up in the Cockpit Country. As he talked, he was staring nervously at the crowd below. "Will, things are getting out of hand up here. You there? Can you hear me?"

"Yeah. Go ahead."

"I don't like this show of force idea. A bunch of those people are waving guns while someone else is speaking."

"You want me up there?"

"Too late, Will. It's a three hour drive up a bad road. Even if I sent the helicopter back, it'd take about an hour, round trip. I'll just do what I can. There are a couple of the Montego Bay cops down there. I'll get with them."

Will nodded his understanding, clicked off his phone and walked back to his playing partners, a frown covering his face.

Accompong was named after Cudjoe's brother, who ascended to chief of the Maroons after Cudjoe's death. White men, and even Jamaicans, were not welcome except on Cudjoe Day. In fact, there was a large double gate across the road that was usually locked. To get there, a visitor passed shacks, shanties, small fields filled with banana trees, and fields where marijuana was grown as a cash crop. It was illegal in other parts of Jamaica, but Cudjoe's treaty with the British was honored. That meant that for any crime other than murder, the Maroon Council handled criminal matters. Something as minor as growing and selling a little ganja was not worthy of their attention.

Accompong had electricity in most of its houses, and some of the Maroons had cell phones. Otherwise, there was no gesture to anything modern; no indoor plumbing and certainly no air conditioning. A few of the Maroons moved into other places like Montego Bay when they were grown. The ones that remained eked out a living from the land and the forest where they found edible plants, roots, berries, nuts, and fruit. There were also many streams in the Cockpit Country, and fish were plentiful. In an earlier time they hunted boar, but that was long ago and now the boars had been hunted to extinction.

Kaven knew about the Cudjoe Day celebration and hoped to find a holiday atmosphere with only a few firecrackers. Unfortunately, those celebrations were in the past. As his helicopter circled, he could see men with rifles and AK-47s pointed at the helicopter. A tall black man, dressed in a suit and tie, stood in front of a monument to Cudjoe that described his exploits as the fearless Maroon leader who had driven the British from their forest. He was speaking into a microphone. In front of him were two Montego Bay police officers dressed in full uniform. They, too, were Maroons, recruited for the day by the speaker, Colonel Rafael Broderick.

In earlier times, Colonel Broderick would have been called their chief, but that changed when the British took over the island. Now, their leader had a different title and was elected every five years. Colonel Broderick had abandoned the Cockpit Country when he was a young man and immigrated to Canada, where he worked for the Canadian railroad for twenty-five years. Once he had earned a pension, he returned to his native village where the pension made him one of the wealthiest men in the area. He had no wife, but rumor was he left a wife and three grown children in Canada. Shortly after his return to the land of the Maroons he had taken a mistress in a neighboring village. The mistress was a Muda, a woman said to be possessed with certain occult powers. She bore him a child, a daughter, before she died from complications of the birth. It was said that he was also skilled in the occult and was an accomplished bush doctor who treated Maroons from throughout the island seeking to be cured with roots, leaves, and dark potions that he mixed to treat the diseases of his people.

As Colonel Broderick expected, current events turned out hundreds of Maroons for this Cudjoe Day, the largest crowd in years. It was his opportunity to bring them together against what the Council perceived as a common enemy. When he rose, silence settled upon the Maroons, many of whom had come to their first Cudjoe Day celebration in many years because they had heard about the giant American company and its plans to level their rainforest.

"My fellow Maroons and guests, thank you for coming. This is the largest turnout for a Cudjoe Day celebration that I've ever seen. We all know the reason for the turnout, don't we? Look around you. We fought for this land."

As Colonel Broderick spoke, he waved his arm to direct the audience to the mountains and rainforest that surrounded them. Blue sky framed mountains of green as far as the eye could see.

"All of this is ours. We have a treaty with the British." He paused. "No, we have a treaty with the British that *was authorized* by King George the second, the ruler of the British Empire. We own this land. We have Cudjoe and his brethren to thank."

The crowd erupted. "Cudjoe, Cudjoe, Cudjoe!"

"With the ownership of this land comes a serious responsibility. It is our solemn duty to protect our rainforest. We know the benefits the rainforest brings us…long life, good health. Only recently have other men in faraway lands learned what we already knew. We can cure their diseases and maladies just like we cure our own. Working with bio-scientists we can make a small profit to help all of us live better and provide medicines for the world. That's been our goal for the past ten years. Progress is slow, but we are moving in the right direction."

Colonel Broderick's voice became very solemn. "Unfortunately, just as we are on the verge of making the lives of the Maroons better and benefitting mankind, a giant American corporation, Global American Metals, has swooped in to put a bauxite mine right in the heart of the Cockpit Country. Global has done this all over the world. They care nothing about people like us. They are concerned only with their own profits."

The crowd had been quiet. Now a few voices began to shout about going to war with Global. Others joined them. Colonel Broderick gestured for silence.

"This has been our country for three hundred years." His voice became loud and angry. "Global American Metals did not consult us. Instead they went to the Ministry of Mines in Kingston, knowing full well that we have sovereign rights to all the Cockpit Country. I tried to call Alexa Pritchard, Global's president. She refused my calls. Now, one of her helicopters is circling our village…and on Cudjoe Day." He waved his fist at the helicopter. "She and her

23

company have no respect for us."

The shouts from the crowd reverberated from the mountains. Two young Maroons fired their rifles in the air. The helicopter pilot turned to Kaven.

"What you want me to do, mon? We should get our asses out of here."

Kaven gulped down the fear that was gurgling up in his throat. "No. I have to speak to these people." Pointing to a wide spot in the village road about a hundred yards from the crowd, he said, "Put us down there."

The pilot shook his head in disbelief but did as he was told.

While the helicopter approached, Colonel Broderick continued. "Our ancestors killed one white witch long ago. If we must go to war with this American white witch to save our land, we'll do it."

Almost with one voice the crowd began to shout, "Kill the witch. Kill the witch. Cudjoe! Cudjoe! Save our rainforest! Kill the witch!"

CHAPTER 7

The three golfers were chipping onto the eighth green when a powerful gust of wind howled in from the ocean. All three caps went flying. The wind pulled the flag from the hole and hurled it toward Rodney who barely ducked in time. The golf cart containing Will and Manny's clubs suddenly began to roll backwards down the path away from the green. Will saw what was happening and chased after it, catching up just as it was about to go over an embankment and down a hill. He leaped in and hit the brake. Once he was in control, he drove it back to the green.

"Manny, you forget to set the brake?"

"No way, man. I braked it. Must be more of the curse of the White Witch." Manny laughed.

The golfers were retrieving their caps and Rodney replaced the flag when he noticed a large black man, dressed in greens keeper coveralls and carrying a rake, standing on the edge of the forest beside a sand trap. That guy wasn't there twenty seconds ago, Rodney thought. He seemed to have appeared out of nowhere.

"You gentlemen should not be speaking badly about Miss Annie," the gardener said in near perfect English with a bass voice that carried down the mountain. "You're on her plantation. She hears every word."

The golfers stared at the greens keeper. Rodney nodded his understanding as they turned to their carts. When Rodney looked back, the greens keeper had vanished.

"Damn, that big guy just evaporated. Don't tell me Annie Palmer is a magician, too."

"No doubt she was a voodoo priestess," Will said. "Supposedly she could levitate objects and hurl them across the room with her mystical powers. I don't know that she could levitate a two-hundred and fifty-pound man and make him disappear. Still, I wouldn't rule it out. On the other hand, maybe he just stepped back into the jungle when we were distracted, and I note that you used the present tense when you referred to Annie Palmer. You believe that she's still around what used to be her plantation?"

"Damned if I know," Rodney said. "Maybe she conjured up that wind and used it to throw the flag at me. Okay, so, maybe I'm getting just a little nervous. Still, it doesn't hurt to be careful around this kind of shit."

"I'm with Rodney," Manny said. "We Mexicans have our own voodoo religion. It's called Santeria. Not practiced much in the United States, but I have some relatives in Mexico who are convinced that a Santeria priest can cast a spell that can lead to sickness or death. I don't buy into that shit. Still, variations of voodoo are practiced in many countries. Hell, even the Catholics perform exorcisms and drive out demons. Who am I to say that there's nothing to the supernatural? Just may be that Miss Annie drops by her old stomping grounds ever so often. If she does, I damn sure don't want to be around."

CHAPTER 8

Colonel Broderick had to raise his hands for silence three more times. "If our rainforest is destroyed by this American white witch, we cannot survive as a people. Certainly, we cannot rely on doctors down in Montego Bay to cure our ailments. As long as our bush doctors can use our rainforest to make medicines, we don't need them. Besides, we can't afford them."

"Not unless there's one that will take marijuana in payment," a voice in the crowd shouted. That brought laughs from many, including Colonel Broderick.

As he spoke, the sound of the helicopter grew louder. It descended and landed in the wide space in the road. Young men in the crowd surged toward the helicopter, guns in hand.

"Mon, you sure you want to do this?" the pilot asked.

"I must try. It's my job," Kaven replied as he surveyed the crowd, finally unfastening his seat belt and unlatching the door. As soon as he did, the young Maroons pulled open the door and jerked him from the helicopter. One of them stuck a pistol to his head.

Before the situation could get worse, Colonel Broderick yelled. "Bring him to me. Don't hurt him. Up here now."

Kaven struggled as the Maroons pushed him toward the platform. One intentionally shoved him face forward to the ground. When he got up, his pants were ripped, and blood was trickling down his left arm. He stumbled toward the platform, dazed and wondering what was in store for him. When he was shoved up the two steps, Colonel Broderick demanded, "Why are you here? This celebration is not for Global or its employees."

Kaven held his hand over his bleeding arm and tried to control a cracking voice as he replied. "I understand, Colonel Broderick. Ms. Pritchard thought that I might be able to explain some things. May I be permitted to say a word on behalf of Global American?"

"No, No," one of the young Maroons cried. "He's the enemy. Death to our enemies."

Colonel Broderick again motioned for silence. "Quiet, my friends. Let's hear what he has to say. Ms. Pritchard won't show her face. At least this young man is willing to talk to us."

Colonel Broderick handed the microphone to Kaven amid boos and catcalls.

Kaven had been in public relations for Global for five years and had spoken to countless audiences, many of them rowdy and rude, particularly the environmentalists who picketed the Global headquarters; never, though, had he faced such a hostile one with guns raised in the air. He did his best to compose himself while holding his hand over the bleeding arm.

"Thank you, Colonel Broderick. First, let me say that I am a Jamaican, too."

"You ain't a Jamaican anymore, mon," a voice yelled from the crowd. "You sold out. Look at that logo on your shirt."

"Yeah, why don't you take the witch's company and get the hell out of our Cockpit Country," a second voice shouted.

Crude protest signs were waved: *Fight to the Death. Cudjoe Lives.* Kaven looked toward the police officers, hoping for some help, but they merely gazed over the crowd. Colonel Broderick came to his aid and once more motioned for silence.

"Please, please, hear me out," Kaven pleaded. "Global American is known throughout the world as a good corporate citizen. All of you will have jobs. We'll take part of our profits and build schools, pay teachers. We'll even build you a hospital."

"No," Colonel Broderick erupted, having heard enough. "You and Ms. Pritchard don't understand. It's not a question of jobs and hospitals. Our rainforest is not for sale at any price. You'll never strip mine it."

Reflecting the anger spilling from Colonel Broderick, the crowd started yelling again. Some hurled rocks toward Kaven who managed to dodge several until one hit him in the forehead, bringing blood that dripped into his right eye. Finally, the police realized the situation was about to get out of hand. They pulled their weapons and fired over the crowd. The sound of gunfire had an effect just opposite from the one the cops had hoped for. Instead of restoring order, the Maroons started firing back until a five-year-old girl standing close to the platform in her Sunday dress was hit and crumpled to the ground, a bullet in her chest.

Seeing that there could be more deaths, one of the police officers grabbed Kaven and pushed through the crowd, gun drawn, with Kaven close behind. As they approached the helicopter, the pilot started the engine. The Maroons saw that the Global mouthpiece was about to get away. They turned their weapons on the helicopter and peppered it with bullets until the engine whined to a stop.

The police officer redirected Kaven toward his car. When they were about to break free from the throng, an old woman reached into her dress and retrieved a small bottle. She uncorked it and threw the contents on Kaven.

"You're not welcome in the Cockpit Country," she cackled. "My powers are far stronger than those of your white witch. My powers will protect the land of our ancestors from you and your company." She pointed a gnarled finger at Kaven. "I curse you and everyone in Global. Mark my words. There will be death. Tell that to your Ms. Pritchard."

Kaven stared at the old woman, uncertain what to do. He glanced at his shirt and realized she had thrown blood on him, most of which landed on the Global logo. He briefly tried to wipe it off, somehow thinking that if he could cleanse his shirt it would break the curse. He heard the officer yelling at him. He turned and sprinted toward the police car. Bullets flew around him. Once in the car, the officer said to duck below the windows and started the engine. They raced through the gate from Accompong and down a narrow road as dark clouds appeared above the mountains.

CHAPTER 9

The squall had been in the Atlantic for several days, following a meandering course. The best estimates from the computers were that it would hit the Bahamas and then Florida. It was of little concern since it was only a tropical storm. Surprisingly, it veered south and increased to a Category I as it swirled offshore Jamaica. The three golfers were on the ninth tee when the rain was driven sideways into them by a fifty mile an hour gust. Will pointed to the White Witch Club House and both carts made a beeline for it. They made it to the parking lot below the club house, abandoned their carts and clubs to an attendant, and dashed for the veranda where plastic panels blocked the rain and wind but allowed them to watch the storm toss the trees to and fro as coconuts popped and cracked on the driveway. They found a table next to the plastic panels and waited to be served.

"Shit," Manny said. "How the hell did we not know this was coming?"

"I don't know about you guys," Will responded, 'but I watched the news last night. It was still a tropical storm and headed north of here. I didn't even turn on the television this morning."

"Me either," Rodney added. "Besides, if we were as wrong as the weather forecasters, we'd all be out of jobs."

"Okay, okay, already," Manny said. "Would someone please tell the White Witch we're sorry? I'll never badmouth her again."

As he spoke, a beautiful Jamaican woman approached. Her long, brown hair framed a face with perfect features: well defined nose, sensuous lips, skin a lightly tinted brown, and dark eyes framed with long, natural eyelashes.

"My apologies for the storm. We always try to have perfect weather for our guests. Can I get you something to drink while you wait it out?"

"I'm for that, sweetie, but first you must tell us your name," Manny replied.

She spoke without a smile, like she was accustomed to cutting off overly friendly guests. "My name is Vertise."

"You know this white witch?"

"I'm quite familiar with the legend of Annie Palmer."

"I think she's the one who screwed up my golf game."

This time Vertise allowed a small smile. "The White Witch has been accused of many things, but messing with one's golf game isn't one of them. I believe you must take credit for that yourself."

"Okay, guys, enough small talk with this lovely lady," Will interrupted. "Miss, if you don't mind, please just bring us three Red Stripes and three cheeseburgers, medium."

Vertise nodded and returned almost immediately with three beers and tall beer glasses, which she placed in front of the guests without a word and returned to the bar.

Will dug into his pocket for his cell, found it, and punched the screen to re-call Kaven. "Dammit. Call failed. All we've got to deal with is a storm beyond the veranda. We haven't heard from Kaven. He may have a little more on his plate. I'm beginning to worry."

"There's nothing you can do about Kaven now. He's a local. He'll take care of himself," Rodney said.

Manny lifted his beer to the storm. "Then, here's to the White Witch, wherever you are."

As he finished his toast, a bolt of lightning hit, and the lights went out. Vertise hurried to their table. "Gentlemen, the beers are on the house. We've cancelled the cheeseburgers. That foursome that was behind you chose to go directly back to the hotel. You are the last guests. Please follow me to the shuttle at the front of the club. We'll try to get you to the Ritz before the storm gets worse."

Will and Rodney rose as Manny finished the last of his beer. When they climbed into the shuttle, they were startled to see that the groundskeeper from the eighth green was now driving the shuttle.

Manny asked him, "You once work for David Copperfield? You're a mighty big man to do that disappearing act."

The driver kept his thoughts to himself, looked straight ahead, and said nothing. The golfers took seats three rows back from the driver and Vertise sat at the rear, clearly wanting nothing to do with them.

"Quiet, guys," Manny whispered as he gestured to the driver. "He will report anything we say to Miss Annie."

CHAPTER 10

The storm hit the Cockpit Country with a force little diminished from when it crashed ashore. Wind drove the rain sideways into leaking shacks that dotted the road. A mangy goat, tied to a stake, stood forlornly with its butt to the storm, just trying to keep its balance. Small creeks that hadn't been there an hour before formed and made their way down the mountains and across the road. Palm trees swayed and then cracked as they toppled to the ground. One driver was foolish enough to be out in the storm.

The officer, with Kaven as a passenger, was forcing his police car as fast as he could down the mountain, uncertain if some Maroons might be close behind. He was barely able to maintain control as the tires squealed around the curves of the potholed and slippery mountain road.

Maybe I should have taken my chances with the Maroons, Kaven thought as he pulled his seat belt tight and held onto the center console for support.

The car had just survived a double curve. The officer was straightening the wheels when Kaven shouted, "Look out! There's a giant boa constrictor on the road."

The officer slammed on his brakes and tried without success to maintain control when he swerved to avoid the huge yellow snake. He missed the serpent but careened off the road, down the mountain, and through the jungle, crashing through underbrush and uprooting trees before coming to a stop with the car lying on the driver's side. Kaven managed to get his door open and stumble out. He reached back to give the officer a hand. Kaven covered his eyes with one arm to fend off the driving rain and limped back up the hill, following the path just cut through the jungle by the car. The officer stumbled behind him. The jungle floor was even more slippery than the highway, and several times Kaven had to grab for a vine to keep from sliding back to the car or beyond. When they finally found the pavement, the boa had disappeared.

Kaven checked to see if the officer was still behind him, then looked down at the red blotch still covering the logo on his shirt. He stared up the mountain toward Accompong, wondering if there was a connection between the old woman, her curse, and what just happened.

Kaven and the police officer huddled under a group of palm trees for some slight protection from the wind and rain, as Kaven tried without success to raise Will on his cell. The officer had a similar result with both his cell and his police walkie-talkie. They were prepared to start walking down the road in hopes of finding better shelter when the second policeman rounded the curve, saw them, and screeched to a halt. The helicopter pilot was with him.

"You guys all right?"

"Yeah, I think so," Kaven replied. "At least nothing's broken."

"What happened?"

"Damn yellow boa was crossing the road as I rounded the curve," the first cop replied. "I swerved to avoid the snake and spun out. Car's down there. You want to have a look?"

"Not in this storm. Get in. We'll drop Tillman at his hotel and then head to the station to fill out reports. I'm not looking forward to telling Chief Harper what happened."

The first officer took the passenger front seat as Kaven climbed into the back, again tightening his seat belt until he could barely breathe. "Things settle down up there after I got out?" Kaven asked.

"Some," the driver replied. "Those young Maroons were still milling around, waving their guns, and cussing Global American. You better tell your people there is going to be trouble."

"Wait just a damn minute," Kaven said. "I'm a native of this island. I know it's nearly impossible to get a permit to carry a pistol much less an AK-47. Why didn't you just arrest them, confiscate their guns or something?"

The first policeman shrugged his shoulders. "We can't do shit up there except in the case of murder. The Maroons are the law up there. Besides, it would take a small army to round up those guns. Best to leave them alone as long as they don't bring weapons into Montego Bay."

"What about the little girl?" Kaven asked.

"She's dead. Probably accidental. We couldn't identify the shooter. The Maroons are blaming your company."

Becoming more concerned, Kaven leaned forward and raised his voice. "Wait a minute. I was the only Global employee up there. You know I didn't have a gun."

"Not saying they're right, mon," the driver replied. "Just telling you what they're saying."

Kaven slumped back into his seat and stared out the window as he mumbled to no one in particular, "Shit, shit, shit."

CHAPTER 11

The groundskeeper carefully maneuvered the shuttle down the hill, weaving between fallen branches and trees.

"Okay, we're almost down," Will announced. "I can see the highway. Five more minutes and I'm buying drinks at the Ritz."

Suddenly, lightning struck close to the shuttle with a terrifying blast that had everyone diving for the floor. Just as they thought they were safe, a utility pole toppled in front of the shuttle, missing it by only a few feet. The utility pole pulled live electrical lines with it, now loose, crackling and popping as they were whipped by the eighty-five mile an hour winds. Vertise made her way to the front of the bus.

"Please follow me. I know a trail from here over to the Rose Hall Mansion. It will be safer to sit out the storm there."

Manny looked at Will and Rodney. "I think she's right, provided we just don't get hit by lightning or a tree on the way."

Will pulled his windbreaker over his head and followed Vertise with the others trailing behind. When they exited the bus, an electric line popped within a foot of Will, and he was thrown several feet into the jungle. Dodging the lines, the others rushed to his side.

"Will, you okay?" Rodney asked.

Will stumbled to his feet and nodded his head. "Yeah, I think so. Probably a good thing these golf shoes have rubber soles. Let's get the hell out of here."

Satisfied that Will could walk, Vertise motioned them toward a trail almost hidden by undergrowth. Rodney brought up the rear and glanced back to the bus. The driver had disappeared. Rodney hurried to catch up to the others. "I've had enough of the white bitch for one day. Now we're going to her goddamn mansion. Jesus Christ."

They broke from the jungle into a clearing where the mansion sat in splendor. When the owners of the Ritz Carlton bought five thousand acres outside of Montego Bay, they had no idea they were buying a former slave plantation and, in fact, didn't even know that Rose Hall was on the property. Once they discovered they owned it, they spent millions of dollars and provided loving care to have it restored and furnished with authentic period pieces.

Manny looked up at the three-story house. "Wow. There must have been some kind of money in sugar cane back in those times."

"It certainly helped that the owners didn't have to pay the help," Vertise replied without a hint of humor in her voice.

Vertise led the golfers up the steps to the main level. "Stay under the veranda. I'll go around to the back. There's a key hidden."

"Just how the hell does she know there's a hidden key? What else does she know about the mansion and its inhabitants?" Rodney asked.

Before Will could reply, one of the double front doors opened and Vertise admitted the golfers to the great ballroom, thirty by thirty feet with a twenty-foot ceiling. All three golfers studied the room in amazement as they took in the multiple sitting areas, each with matching furniture, portraits and tapestries on the walls, and doors leading to unknown rooms. To their right was a massive fireplace.

As she ushered them in, Vertise said, "Welcome to Rose Hall, gentlemen."

"Boy," Manny said. "Miss Annie must have thrown some fantastic parties. How come no one's home?"

"The employees of the mansion always leave by five. They won't work after dark," Vertise replied. "They believe it's Miss Annie's time to roam the mansion. Same is true in storms. When there's no electricity, they lock up and get down the hill as fast as they can. They also believe that Annie Palmer can also conjure up a storm."

"Wait a minute," Rodney countered. "You saying that she's around here somewhere right now?"

"Believe what you choose. I'll light some candles. Who knows? Maybe they'll keep Miss Annie away."

Vertise walked to the fireplace where she took a modern fire starter and walked around the room lighting candles. As she made her way around the room, Rodney started to sit in one of the two-hundred-year-old chairs.

"Rodney, get the hell out of that chair," Will commanded. "You're soaked. Talk about pissing Miss Annie off."

Rodney leaped from the chair and turned to brush any drops of water from it. "Sorry. Sorry. Please, I didn't mean any harm," Rodney said, not sure if Will was serious about pissing Annie off or not. He removed his windbreaker and sat, instead, on the floor. Manny did likewise. Will watched as Vertise completed the candle lighting and disappeared through a door to the back of the house. Once she was gone, a wind came from nowhere and whistled through the room, dousing every candle that Vertise had lighted.

"Jeez, that's just a little too damn much," Manny exclaimed. "Anybody see an open window?"

Will was taking off his windbreaker when he retorted, "Nope. Sealed like a tomb."

"Thanks a lot," Rodney replied nervously as he searched the room with his eyes, looking for some logical reason for the candles to blow out. "Couldn't you come up with some other analogy?"

"Okay, sealed like a can of sardines," Will said. His eyes twinkled since he certainly was not buying into the idea of a haunted mansion. "Come on, Rodney. Relax. At least we're out of the storm."

Will walked to the mantle where Vertise had placed the fire starter, took it, and retraced Vertise's steps, again lighting the candles. As he passed an oval mirror on the wall, Manny did a double take. "Shit! Rodney, did you see that? When Will walked passed that mirror, it wasn't his reflection. It was a young woman, black hair pulled back in a bun, white shirt with lace around the neck. You saw it, didn't you, Rodney?"

"Grow up, guys. It was probably just a reflection from the window," Will said, growing a little weary of his two friends and their concerns about the white witch.

Rodney got up and walked to the mirror, trying to stare through it. "No, Will. Manny's right. It was a woman, just like Manny said. No damn wonder the help leaves before dark every night."

Vertise returned through the back door with hand towels and passed them around. "Here, I got these from downstairs. Sorry they're so small. They turned Annie's dungeon into a tourist shop with an adjoining bar. I also work there occasionally."

Rodney finished drying himself as best he could. "Damn, if there's a bar down there, why are we up here?"

"Sorry, the liquor is locked up after hours. I don't have a key."

"Hell, probably locked up so Annie doesn't go on a drunken binge." Manny managed a slight laugh.

Suddenly, there was a loud crash from a small room off to the side. All four of the storm refugees jumped, even Vertise.

"I'm not liking this place. What was that?" Rodney asked, fear beginning to etch his face.

"Maybe Annie broke into the schnapps and is throwing furniture around," Will cracked.

Vertise led the way to the adjoining room. "This is the library." She looked at a chair in the middle of the room. "Aha, this is one of our period pieces. You see it now as a chair. When I pull this handle at the base, it flips up into a step stool. Watch." Vertise pulled the lever and pushed the back of the chair forward. When it stopped, there were six steps instead of a chair. She pulled the handle and it returned to the chair position. "Miss Annie could use it to get to the higher shelves. When we lock up for the night, we leave it in the step stool position. Something caused it to fall back into its position as a chair."

"Looks to me like Miss Annie finished her first patrol of the night and wanted to sit a while," Will concluded.

"Dammit, Will. Stop screwing around. We're in a damn haunted mansion in the middle of a storm. It ain't funny," Rodney replied as he looked anxiously around the library.

Will walked over, made sure his butt was reasonably dry, sat in the chair and teased, "You weenie, you think the big, bad witch is going to get us." He stretched out his legs and leaned back. "I could catch forty winks right here. Annie could curl up in my lap."

As Will spoke, a cold draft blew into the room. "Damn, there it is again," Manny said. "What's causing that?"

"It's a big old mansion. There may still be a few places where the wind can blow through," Vertise said. "We have had some ghost hunters visit from time to time. Some of them say that the chilly wind is a sign that Annie is walking through the room."

"Oh, shit," Rodney muttered.

"You gentlemen follow me back into the ballroom. I'll light a fire to help us dry out." Vertise led them back to the giant room and turned a knob on the wall beside the fireplace. A gas fire roared into life. "Not much use for a fire in Jamaica, but from what I understand, the British couldn't conceive of a room like this without a fireplace. When the mansion was restored, they kept the fireplace but installed gas fired logs. Sit close and maybe you'll be dry by the time the storm passes."

The three men arranged themselves on the floor around the fireplace as Vertise seated herself on the hearth.

They all were quiet for a few minutes while they listened to the wind wailing outside and rain being driven against the windows. They occasionally heard creaking from elsewhere in the house that caused Rodney to study the room to see if Miss Annie was joining them. Finally, Manny spoke. "Look, Vertise, you're a great hostess, and we appreciate you getting us out of the storm, only we don't know anything about you."

Vertise smiled as she began to gain a level of comfort with her guests. "As you know, my name is Vertise. I know your names since I've been hearing each of you speak to each other. I'm from this area originally. I worked in New York until last year when I returned to write for the *Montego Bay Monitor*. I tend bar to make ends meet."

"Maybe you can tell us the real story about Miss Annie and this mansion," Rodney said. "Seems like everywhere I go around Montego Bay, there's something about this White Witch. And that's a helluva name for a golf course."

"And on the logo golf balls, the 't' in witch is a dagger. That's even more weird," Manny added.

Vertise looked out the window at the still raging storm. "No doubt that the hotel, and golf course, and tourist industry try to capitalize on the legend of Annie Palmer. Just the fact that people still talk about her, and some even fear her after two hundred years, lends some credence to the mystery of her life and death. Since it appears that we're going to be here a while, I'll tell you what I know. I should warn you that this is part truth and part legend."

Vertise shifted her position to better face the three men seated in front of her and began. "Annie Palmer was from Scotland. When she was ten she moved with her parents to Haiti. Her parents died from a plague, and she was raised by a voodoo priestess who taught her the deepest, darkest secrets of the occult."

"How did she get here, I mean, to Jamaica?" Manny asked.

"The owner of this plantation, a much older gentleman, heard about this beautiful girl in Haiti. He sailed there and brought her back as his bride. She was eighteen at the time. Not long after she took over as mistress of the Rose Hall Plantation, she poisoned him with arsenic. It was her first murder, as far as anyone knows."

"Just a minute, murder?" Rodney asked. "And what do you mean first?" Rodney's eyes again darted around the room, looking for signs of the White Witch.

"Please, let me finish," Vertise continued. "Over the next several years she took two other husbands. She also killed both of them, one with a knife while he slept. As to the third, she enlisted the help of an overseer to strangle him."

"Looks to me like they could have just as easily dubbed her the *Black Widow*," Will joked.

"Sir, this really is not meant to be funny. In a country where there were many slave plantations, she was notorious for her cruelty. There was a gallows out in the back yard and a flogging post. As a petite white woman, she used cruelty, and yes, voodoo, to maintain control of her slaves. Fear was her greatest weapon and she knew how to use it."

"I suspect she couldn't find another husband after three died under strange circumstances," Will commented with a little more seriousness in his voice.

"Speaking of the husbands, there are three coconut trees growing on the beach just at the bottom of the hill. Supposedly, the three husbands are buried under those trees, but we're not quite through with her lovers."

Vertise then described how Annie Palmer romanced and then tortured and killed slaves. When she paused, a lightning bolt thundered down just outside the window. Rodney jumped to his feet. "I've had enough. I'm out of here. I'd rather take my chances with the storm."

"Sit down, Rodney," Will commanded. "Most of this is probably just legend like Vertise said."

"No, Mr. Taylor, most of what I have told you is true. Only a small part is legend. If you want to hear the whole story, please remain silent. I'm almost done."

Vertise told the three men the story of the overseer sacrificing his own life to kill the White Witch and avenge the death of his daughter's fiancé.

When she finished the story, Rodney took off his golf cap and stared at the White Witch logo. Then he flipped to the back where there was an emblem of a dagger. After studying the cap, he refused to place it on his head; instead, he stuck it in his back pocket.

"Wait," Will said. "Let me guess. The slaves screwed it up, didn't they?"

Vertise smiled as she glanced out the window to check the storm. "You must have heard the story before, Mr. Taylor. They tossed her body in the grave, piled some dirt on it, and took off running. Those who have studied *Obeah* will tell you that a voodoo priestess must be buried according to century's old protocols. Otherwise she will never find her final rest."

"Wait a second," Rodney interrupted. "Stuff was flying around by itself. I don't get it. Oh, my God, what the heck is that?"

Manny had his jacket on the end of a cane he found leaning against the fireplace and was waving it back and forth, giving the appearance of a ghost. Manny smiled at Rodney.

"Asshole," Rodney yelled.

Vertise completed her survey of the storm and faced the three men. "Gentlemen, we do try to keep our voices under control in this house and profanity is not permitted."

"My most sincere apologies, Vertise," Manny replied. "I caused the outburst."

"I think the storm is passing. If I can find my cell phone, and if there is service, we can get a taxi to go back to the hotel. Please follow me. We'll go downstairs and out through the bar to a covered driveway."

Vertise blew out all the candles but one and used it to provide light as they made their way to the back stairway. Will wondered why she didn't just turn on her cellphone light, but figured the candle was for effect and followed with Manny and Rodney bringing up the rear. Rodney tried to peer through the flickering shadows, half expecting Annie Palmer to join them at any minute.

"Watch it," Vertise cried, pointing to the floor to a bear trap in an open position, its saw tooth blades ready to clamp down on the foot of any animal or person. "Strange, I walked by here to go downstairs earlier and don't recall it being open. In fact, it's never supposed to be open."

"Okay," Manny said, "I've got a stupid question. I never heard of there being bears on this island; so, why did Annie have a bear trap?"

"Also," Will followed up, "What's it doing in the house?"

"There were bears here hundreds of years ago, but they were hunted to extinction long before the English occupied the island. In Miss Annie's day, she had this trap out on the back lawn. If a slave did something that she thought called for his death, sometimes she would have the other slaves force his leg into the bear trap and snap it shut. The condemned slave would suffer for days before dying. The other slaves were barred from getting close to him or providing even water. She wanted them to see what fate might befall them if they erred. Given a choice between the gallows or the bear trap, a slave would always take the gallows. Now, we leave it here for visitors to have a better understanding of the evil that was Annie Palmer. Only it never should have been opened..." Her voice trailed off.

"Believe me," Rodney said, "I'm beginning to get the idea."

The three men continued to follow Vertise down the stairs. When they got to the dungeon, now turned into a bar, Rodney edged up to walk beside their guide. Will smiled when he noted the change in positions.

Rodney whispered to Vertise, "Is there any other spooky stuff that goes on around here?"

Vertise smiled. "Since you ask, sometimes people have heard rapid footsteps going across the room we were just in and knocking on walls; I've been behind the bar when water just started running from the tap. Occasionally, visitors hear whispered voices in the dungeon. Some of them claim the voices are cries for help."

Rodney heard enough. He bolted for the door and was waiting for the others when they exited. Once outside, they were under a covered driveway where Vertise could call a taxi. Rodney walked in a circle, staring into the darkness, fearful that the *White Witch* would step from the shadows at any moment, dagger in hand.

CHAPTER 12

The taxi dropped the foursome at the front entrance to the Ritz. The three men and Vertise hurried to the bar, a spacious room with a high ceiling, dark wood paneled walls, discreet indirect lighting, plush, brown carpet, and tables for probably a hundred and fifty guests. A pianist and a bass player accompanied a singer in one corner. The waiters served drinks and cigars, mainly Cuban brands.

After being shown to a table, Vertise ordered white wine. Will and Manny chose Red Stripes. Rodney went for the hard stuff, a double martini on the rocks. When the waiter brought drinks, Rodney downed his in two gulps and ordered another before the waiter left the table.

"Hey, man," Will cautioned, "Take it easy."

"Hell, that was easy. I'll need three or four more just to sleep tonight."

"Anything more we should know about Rose Hall?" Manny changed the subject.

Vertise shook her head. "I think you've gotten a pretty good idea about the place. The Mansion has become a very popular tourist attraction."

"Yeah," Will replied, "I hear that every cruise ship that stops here has a special mansion ghost tour."

"Here's one more little-known fact. Johnny Cash had a house just up the hill from Rose Hall. He became fascinated with the story and wrote *The Ballad of Annie Palmer*, even recorded it on one of his albums in the seventies."

"Now tell us the truth, Vertise," Rodney said between gulps. "Would you go up there at night?"

"I was educated in the United States and worked for the *New York Times* until last year. Still, I don't push my luck, if you know what I mean." She looked down as she continued. "There are plenty of other places to go after dark."

Will glanced toward the door to the lobby and saw Kaven standing in the doorway, his eyes searching the tables. Will stood and waved at Kaven who wove his way between the tables and pulled up a chair. The waiter appeared immediately, somewhat taken aback by Kaven's appearance and not sure if he should be calling security. Kaven had a deep cut on his face, scratches like he had fought his way out of a briar patch on his arms, rips on his pants, and a splash of something red across the front of his shirt. Kaven ordered a double scotch. Will introduced Vertise and explained where Kaven had been that day.

"Looks like I should have gotten you a bodyguard."

"Yeah, it wasn't the day I expected. These people are going to be trouble, Will— big time trouble. I was lucky to get out of there with my life. I told you that I had to take one of Alexa's damn helicopters."

"Hell, I'm still surprised she didn't send a whole fleet of them."

"Even one wasn't a wise choice. Just pissed off the Maroons. They pulled me out of the chopper as soon as we landed. Then Colonel Broderick had me dragged up to a platform."

At the mention of Colonel Broderick's name, Vertise lowered her eyes and stared into her wine.

"I tried to explain about our company. Whatever I said just upset them even more. Colonel Broderick started yelling at me. Shots were fired. A little girl was hit. A cop tried to get me back to the chopper. We made it, but too late. By then, it was riddled with bullets."

"Shit, and I thought we had a bad day," Rodney said. "How'd you get out?"

"Cop led interference to his car. I got hit with some rocks. Some old woman threw blood on my shirt. See here. She even managed to cover most of the Global logo. On top of that, on the way down the mountain in the storm, we managed to roll the cop car."

"How the hell did that happen?" Manny asked.

"Road was wet. Waiter, can I have another double please? We came around a curve and there's this enormous yellow boa on the road. Cop tried to dodge it and we lost control, skidded down an embankment, and rolled the car. Climbed back up to the road about the time the second cop was coming down."

"What happened to the pilot?" Will asked.

"He was with the second cop. He's okay."

As he paused, Vertise leaned over and put her hand on Kaven's hand. "You must listen very carefully. That old woman was a voodoo muda. I know her. She put a curse on you and your company. Take my warning seriously...please."

"No way," Will said. "Voodoo's not for real. Just a bunch of mind games. Besides, the cops here say they wiped out the practice a hundred years ago."

Vertise slowly sipped her wine and shook her head at Will's comments. Kaven picked up his second double and downed it in one gulp. Without saying another word, he pushed back his chair and hurried out of the bar.

CHAPTER 13

Kaven joined other guests waiting for the elevator. When the elevator door opened, he was the only one to enter since the others elected not to ride with what appeared to be a street person. He stumbled as he left the elevator, wondering how two drinks could have such an effect. At the door, he fumbled for his key card, found it, and tried three times before the green light flashed permission for him to enter.

When he shut the door, he bolted it and hooked the chain. Next, he turned on all the lights. He searched the bathroom, checking the shower and the separate toilet area. He flung open the door to the closet to find it empty. He looked under the bed. He opened the glass doors to the balcony overlooking the ocean. Satisfied that no one was there, he secured the balcony doors and pulled the curtains. Next, he went to the mini-bar and extracted two small bottles of scotch. He opened and downed one as he stood in front of the mirror, sizing up the various cuts and bruises on his flesh as well as the rips and tears on his shirt and pants. Dammit, he thought, I wish I had stayed in Baltimore. I never should have returned to this damn island. He collapsed on the bed fully clothed, with the second bottle of scotch, unopened, still in his hand and stared at the ceiling, hoping that sleep might come.

***

A green Volkswagen turned off the highway a few miles east of the Ritz and into a parking lot in front of a bamboo thatched beach bar. Parts of the roof were missing following the storm, but the lights glowing from the inside indicated it was back in business. One old Toyota pickup and a nondescript sedan occupied the lot. The bar faced a deserted beach where the hurricane had washed up a few weather-beaten boards, seaweed, and a variety of beer and soft drink cans. A handful of fishing boats had been anchored forty yards offshore and survived the hurricane. Now, they rocked briskly in four and five-foot waves that passed among them before crashing on shore in front of the bar. The bar had no name. It didn't seek out the tourist trade. Locals knew it was there and when it was open. That's all that mattered to the owner.

Vertise locked her car and walked on stepping stones to the beach side. The bar was curved and had room for ten well-worn stools. Three tables with linoleum tops, surrounded with metal chairs, fronted the bar. Devon, the owner, stood behind the bar drinking a Red Stripe and smoking a cigar as he talked with Jorell, the groundskeeper from the Ritz. Sounds from a Bob Marley song came from two speakers hanging from the ceiling.

"Hey, Vertise. Where you been girl?" Devon asked. "You want another bartending job? I could use some time off."

"No thanks, Devon. I just need to talk to Jorell about something and saw his pickup in the parking lot."

"Get you anything to drink?"

"How about a bottle of water?"

"You know I can give you a Red Stripe for the same price."

"Doesn't matter. Water's fine."

Devon turned to a refrigerator, pulled out a bottle, and set it in front of Vertise. "I'll be in back if you need anything." Devon excused himself and went through a beaded doorway, leaving Vertise and Jorell alone.

Jorell shifted his bulk on the small stool to better face Vertise. "What's up?"

"I'm worried about Kaven Tillman. I don't really know him, but his Jamaican accent comes through even after five years in the states. He seems to be a nice guy in a job that may have just gotten too big for him. You ever heard of him?"

"Sure. If it's the same Kaven I'm thinking about, me and him went to high school together. Both of us grew up in Negril. He went to college, and then I heard he went to work for Global American somewhere in the United States."

Vertise nodded. "It must be the same guy." She explained Kaven's day as best she knew it. "I think his life is in danger. Could be some of the young Maroons, I don't know. I've got certain instincts. Bells are going off in my head. I tried to call his room when I left the Ritz. Couldn't get through. The man at the front desk said their phones were down from the storm. He couldn't say when they might be back up. Global has a security guy, Will something. Seems to be pretty sharp, but he doesn't know the island and the Maroons." She hesitated. "If he gets killed by the Maroons, or someone else for that matter, Global will be coming after the Maroons. I've researched Alexa Pritchard. She believes in an 'eye for an eye.' Jorell, you know we can't let that happen. I want to wage this war with my column, not with guns."

Jorell gazed out at the waves lapping to shore for a while and then spoke. "I've got a gun in the tool shed at the mansion. I suppose I could loan it to Kaven for a while."

Vertise seized the opportunity "Let's go get it. I'll take it back to the hotel. Maybe I can talk him into carrying it. I'll pay Devon and meet you in the parking lot."

Jorell nodded and slipped from his stool. Vertise fumbled in her purse for money, found it, and called to Devon for change. When she got to the parking lot, she could see the taillights of Jorell's pickup heading west. She started to get into her car when she noticed the back-left tire was flat. Someone had punctured the sidewall with a knife. *Who would do this? There were only three people in the bar. She had just left Devon. Why would Jorell give her a flat tire? Or was it someone who recognized her car from the highway? If so, why puncture her tire?* Kicking the tire in disgust, she went to the front of the Volkswagen and opened the trunk to retrieve the spare tire and jack. Answers would have to wait for a later time. For now, she had a tire to change.

CHAPTER 14

Jorell finished a call as he headed west on the highway. "Understood. I'll take care of it." Then he speed-dialed the Ritz. Pleased to find that an operator answered, he said, "Kaven Tillman's room, please."

Kaven was lying, still fully clothed, on his bed when the phone jangled him out of a light sleep. "Yeah," he answered.

"Kaven, this is Jorell. Mon, it's been a long time. I heard you were back on the island."

Now awake, Kaven said, "Is this Jorell from high school?"

"One and the same."

Suddenly cautious, Kaven asked, "If this is the Jorell I know, what position did you play on our football team?"

Jorell smiled. "I was the big guy that played middle defender. You were the fast one, usually played right wing." Kaven relaxed.

"Why the hell are you calling me in the middle of the night?"

"Heard you had a little trouble up at Accompong."

Kaven rose and paced the room. "Wait a minute. That just happened a few hours ago. How did you learn about it so quick?"

"Come on, Kaven, I know some of the Maroons. Word travels fast on this island. Now, you need to listen to me. We go back a long way. Your life is in danger if you stay in Jamaica. You need to get the first plane out of here in the morning."

Kaven shook his head as if Jorell were in the room. "Can't do that. My job's here now."

"Okay. Don't say I didn't warn you. Here's what you must do. I work for the Ritz as a groundskeeper at Rose Hall and the golf course. In fact, I saw some of your co-workers this afternoon. If those young Maroons are coming for you, they have a small arsenal up in Accompong. You need to be carrying a gun."

Kaven again shook his head as his voice raised. "Dammit, Jorell, I can't do that. You know that if I got caught with a gun on me, I'd be doing time."

Jorell raised his voice in return. "And if you don't carry a gun, every time you step out of that hotel, you're putting your life in danger. I've got one that I hide in the tool shed at Rose Hall. It's yours for now. Meet me on the steps of the mansion in thirty minutes. I'll leave the front gate unlocked." Jorell clicked off the phone as he turned into the front drive of the mansion and dropped from his truck to unlock the gate.

Kaven stared at the phone and wondered what to do. He started to call Will's room, but glanced at the clock and realized it was two a.m. He looked in the mirror and saw he still had the tattered and torn clothes he had been wearing earlier that day, including the shirt with blood splotched across the Global logo. He stripped off the shirt and his pants, replacing them with a clean shirt, this one with no logo, and jeans. He grabbed his key card and wallet and walked to the door and paused. He walked back through the room to the balcony where he could see the moon glistening on the waves as they crashed on shore. He considered his options. The Maroons could be waiting just outside the hotel. But Jorell was an old friend and, as best he could recall, Jorell was not a Maroon. Besides the Rose Hall Mansion is part of the Ritz complex. They probably have a couple of guards roaming the property. And while personal weapons were illegal, the chances of his getting caught were slim. Last, he thought about the stories that he had known since he was a boy about Annie Palmer and the legend of the White Witch. A minute later he took a deep breath, exhaled, and left the room.

Kaven stepped from the elevator on the main floor. He stopped to study a three-dimensional rendition of the Ritz property. When he determined that the Rose Hall Mansion was just across the street and up the hill, he set off toward the front entrance.

The attendant at the front desk was not accustomed to seeing guests leave at this hour of the morning. "Sir, can I help you?"

Kaven ignored him.

When he arrived at the front door, a bellman asked, "Sir, can I call you a taxi?"

Kaven shook his head and walked down the driveway, breathing in the scent of tropical flowers. When he approached the guardhouse, the guard said, with a sense of urgency in his voice, "Sir, it's too late for tourists to be out alone. Street gangs cruise the highway this time of night looking for tourists in rental vehicles. You will be even more of a target if you're walking alone. There's nothing out there that won't wait until morning."

Kaven ignored him.

"At least let me call a cab."

Kaven kept walking and crossed the highway. On the other side, he looked both directions and turned left. He walked about a hundred yards through a night where clouds had now drifted over the moon, leaving only shadows that seemed to take on a life of their own. The only sounds he heard came from night birds and the occasional crackling of limbs, weakened from the storm. After listening to the guard, he was relieved that the highway was deserted. When he reached the drive to the mansion, he found it as Jorell had said. The gate, usually locked, had been opened. He could make out a sign that announced the entrance to the Rose Hall Mansion. He presumed that it had been lighted, but the storm darkened it.

Kaven hesitated at the entrance, wondering once again if he was doing the right thing. He again glanced both ways on the highway and tilted his head until he could see the mansion looming in the shadows toward the top of the hill. Now he could hear waves crashing to shore behind him, along with the creaking of palm trees still responding to the remaining gusts of the hurricane. He tried to put thoughts of Annie Palmer roaming the grounds out of his mind and started a slow trek up the hill.

As he walked, he had to focus on the road that was strewn with downed trees and limbs, along with power lines that no longer carried electricity but could still be a hazard he could trip over. Off in the bushes he heard something. A person? An animal? He stopped and listened quietly. Nothing. He continued to walk. Now he was certain he heard footsteps. He whirled and saw nobody. "What the hell am I doing here in the middle of the night?" Kaven mumbled to no one but himself.

As he climbed the hill, the mansion loomed larger. Strange, he thought, he had only vaguely heard of Annie Palmer before he left for Maryland. He remembered his mother talking about her. Of course, he grew up down the road in Negril. Or maybe it was when the Ritz bought the property and restored it, that her legend grew. On the other hand, he knew there were many islanders who still were raised to believe that Annie Palmer roamed these parts every night. Right about now. Shit!

Now all Kaven could think about was the White Witch and the number of people that died at her command on these very grounds two hundred years before. Again, he considered turning back, but didn't. He was convinced that after what had happened in Accompong, he needed a gun. When he arrived at the front steps, he stopped to catch his breath and then listened. There was only silence.

"Hello."

Silence.

"Jorell? Where are you?"

Silence.

"Anybody?"

A crack of a branch under someone's foot sounded like a bolt of lightning.

"Who's that? I've got a gun. Jorell, you there?"

The next sound was a rush of steps. When he turned, Kaven was hit over the head with a large rock. Passing into unconsciousness, his last thought was that he should have called Will.

CHAPTER 15

Will stayed for another drink with Rodney and Manny after Kaven had stumbled off to his room and Vertise said her goodbyes. He wanted to make sure that his colleagues had not suffered any ill effects from the events of the day. "Okay, Rodney, I think you've had about enough. You won't be able to see a computer keyboard if you have another martini."

"Sorry. This whole day spooked me out. Maybe I'll settle for a cigar as a nightcap." He motioned to the waiter and requested a selection of cigars. He returned with an assortment of Cuba's finest.

"I don't know a damn thing about cigars. You pick. What's your name?"

"Dennard, sir. I suggest this one. It's full bodied, slightly aromatic, just the thing to finish off the night. May I light it for you?"

Rodney nodded as Dennard clipped the cigar, handed it to Rodney and held a flame to it while Rodney puffed. Rodney broke out in a fit of coughing and pronounced it excellent.

"Manny," Will asked, "You okay with what happened today?"

"Yeah, mon. You notice I called you 'mon.' I'm a quick study. Everything's cool. Hurricanes, like shit, just happen. As to the mansion, it's a really crazy story. I'd like to figure out what part is real and what part is legend. And I'm amazed by Vertise. You don't often find that kind of brains and beauty in the same package. I'll have one more Red Stripe and then turn in."

Will switched to brandy for his last drink. He and Manny finished their drinks while Rodney figured out how to puff on a cigar without inhaling. Since they were about to close the bar, Will called for a check. "Okay, guys, tomorrow we go on the clock. We already know we're facing some problems we didn't anticipate. Alexa should have warned us, but she probably just figured that Global could deal with a bunch of semi-literate natives living in the mountains by themselves. Maybe she didn't know that they had fought for their country for a couple of hundred years and won. Let's get a good night's sleep. We'll plan our day over breakfast. And I promise we'll finish playing the White Witch before we leave here."

Suddenly, Rodney coughed. "Dammit, Will. I told you I don't want anything more to do with that white bitch. Don't even mention Miss Annie to me in polite conversation."

Will returned to his room, too wound up to sleep. He stripped to his underwear and flipped channels on a large screen HD television until he ran across *First Blood* with Sylvester Stallone. Having lived that life for a few years, he never passed up the opportunity to watch it again. He settled back and had drifted off to sleep when his cell chimed. He glanced at the television to make sure it was not coming from there and found Fred Astaire waltzing Ginger Rogers around a ballroom. He turned off the television and reached for his phone.

"Taylor."

"Will, Alexa here." It was nearly three in the morning and Alexa was still at her desk. Smoke drifted from a cigarette in her ash tray while she sucked on a Tootsie Pop. She was on the speaker phone. When Will answered, she walked to her window and stared at the lights of Baltimore.

Will turned on the nightstand light, glanced at the clock, and swung his feet into a sitting position on the side of the bed. "Yes, ma'am. Little late for a booty call."

"Cut the crap. Kaven was just found at Rose Hall. He's dead."

"What? Are you sure? I just saw him a few hours ago." Will got to his feet and began pacing the room. "Shit."

"Must be those goddamn Maroons. He called me last night once he got back from Accompong. He told me about what happened up there. By the way, they let the pilot go. They said they had no beef with him."

"So I heard. What was Kaven doing at Rose Hall? When I saw him, he was going to his room."

"How the hell should I know? I got a call from some local detective. They found his employee identification in his wallet. When the detective called here, the operator knew I was still in my office and put the call through to me. You need to get to Rose Hall now."

"Yes, ma'am," Will agreed.

"And I'm flying down there tomorrow before this gets any more out of hand. See if you can keep anybody else from being killed until I get there."

Will's cell went dead. He put it on the nightstand and picked up the hotel phone. Pleased to find it working, he punched the key for valet parking.

"Good evening, Mr. Taylor. How can I be of assistance?"

"Bring my company Land Rover to the front as quickly as possible."

Getting assurance that it would be there when he got downstairs, Will hung up and walked to the bathroom. Five minutes later he was met at the hotel entrance by a valet.

"Can I give you directions, Mr. Taylor? It's a little late at night."

"No thanks. I know exactly where I'm going." Will got in the car, fastened his seat belt, and left the hotel.

CHAPTER 16

When Will got to Rose Hall, he turned onto the road they had just come down the evening before. At the top of the hill he could see the mansion, now well lighted. He dodged tree limbs and utility wires and parked among several other vehicles. Police cars were positioned so that their headlights focused on the steps of the mansion where Will could see the yellow police crime scene tape. He walked up a path from the parking lot between the police cars that faced the mansion to the yellow tape where an officer stood watch. The officer came to attention as Will approached.

"Sorry, mon. I can't let you past here. We're investigating a murder."

Will kept his voice even but controlling. "I know, officer. That's why I'm here. Name's William Taylor. I'm head of security for Global American Metals. Here's my identification." Will tried to hand him an ID. The officer just shook his head. "Officer, the dead man is one of Global's employees. Can you get someone in authority to let me up there?"

Before the officer could reply, Miles Harper, the St. James Parish Chief of Detectives, approached. Harper was a lean, fit man with a shaved head and a no-nonsense manner. He was dressed in a brown suit, yellow shirt, and matching tie. He looked like he just stepped out of *GQ Magazine*, even at three in the morning.

"Mr. Taylor, I'm Miles Harper, Chief of Detectives in this parish. I was told by your company to expect you."

Will extended his right hand. Harper ignored it. Instead, he nodded at the officer and motioned for Will to follow him. Harper went up a dozen steps and turned to Will as he stood beside Kaven's body, sprawled on his back with a dagger in his chest. Will bent over for a closer look and found that the handle of the dagger was in the shape of a snake. At the top of the handle was the snake's head. The snake's eyes were two bright rubies.

"Shit," Will muttered, "He was almost killed because of one snake on the road today and now someone finished the job with a, what would you call this, a snake dagger?"

"That's as good a name as any, Mr. Taylor. My officers reported what went on up in Accompong and the incident with the boa."

Will continued to study the body. "Looks like he's been dead a couple of hours. I last saw him about ten last night. Who found him?"

"The hotel has a security guard that roams the mansion grounds and up to the club house in a golf cart. He spotted the body."

"Where's your coroner?"

"He's a local Justice of the Peace, not a medical doctor. He won't set foot on these steps until morning. My men here won't go past the tape either. They believe the White Witch did it."

Will shook his head in disbelief. "Come on, Chief, this is the twenty-first century."

"Old beliefs die hard, Mr. Taylor. Come on. Let me show you something."

Harper stepped around the body and climbed the steps with Will behind him. Entering the ballroom, Will said, "I was just in this room yesterday evening during the storm."

Harper turned to study Will. "Would you care to explain?"

Will covered the details of the previous day and their time in the mansion while they waited out the storm. "You know a woman named Vertise?"

Harper nodded his head. "She's a local. Works for the paper and tends bar for the hotel. Since you were in this room a few hours ago, come over here." Harper led Will to a glass display against one wall with pictures of two snake daggers above it along with the history of the daggers. The glass had been broken and the daggers were gone.

"You see this case when you were up here?"

Will studied it and thought back to the day before. "Can't say I did, Chief. It was pretty dark in here, lit only by candles since the storm knocked out power. I wandered around the room but never glanced toward this case. And I don't believe anyone else mentioned it. Now that I think about it, Vertise told us the legend of Annie Palmer and her using a snake dagger to kill an overseer.

Surprising that she didn't show us these daggers when she was telling the story."

"Interesting," mused Harper. "You have any idea why your man would come up here in the middle of the night?"

"Not a clue. Have you checked his cell phone? He always carried it."

"Yeah. The last calls were with you yesterday afternoon and one with Ms. Pritchard later in the evening."

Will nodded. "He called me from Accompong, warning me of trouble up there. I should have gone with him."

Harper shook his head. "Whether you were there or not wouldn't have made any difference. Just would have been one more person that was in my police car that rolled, assuming, of course, you didn't take a bullet up on the mountain."

"Understood."

"How did you get in the mansion?"

"Vertise said she knew where a key was hidden and let us in."

"Strange that she could get into the locked mansion. It was my understanding that only the manager of Rose Hall had a key. He locked it and left when the storm was hitting. The hotel spent a fortune on period pieces to recreate how it looked two hundred years ago. One of his jobs is to make sure they are not stolen."

"Any signs of a break-in?" Will asked.

"This is not for publication, you understand, but when I got here the mansion was locked and the lights were off."

"So, you're saying that someone got into the mansion, stole two daggers, let themselves back out, killed Kaven, and left no trace." Will paused to absorb all that he had just said. "Wait a minute. If someone wanted to kill Kaven, why not just use a gun? Why go to all the trouble of getting that dagger to do it?"

"I've been wrestling with that very question," Harper said. "It's illegal for a private citizen to own a gun in Jamaica, but that doesn't mean they are not available if you know the right people. My working hypothesis is that the killer or killers wanted the public to think voodoo was involved, or maybe even the White Witch. The only other possibility that comes to mind is that the Maroons are trying to send a message to Global. They tried to kill Tillman in Accompong and failed. Maybe the message is that they finish what they start. Either way, someone is trying to make trouble for your company. I have another problem that may not be apparent."

Will looked quizzically at the detective.

"As you can see, there were two snake daggers in this case. One's accounted for out on the steps. The other is gone. Nearly everyone around here thinks that they are voodoo daggers with magical powers. They were found in an overseer's grave during the restoration of the mansion thirty years ago."

"Does 'everyone' include you? Looks to me like the killer or killers are just trying to mess with the minds of my co-workers, maybe keep some locals from hiring on with us."

Harper stuck his hands in his pockets. "Not up to me to decide if they're magic or not. I've got a murder with one of those daggers. My job is to solve the murder and along the way, find that other dagger before someone uses it."

Will's eyes searched the room in a futile effort to see any clues to the crime. Then he focused on the chief. "Look, I'm going to need a gun. My company is obviously under attack. I'm licensed to carry back home."

"No way, Mr. Taylor," Harper exploded. "Foreigners are not permitted to have guns in Jamaica. For that matter, as I just told you, neither are Jamaicans. And I want you to stay the hell out of my investigation. We don't need your help. Understand?"

"Yeah, I understand. You know that each of our mines on this island is permitted a certain number of guns for our guards. I'll just get one of those."

"The hell you will. Don't you dare go behind my back. Those guns never leave mine property. I have an officer that inventories them. If one turns up missing, I'll confiscate every damn weapon that Global has and put you under house arrest. Clear, Mr. Taylor?"

Will clinched his fists and tried to hold back the anger that was apparent in his face. Without another word, he turned and stormed out of the mansion, pausing only to gaze at Kaven and say a prayer for him and his family. At the bottom of the steps, he got in his car and glanced toward the mansion. The lights from his car somehow caught the ruby eyes of the snake, making them appear briefly to be alive. Will shook his head, put the car in reverse, and returned to the hotel.

CHAPTER 20

Will handed his Land Rover over to the valet and went to his room. It was still only five o'clock. He wanted to alert Manny and Rodney to the events of the night but decided to wait until seven to roust them out of bed. He ordered a pot of coffee and a basket of rolls from room service and stepped to the bathroom where he took a long, hot shower and shaved. When he heard a knock at the door, he donned the Ritz robe and asked the bellman to roll the cart onto the balcony where the first light of day was illuminating the ocean. He tipped the bellman and checked to make sure the door locked when he left. Will poured black coffee and took a sip, smiling at the robust flavor of the Jamaican brew. Next, he buttered a roll and sat back to watch the beginning of the day while he thought about the events of the early morning.

Who wanted Kaven dead? The Maroons were at the top of the list. But why choose Kaven to make a statement? They could have figured out some way to kill him up at Accompong. No, they wouldn't do it up there, not on their home turf. Or maybe it is some old enemy from Kaven's former days on the island. And why would Kaven go up to Rose Hall in the middle of the night? He had to have gotten a call, but the phones were down in the hotel for most of the night. I'll need to check with the hotel about whether and when a call went through to his room. Surely he would have contacted me, unless…unless he knew the person who talked him into going to Rose Hall. And why was he killed with a snake dagger? Obviously, voodoo still exists on this island. Still, I'm not going to put two-hundred-year-old Annie Palmer on my list of suspects. On the other hand, his death at Rose Hall with a snake dagger will be in all the island newspapers in a matter of hours. Maybe the message is that anyone who goes to work for Global may suffer the same fate. Then there's Miles Harper. It's his jurisdiction and he doesn't want me involved. Fat chance of that. Kaven was my friend. We used to have a beer after work every week or two. Good guy. Shouldn't have met a violent death. And so young. Shit, I'll conduct my own investigation, starting with the hotel this morning and probably backtracking to Accompong before the day is over. Harper can do what he damn well pleases.

Will glanced at his watch. It was not quite seven, but close enough to call Manny and Rodney and ask them to meet him in the dining room in thirty minutes. He chose a table overlooking the Caribbean. He was perusing the menu when Rodney joined him with Manny following close behind.

"What's up?" Rodney asked. "I didn't figure we'd have breakfast until about nine."

Will took a sip of black coffee. "Bad news. Kaven was killed last night. Or I should say early this morning."

"How could that be?" Manny asked. "We all saw him leaving for his room. Someone break into his room? Why?"

Will raised his hand for silence. "Hold on. You're right that he went to his room. Sometime during the night, he went to Rose Hall. A security guard making his rounds in a golf cart spotted him on the steps leading to the front door."

"How the hell did he get there?" Manny asked.

"I'll be talking to some folks at the hotel when we finish breakfast. I presume he must have walked up the hill to the mansion."

"That's crazy. No one in their right mind would have gone up there at night. I don't believe that Annie Palmer is out, roaming her property. Still, what Vertise said yesterday kind of worried me," Rodney said.

Manny nodded his agreement as the waiter filled his coffee cup.

"There's one more thing. He was killed with a snake dagger through the heart."

Rodney choked on his coffee, almost spewing it across the white table cloth.

"Will, give it to us straight," Manny said. Are the three of us in danger?"

Will stared out the window before speaking. "I wish I could say we're not, but right now I have no idea."

"Well, that's just goddamn great," Manny said. "I came down here to open a mine and now I may be the next one killed."

"I saw a cabinet yesterday afternoon," Rodney said. "It was over against the wall. Had two daggers enclosed in glass. Both seemed identical, with a snake wrapping itself around the handle. The eyes were some kind of red stone."

"I missed it," Will said, "Not that I would have thought anything about two knives in that place."

There was silence around the table. Each of the men allowed the events to sink in until Rodney spoke. "Now, I am a little freaked out. Did Kaven have any old enemies on the island? Could it have been those Maroons? Only, they could have killed him when he and that cop were coming down the mountain."

"They ran off the road to avoid a yellow boa," Manny interrupted. "You think that that old voodoo woman put that snake there?"

Will flattened his hands on the table. "Hold on, guys. We're speculating when we have only one fact: Kaven is dead on the steps of the mansion with a dagger in his chest. And, I almost forgot. He also had a blunt trauma wound to his head, probably from a rock. Here's what I'm doing today. By the time we finish breakfast, I should be able to round up a manager or assistant manager. After I find out what I can at the hotel, I'm taking a drive up to Accompong."

"Maybe I ought to go with you," Manny said. "I already have a bulldozer doing some preliminary clearing. I was planning to check up there anyway."

Will thought about Manny's offer and then agreed. "Now, I need to know what we're doing up there as much as you. We'll be unarmed. So, two men will hardly be another show of force. By the way, Alexa will be here sometime today. I expect a command performance."

"I just lost my appetite," Rodney said. "We computer geeks are not used to having to deal with murder. I'll miss Kaven. We met most Sunday mornings at that Starbucks by the park. Then we'd go over to one of those concrete tables and play chess for two or three hours." Rodney smiled. "That son of a bitch. The last time we played, he whipped my ass. Then he goes and gets himself killed. I can't even get a rematch. What do you want me to do?"

"Hang out in your room. Do not go anywhere else. Now, you may have lost your appetite; only, Manny and I may not get another meal before nightfall. So, we're going to order. Your choice to stay or go to your room."

Rodney rubbed his face with the palms of his hands. "I might as well have something since I'm here. And I damn sure expect to see the two of you back here tonight. Understood?"

CHAPTER 18

After breakfast Rodney went to his room. Manny did the same and was told to await a call from Will, who walked to the reception desk. An attractive young lady, whose name tag identified her as Catherine, smiled as he approached.

"Good morning, Catherine. I'm Will Taylor." He handed her his business card. "I'm vice-president of Global American Metals security and a guest of this hotel. One of our co-workers, Kaven Tillman, was killed at the Rose Hall Mansion sometime during the night."

The desk attendant brought her hand to her mouth. "I just heard about that when I came on duty. We have our hotel head of security on it, too."

"I'll be conducting my own investigation. Could I speak to the manager on duty and your head of security?"

"Certainly, I'll call our manager." She hesitated. "Can I say one thing?"

Will nodded.

"No one should be at that mansion after dark. I've lived here my entire life. When I was a little girl, my mother warned me to never go close to it at night. Many of us believe that Annie Palmer roams the grounds. She still believes it's her house and will do whatever necessary to protect it."

She turned to the phone. Within a minute a handsome black man, dressed in a Brooks Brothers suit, blue shirt, and dark striped tie approached and extended his hand. "Mr. Taylor, I'm Alfred Sampson. I've called our head of security. Please follow me back to my office."

Sampson led the way a few steps to a paneled door that opened into a secretarial/reception area and through it into his office, one that was comfortable but not extravagant. "Can I get you coffee?" Sampson asked as he pointed to one of the guest chairs.

"No thanks. I love your coffee, but I've been drinking it since about five this morning."

There was a knock on the door, and a man who looked as if he could have played linebacker in the NFL entered. "Mr. Taylor, this is Johnson Murphy, our director of security. Please have a seat, John." He turned to Will. "First, let me say how sorry I am about Mr. Tillman's death. We will do anything we can to assist in finding his killer."

The deep voice of Murphy interrupted. "I've already been on it. Here's what I've found so far." He handed Will several sheets of paper. Will paged through them as he talked. "First, our hotel phones were back up at 1:22 a.m. At 1:53 Mr. Tillman received a call in his room. The length of the call was 93 seconds."

"If I can interrupt," Will said, "do you have any way to trace the caller?"

Murphy shook his head. "Afraid not. Came from a cell phone. That's all we can determine. I'm afraid our phone tracking systems are not as modern as yours in the States. He left his room five minutes later. Next, I have already taken statements from the front desk attendant, the bellman, and the security guard at the entrance to the hotel. As you can see, they are almost identical. All three encouraged Mr. Tillman not to leave the hotel alone, to at least get a taxi. He ignored them. He was last seen by the front gate security guard crossing the highway and walking in the direction of Rose Hall."

"Did you alert the guard at the mansion?"

Murphy shook his head. "We had no idea where he was going. In hindsight, maybe we should have. But the fact of the matter is that we cannot be responsible for our guests once they leave the hotel property."

Will nodded his understanding and turned to Sampson. "What about this Annie Palmer and her legend? It started popping up yesterday, even while we were out on the golf course."

Sampson folded his hands on his desk. "Voodoo was practiced on this island for a couple of hundred years. The actual name of the religion practiced then was *Obeah*. Voodoo is the common slang term. It doesn't exist now. You can ask Chief Harper. Oh, there may be some natives who still believe in the powers of the occult, but not among the educated. As to Annie Palmer, we certainly would not have spent millions restoring the mansion and put a championship golf course on the old plantation property if we believed that the property was truly haunted. Old myths die hard." He paused. "I must say, we are somewhat responsible for perpetuating the myth. It's good for business. But, if something goes bump in the night at the mansion, you can rest assured that it's not Miss Annie roaming around and knocking over lamps."

Will noticed that Murphy remained strangely silent as his boss discredited the legend. He would need to take Murphy aside some time soon to get his take on Annie and the snake daggers.

CHAPTER 22

Will called Manny from a house phone and told him to meet at the valet parking service. When Will asked for his car, a valet ran to retrieve it. While he waited, he turned to the head valet. "Can I have a map that will show me how to get to Accompong?"

The valet shook his head. "Sir, I would not recommend that any white man go into the Cockpit Country. Too dangerous. I have some friends who work in Montego Bay They're Maroons. They tell me the people up there are riled up about a bauxite mine stripping away their ancestral home."

Will nodded his understanding as the Range Rover was brought to the front of the hotel at the same time as Manny walked out. "Appreciate that, but we're not looking to cause trouble. I have to track down whoever killed Kaven Tillman last night at the mansion. He was up in Accompong yesterday. I need to talk to Colonel Broderick. But thanks for your advice." Will handed the valet five American dollars. The valet shook his head as he handed him a map. Will and Manny fastened their seat belts when Will turned right onto the North Coast Highway.

"You know where we're going?" Manny asked.

"Not exactly. The hotel security guard said to follow the highway through Montego Bay toward Negril and veer left up the mountain. Paved, pothole-filled road. Should take about two hours."

"Good directions. This map is not all that clear, but that should be about right. Look for any signs that point us toward Accompong."

They drove through a construction zone, around and past barricades and orange barrels. When they passed a shack on the left, Manny said, "Hey, that's

Scochie's. We'll need to stop on the way back. Reputation is that it's the best jerk chicken on the island. A couple of those and a six pack of Red Stripes and we'll be set for the night." His voice dropped. "I only wish that Kaven was here to share it with us."

Will nodded as they passed by what was known as the Hip Strip, several blocks of restaurants, bars, and tourist traps. The better restaurants opened onto the water. Once the sun set, dope dealers with one or more gold teeth appeared on their corners along with whores who would do nearly anything for a few dollars. Fortunately, they generally left the tourists from the cruise ships alone unless approached. That was their understanding with the local police...ply your trade, sell your dope, but don't piss off the tourists who were the bread and butter of the Montego Bay.

Beyond the strip they came to a fork in the road. A sign pointed to the highway to the west, headed for Negril. Another pointed up the mountain to Accompong. When they turned, they left tourist Jamaica behind. On either side of the road were tin shanties that did little to keep out the wind and rain. The side streets were mud. Small children ran up and down clad only in diapers or nothing at all. Women, some young and some old, sat on old wooden chairs, watching the children and smoking weed. Will wondered where they got the money for even such a meager existence. After a few miles, they started climbing the mountain, dodging potholes and minor landslides that covered parts of the road after the heavy rains of the past week.

"Watch out," Manny yelled.

A goat had chosen that moment to mosey across the road. Will slammed on his brakes and felt the rear of the Land Rover fish tail. "All right, we both better keep our eyes open. I don't want my obituary to read, *He Dodged a Goat. The Goat Lived. He Didn't.*"

Winding up the mountain, they found the jungle cleared in several areas. Crops were growing in fields right beside the road. While they saw some corn and other vegetables, nearly every square foot was filled with marijuana. Toward the back of each field was a shack, probably occupied by the farmer and his family. Will found it interesting that no one seemed to be concerned about the growing of dope. He flagged his memory to ask Harper about it when he saw him again.

Going around a curve, they spotted what appeared to be a convenience store, or at least a store with a few groceries. They turned onto the dirt parking lot and locked the car before they entered. An old man sat on a stool, puffing on a spliff. He nodded but said nothing. Will looked around and spotted a small refrigerator where he extracted two bottles of water. The old man held up three fingers. Will left a five on the counter and asked, "How far to Accompong?"

The old man took the five and stuck it in his pocket. He shrugged his shoulders and pointed up the mountain. "Not far." Then his voice dropped. "Only they don't like white men up there. You be careful."

About two hundred yards beyond the store, both men spotted tire tracks veering from the oncoming lane down an embankment. Manny yelled, "Stop," but Will was hitting the brake a split second before Manny's yell.

"Must be where the police car went over the side," Manny said.

"I'll get as far to the left as I can without getting off the pavement."

The outside edge of the tires barely touched the mud beside the road. Will cussed as he stepped from the car and almost slid over the embankment. Manny walked around the front of the car. "I see the police car about forty yards down there. It's lying on its side up against a giant tree of some kind. Damn sure lucky the tree stopped them. Doesn't look like anything else to slow them for another hundred yards."

"We're going down there to take a look."

"What are we looking for?"

Will shook his head. "Damned if I know. I'll tell you when I see something."

Using branches of trees and bushes for support, they made their way down. Manny grabbed the wrong branch at one point. It broke off in his hand. He found himself sliding down the muddy slope until he managed to grab a tree trunk as he went by. Will tried to hurry to him, but was also worried that he could face a similar problem. When he got to Manny, he was wrapped around the tree, using both arms and legs.

"You okay?" Will asked.

"I don't think anything is broken."

Will directed Manny to follow him. When they came close to the police car, they found little more than a frame. The tires and wheels had been stripped. The engine was gone. The lights, both front and rear, were taken. The same with all the windows. Looking inside, the seats had vanished along with the radio.

"I understand how they took all this other stuff, but that engine had to weigh several hundred pounds" Will said. "Maybe they threw a chain over a branch of that tree and…shit, there's a yellow boa up there, wrapped around the lowest branch. To hell with any more investigating. Let's get out of here."

Manny didn't have to be told twice. He was already halfway up the hill when Will took off after him. They made it to the road. Both bent over to catch their breath when they heard someone laughing at them. Will raised his head to see Chief Miles Harper, pointing down the hill. "You boys scared of a little snake. Wrapped around that branch, he's not going anywhere for a good while." The tone of his voice changed. "Taylor, I told you to stay the hell out of my murder investigation."

Will took a moment until his breath returned. "Why, Chief, we're just out for a drive, doing the tourist thing. By the way, you've got some very efficient vultures around these parts. Stripped that car down to the bare bones in less than a day."

"Every part on that car has an ID number. They'll turn up shortly and we'll arrest a few thieves. Still, all they did was steal some parts." He pointed at Will. "Hear me good. I'll say it again. This is my show and I don't want you tampering with any evidence. Get on back down to Montego Bay. That clear?"

Will shook his head. "Sorry, Chief, but I figure we are now in Cockpit Country. Unless you're charging us with murder, we'll be on our way. As I understand it, Colonel Broderick is the judge and jury up here. You have a good day."

Harper's face scowled with anger. He walked the few feet between him and Will until they were nose-to-nose. "You apparently don't understand the Queen's English. You will not go any farther up this mountain until I say it's okay. Understood now?"

Will stepped back and composed himself. "Tell you what, I'll give you a couple of days. If you don't have any hard leads on Kaven's murder, all bets are off." Will turned to his car and Manny climbed in the other side. He turned the car around and started down the mountain.

"You sure you're doing the right thing?" Manny asked.

Will shook his head. "Not really, but the murder was down at the mansion. We have plenty to do there and in Montego Bay. We'll give Harper some time to get his shit together. If he's still clueless, we'll ignore his damn orders. I'll alert Global's legal department to have local counsel on standby if he throws us in the hoosegow."

70

CHAPTER 20

They made their way back to Montego Bay without incident. Will told Manny that he was dropping him at the hotel and then going back to the Hip Strip for an appointment.

"Stop," Manny yelled. "There's Scochie's. If you are eating back at the strip, I want to buy a couple of chickens and two six packs of Red Stripe. Rodney and I can sit out on the balcony, chow down on jerk chicken, and get a little mellow as we watch the sun slide into the ocean."

Will turned into the gravel drive and stopped in front of a wall. They smelled the chicken on the other side and walked to one end to find the entrance. Beyond the wall was a bar with eight stools that appeared to be on their last legs. Across a small courtyard was a window where customers could place orders. Manny ordered two chickens to go and two six packs of Red Stripe. Before he finished his order, Will interjected, "Make that three chickens, one to eat here."

The elderly woman behind the counter handed over twelve Red Stripes and took Will's money. He told her to keep the change but to let them know when the one to be eaten here was ready. They took their beer and found a small table with a thatched umbrella to shield the afternoon sun. They had barely finished one beer when the woman motioned that their order was ready. She handed Manny the chicken wrapped in foil and a few sheets of butcher paper along with napkins. When Manny set the chicken on the table, Will allowed the aroma to drift over him. "Hell, that smells so good I may forget my appointment and see how many of these I can devour."

Instead he took a few bites and shoved the remainder to Manny. "I'd like to eat it all, but I have a lunch appointment."

Manny wiped his mouth and said, "Just more for me."

While Manny finished the chicken, Will had a second beer. "I need to get going. You and Rodney enjoy the rest back at the hotel."

Will made the five-minute drive to the Ritz, dropped Manny off, and headed back to the Hip Strip. He valeted in front of Margarita's Cafe and entered a restaurant that opened out to the ocean. At mid-afternoon the place was near deserted; so, he wandered around looking at the guitars and other memorabilia on the walls, along with photos of Jimmy Buffett and the Coral Reefer Band. Nothing was said about Buffett owning the place, but his history in Jamaica was well known and Will figured he must have a piece of the action.

After fifteen minutes, he asked to be seated at a table beside the water where he could watch the waves pounding below the restaurant and the boats gliding by farther out at sea. When he looked again toward the entrance, he saw Vertise hurrying through the door and nodding to the head waiter as she made her way through the empty tables.

"I'm so sorry," she said as she shook Will's hand and took a seat opposite him. "I had to finish a story, and my editor made me make minor corrections three times. Somehow, he forgets that I graduated with honors and don't really need his copy-editing. Can I get a glass of Chardonnay?"

Will looked at the waiter who was hovering near them. "A glass of your best Chardonnay for the lady. I'll have a vodka martini on the rocks, a little dirty with two olives. Do you have 10th Mountain vodka?"

The waiter shook his head. "No sir. I've heard good things about it, but we don't serve it."

"Then make mine with Grey Goose...and light on the Vermouth."

After the waiter served their drinks, Will and Vertise ordered lunch and quietly sipped their drinks while they watched the ships and sailboats. Soon the waiter returned with a club sandwich for Vertise and a hamburger for Will.

"Oh," Vertise said as she reached into her purse. "Here's the story I was finishing. It will be in the morning edition."

Will glanced through it. "So, it's about that young girl killed up at the Cudjoe Day celebration. You know who did it?"

Vertise sipped her wine. "I know who didn't. It wasn't Kaven. He didn't even have a gun. Blaming him is just throwing up a smoke screen."

"What about the story of his death?"

"I did that one first. It's just factual—an interview with Harper, photos of the mansion. No leads on who did it yet. I wish I could tell you more."

Will put down his martini and stared into Vertise's face. "Look, Kaven was my friend. There seems to be a cover-up here…"

Before he could say anything more, Vertise interrupted. "No way, Mr. Taylor. I research the facts and I write the story. No slanting any direction. Look, I'm a Maroon, too, a descendant of slaves. One of my ancestors was killed by the white witch. That's why my editor assigned this story to me. I'm reporting the facts, nothing more, nothing less."

Silence again as Will drummed his fingers on the table. "You said something yesterday about living in the states?"

Vertise took a bite from her club sandwich before speaking. "As a girl, all I wanted was to get off this island. I graduated at the top of my class and earned a scholarship to any school in the United States. I chose Columbia because I wanted to live in the big city. I majored in journalism, got a job with the *Times* and never expected to set foot on this island again."

"What changed your mind? Now you're working for a two-bit local paper and bartending to make ends meet."

Vertise thought for a moment. "Your company changed my mind."

"My company? You're kidding."

Vertise shook her head. "Up there in the Cockpit Country is our most valuable resource. It's not bauxite. It's the rainforest. Its many treasures have yet to be documented. I came back to keep your company and its efforts to destroy the rainforest on the front page of the paper."

Will gulped the remainder of his martini and ordered another. "Whoa. Just a minute. When we put a mine anywhere in the world, we also budget for restoration. We return the land to how it was before."

Vertise slammed down her water. "That's bullshit. I've studied your company's operations. You'll come in with a few truckloads of dirt, throw down a few seeds, pat yourselves on the back and leave." Tears filled her eyes. "Only, our forest will be gone forever."

Will tried to control the anger that was causing his voice to rise. "We have a wall back in Maryland filled with letters of gratitude from public officials on five continents."

"I'm sure you do. You leave those same officials with pockets overflowing with money," Vertise hissed. "The Cockpit Country will look like the surface of the moon. It's my people who will suffer, not the politicians in Kingston."

"Wait just a damn minute."

"No. You wait." Vertise said. She stood, shoved her chair back and threw her napkin on the table. "You need to stop your company before they do any more damage. I know your Ms. Pritchard has paid...bribed...the Minister of Mines and I'm close to proving it."

She turned and stormed from the restaurant, passing the waiter who was bringing Will's second martini. He looked at Vertise and back at Will. "Sir, will you still be having this?"

"No, but if you don't mind, I just need to sit here a few minutes more."

Will considered what Vertise had said. *No doubt Alexa was ruthless, but had she really been paying off officials in other countries? Was she doing it here? If so, how did she do it? Bags of cash? Swiss bank accounts? My mind doesn't work that way. How do you even approach someone about taking a bribe? If it's true, how does a reporter like Vertise trace a bribe?* Will looked at his watch and realized that he needed to make the short drive to the airport. Alexa was due to arrive soon.

Will parked the Land Rover in a space reserved for vehicles in front of a small white building that served as a corporate terminal. He walked inside to find a young man dressed in a white shirt and black tie behind the counter. "What time is the Global American Metals jet due to arrive?"

The man looked up from his computer. "It's on its final approach now." He nodded to a glass door at the back. "If you step out that door, you can see it land. It'll park right out there."

Will nodded and pushed through the door. A Boeing 727 with the Global logo was touching down. The pilot used most of the runway to slow the plane, then he turned and taxied to the terminal where Will stood. The first officer nodded at him as they stopped. Will had traveled on that plane a few times over the years and was acquainted with the crew. He watched as the engines wound down. Next, the passenger door opened. Two attendants pushed portable steps up to the door and stepped back for Will to mount the steps into the cabin. Will glanced toward the front where there were several leather-covered chairs that he knew could swivel 360 degrees. Among them were coffee and side tables. He turned to the back and saw Alexa Pritchard behind her desk, talking on her phone and sucking on a Tootsie Pop. She motioned for him to take a seat opposite her. She ended her call, tossed the remainder of the Tootsie Pop in a trash can, and lit a cigarette using a gold lighter with a Global logo. She sucked in the smoke. When she exhaled, she broke into a fit of coughing interspersed by gasps for air.

"Shit, I can't even breathe on this island." She reached for a bottle of water on her desk, unscrewed the cap, and drank from it. When she was sure the coughing had passed, she said, "How the hell did you let this get out of hand so quickly? One riot, one little girl dead, Kaven dead. You're supposed to be my head of security. Hell, I could have hired a rent-a-cop for a tenth of your salary and not been any worse off."

Will didn't reply at first. Instead, he walked to a bar to Alexa's right, filled a glass with three fingers of bourbon, and downed it in one gulp. "Dammit, Alexa, I've been here for two days. If anyone should have seen this coming, it was you."

Alexa rose to stand behind her desk. Her voice was quiet but intense. "All right, Will. But you need to put a lid on this and make sure there are no more problems. We need this mine. Our profits depend on it. Understand?"

Will poured another drink. "And I presume that will ensure that you will become CEO?"

"If I do, I'll take my friends up the ladder with me. That could include you."

"And what about Kaven?"

"I don't give a damn about him. Send some flowers from Global. Cover his casket. I don't care. I'm going to the Kingston office. I'll be there until you get this under control."

Will stared at his boss, then turned and walked to the door where he exited. As he descended the stairs, he heard more coughing.

CHAPTER 21

When Will returned to the hotel, he called Manny and Rodney and asked them to meet him for dinner at seven. Manny arrived right behind Will.

"After that jerk chicken and several beers, I'm good for a salad and that's about it."

The host led them to a table in the center of the room. Will shook his head. "Can we have that one over in the corner?" Will had something to discuss that he did not want to be overheard. The host nodded and led them to Will's table of choice. Rodney joined them, exclaiming about Scochie's chicken. Rodney and Manny ordered a side salad and iced tea. Will chose a small steak, medium rare. After the waiter left, Will leaned toward his friends and lowered his voice.

"We may have another problem that could blow the lid off this whole damn Jamaica operation. I was trying to have lunch with Vertise today when she launched into an attack on Alexa. She says that our esteemed president has bribed her way around the world, paying officials whatever it takes to get them to approve our mines. Vertise claims she knows that Alexa has paid off Jamaica's Minister of Mining. Supposedly, she's close to having proof."

Manny and Rodney stared at Will, not sure what to say. Finally, Manny spoke. "Maybe we just ought to take the next plane out of here in the morning. Get the hell out of Dodge."

"Yeah," Rodney said. "If those Maroons get wind of anything like that, they'll come storming down the mountain and head to Kingston, looking for the Minister's head, maybe Alexa's, too."

"Maybe ours," Manny added.

Will lowered his voice even more. "And it can get a lot worse. You guys ever heard of the Foreign Corrupt Practices Act?"

Manny and Rodney shook their heads.

"The United States has laws that make it illegal to get business in a foreign country with bribes. There are corporate officers who have gone to jail for doing it and their companies have been fined tens of millions of dollars."

Rodney shook his head and started to rise. "I'm packing my bags. Maybe I'll just turn in my resignation when I get back home. I won't have any problem getting a job with another company."

"Sit down, Rodney," Will said. "Don't jump ship too soon. Let's do a little investigating of our own. Besides, with Trump in office, the Foreign Corrupt Practices Act may soon be a thing of the past. He claims it puts United States at a competitive disadvantage in countries whose officials have their hands out. Can you get into the company computer system and see if there are any strange payments in other countries, initiated by Alexa?"

Rodney stared off into space. "Yeah, I can do that."

"Can you do that without leaving a trail?"

"Sure."

"Start with Jamaica and see what you can find. How long will it take?"

Rodney thought again. "Could be a day. Could be a week. No way to know."

"Then I want you to hole up in your room, starting tonight. Call me when you have something." Will pushed back his chair. "I'm going into town. You don't want to know why."

CHAPTER 22

Will needed a gun. To hell with Miles Harper. Things were rapidly spinning out of control. Maybe he would never use it, but if he found himself in a dangerous situation he wanted to be prepared. The question was where to buy a one. He turned onto the Hip Strip and decided to start there. After all, everything else was for sale once the sun went down. He found a parking place, locked his car, and studied the activity on the strip. On the corner to his right were several women of the night, breasts pushed high by bras, skirts that barely covered their butts, and spiked four-inch heels. He looked the other way and saw a couple of local men leaning against a building and smoking something. He headed in their direction. As he approached, one of them stepped out to confront him. He was decently dressed— black pants, black coat, black snap-brimmed hat—on second thought, definitely a sharp dresser.

"Evening, mon. Name's Judean. I saw you parking. Nice set of wheels. We don't see many Land Rovers around here. How can I help you? Ganja? Coke? Maybe a beautiful woman?"

"Not interested in any of that."

Judean shrugged his shoulders and started to walk away.

"Hold on a minute," Will said. Judean turned to him. "How about a gun? Can you make that happen?"

Judean stepped closer. "Mon, guns are illegal here. I may be able to get you one, but it's going to be expensive. Maybe a thousand, maybe two. Can you handle that?"

Will nodded.

"Then I know an old man, not far from here. Permit me to make a call, make sure he's available." He stepped away and turned his back as he extracted his cell phone from his pocket. After a minute, he placed the phone back in his pocket. "You're in luck, mon. He can talk. Follow me across the street and up the hill a way."

Will followed the Jamaican across the street and up a dirt road that turned to the left as the lights from the strip faded. Will had spent too many years in the military not to understand that he could be walking into an ambush. His senses went on high alert. His muscles tensed until he forced them to relax. Once they made the turn, the only illumination came from interior lights in some small houses. Judean led him into an alley. Will considered turning back, but he really needed a gun. Judean motioned Will forward as he backed up to the wall of a house. Three young toughs stepped from the shadows; two had switchblades and one a machete. Will turned to see Judean retrieving another machete that had been leaning against the house.

"You see, mon, I told you that guns were expensive. We need your wallet, gold watch, cell phone, and the keys to that Rover."

Will sized up the situation. He reached into his back pocket for his wallet and pitched it to the ground between him and the three toughs. When the one with the machete bent over to pick up the wallet, Will kicked him in the head. Next, he spun and in one violent motion, karate kicked Judean in the knee. Will heard the knee snap. Judean collapsed, moaning and holding his knee. That left the two with the switchblades who were grinning as they walked toward him, one of them pitching his knife from one hand to the other.

"Look, boys, I don't really want to hurt you. If you'll just turn around and disappear into the dark, I won't come after you."

They looked at him like he was mad. They were armed. He had nothing. Not even a fair fight. Of course, they were right, but they didn't realize the deck was stacked against them. They continued to move forward. In less than the blink of an eye, Will brought his hand down on the arm of the one to the left. As he did so, he twisted the hand of the assailant until he dropped the knife and fell to the ground, writhing in pain. The other one looked at his three friends lying on the ground and bolted around Will, running for the strip. Will walked to where Judean was lying on the ground. He picked up Judean's weapon and put the blade on his neck. "Now, where's the old man? You want out of this alley alive, you'll tell me. Otherwise, I start carving." He pulled the machete across the neck just enough to draw a little blood.

"That won't be necessary," a man said as he stepped from the shadows. He was black, stooped in the shoulders, and walked with a cane. "I'm the one you're looking for. Leave these young men alone. I believe they have learned their lesson and will be more choosey as to who they try to rob in the future. Step into my house. I can supply you with a Sig, a Glock, you name it."

Once in the house, the old man sat behind a desk, unlocked a drawer, and retrieved several guns that he placed on the desk. Will studied each of them and picked the Glock. He hefted it, then checked the sight and trigger. "I'll take it. I'll need two clips and four boxes of ammo and a silencer."

The old man looked at him. "That'll cost you $1500."

Will pulled a wad of bills from his pocket and peeled off the $1500. He loaded one clip and put the other and the remaining shells and the silencer in various pockets. When he left the house, he walked by one of the toughs and Judean, who were still lying in the alley. The third had disappeared. As a parting gesture, he kicked both in the ribs and walked toward the strip, thinking he was now a little more prepared for what the future might bring.

CHAPTER 23

Will turned the Land Rover over to the valet at the hotel. He rode the elevator to the fourth floor where he knew that Manny and Rodney shared a suite. When he knocked on the door, Manny opened it.

Manny was watching a cricket game while Rodney hovered over his computer. The sliding doors to the balcony were open and the sounds of waves and chirping frogs drifted into the room. Will's clothes were dirty, and his shirt had a long rip in the front.

"What the hell happened to the other guy?" Manny asked.

"Other guys. There were four them. Let's just say that they got the worst of it." Will reached into his back pocket and dropped the Glock on the table. Rodney looked up from his computer, concern framing his face.

"That's illegal. Could land you in jail."

"Look, guys, I'm sorry to say this, but I don't think the violence is over. It's only going to get worse. I have to figure out what is going on before we lose more employees. Yeah, the gun's illegal, but when I weigh the chances of me getting caught carrying it against getting attacked by some damn Maroons or street thugs, I'll take that chance. I don't want to get in a gunfight with only my bare hands as weapons."

Rodney turned his computer around so that Will could see the screen. "This turned out to be much easier than I thought. Of course, I'm the in-house computer guy. Only, you're not going to like what I found."

Will paced the room, hands in his pockets while he thought. "Maybe I don't want to know what you found. Just shut it down and keep it to yourself."

Rodney was a meek, usually quiet, person. Now he wasn't. He stood and raised his voice. "No, Will, you've got to look at this screen. I've tracked payoffs coming from Pritchard's office to the Jamaican Minister of Mines, close to a half million."

"Shit."

"And there are similar payments in at least twenty other countries."

"I guess it's not surprising. Alexa has built this company by pretending that the Foreign Corrupt Practices Act doesn't exist, or maybe it doesn't apply to her."

"That's for damn sure," Manny said. "She could spend the rest of her life in prison. No damn wonder she got her ass down here so quickly."

"There's more, Will," Rodney said. "I found her stock options. Once our stock hits a hundred dollars, she can cash in for a cool half a billion."

"Cha-ching. Hell, I've got that in my money belt," Manny joked. "What? You guys didn't bring five hundred million with you? Cheapskates."

"Shut up, Manny," Rodney said. "I also found an email to her brother, a hedge fund manager, where she said the Jamaican project will drive the stock to a hundred bucks. That's insider information. She and her brother could both go to prison on that alone. Just remember what happened to Martha Stewart. Additionally, it looks like she's trying to manipulate the price of bauxite."

"That shouldn't be too hard. The bauxite market is relatively small and Global is damn sure the biggest player in the world."

Rodney walked toward the balcony and motioned Will to follow him. "Okay, now I'm worried. I got onto some company sites that I shouldn't be on. Then we learn that this has been going on for years all over the world. If Alexa figures out I'm the hacker, I could be on her hit list."

"Dammit, Rodney. Didn't you just tell me a few hours ago that no one could follow your trail?"

Rodney nodded. "That's what I said, but I didn't know how big this was going to be. I think I covered my tracks, but you just never know in the computer world these days."

"Who else could do what you just did?"

"Probably no one outside the company, at least not as easily, maybe two others inside."

"Would those two have any reason to follow in your footsteps?"

Manny hesitated and then said, "No. Not unless Alexa ordered a search."

"Then let's proceed on the assumption that she won't. I want you monitoring the computer system. Let me know if you see the slightest hint that she's on our trail." Will walked back into the room. "Manny, you and I are going into enemy territory tomorrow. Time to pay a visit to Colonel Broderick."

CHAPTER 24

Will arranged to have a rental car the next morning, figuring that having a Range Rover with the Global logo was akin to waving a red cape at a raging bull. They left at eight and wound their way through Montego Bay and up the mountain. Manny kept an eye out for boas and saw none. They received a few questioning stares from people along the road, but nothing more. When they arrived at Accompong they found the gates to the village open. The paved road ended at the gates, and they traveled across a gravel road for fifty yards or so. The village appeared to be deserted.

"Any suggestions about where to park?" Will asked.

"Seems to be a parking area in front of that monument. How about there?"

Will agreed. They exited and read the plaque on the monument. It was about Cudjoe and described his leadership in the fight for independence for the Maroons and for their right to own the Cockpit Country. By the time they finished, half a dozen young men surrounded them. They were dressed in jeans, T-shirts with major league baseball and NFL football logos on them, and expensive running shoes. None brandished weapons. Beyond them were small houses, mainly cinderblock. All had satellite dishes, and all had outdoor privies. Will noticed that a couple of the young men had cell phones bulging from their pockets. It was a strange juxtaposition of old and new.

One of them stepped forward. "What you want, mon?"

Trying to be extremely polite, Will said, "We would like an audience with Colonel Broderick?"

"You have an appointment?"

"No. We only want a few minutes of his time. Could you see if he is available?"

"No need, mon. He won't see no white man unless he invites them. You should just get back in the car and head down the mountain. Didn't you see that sign beside the gate? *WE DON'T INVITE. YOU DON'T COME.*

As he talked, the other men pushed forward until there was no place to turn. Will said, "Thank you. We'll come back another day." He and Manny got in the car and slowly exited through the gates and made their way back down the mountain.

When the young Maroons were satisfied that the strangers were not returning, they walked across the gravel area to the community hall, a white building, larger than the houses. It contained several folding tables and metal chairs, enough for about forty people. The floor was concrete. There was a large map of the Cockpit Country on one wall. On the other was a document labeled "TREATY." At the back, Colonel Broderick sat drinking coffee and talking to three of the elders. He motioned them forward and pointed to a row of chairs facing his table.

"What did those men want?"

Lawrence, the spokesman for the young Maroons, said, "We didn't give them a chance to talk. They wanted an audience with you, and we ran them off."

The colonel scratched his goatee. "Probably some men from Global. You did right."

"Colonel, if I can speak freely?"

Broderick nodded for him to continue.

"We need to declare war on Global American Metals. The treaty on that wall makes it clear that we are a free state. We must defend what is ours or have it destroyed by a greedy American corporation."

"They're a multi-national corporation," Broderick replied. "They make forty billion dollars every year. They could hire a mercenary force that would outnumber us ten to one."

"Colonel, the British outnumbered us a hundred to one, and we still defeated them. We haven't forgotten how to wage guerilla warfare. It's our jungle. We know the trails. We can hit and run like Cudjoe did three hundred years ago."

Colonel Broderick looked at the other elders who were nodding their agreement. "All right, gentlemen. We'll declare war. If nothing else, it should attract international attention. The more environmentalists and bio-scientists we can get to join our cause, the better our chance. Just one thing. You can rattle your swords, but no one dies on either side unless I give the okay."

Two of the young Maroons could be seen shaking their heads.

That night Lawrence and Aaron hiked on trails through the forest to where Global had already started bulldozing trees and undergrowth. The bulldozer and a pickup were parked in the clearing, surrounded by downed trees. A guardhouse displayed the only light. Inside was a man, fast asleep. Aaron picked up a two by four and clubbed the sleeping guard.

"The keys must be in here," Aaron said. He opened drawers until he found a key ring and showed it to Lawrence. Lawrence walked to the bulldozer, inserted a key, and brought the sleeping giant to life with a roar. He studied the gears for a moment and then shoved it into a forward position and pushed on the gas. It rumbled toward a cliff. At the last second, Lawrence leaped from the dozer, just before it tumbled over the cliff to rocks two hundred feet below.

Lawrence walked back to the guardhouse. Aaron pointed to the man lying on the floor. "He's dead. The colonel is going to be pissed."

"Shit happens, mon. Shit happens, particularly in war. He'll get over it."

CHAPTER 25

Will joined Manny and Rodney for breakfast. As he took a seat, he pitched a copy of the *Monitor* on the table. "Sorry I'm late. I just took a call from the day shift up at the Cockpit mine. Our guard was bludgeoned to death last night."

Rodney brought his hand to his mouth and stared, speechless. Manny remained stoic. "And someone drove our dozer over a cliff," Will continued. "It's now lying at the bottom of the ravine."

"Shit," Manny finally said. "I hired that guard myself. Young man, married with a couple of kids. Just looking for a way to make a living."

"And that's two of our people in two days," Rodney added.

"I assume the dozer is totaled," Manny said. "We don't have another dozer to replace it anywhere on the island. We've got a couple in other mines, but to pull one of them away would cut down production."

"Robbing Peter to pay Paul won't do us any good. How long before we can get another one shipped from the States?" Will asked.

"At least two weeks."

Will pointed at the *Monitor*. "You guys see this?" The headline on the story with Vertise's byline read, MAROONS DECLARE WAR ON GLOBAL AMERICAN METALS. Colonel Broderick was quoted in the story, saying that they know how to fight a guerilla war. They beat the British into submission three hundred years ago. They are ready to do it again with this international corporation.

"I guess what happened up there last night was the first round," Manny said. "How the hell did Vertise get the story so fast and get it in today's first edition?"

"She told me she was a Maroon. They probably called her. We have to take this seriously. And considering what happened to Kaven, this may be round two. While I'm driving to Nigril, I'll call Pritchard to tell her that we need to beef up security anywhere we have employees. Forget about all three of us going to the funeral. Manny, you take Rodney and survey the damage."

Rodney noticeably cringed. "Do I really have to go?"

"Yes, you do. Manny knows our back road into the site. You won't be going through Accompong. Manny, come to my room and I'll get you my Glock. Only keep it concealed unless you absolutely must use it. I don't want you in Harper's jail. Understand?"

Manny nodded. "Yeah, I got it. And I have a Glock back in the States. So, it should be no problem."

Will handed off the gun in his room and called for his car to be brought to the front.

He tipped the valet and nodded to the guard at the front gate before turning right on the highway. He passed through Montego Bay and took the right fork when he came to the turnoff to the Cockpit Country. He was circling the western end of the island to the town of Negril. Jimmy Buffett had made the town famous, or maybe infamous might be the better word, when he wrote a song about flying his seaplane to Negril to buy some jerk chicken, and the local authorities—thinking he was a drug dealer—tried to shoot his plane out of the sky. On this day, though, Will was not thinking about Jimmy Buffett. Kaven had grown up there and would be buried at the local cemetery. He thought about how quickly things had changed. Flying to the island, he had figured on confirming security was in place and then getting in a little golf and a day or two on the beach before flying back to Maryland. Now he was on the front lines of what the Maroons were calling a war. He presumed that he would be the commander in charge of the Global forces unless Alexa said otherwise. That reminded him that he had not yet checked in with her about the events of the night and the declaration of war. He retrieved his cell phone and pushed Alexa's speed dial. Nothing happened. He glanced at his phone and realized he had no service. Maybe there would be service in Negril, maybe not. Nothing he could do but focus on the winding road and enjoy the scenery.

After about an hour, he approached the town. To his right he saw a white sand beach with several resorts. As he approached the town center, he spotted a cemetery on a hill to the left and turned toward it. He didn't know if it was the right one, or for that matter, if Negril had more than one. He only knew there was to be a graveside service that was to begin at ten. Turning into the cemetery, he parked among several other cars and made his way to a group of people seated on white folding chairs and talking quietly among themselves as they waited for the service to begin. The casket was open; so, Will took the opportunity to view the body, partly to pay his respects and also to confirm that it was Kaven. It was. He stood beside the casket with his head lowered, then turned to find a seat in the back row. When he did, he glanced at a woman dressed in black on the front row. Must be Kaven's mother, he thought.

The ocean could be seen from the cemetery. Waves were forming in the distance and raced toward the white sand before they broke about thirty yards out and ripples made their way to the beach. Will was lost in thought when he heard a man's voice ask those gathered to stand for a prayer. When he finished, he invited the mourners to take their seats as he launched into a eulogy about Kaven, who he had known since he was a boy attending church. As he praised the deceased, Kaven's mother sobbed loudly. She was comforted by those around her, but the crying continued. When the preacher was finished, several others stood to describe their relationship with Kaven and what a fine young man he was. The service ended when a woman with a beautiful soprano voice, sang *The Lord's Prayer*. Will joined others in line to pay their respects to Ms. Tillman.

When he faced her, he said, "Ms. Tillman, I'm Will Taylor. I work for Global American Metals. Kaven was a friend of mine. I am saddened by his death. We will find the person who took his life."

Ms. Tillman raised her head to look at Will. After wiping her eyes, she said, "Thank you, sir. I hope you can do just that." Then she motioned for him to lean closer. "You must know that I believe that it was the White Witch. He never should have been up there at night."

CHAPTER 26

When Will approached Montego Bay, he checked his cell to find he had service and speed dialed Pritchard. In her Kingston office, Alexa glanced at the caller ID. "Dammit, do I need to get someone in here to do your job? Now we have another employee dead, and our Cockpit operation is down for at least two weeks while we get another damn bulldozer in here."

"Alexa, would you please calm down. I've got Manny and Rodney up there this morning. The problem is we need more security there and everywhere we have operations. That, by the way, includes your office in Kingston and the hangar where you have that company plane parked. You get me twenty more guards. I'll place them where they'll do the most good. I'll have to get permission from Miles Harper for them to be armed."

Alexa's voice lowered. "You worried about those Maroons declaring war?"

"Hell, yes. Like you said, we've had two men killed. No doubt in my mind that the Maroons killed our guard. Not that certain about Kaven. Still, we better take them seriously."

Pritchard drummed her fingers on the desk while she thought. "I'll get the men. Our local security service can provide some good ones who know the territory. Harper called my secretary this morning, wanting to know how to get hold of you. You better go see him in person. And give him your cell number so he won't be bugging my staff."

Next, Will tried to call Manny and Rodney. Neither of the men answered. They could be in danger, Will thought. Or, they could be in a cell phone dead zone. Will elected to assume the best and decided to call them later. Will's thoughts were interrupted by his stomach, reminding him that he had not eaten in several hours. He spotted a cafe that seemed to be busy and parked on the street close to it. He sat on the front patio under an umbrella so that he could keep an eye on his car. When the waiter brought a menu, he glanced at it and ordered fried shrimp. While he waited, he considered where to put the new guards. Figuring that he would have them work twelve hours on and twelve off, that gave him ten spots. Three would patrol the Cockpit project, one each at Global's other two island mines, two at Discovery Bay, the port between Montego Bay and Ocho Rios where the train brought the bauxite down from the mines, one at Pritchard's office building in Kingston, one at the hangar, and one to relieve the others when they were off a day. When his lunch came, he glanced at his watch and decided to eat in a hurry. In fifteen minutes he finished, paid the bill and was on his way to his car when he stopped and backtracked. He knew the police station was close but didn't know how to get there. The waiter told him to go three blocks, take a left and look for a concrete building on the right with a sign identifying it as the police station. Will followed the directions and found a concrete block building surrounded by a parking lot full of cars. He drove around for five minutes before finding a spot that had just been vacated. The entrance to the building had a faded sign announcing it was the St. James Parish Police Department.

When he entered, he was met by a mass of people. All seemed to be talking with raised voices. The smell of unwashed bodies was almost overwhelming. People sat on a few wooden benches, lined the walls and milled up and down the hall. To Will's right was a woman sitting behind a dilapidated metal desk. Occasionally, she would call out a name. That person, along with other family members, would be directed through a door behind her to meet with a brother, son, husband, or wife who was incarcerated.

Will made his way to the woman who looked at him with tired eyes. "What do you want?"

"I'm here to see Chief Harper."

She pointed to double doors at the opposite end of the hall. "I think I saw him heading to the police cafeteria, probably getting a late lunch. Go through those doors."

Will thanked her and fought through the crowded hallway. A sign above the doors said: "Police Cafeteria. No Public Admission." When Will pulled open the door, he saw metal tables and chairs scattered around a large room. At one end was a steam table where hot meals were served, probably three times a day.

But what caught his eye was a fully stocked bar at the other end with six bar stools. Sitting on one of them was a policeman in uniform with an AK-47 hanging from his shoulder. In his left hand was a dark liquid, probably bourbon or scotch. Seated almost directly behind him was Miles Harper. Harper had a mouthful of food and motioned him to take a seat.

"Sure hope that guy is going off duty and not starting his shift."

Harper swallowed and took a drink of water. "He's off duty. A lot of our officers live in the barracks behind this building. Since we know they're going to drink, we decided years ago to have them drink here rather than out among the public. For the ones that live in the barracks, we don't have to worry about them driving. They can just walk across the parking lot."

"I heard you were looking for me. Tell me what's on your mind. Then I've got an issue or two to put on the table."

Harper wiped his mouth with his napkin and motioned for a woman who was hovering near the table to clear it. When she was gone, he said, "There's an old man that lives just up the hill from the Strip. We know he sells a few guns and we let him do it because he's a useful informant. We have an officer drop by there every couple of weeks to see who he's selling to. Just yesterday he said that he had sold a Glock to a man that he described as looking a lot like you."

"Oh, come on, now, Chief," Will said with a grin, "you know all us white guys look alike."

Harper shook his head. "I'm being dead serious here. We also learned that four street punks were beaten up badly. Don't suppose you know anything about that either?"

Will shook his head. "Nope, not a thing."

"You have any special ops training?"

"Let's just say that I can handle myself."

"Just what I figured. Where did you get that bruise under your eye?"

Will shrugged his shoulders. "Slipped getting out of the shower."

Harper saw the conversation was going nowhere. "Taylor, just let me remind you that what I said still goes. You get stopped with a gun on you, it will be my pleasure to put you in our lovely jail for a while."

Will stood and turned his hands palms up. "You want to search me now?"

"Sit down. I think you're smarter than to bring a gun into the police station."

Will took his seat. "My turn, now, Chief?"

Harper nodded his head.

"Let me cut to the bottom line," Will said. "I went to Kaven Tillman's funeral this morning. And, I'm sure you know that one of our guards up at the Cockpit project was killed last night and a dozer worth several hundred thousand dollars was driven off a cliff. Then I learn that Colonel Broderick has declared war. I don't think you have the manpower to do your job."

Harper glared at Will. "I sent two cops up to the Cockpit project this morning. I'm on top of it."

Will shook his head. "Sorry, Chief. That doesn't give me the comfort level I need. We don't know when or where the Maroons will strike next."

"You don't know the killings were done by Maroons."

"You're right. Kaven's death is still unsolved. Only, you and I both know that guard up in the mountains must have been killed by some of the Maroons. So, here's what I've done. I have twenty more security guards starting tomorrow. I plan to station them at various Global sites around the island." Will paused. "And they need weapons."

Harper pounded the table so hard that the cop at the bar turned to see if he needed help. Harper waved him off. "Dammit, Taylor, I'm not going to authorize any more gun permits to Global."

"Wrong. You know our guards are armed. You told me you check their weapons regularly. Just tell me how you want to handle this. My company is under attack. We can't defend ourselves with our bare hands."

Harper rubbed his face and then his bald head as he thought. "Okay, here's how it's going to be. We don't have the resources to check out these guys. I want you to do it."

"Won't be necessary. They are all local, coming from that same security service that Global has used for years."

"Tell your guy to bring their names to my secretary. I'll expedite it from my end. Also, identify what weapons they expect to be carrying. We'll set up a file on each of them, including authorized weapons. For God's sake, Taylor, tell your men not to start a war with the Maroons."

Will rose and shook Harper's hand. "Understood. Only, if they insist on going to war, we won't have any choice."

CHAPTER 27

A black Lincoln with government license plates rolled to a stop in front of the office building that housed Global's Jamaican headquarters in Kingston. The driver put it in park and hustled around to the rear passenger door. Richard Snyder, Jamaica's Minister of Mining, a short, overweight man with a bald head and goatee, took the driver's hand as he huffed his way out of the car and walked into the building. He pushed the button to go to the eighth floor and was pleased that it took a few moments for the elevator to arrive. He used that time to take a few deep breaths and wipe his face with a handkerchief. When he arrived at the eighth floor, the elevator opened to a tastefully decorated reception area with the Global logo on the wall above the receptionist. Snyder handed her his card.

"Ms. Pritchard is expecting you," she said with a smile. "Please follow me."

She opened one of two double doors and stepped aside to allow Snyder to enter a large corner office with a view of the Kingston Harbor, where Pritchard was in conversation on the phone. When she saw him, she said, "I'll have to call you back," and hung up. She motioned Snyder to the one chair that was in front of her desk. Before she could say anything, she started coughing. She reached into a drawer for a cough drop and waited a few seconds for it to take effect. "MISTER Snyder."

"Yes, ma'am."

"I paid you $500,000 dollars. You haven't forgotten that, have you?"

"No, ma'am."

"You recall me telling you that it was critical to my company to get that Cockpit mine up and running as quickly as possible?"

Beads of sweat were popping out on Snyder's forehead when he said, "Correct."

"Why the hell didn't you tell me the Maroons were going to start a war?"

"Ms. Pritchard, I can assure you that they're just stirring things up for a while. Once they let off a little steam, they should settle down. May I say, ma'am, that you don't look well. Have you seen a doctor?"

"Don't have time for doctors. Must be something on this island I'm allergic to."

"I can get you in to see my doctor. He's very good."

"Dammit, don't distract me. I can take care of myself." She paused to unwrap a Tootsie Pop. "While your Maroons are settling down, as you call it, that declaration of war is hitting the media around the world. They're making Global American look like we're taking some poor natives' precious rainforest."

"But, Ms. Pritchard, isn't that what you are doing?"

"Hell, yes. I've got publicity people back in Maryland who can put the proper spin on what we're doing. You know, more jobs, more schools, better health care." She paused. "That was intended to be Kaven Tillman's job..." Her voice trailed off. "The problem now is this woman named Vertise beat us to the punch. We've got damn tree huggers picketing our headquarters in Baltimore today."

"I'll get right on it. Maybe Colonel Broderick can be bought. If not, I'll figure out another way to take him out of the picture."

"And who the hell is this Vertise? Her columns in the *Monitor* are on the internet. The New York Times called my office this morning, wanting to do a story on the Bauxite War. She may be a bigger problem than the Maroons."

"Local woman. Got her degree somewhere in the States. And, if I'm not mistaken, she worked for the *New York Times* before she returned to the island."

"Well, isn't that just great?" Pritchard paused to toss her Tootsie Pop in the trash and lighted a cigarette. "She probably has a direct line to the *Times* editor."

"Look, I'll talk to her editor here. In the meantime, may I suggest that you crank up that publicity machine. A press release every couple of days about jobs, economic impact, and so forth would be good."

Pritchard twirled her chair to stare out the window at the harbor.

Finally, Snyder rose and said, "I suppose I better leave."

"No," Pritchard said, as she turned again to face him. "I was just thinking. You might as well know this. Someone hacked into our server. I've got a team in

Baltimore trying to trace the culprit. It's pretty clear that he discovered the half million in payments to your Swiss bank account. Hopefully, he can't get past the Swiss security and the fire walls they have created."

Snyder began to tremble. "If that gets out, I'm through. I'll spend the rest of my life in prison."

"Why do you think I'm telling you? Until we put a lid on Vertise and the Maroons, you're at risk. Maybe we are all at risk. I want your attention focused on this and nothing else. And there's one more thing. My vice president of security is here. Name's Will Taylor. Smart son of a bitch. Smart enough that he might be able to put all the pieces of the puzzle together."

"Why don't you just send him back to the mainland?"

"Come on, Snyder. Get your head out of your ass. How's it going to look if I send my head of security home while there's a riot here? But, I want him out of the picture. You're going to arrange to have him laid up in a hospital for a while. Not killed, just a few broken bones that will keep him there until we can get this under control. You can do that, right?"

"Trust me, Ms. Pritchard. You'll get your mine like I promised. And I'll take care of the Maroons as well as Mr. Taylor…and the reporter, too."

CHAPTER 28

Will and Manny parked the Land Rover in front of the small building with *Montego Bay Monitor* etched on one of two glass windows that fronted the street. When they entered, they saw people at a few desks with old computers on them. The only one that looked up was Vertise who was working on a new laptop in the center of the room. Will walked to face her desk. She kept on typing.

"Look," Will said, "I'm sorry. I was an ass. I need to see what's going on up there in the Cockpit Country. We tried once, but some young guns ran us off."

Vertise kept on typing.

"With the number of stories you're writing, I figure you must know someone up there. I was hoping that you could get us past the palace guard. I would really like to see your rainforest."

Vertise stopped typing and looked at Will and Manny. "I just might know someone up there. After all, I am a Maroon. Two points I want to make. One is to prove that the Maroons own the rainforest. The second is to show you the value of what is there. If I can do both, will you stop the mine?"

"I don't have that authority. But, I'll promise to report everything I learn to Ms. Pritchard and advocate for a change of our position, if that's what I truly believe."

Vertise pursed her lips as she thought. "Okay. Nothing ventured, nothing gained. Have a seat up at the front while I finish this story. Shouldn't take more than fifteen or twenty minutes."

When they walked out to the Land Rover, Manny said, "Shouldn't we go by the airport and get a rental car to go up there?"

"Didn't do us any good last time," Will replied.

"Then, I'm going to do this." He pulled the magnetic Global logo off the passenger side and walked around to do the same on the driver's side. Then, he pitched them in the rear compartment.

Will nodded his agreement. With Vertise in the front passenger seat and Manny in the back, they drove up the mountain in silence. When Will saw the place where the cop car crashed down the mountain, he stopped.

"If you'll get out, I'll show you what's left of the cop car."

They walked to the edge of the pavement and looked down. The bones of the car were still there. The yellow boa was sleeping on top of it. "Kaven and the cop could have been killed. And, by the way, I don't like any snake, particularly big ones."

Vertise was quiet.

"What's up with you?" Will asked.

"That snake. I know you don't believe in voodoo, but that snake still hanging around here is a very bad sign for you and your company."

"Here's what I think about that snake." Will picked up a baseball size rock, took several steps down the embankment and threw the rock toward the snake. It bounced off the car, but startled the snake enough that it slithered down the other side and disappeared into the undergrowth. "Spell broken," Will said as he climbed back up to the car.

"You wish," Vertise said. "You really should take this more seriously. There are ways to break a spell, but throwing rocks at a yellow boa is not one of them."

"This is scaring the shit out of me," Manny said.

"There you go. Manny's taking it serious enough for both of us," Will said.

"I give up," Vertise said.

When they got to Accompong, the gates were still open.

"Don't they ever lock it?" Will asked.

"Usually only at night," Vertise replied.

Vertise directed them to park in front of the Cudjoe monument. Several young Maroons, a couple with weapons, surrounded the car. Will reached over to open the glove compartment and retrieve his Glock. Vertise shook her head and shut it. "I'll deal with them."

They exited the car and one of the Maroons hugged Vertise. Will and Manny looked at each other in surprise, not sure what was going on.

The Maroon who hugged her smiled. "Ain't seen you up here in a couple of months."

"I've been around, trying to do my part."

"Yeah," a second Maroon said, "I've got a stack of newspapers in my house. Every one of them has a story with your byline about the Cockpit Country. We appreciate what you're doing."

"These are my friends, Will and Manny." She turned to Will and Manny. "Lawrence and Aaron are two of the most active of the Maroons in trying to preserve our rainforest.

Lawrence stared at Will and Manny. "We just ran these two off a couple of days ago. Why you hanging out with them?"

"Consider it an education. I'm going to show them around. Try to convince them that what we have up here is worth dying for. I want to start with the treaty."

Lawrence nodded and led them across the road to the meeting hall. Vertise stopped just past the door and pointed to the wall. "This is an enlarged copy of the treaty between Cudjoe and the British general, signed in 1739. The original is kept in a safe place, known only to Colonel Broderick and two other elders.

"As I told you the other evening in the mansion, the Maroons had been waging guerilla warfare, first against the Spanish and then the British. The British general finally called for a peace conference. I'll show you the place later on. He wanted the land along the ocean, where sugar cane could be grown. He didn't give a damn about this forest. Figured it was a fair trade and would end the Maroons raiding parties. From their standpoint, the Maroons just wanted to be left alone."

Manny had been studying the map while she talked. "Damn, this says that the Maroons own the land as far as the eye can see. That's not very specific."

"Maybe not today, but this was in 1739. The conveyed land was all mountains and valleys. No way to be more specific. Must have seemed reasonable at the time."

"Anyone ever figured out what that included?" Manny asked.

"It's believed to be 150,000 acres, which includes where Global is trying to open the Cockpit mine.

"Only, this says 1500 acres."

"That's a typo. We have another document signed by Cudjoe, confirming it's 150,000 acres."

Will had been silent while he studied the treaty and listened to Vertise. Now he spoke. "But, Global has a permit to mine a couple of thousand acres of minerals up here. It's an official document, signed by some guy named Snyder who claims to be The Minister of Mines. Are you saying that he doesn't know about the Maroons' rights to this land?"

Vertise's eyes narrowed. "Of course, he does." She motioned them to join her at one of the tables. "Aaron, can you get us some bottles of water?"

"Look, this is a Caribbean island. If you want something done, you bribe the right official. I've told you I'm close to proving that Snyder took a half a million. Once that happened, the permit was executed. You see our treaty. That permit is not worth the paper it's written on, but now your Ms. Pritchard can wave it in front of television cameras and swear that Global has the legal right to mine the land they're about to destroy."

Will rose and walked back to study the treaty again. "Okay, I'm close to being convinced. Still, I'd like to run all of this by one of our lawyers."

They heard footsteps on the gravel. Colonel Broderick entered the building with several younger Maroons. Broderick was wearing jeans, a Dallas Cowboys T-shirt, and Reeboks.

"Hi, Dad. These are my friends, Will and Manny."

Broderick bent to give Vertise a kiss on the forehead before turning to Will and Manny.

"Dad?" Will asked. "Colonel Broderick is your dad?"

"My, my, what a quick study you are," Vertise said.

"He really is your father?" Manny said, not sure what to believe.

"Mr. Taylor," Broderick said, "I know you are head of security and Mr. Rodriquez oversees the mine. You're employed by our enemy. If you weren't with Vertise, I would have you tossed out like I did the other day."

"Dad, calm down," Vertise said. "They're not here in any official capacity. They want to understand our side of the dispute. I'm going to take them on some of the Maroon trails, show them what we are trying to protect. Probably show them the Peace Cave. You want to come along?"

Broderick shook his head. "I'll stay here, but I want Lawrence and Aaron to go."

Lawrence nodded. He shouldered an AK-47 while Aaron grabbed a machete. They left the meeting hall and walked to the edge of the village where a trail wound through the forest. Vertise led the way with Will beside her. Manny followed. Lawrence and Aaron stayed about five yards back. Manny occasionally glanced at the two Maroons, worried that they were being led into the forest where they would be killed and thrown over a cliff. At one point, Will reached under his shirt for his Glock, then remembered Vertise insisted he leave it in the car. Trees towered over them, forming a canopy. A variety of bushes lined the trail, some with flowers, some with berries, some with distinct aromas.

"Where did the Maroon name come from?" Will asked.

"It's a shortened version of a Spanish word, Cimarron, which means wild or untamed."

Manny glanced again at Lawrence and Aaron. "Could be a good description of some of your buddies today."

Vertise's voice hardened. "They were all descendants of a people who were ripped from their homes in Africa and sold into the slave trade. They were abused, whipped, starved, raped, and killed. Even after enduring incredible hardships, they still had the determination to fight for what they believed was right. They were willing to risk it all to be a free people. They succeeded and lived quietly up here for three hundred years until your company arrived. Now, it appears that, once again, they must resume that fight unless Global decides to look elsewhere for its bauxite."

Neither Will nor Manny replied. Instead they walked in silence down the trail, appreciating the beauty of the mountainous terrain with silence broken only by the call of a bird or the sound of an animal somewhere in the underbrush. Vertise stopped to pick a few leaves from a bush.

"We boil these to make a tea to control high blood pressure." She handed the leaves to Will who put one in his mouth and grimaced at the taste.

Vertise saw his grimace and said, "Bitter, huh? When we drink the tea, we put a little honey in it."

She walked across the trail and found a stick to dig beside a plant and break off a root. "Arthritis? This will put the spring back in your step."

"And these red berries will knock out a cold or the flu."

"You've got a regular outdoor pharmacy here," Manny said.

"Where do you think so many of your modern medicines came from, these kinds of forests and jungles." Vertise replied. "Your mine will destroy much of this one. Unfortunately, this destruction is going on all over the world: South America, Africa, India, you name it. The jungles are going up in smoke."

Manny slowly turned around, taking in the environment that surrounded him. "I actually had a double major in mining and earth sciences. I became a mining engineer because the money was better. I understand what you are saying."

Vertise continued. "We live long lives up here and hardly ever see a medical doctor. Our bush doctors take care of us. My dad is one. Take a guess at his age."

"Wild guess, maybe sixty, maybe a few years younger," Will replied.

"He'll be eighty in a couple of months. Nearly everyone in my family lives to be a hundred. And our men don't need any of those little blue pills."

"You have some root or herb that I might use in that department?" Manny asked.

Vertise stepped back up the trail to where Lawrence and Aaron stood. She kneeled at another bush. After she had exposed a root, she motioned to Aaron to hand her his machete. After a few short swings, she stood with the root in her hand. She gave Aaron the machete and handed Manny the root. "Chew on a piece of this tonight."

Manny studied the root and turned it slowly in his hand. "I believe you, but I think I'll stick to the little blue pills."

He started to hand the root back to Vertise when Aaron said, "Here, I'll take that."

Then he looked a little embarrassed. "I'll give it to my dad."

They walked in silence. Will likened the canopied trail to a cathedral—walking it akin to a religious experience. He felt a sense of reverence, a sense of awe. When they came to a fork in the trail, Vertise said, "The one to the left winds down the mountain and actually comes out just above the Rose Hall Mansion. One of my ancestors, a great grandmother, so to speak, escaped from the White Witch. Her dad took her out one night and showed her the trail to the Cockpit Country. She was pregnant at the time. The next night, he killed the White Witch. Two hundred years later, that's why I am here."

"So, you're saying that your ancestors were slaves of the White Witch?"

Vertise grimaced and said, "It's not something I care to talk about, but it's a part of where I'm from." She pointed to the fork that went up the mountain. "Now we're going to climb a while to get to the Peace Cave."

Boy, she was right about climbing, Will thought, as the trail became steep and covered with rocks.

"Hey, I need to stop and get my breath. Is here okay?" Manny asked.

Vertise nodded. Manny slumped onto a small boulder and put his hands on his knees while he breathed. Will was slightly winded, but could stand and talk.

Vertise, Lawrence and Aaron appeared to have been just walking along a beach.

Vertise took the opportunity to fish for information. "What can you tell me about Ms. Pritchard?"

Will hesitated. "Okay, I'll answer as long as it's off the record. I think you reporters call it background, or something like that."

"Agreed."

"Alexa is a hard woman, driven to succeed. She's about sixty. I think I heard that she was married once, but quickly divorced. She was an orphan and worked her way through a small college. No Ivy League background or anything like that. She has no children. Global American is her life. In fact, it's really all she lives for. She doesn't play golf, or bridge, or go on vacations. She works, usually twelve or fifteen hours a day. She smokes—and way too much. She wouldn't be able to walk halfway up this trail without collapsing. Now understand that she is the president of Global. She reports to a CEO and a board. The CEO is not really involved in the operation of the company. He probably reads the financial statements. If the numbers look good, he leaves her alone."

"What's your relationship with her?"

"I suppose you could say it's tenuous. She thinks I'm a wise ass."

"She ever threaten to fire you?"

"Usually two or three times a month." Will grinned. "That's not going to happen. I do a damn fine job. Of course, it doesn't hurt that my old man is best friends with the CEO."

Vertise thought for a moment and was about to turn away.

"Fair's fair. Tell me more about you."

"I was born in Accompong, delivered by a midwife. Breech birth. My mother died."

"I'm sorry."

"It was a long time ago. I was raised mainly by my father. In the sixth grade, I was one of the fortunate ones who were bused into Montego Bay every day for school. That was a life-changing event. You know I majored in journalism at Columbia. Once I hit New York, I never wanted to set foot in Jamaica again. You probably heard that song about 'Happiness is leaving Lubbock in my rear-view mirror.' That was my mindset, only replace Lubbock with Jamaica."

"And it was my company that brought you back? Are you here for good?"

"I'm here until we drive Global from the island. I'm the voice of the Maroons, but also environmentalists and scientists all over the world. The more stories I can write, the more I hope to focus world attention on what is going on here and in rainforests in the rest of the world. As to whether I'm back here for good, it's not up for discussion. I'll make that decision when I fulfill my mission." She turned to Manny. "You ready to keep going now?"

Manny pushed himself from the rock, wiped his forehead with the tail of his shirt and said, "Let's do it."

They hiked for another half hour. Soon they could see the mountains and valleys, green with trees and plants as far as the eye could see. They rounded a bend in the trail and were captivated by one of the most magnificent views of the hike, a cave with a mouth probably twenty feet by twenty feet with a spring flowing from it. The sky was azure, the color of peacock eggs. A few white clouds seemed to be tethered in place by an invisible wire. The spring water cascaded through a small crevice that grew to a massive canyon at the bottom of the cliff as it met other streams that grew into a roaring river on the way to the sea. The vegetation was the greenest Manny had ever seen, reminding him that the soil must be rich in nutrients. He blinked, and the vision changed to a barren landscape, it, too, being seen for miles. It was the image he pictured after Global had stripped the vegetation from the land. He blinked that vision away and saw again the green forest down below. He realized that he could not be a part of such destruction, no matter how much he was paid.

Vertise had been quiet, allowing Manny and Will to take in the panorama. Lawrence and Aaron had retired to the shade at the entrance of the cave and talked quietly between themselves. She pointed to the cave. "This is the Peace Cave. After decades of fighting, in 1739 the British knew they could not win. The British General and Cudjoe met here. Cudjoe insisted that the meeting be on Maroon land and picked this spot. The Maroons performed weddings and held other ceremonies here. He came up here the night before, alone, made a small campfire, and chanted that the spirits would be with him in the negotiations. When the general and his entourage arrived the next morning, they were surprised to find only one man to represent the Maroons.

"Do you not have staff or aides, Captain Cudjoe?"

Cudjoe was not a big man, but his presence was commanding. He faced the general. "Sir, I need no one to advise me. I speak for the Maroons." He walked to the campfire and picked up a pot with tongs. "I made some tea. I'm sorry that I did not know you would have so many people. I have six earthen cups. Perhaps you can share five of them." He carefully poured the tea into the cups and handed them to the

General who chose the recipients. "I made this myself from herbs growing near the cave. The water is fresh from the stream. You should like it."

The general took a sip and nodded his approval. "You know that we British are fond of our tea. If I could trouble you for the recipe, it would be much appreciated. Now, shall we get down to business?"

Cudjoe sipped his tea with both hands, placed his cup on a rock beside where he sat and replied, "We shall."

"Captain, the Spanish before us and now our British troops have been fighting with your men for over two hundred years. I don't see an end in sight. I'm ready to stop the killing."

Cudjoe nodded. "I'm listening."

The General waved his hand across the landscape. "This is beautiful, and I hear the hunting of boar is good. Only, that's not why we are here. We want the land down by the sea where we can grow sugar cane and bananas to be shipped back to England or sold at auction. As I understand it, you don't care about that land."

Cudjoe nodded.

"Here's what I propose. You take this land."

"I want it as far as the eye can see from this spot."

"Understood. You acknowledge that we own the land down below. You cease your raids on our troops and our people. We'll leave you alone up here."

Cudjoe thought for a moment. "We need sovereignty over our land. We make the laws, we enforce them. We want nothing to do with the British. If you agree, then have one of your men draft a treaty between two sovereign nations and we each will sign it."

The general motioned to one of his men who came forward with a quill, ink and parchment. The general dictated the terms of the agreement and handed it to Cudjoe.

"I heard what you said and agree with it. While I speak English, I do not read and write it. I am relying on your word as a gentleman that this treaty is as you represent."

"You have my word, Captain Cudjoe."

"Then I will make my mark and you can sign below."

Once done, they rose and shook hands. "We wish you well with your property."

Cudjoe shook his head. "Not our property or land, but our country, now and forever."

After Vertise finished, the only sound was the brook flowing downhill and the wind whispering through the trees.

Finally, Manny spoke. "And that treaty on the wall is what was signed up here?"

"It's a copy, but it's authentic right down to Cudjoe's mark. And it's still in force."

"Wow, I've got to do some heavy duty thinking. You, too, Will."

"I'm just the security guy, but I'll be your sounding board. And whatever you decide, I'll try to influence Alexa." He paused and turned to Vertise. "Don't get your hopes up."

Vertise rose. "Gentlemen, shall we start down. I promise the walk will be easier."

Manny glanced back and saw that Lawrence and Aaron were again close behind and wondered what they might do if Vertise was not present.

CHAPTER 29

The five walked in silence until they were about a half mile from Accompong. Will stopped. "I think I hear trucks over that way—not big ones, probably just pickups, and chain saws."

"Yeah," Manny said, "that's where they're clearing for our mine. The dozer is at the bottom of a cliff."

"Is there a way we can get over there?" Will asked Vertise.

"Sure. The trail's narrow, but we can make it."

After a half mile, they stepped from the forest onto several acres of barren land. On the far side, they could see men with chain saws cutting downed trees into lengths to be burned. While Will absorbed what had happened to the forest, a pickup raced from a small metal building, probably a temporary office, and slid to a stop a few feet from them.

"I was up here, but I don't recognize those two guys in the pickup," Manny said. The driver slammed on the brakes and the two men leaped from it, each carrying a Sig Sauer pistol. The driver shouted, "You need to turn around and go back to wherever you came from. This is private property."

"I'm Will Taylor. Do you know who I am?"

"Don't know and don't care. I'm following my orders. Like I just said, get off this property." He pointed to the sign a few feet to his right at the edge of the clearing: TRESPASSERS WILL BE SHOT. Will stepped forward as if he could not read the sign. When he drew even with the driver, he whipped out his right hand, seized the driver's gun hand, and twisted it behind his back, causing him to drop the gun in the process. Then he twisted more until the driver collapsed to the ground. The other guard watched, uncertain as to what he should do.

"What are you looking at?" Will yelled at him. "If you don't want the same treatment, you better get your ass out of here."

"Yes, sir. I'll be going over to check on those tree cutters. Okay if I put my friend in the truck?"

Will nodded. "Only both of you leave your guns on the ground here in front of me."

After they had driven away, Vertise said, "All I can say is I hope you're on our side if we get into a fight."

"Old skills I learned in the Navy. It's been a while. Reflexes aren't as good as back then, but I can hold my own. Manny, I want you to contact your foreman and tell him that there is a moratorium on this project until further notice."

"You think Ms. Pritchard will go along with that?"

He turned to face Manny, hands on hips. "Of course not, but it will give me a little time to digest what we learned today, a couple of days at most."

Vertise beamed her agreement. Lawrence and Aaron could not believe what they just saw: A Global company man shutting down the whole operation.

***

Will, Manny and Vertise were in the Land Rover on the way down the mountain from Accompong.

"You learn anything up there today, Will?" Vertise asked.

"Yeah, but even though I told those men to stop working, I'm still on the fence. Like I said, Pritchard will have them back working in a couple of days. Hell, maybe even tomorrow."

Manny had been quiet. "I've made up my mind. I'm not working on that mine. If I get fired, so be it. In fact, I'm sure I will. I think I'll switch to earth science, maybe do some good for the planet."

Will glanced in the rear-view mirror to see if Manny was for real. When he did, he saw a black Hummer turn onto the road behind them and accelerate rapidly. "We've got a tail; make sure your seat belts are on tight and hold wherever you can."

The Hummer was at ram speed. Will waited until it was within a few feet, then jerked the wheel to swerve into the other lane. The Hummer shot by them. Now Will was in charge. He waited until the next curve and when the Hummer turned into it, he eased alongside the left rear fender and yanked the wheel, causing his right front bumper and fender to collide with the Hummer. Then he

108

hit his brakes and watched as the Hummer spun out of control and down the embankment, bouncing from tree to tree at first, like a pinball, before flipping on its side. Will raced past and continued down the hill.

"You two okay?" he asked.

"Other than a slight heart attack, I'm fine," Manny said. "No, I'm just kidding. I'm good."

'Same here," Vertise said. "Where did you learn that little maneuver?"

"Thought about being a NASCAR driver in my younger days. Took a few racing courses. Then, in the SEALs we went out on the defensive driving course every so often. Not my best driving, but mission accomplished. We have a smashed fender, but it's not interfering with the handling. Either of you get a look at the driver?"

"Going too fast," Manny replied.

"He had a cap pulled low on his head. I couldn't even tell if he was black or white," Vertise said.

"Vertise, you think those were Maroons?" Manny asked.

"No way. My dad and friends knew I was in this car. They wouldn't be trying to hurt me. And, as far as I know, the Maroons don't own a Hummer. They couldn't afford one."

"Then I suppose that narrows it down to Alexa. Would she really try to kill us?" Manny asked.

"No doubt I've been a pain in her ass, and maybe she thinks I've even gone rogue on her. She is damn sure worried about the mine and our two dead men; figures this mine is her express pass to the top rung on the ladder. Desperation can make people do desperate acts; so, I don't rule her out. No doubt she's pissed at Vertise. There's one other possibility. One of our competitors was mighty upset when we secured this contract. They knew about the bauxite up in the Cockpit Country, but didn't believe there was a way to get a permit for enough land to make it profitable. Alexa one-upped them. Could be they are not taking the defeat lying down. So, let's leave Alexa at the top of the list and assume she hired someone to scare us, not kill us. We'll give her the benefit of the doubt for now, but hold off on a final decision for a few days. We'll see how things play out. One thing is for sure. We must assume we're all being followed by someone every time we leave the hotel or, Vertise, you leave your condo."

CHAPTER 30

Will and Vertise were sitting on the deck of the hotel, between the giant pool and the ocean, sipping drinks before ordering dinner and watching the moon and its reflection on the water.

Will took a strong drink of his bourbon on the rocks. "Turns out this is a helluva lot more than I bargained for."

"Yeah. We could've been killed." She reached across the table to put her hand over his. "Thanks for saving my life today."

"Your life? Hell, I was trying to save mine, too."

Their waiter had been hovering near the table and took this opportunity to approach. "Are you ready to order?"

Vertise nodded. "I'll have the shrimp Caesar salad as my main course."

"Sir?"

"Make mine that big filet, rare, a baked potato with everything on it, and a bowl of your onion soup."

After the waiter left, Vertise said, "We need you on our side."

"Sorry, right now I am not on anyone's side. I'm staying focused on who's behind these murders and acts of violence. Once I've figured that out and put a stop to it, I'll know who is right and wrong. Then I can choose a side if I think it's necessary. Look to your right. You see the lights of a small boat way off shore. Care to take a guess as to what's going on out there?"

Vertise studied the lights for a while before she spoke. "Another of our reporters has been working on a story. He says that about once a week a boat loaded to the gills with marijuana meets up with some gunrunners offshore. They trade guns for ganja."

"Who is getting the guns?"

"Mostly street gangs. Some may end up with the Maroons. You saw Lawrence carrying that AK-47. He didn't buy that with money from any honest work. He's an overseer on one of those farms you saw from the highway to Accompong. Most likely, he gets paid in marijuana."

"Then, I've got to put the Maroons, at least some of them, back on my list. They may be taking orders from someone other than your father."

Vertise sipped from her white wine, then asked, "What made you join Global?"

Will motioned for the waiter to refill their drinks and watched as he disappeared to the outdoor bar. "Short version. After high school, I went directly into the Navy. I wasn't ready for college at eighteen. That led to the SEALs where I spent six years before I decided it was time to move on. During that time, I completed two years of college. When I was mustered out of the Navy, I went to Duke and completed my bachelor's in three semesters. When I graduated from Duke law school, I joined a trial firm in Richmond, Virginia. Liked the trial work, something like combat without the guns. After four years I was invited to join Global as vice president of worldwide security. Didn't hurt that my old man and Alexa's boss were in Nam together. Security was a division of the law department; so, I figured that I would eventually return to trying lawsuits. That was near six years ago. Hasn't happened yet."

"Can I ask a personal question?"

"Sure."

"Are you happy with your work?"

Will leaned back in his chair and rubbed his cheek with one hand as he thought. "Interesting you should ask. Just before I got on the flight to Jamaica, I had lunch with my parents and that subject came up. The short answer is not really. I'm well paid, but I now realize that I'm not cut out for the cutthroat corporate world. Besides that, I don't really like Alexa Pritchard or her management style. Long story short, I think I'm through with Global once I've got control of the situation here."

Vertise let a slight smile cross her face. "I knew that there was a heart beating somewhere behind that tough exterior."

The waiter brought dinner. They made small talk as they ate. While they were drinking their after-dinner coffee, Will said, "Look, Manny and Rodney are scared. They think that old woman has all the Global employees under a spell. Rodney won't even leave the hotel."

Vertise smiled. "They're right, you know. Only, I can take care of it. Let's go."

As Will reached over to pull her chair back, she stood and kissed him on the cheek. "And I expect you to keep an open mind."

"Deal."

When they arrived at the front desk, Will asked that his car be brought around. He then called the room shared by Manny and Rodney on a house phone. Manny answered. "Meet me at the front. Vertise says she can un-spell us."

"I don't understand."

"Just get down here," Will said.

Manny arrived as the valet delivered the Land Rover. The valet opened the door for Vertise and then turned to Will. "Mr. Taylor, you've got damage on that front fender. Our service didn't do that."

"I know. I dodged a goat that wandered onto the highway this afternoon. My fault, not yours."

Manny climbed into the back seat.

"Where's Rodney?" Will asked as they strapped their seat belts and started around the circle.

"Don't know," Manny replied. "He wasn't in the room when we came back from Accompong, and I haven't seen him all evening. Figured he must have met up with you. Oh, and he doesn't answer his cell either."

"That's troubling," Will said. "I told him not to go anywhere without telling me."

Vertise directed them away from the water and up a road lined with shacks. The road was dark. Their headlights illuminated people walking in the dark. Old cars were parked haphazardly, making it difficult for Will to weave among them. They passed what must have been a neighborhood bar, small and open to the street. Three bar stools fronted a counter. Behind it was a Red Stripe sign. Manny was getting nervous.

"Vertise, you sure you know where you're going?" Manny asked.

"Almost there." After another block, she said, "Stop in front of that next house on the right."

In contrast to the rest of the neighborhood, the house was well maintained. The front yard was fenced. In the center of the yard was a water basin on a pedestal with several bottles hanging on strings below it.

"Is that a bird bath?" Manny asked.

Vertise shook her head. "That's an announcement that a voodoo muda lives here. The three candles in the window are telling us that she is open for business."

As they exited the Land Rover, Will asked, "Is it safe to leave the car parked on this street."

"No worries. It's in front of the muda's house. No one will disturb it."

Vertise led the way through the front gate and up to the porch. Manny looked up and down the street, obviously worried that there may be trouble awaiting them in the dark. Vertise knocked on the door. It was opened by an old woman, no more than five feet tall, wearing gold rimmed glasses, faded jeans, and an *Usain Bolt* T-shirt. Her feet were bare. When she saw Vertise, she smiled and gave her a warm hug.

With a twinkle in her eye, she said to Vertise, "You not dead yet?"

Vertise grinned. "That's a question I ought to be asking you, old woman." She turned to Will and Manny. "This is Muda Katherine. Katherine, these are my friends, Will and Manny. They need your help."

"I was about ready to blow out the candles and call it a night." She studied the two men. "I can see that someone put a spell on them. Come in and let's see what I can do."

She led them to a round table with four chairs in the middle of the room. A candelabra on the table provided the only illumination. As they settled into chairs, Muda Katherine walked over to a switch by the front door, flipped it, and the room was flooded with light. "Some of my local clients aren't all that well educated. They expect a little magic. With them I just light the place with the candles. Since you're with Vertise, I suspect you're more interested in results."

"It was the old muda up in Accompong," Vertise said. "The curse was put on them and their co-workers with Global American Metals. Their friend named Rodney is fearing for his life."

"I know that crazy old woman."

"We'll pay anything," Manny interrupted.

"I can take care of your problem. What you pay is up to you. Just drop your payment in that crystal bowl by the front door when you leave."

The old woman stepped to a bookcase against the wall that was filled with an assortment of bottles in various shapes and sizes. Each had a label with handwriting on it. She took one from the shelf, studied it, and replaced it. She looked at about a half a dozen before selecting two. She held one in each hand, and a guttural sound came from her throat followed by a loud cough.

Manny had been watching carefully. "Was that a magic incantation you were saying over those bottles?"

"No," Muda Katherine said with a smile. "I was just clearing my throat. Must be allergies or something."

She took an empty bottle that was sitting in the center of the table and simultaneously poured the contents of each bottle into it. When she did so, smoke spilled from the bottle. She handed the bottle to Manny. "You like the smoke effect? It's just for show. I put a little pill in the bottle on the table before you arrived. It reacted to the liquids in the other two bottles. Helps convince the locals they're getting their money's worth. Now, take two sips from the bottle in your hand, not three, only two."

Manny hesitated, staring at the bottle, until Will grabbed it and took the required two swallows. His lips pursed like he had just eaten a lemon when he handed the bottle to Manny. Manny quickly took two swallows and set the bottle on the table. Muda Katherine corked the bottle and returned it to Manny.

"When you find your friend, have him take two swallows. Then throw the rest down the toilet. That old Accompong Muda's spell will be broken. The three of you will no longer be cursed." She paused and pointed a finger at Manny. "Except for you. You're screwed."

"Really? Oh shit."

"Ha, ha, just joking. Your spells are broken, once you drop something in the bowl, of course."

"What about the rest of the Global employees?" Manny asked.

"I wasn't asked to break their spells. I wouldn't do it anyway. I don't like what your company is doing to the Cockpit Country. I helped you because Vertise is my friend."

"What exactly happens when someone is under one of these curses? I mean, I understand we're okay, but what about the other Global employees?"

Muda Katherine scratched the side of her face as she thought. "That old muda's not real strong. With her powers, you can expect headaches, violent coughing, stomach cramps, vomiting, rashes, that kind of thing. Could be some deaths, but only a few."

114

"You know about snake daggers, Muda Katherine?"

"Like the one that killed Kaven at Rose Hall? Those snake daggers that were buried with the overseer have magical powers. I understand one is missing. I urge you to find it before someone else does and uses it against you."

Will nodded. They rose from their chairs and thanked Muda Katherine. Manny dropped two one hundred-dollar bills in the bowl on the way out. He smiled as he did so, hoping that the spell was broken for good.

CHAPTER 31

The bartender at the outdoor bar looked at his lone customer at the far end and decided to intervene. He walked to stand in front of the customer who was staring into an empty glass that had contained vodka on the rocks. "Sir, that's your fifth double in two hours. You're not driving tonight, are you?"

Rodney looked up from his empty glass and took a moment to focus on the bartender. "I only have to drive the elevator to my floor," he slurred. "I think I can push the right button."

The bartender turned to walk away. "Give me one more double on the rocks, then I'll head up to my room. Say, you know anything about the White Witch?"

The bartender turned back to his customer. "Certainly. Our golf course is named after her and the hotel restored her mansion. Why do you ask?"

"Some, some, somebody is trying to kill me and my friends. I figure it's either her or some of those damn morons."

"You mean Maroons, sir?"

"Yeah, I mean Maroons. Anyway, someone is trying to kill us. You heard about the man that was found on the mansion steps?"

"Of course," the bartender replied as he placed a double vodka in front of the customer.

"He was my friend. We worked for the same company. Now I'm worried about my other two co-workers. I was out walking on the beach when I must have dropped my cell. Too damn dark to find it. I'll check the beach in the morning. They could have been killed tonight, too."

The bartender handed him his bill. "If one of them was Mr. Taylor, he and

Ms. Broderick were here and left probably about ten minutes before you walked up from the beach. Certainly, he seemed to be in good health."

Rodney slowly absorbed what the bartender told him and said, "Well, that's good news, in fact, damn good news. Means Manny is probably okay, too. Now, let me sign this tab."

Rodney signed it and added a twenty percent tip. When he rose, he tripped over a chair and fell to his knees.

"Sir, would you like for me to get someone from security to walk you to your room and make sure everything is okay?"

Rodney pushed himself up and stumbled into the shadows. "No, I'll be good. Just have to go over two buildings."

Rodney weaved his way along the sidewalk that fronted the ocean, passed by his building, and soon found himself beyond the hotel property. He looked back. "Shit. I went two buildings too far. "

He tried to walk a straight line to the path that led to his building. He fumbled in his pocket for the room key that would unlock the outer door. After a couple of tries, he succeeded. The elevator opened as soon as he pushed the button. He looked in the mirror that was the back wall of the elevator as it rose to the fourth floor. "You're one drunk bastard," he mumbled to his image in the mirror. He hoped that Manny would be in the room. He pushed his room key into the slot and pitched it on the entry table as he turned on the lights. He started for his bedroom when a giant black man wearing a bellman's uniform appeared in the doorway. Before he could say anything, the man rushed to confront him and plunged a knife into his side. Rodney cried out in pain.

"Take what you want. My wallet is in my pocket. You want my computer? It's on the desk."

The bellman planted a big fist under his chin that sent Rodney sprawling to the floor. The bellman picked him up like he was a little kid and walked to the balcony. Rodney realized what was happening. "No, No. Please don't do it."

"Shut up. Your whining won't do any good."

The bellman tossed him over the rail. He watched as Rodney fell the four floors and landed in a flower bed below. When he was satisfied there were no signs of movement, he turned back into the room.

CHAPTER 32

When they arrived at the hotel, Vertise directed them to a side parking lot for employees. "I can certainly say that this is a day that I will not forget."

"You want us to follow you home?"

"No. I'm not worried. Thanks for everything."

Will and Manny watched as she got in her Volkswagen and left the parking lot. Driving to the front of the hotel, Will said, "I'm a little worried about Rodney. He hasn't answered his cell all night."

Walking to the elevator, Manny asked, "You heading to your room?"

"I think I'll drop by yours first, just to check on Rodney. Not like him to go off the grid for so many hours."

Manny pushed the door to the room open and stepped back in horror. The room looked as if it had been hit by a tornado. The television screen was in pieces with a lamp below it. The coffee table glass was shattered. Furniture was overturned. The screen door to the balcony was ripped. A trail of blood led to the door.

"Stand back, Manny," Will said as he reached for his gun and eased into the room. Rodney was nowhere to be found. Will opened what was left of the screen door and stepped onto the balcony. No Rodney. He looked down from the balcony and saw a body sprawled on the flower bed below. "Manny, stay inside. You don't need to look."

Manny ignored him and walked to look at Rodney. He reached in his pocket and took the bottle the muda had given him, pulled the cork, and poured it over the balcony. Then he tossed the bottle before turning to Will. "His computer is gone. Dammit, it's your fault. It was your job to protect us.

Now what do we do?" Manny collapsed into a chair on the balcony and buried his face in his hands.

Will headed for the hallway. Manny saw what he was doing and followed. Will pushed the button for the elevator. When it didn't arrive in seconds, he turned and dashed for the stairs. He took them two at a time until he hit the ground floor and went out into the night. When he got to Rodney, Will felt his neck. "Manny, he's still got a pulse. Call the front desk."

Fifteen minutes later an ambulance could be heard in the distance. As it drew closer, it circled around the hotel on a service drive and made its way up the sidewalk. The driver left the headlights on as he pushed the button to silence the siren and douse the flashing lights. He jumped from the ambulance while his partner leaped from the other side with a medical bag and oxygen tank in hand.

By then a crowd was gathering. The driver, whose name tag read Bryan Williams, said, "Would you please back up?"

Will and Manny backed away with the others. Bryan's partner was a very efficient woman he called Louise. "Check his vitals," he ordered.

She put her hand to his neck. "Pulse is erratic and thready, about forty-five." She applied a blood pressure cuff and put her stethoscope to his arm. She pumped the cuff and listened carefully. "Blood pressure is sixty over forty and dropping."

"The wound in his gut is on the right side. It's oozing some, but doesn't appear to be life threatening. I'm putting the oxygen mask on. Then, I'll pack the wound with gauze and tape it. Get the board and let's get him strapped on. Once we get him in the truck, we'll give him some dopamine to try to get his pressure stabilized."

While Louise went to get the backboard, Bryan asked, "Who found him?"

"I did," Will said. "His room was up on the fourth floor. Judging from the condition of the room, someone threw him off the balcony. Any chance of him living?"

Bryan shook his head. "Slim, but we'll do our best. Looks like the leg is broken. I suspect a rib punctured his lung. That knife wound doesn't appear to be life-threatening. I don't see any signs of a skull fracture, but it's pretty dark out here. Imaging will tell us the condition of his brain." He paused. "Frankly, I'm surprised he's not dead."

Louise returned with the board and a neck collar. She carefully placed the collar. Next, she and Bryan readied to move him to the board. "Would you help us by lifting his feet?" he asked Will. Will did as he was instructed, and the two EMTs gently moved Rodney onto the board and secured him with straps. Next, Louise returned with a gurney. They moved him to the gurney and raised it to the level of the back of the ambulance, then moved him to the open doors and pushed the gurney into the back. Louise jumped in behind him. Bryan closed the doors.

"The cops will be here shortly. Tell them we're taking him to the Montego Bay Hospital."

Bryan jumped into the driver's seat, buckled his seat belt, shut the door, started the engine, and the ambulance took off with lights flashing and siren screeching over the normally quiet back lawn of the hotel.

"Shouldn't we head to the hospital?" Manny asked.

"They won't know anything until the doctor checks him over and they do some imaging. Harper or some of his guys ought to be here any time. Let's wait a few minutes and tell them what we know. We can check out the area while we wait."

Manny agreed.

Will used his cell phone flashlight to illuminate the flower bed and started searching for any clues. Manny saw what he was doing and did the same. Other guests tried to join in, but Will shooed them away, saying it was a crime scene. Will had just found a cufflink under a bush when Harper burst into view.

"Dammit, Taylor, what the hell are you doing to my crime scene? You've probably already compromised critical evidence."

Taylor faced off with Harper. "I've had enough of you. While we were waiting for you to get here, I called the ambulance and got Rodney, another Global employee who may yet die, in the hands of the EMTs and on the way to the Montego Bay Hospital. You can check his room when you get finished. You'll find one unholy mess. I just found this on the ground under that bush. Connected? I don't know, but you ought to put it in an evidence bag.

"Look, Harper, Rodney had a wound in his gut. Did it come from a snake dagger? Damned if I know. It sure as hell could have. I'm a pretty smart man. I don't believe in voodoo. Fact is I never encountered it until I got here. On the other hand, Manny and I just paid two hundred dollars to have a curse removed by an old woman up in the hills. Is that crazy? Maybe it's insurance, just in case. These snake daggers may have our names on them for all I know. We know one was used on Kaven. I don't believe a snake dagger is any different from a KA-

BAR or a kitchen knife for that matter. In the right hands any one of them is a lethal weapon. Was one used on Rodney? Who the hell knows?"

"There are actually three snake daggers," Harper said quietly. "Legend has it that Annie was buried with the one that had the most mystical power. Supposedly, it was moved with her to that crypt at the mansion and is interred with her remains."

Will looked at Manny and back at Harper. "Well, that's just great. So, we have not one, but two daggers to worry about, including one that is all powerful. Look Harper, I have carried a knife and used it a few times. The knife didn't have anything mystical about it, but in my hands, it became a lethal weapon. If someone gets his hands on one of those snake daggers, I'm not worried about the knife, but if that guy thinks that he has just become Superman, it could be a problem."

"You can rest easy about the dagger that was buried with Annie Palmer. First, graves are sacred in Jamaica. If someone disturbs a grave, it's automatic prison time. Second, no one is going to touch it if it is buried with the White Witch. My understanding is that another *Obeah* priest or priestess would be the only persons who would disturb her tomb."

"That doesn't really increase our comfort level, knowing another friend is near death. I know you're going to want to check out Rodney's room. Manny and I are going to the hospital. Can you tell us how to get there?"

"You've been to the police station. On that same street, just two blocks away."

Will nodded. "We'll be there for a while. If you have any questions for us, you have my cell number."

When they passed the police station, Will said, "In that building is one of the best stocked bars on the whole damn island."

"I don't understand," Manny said.

"One of the perks of being a police officer. The drinks are compliments of the taxpayers."

Will drove two more blocks and found the hospital. He figured that Rodney would still be in the emergency room. Hopefully, someone there could tell him Rodney's status. He parked in a space that was reserved for physicians. When they walked through double doors, they found an emergency room that was surprisingly deserted. Only two people were sleeping in chairs, awaiting word on some friend or loved one. Will walked to the desk and handed his card to the woman behind it.

"Name's Will Taylor. I'm with Global American Metals. One of my associates was brought here in the past hour or so. Name's Rodney Gore. He was pretty banged up. We need to check on him. I know this is a bit unusual, but he doesn't have any family on the island. I'll be able to report what I learn to them back in the States."

The woman rose and disappeared through two double doors that led to the back. In a few minutes she returned with a short, stocky male nurse. The nurse had Will's card in his hand.

"You're Mr. Taylor?"

"I am. This is Manny Rodriquez, another co-worker."

"I checked his pockets and found an ID from your company. I'll tell you what I know. He broke his right tibia in two places. He has several broken ribs. One of them punctured a lung. The knife didn't hit any vital organs, but caused the loss of about a liter of blood. No fractures on his head, but there is some swelling in the brain that we'll have to monitor. He's in surgery now. We have a general surgeon working on him first. An orthopedic surgeon is standing by. It's going to be several hours before he even gets out of surgery. My guess is that he will be in recovery and critical care for twenty-four to forty-eight hours. I suggest that you check back in the morning, but not before ten. Oh, one other thing. He had a very high blood alcohol level. He must have been drinking for several hours before he fell off that balcony."

"He didn't fall. He was thrown off. Someone was in his room. How else would he have gotten that knife wound?"

The nurse turned to walk back through the doors and shrugged his shoulders. "Not for me to say. Just thought you would want to know the complete story."

Then he was gone.

CHAPTER 33

When they returned to the hotel, they went to the front desk. "Are the police still on the premises?" Manny asked.

"They spent some time in your room, Mr. Rodriquez. They sealed it off and said they would be back in the morning. We moved all your belongings and those of Mr. Gore to a suite next to Mr. Taylor. Here's the key."

Will and Manny agreed that they needed a couple of drinks to help unwind from a stressful day and headed for the bar. When they arrived, even though well past midnight, it was crowded. A piano and bass guitar sounded quietly from the corner of the room. Will ordered 10th Mountain Bourbon and asked to see the cigars. Manny asked about the bourbon and Will explained that some of his military buddies put him onto it. It was distilled in Colorado and was intended to capture the spirit of the legendary 10th Mountain Division that fought in World War II and trained at Camp Hale, not far from what is now the ski resort of Vail. Hearing the story, Manny ordered the same and toasted Will and all of those who had fought for their country. Will accepted the toast.

"And one more toast, or maybe more of a prayer," Will said. "Here's to Rodney, may he have a swift and full recovery."

They ordered Cuban cigars, and after two drinks Manny was getting a little high. Will had been quiet as he enjoyed the fine liquor and cigar. He put down both and took his cell phone from the cocktail table to call Vertise. When she picked up, he said, "Will here. Manny and I are in the hotel bar. We found Rodney four floors below his room in a flower bed."

"My God, Will. I don't know what to say. Is Rodney dead?"

"No, Bad hurt and in surgery at the hospital. Someone had stabbed him and tossed him over the balcony. May have been done with the missing snake dagger or someone wanted us to believe that. Manny's upset, but a couple of shots of bourbon seem to have settled him down."

"Should we be at the hospital?"

"No. They said for us to check in about mid-morning. There's something else. I was talking to Chief Harper about those snake daggers. He says there's another one in Annie Palmer's crypt. I'm not saying that I believe anything about those damn daggers, but let's just say I'm curious. What's the story on that?"

"Pick me up in thirty minutes, and I'll show you. Tell Manny not to worry about going to the mansion at night. I'll protect him."

Will clicked off the phone and pondered her last comment. How the hell could she protect them from the snake daggers?

Vertise was waiting at the curb when they stopped in front of her apartment. She buckled herself in the back seat and said, "No questions. I'll explain everything when we get there."

When they got to the Rose Hall gate, Vertise walked to the pillar on the left and punched in a code. The gates opened without a sound. When Vertise returned to the car, she said, "Follow the road to the front of the mansion. We'll park there."

Once parked, Will locked the Land Rover. Vertise motioned to follow her around the left side of the mansion to a path that led to a small garden area. The full moon shone on a concrete crypt with the image of a woman carved on the top. Her hands were resting on her chest and clutched a snake dagger. Vertise moved to the head of the crypt.

"We're not sure when her body was moved here. Best estimate is about a hundred and fifty years ago."

Will and Manny stared at the crypt until Will asked, "How can you be sure it's Annie Palmer that's in there?"

"About fifty years ago, three most revered mudas visited this tomb on the night of a full moon." She looked up into the sky. "Like tonight."

Manny looked up at the moon and then his eyes searched the forest around them for movement. Next, he turned and studied the mansion. Once he was satisfied they were alone, he again faced Vertise.

"These mudas knew ways to contact any spirit that might be inside the tomb. When they did so, they asked to speak with Annie Palmer. A voice from within the tomb replied that she was Annie Palmer's spirit. They asked a number of questions to this spirit, things that only Annie Palmer would know."

"Such as?" Will asked.

"Where she was born. When she arrived in Jamaica. When and how her parents died. The names of her husbands. She answered all the questions. Of course, she denied that she had killed her husbands or that she tortured slaves."

"What's this got to do with the dagger?" Will asked.

"That was one of the questions the mudas asked. She said that the dagger was in the crypt with her. Then she was quiet. After a time, the mudas left, planning to return the next night."

"Why?" Manny said.

"They intended to paint white crosses on all four sides of the crypt. That would insure that her spirit would remain in the tomb. When they arrived at the crypt, they tried to talk to Annie Palmer, but no one answered. It was clear that her spirit was gone from the tomb. They assumed she was out roaming the grounds or the mansion. Not wanting to bar her spirit from her crypt, they left one side without a cross. That would permit her to come and go as she wanted. Over the years, various people have re-painted the three crosses, but no one has dared to put a cross on the fourth side."

"This is all just a bunch of crap," Will said. "You want me to believe that because these mudas painted only three crosses, the White Witch is roaming around throwing daggers at us?"

Vertise replied calmly. "I'm not asking you to believe anything. Voodoo engenders strong beliefs in certain of its followers. I'm not saying that anyone should believe as they do. Only you should recognize the power of their religion."

Will stared at Vertise with no expression. Manny turned again and looked at the mansion.

"Isn't this just great," Manny said. "Here we are at the Rose Hall Mansion, the home of the White Witch, standing beside her crypt under a full moon. Annie may come walking up any time, snake dagger in hand, looking for her next victim. I'm only two generations removed from Mexico. I had a grandmother who said that she could call up spirits. I blew her off when I was a teenager. Maybe she knew more than I thought."

"Let me try to calm you. Annie Palmer has been dead about two hundred years. There have been hundreds of sightings of her in the mansion and on the grounds of the old plantation. Even some golfers have seen her early in the morning off in the fog that sometimes settles on the course." She looked directly at Manny. "There are no reports of her hurting anyone since she died."

"Yeah, tell that to Kaven and Rodney."

The sound of cars coming up the driveway caught their attention. Then car doors slammed. A male voice said, "That's Taylor's car. They're here somewhere."

"Dammit," Vertise said. "I forgot to lock the gate after we went through. I didn't expect any visitors at this hour of the morning."

Will pulled his Glock and looked around for a safe place. "Do you know them? Recognize any voices?"

"No. They're looking for you. That can't be good. We need to get to the dungeon. There's a secret passage from there."

Manny stared at the mansion, weighing the White Witch against the male voices.

"Come on, Manny," Will said. "We don't have any choice."

Vertise led the way to the back of the mansion and down some stone steps to a small door. She moved her fingers over the bricks to the right of the entrance until she pulled one out and retrieved a key. She opened the door and replaced the key before directing Will and Manny to follow her. Once they were in, she locked the door. Several candles were on a wooden table beside it. She handed one each to Will and Manny. Then she found a match which she lit by striking it on one of the bricks.

Will pulled his cell from his pocket. "I prefer to use the flashlight on this." Manny nodded and retrieved his cell.

"Good idea, but I left mine back at the house," Vertise said, as she used the match to light one candle.

"That door hasn't been opened in years. It leads to a tunnel that comes out on the beach across the highway. Annie Palmer had it built as an escape route if there was ever a slave uprising. See if you can open it."

Will handed her his cell to light the door. Manny clicked his off and put it back in his pocket. Will and Manny grabbed a large ring and tugged. Nothing happened. They twisted the ring and tugged. Still nothing. Finally, Will propped one foot up against the wall, and they tried again. The door creaked at first and began to open.

They entered a tunnel, probably five and a half feet high. Will took his cell back from Vertise. Rats scurried across their path. Spider webs hung from the ceiling. Puddles of stagnant water dotted the dirt floor.

"We're probably the first people in this tunnel since back in Annie Palmer's time," Will said. "Obviously, folks back then were not six feet tall. Give Manny and me a few seconds to pull this door back in place. Maybe they won't spot it at first, and we can buy a little time. Vertise, how are these guys going to get in the mansion?"

"Windows. All they have to do is break one and unlatch it. They will probably look through the house. They may not find this door for a few minutes."

"Manny, I have about a half a charge in my cell. Let's use mine first, and if I run out of battery, we'll switch to yours."

Manny was looking at the tunnel with an engineer's eye. "This damn thing was not very well built, even for two hundred years ago. Not nearly enough support beams. Now a bunch of them are rotted. I know we're in a hurry, but we better take it slow; look for signs of caving, and try not to step in a hole like that one right there." He had Will direct his beam to a hole along the right wall. "Someone steps in something like that, it could sprain an ankle or tear a knee. Take off, Will. Vertise will follow and I'll bring up the rear."

Will crouched to avoid hitting his head. He moved his beam back and forth across the tunnel, walking at a pace that would allow him to spot any dangers.

"Will, you should know that I can handle rats, but I'm scared of spiders," Vertise said. "I may panic if one lands on me."

"Then don't get close to that left wall. There's a big web hanging from a beam in the ceiling right there."

Vertise hugged the right wall as she squeezed past.

"There's a hole up here, goes nearly all the way across. Looks to be several feet deep. I think we can just get by on this side." He edged to the left and tiptoed along a four-inch ledge, bracing a hand on the ceiling for support. When he reached the other side, he held his hand out for Vertise. Once she was across, he did the same for Manny.

Before they could go any farther, they heard creaking from the door they had just been through as it was opened. All three paused to listen. A male voice said, "Why do you think they would be in here? I got claustrophobia. I don't want to go in that damn tunnel."

"Look right there," a second voice said as he shined a flashlight on the floor.

"You see those footprints? You think they were made two hundred years ago? They went this way. You put your claustrophobia up your ass. We're going in."

"I agree," a third man said.

The first man was big, heavy-set with a dark black complexion. The second was short and thin. The third was white, probably American.

"Be easier if you went first. You're short and don't have to stoop."

The second man's hands were shaking. His voice cracked when he replied, "No way, mon. You take the lead or I'm not going in."

"All right," the first man grumbled. "Use your flashlights and keep your guns handy."

Will put his finger to his lips when he heard the voices. "We have a head start," he whispered.

"You still have your gun, don't you, Will?" Manny asked.

Will nodded and turned to lead the way, only now he picked up the pace. Will was thinking that they just might get away safely until they were faced with a cave-in that blocked the entire tunnel. The upper beams had collapsed. "So much for being quiet. Manny, what do you suggest?"

Manny studied the timbers and dirt that blocked their escape. He pointed at one of the beams near the top of the pile. "Will, help me pull that one away from the cave-in."

Will and Manny grabbed the beam, rocked it back and forth for a few seconds, and started to pull. At first it wouldn't budge. They rocked it more. The second time they pulled, it gave way to expose a hole between the dirt and the top of the tunnel. It looked to be about two feet across. The gap between the dirt and the top was six inches or so. Manny looked at the pile. "We need something about the size of a two by four to widen that hole."

Vertise spotted the end of a board at the bottom of the dirt. "Will, see if you can pull this out."

Will bent over and went through the same rocking motion with the board, then pulled hard. A three-foot board came out. He handed it to Manny, who used it to push the dirt from the perimeter of the hole until two shots echoed through the tunnel.

"We better hurry," Will said as he fired a shot back in the direction of the men. "No way I can hit them, just slow them down. Manny, you loosened the dirt, let me see what I can do with my hands." Using both hands Will pulled the dirt toward him until the hole was over a foot between the ceiling and the dirt.

"Vertise, you're the smallest. You go first."

Vertise still held her candle, but realized that it was not adding much to the light from the cell phone. She blew it out. Will helped her up the pile and directed her to use his hands as a step. Vertise shivered with fright as she looked at the dark beyond the hole, but she did as she was told and disappeared to the other side. "Once you get through the hole, it's easy to climb down," she said. "Would someone please hurry and get some light over here?"

Will directed Manny to go next. He climbed the mound of dirt, using a timber for a foothold. He had to wiggle his way through, but made it. Once through, he clicked his cell phone light on. "That's a tight fit. Next time we try this I'm going to lay off the tacos for a few days."

"Okay, I'm going to fire a couple more shots back up the tunnel. Don't be surprised." The shots echoed through the tunnel. Several shots were fired in response. "They're getting closer. Here I come." Will put his gun and cell in pockets and pushed his way through the hole and climbed the few feet down to the other side.

"You two take off. Use Manny's light. I'm going to stay back and try to stall them." Vertise and Manny said nothing, but turned and started making their way through the tunnel. Will doused his light. Soon the male voices were heard, and Will could see light coming through the hole at the top.

"It's a damn cave-in," one said. "Did we miss a side tunnel?"

"No, look up at the top. There's a hole. They must have gone through it."

The big man studied the hole. "You two can make it through. We'll need to widen it more for me." He found the board on the ground and started to work. Will leaned against the wall on the other side, listening and watching as they nearly doubled the size of the hole. The big man turned to the one who complained of claustrophobia and said, "You first."

"Why me?"

The big man pointed his gun. "Because this says so. You have a flashlight. We'll be right behind you. Now, move your ass. We may lose them if we don't pick it up."

Will pointed the Glock at the hole and held his breath. In a matter of seconds, the little man was scrambling through the hole. Will waited, wanting his body to be in a position where he could pull him through and, hopefully seize his gun and flashlight. When he decided the time was right, he fired two shots, one hitting the head and one the neck. When Will was sure the body was not moving, he stepped forward and pulled him to the ground. He found the flashlight and a Sig Sauer.

"You guys listen up. This is Will Taylor. Your friend is dead. Vertise and Manny are now close to the end of the tunnel. I'm going to stay right here as long as it takes. I know there are at least two of you left. If you want to try going through that hole, you'll be lying beside your friend on this side. What's it going to be?"

Will heard whispers coming from the other side, then a voice. "Taylor, we're leaving. We'll be back tomorrow to retrieve the body. I presume you'll be long gone by then. There'll be another day."

Will heard footsteps fading away and the sound of the two men talking. Will thought it could be a ruse and they might still turn around. Still, it was buying him a few minutes. Hopefully, that would be enough lead time. He turned on the flashlight and was pleased to find that it illuminated the tunnel far better than the cell phone. He stuck the Sig in his back pocket and continued through the tunnel.

The two men on the other side watched the light coming through the hole and observed it fading. When it was dark, they backtracked, turned on one flashlight and squeezed through the hole. The big man paused to check the pulse of their comrade and shook his head. Now they needed to double-time as much as possible.

Will was hustling through the tunnel, finding it was easier with a bright flashlight that cast a wide and long beam. Within a matter of minutes, he found Vertise and Manny staring at another solid wooden door. Beside it, hanging from the wall, was a bear trap.

"What happened, Will?"

"I killed one of them who was coming through the hole. The other two claimed they were leaving rather than risk being shot by me. I think they backtracked a little and, by now, are through the hole and headed our direction. What's the deal on this door, and why's a bear trap hanging on the wall?"

"The door is the entrance to the beach. Legend has it that Annie put the bear trap here. If she was being chased through the tunnel, she could set the trap. The first of her pursuers would be caught. By the time he was freed, she would be far down the beach or maybe in a boat, heading for Montego Bay or Ocho Rios."

"Have you tried the door?"

"Worse than the one on the other end," Manny said. "Won't budge."

Will shined his light on the bear trap to study it. The trap was a foot and a half across, hinged in the middle with one-inch metal teeth around the perimeter. A five-foot metal chain ran from it to an eighteen-inch metal peg that could be hammered into the ground. Will pulled the bear trap from the peg on the wall. "Manny, I passed another two by four about thirty feet back. Take this flashlight and find it."

Manny jogged back up the tunnel and returned with the board. "Now what?"

"Let's use this metal peg to hammer one side of the trap's teeth into the crack between the door and the frame. Then, we'll use the board to lever the trap to force the door open."

Manny picked up the trap and positioned it so that several of the teeth were over the crack between the door and frame. Vertise held the flashlight. Will took the metal peg and hammered the trap until the teeth were well into the crack. The noise of the pounding resounded through the tunnel. Once Will was satisfied they had done all they could, he picked up the board and placed it into the trap and up against the door frame. Then he pried. He broke the seal and pried harder until the door released. When the door was open about a foot, Manny looked out.

"Shit, there's a wall of sand beyond the door."

"The tunnel was intended to come out on the beach," Vertise said. "Sand has been washed up against that door for two hundred years. We have to try to dig our way out."

"Give me the board, Manny," Will said as he pulled the door open another foot. Manny handed him the board. "Manny, hold the end of the board up against the sand, and I'll pound on it with the metal peg."

Manny did what he was told. Will beat on the board until he was exhausted and out of breath. "Here, let me take over," Manny said. He did the same until the board was four feet into the sand when it broke through. Manny pulled the board out. Vertise, jumped to the front and began widening the hole with her hands. When she paused for a breath, Will gently shoved her aside and took over the same task. Just as they had a hole in the sand big enough for them to crawl through, they heard voices in the tunnel. Vertise went first, followed by Manny. Will seized the bear trap and pulled it behind him. Then he pulled the door shut and put the metal peg through the ring handle and against the door frame. He hoped it would be enough to keep the killers inside.

Vertise led Will and Manny on a run down the beach back in the direction of the Ritz. When they paused for a breath, Manny asked, "How come you didn't set the trap like the White Witch would have?"

"I can tell you," Vertise said. "Annie would have had some house slaves cover it in a thin layer of dirt, so her enemies wouldn't notice it until the jaws snapped shut around one of their legs. We didn't have time for that. What Will did was perfect. Quick thinking, for sure."

"Back when I was in the SEALs, there were a number of times when my team was trying to extract ourselves from a situation and we had to improvise on the run. Glad it worked out this time. Only, we still don't know who is after us."

CHAPTER 34

The next day Will and Manny met at eleven for a late breakfast, then took the hotel shuttle up to Rose Hall to retrieve the Land Rover. The night before, Vertise had asked a hotel security guard to take her home. She met them at the mansion and led them into the bar where the dungeon used to be and poured three cups of coffee.

Will took a sip from his coffee and set the cup on the bar. "We have another mystery."

Vertise looked at him expectantly.

"Our trip to Rose Hall last night was on very short notice. Think about this. Manny and I were talking about snake daggers, we call you, and we pick you up thirty minutes later. Only the three of us knew where we were going, but a half hour later we're running for our lives." Will shook his head. "Pretty clear that someone is staking out the hotel and followed us when Manny and I left." He looked at Vertise. "You have any other ideas?"

Vertise shook her head and sipped her coffee.

"We can't solve that one right now. Manny and I are heading to the hospital to check on Rodney. You want to go?"

"Of course," Vertise replied. "I'm taking a few days off from bartending until we sort this all out. And I've told the paper to let me run with this story and not assign me anything else for a while. They've agreed."

Will parked in the front visitors' lot. When they entered, Vertise took the lead. "We're here to see Rodney Gore. He was admitted through the emergency room last night."

The receptionist checked her log. "He's still in the ICU. Only family members are permitted to visit."

"If you'll direct us to the ICU, we'll talk to the nurses and, maybe, a doctor."

The receptionist told them the ICU was on the third floor. They remained silent on the elevator, not sure what to expect. Stepping from the elevator, they were confronted with a desk, behind which was a burly nurse with a gruff continence. Vertise recognized her.

"Mary, how are you and your family doing?"

Mary smiled. "Vertise, I knew you were back on the island. I've been reading your stories in the paper. Who are you here to see?"

"It's Rodney Gore. Came in last night."

"He spent most of the night in the OR. You probably know the rules. Only family members permitted beyond those doors."

"Look, Mary. He's from the United States. He doesn't have any family here. These men, Will Taylor and Manuel Rodriquez, are co-workers. They'd like to see him just a few moments to give a report to his parents."

Mary leaned back in her chair as she thought, then put her elbows on her desk. "Okay, just this once. Through those doors. He's in the third bed on the right. He was banged up bad. I don't think the anesthesia has worn off, but you can talk to one of the nurses who is caring for him."

Vertise smiled her thanks and they entered the ICU. They found beds lining both sides of an aisle with curtains separating them. The smell was antiseptic. The sounds were of machines with different beeps emitting from them. Groans and cries of pain pierced the air. Patients were talking when no one was near them. Nurses, dressed in white with white hats, moved from bed to bed. If Mary had not told them that Rodney was in the third bed on the right, they never would have identified him.

Rodney was in casts and bandages from head to toe. His leg was suspended from a pulley. A ventilator mask covered his face. His eyes were shut, but were surrounded by bruises. A nurse was at his side, taking his vital signs. When she finished, she looked at them. "Can I help you?"

"We're here to check on Rodney. Mary said it was okay," Vertise said.

"He survived the surgery. It was long and difficult. He still is heavily sedated."

"Is he going to make it?" Will asked.

"It's touch and go. Too soon to tell, but we can hope. I suggest that you all pray, as will I. Check back tonight if you like."

Vertise, Will and Manny lowered their heads in prayer for a few moments, then turned and left the ICU.

When they drove from the hospital, Will said, "Should I drop you by the mansion so you can get your car?"

"That would be great," Vertise said.

"Hey," Manny interrupted, "I was up early this morning. Couldn't sleep for some reason after our little adventure last night. I walked around the grounds of the hotel. A bunch of the plants there look like some of those you showed us up in the rainforest."

"I'll give you an *A* for our botany lesson in the Cockpit Country. You're right. The Ritz contracted with my dad to transplant certain species here."

"Vertise, have you thought any more about those three men who were trying to kill us last night?"

Vertise shook her head. "I wish I knew. The logical conclusion would be that they're Maroons. If they were, my dad knew nothing about them."

Will remained silent, not sure what to believe any more. "Maroons, maybe. One sounded American. That doesn't fit in the puzzle. They were after me. Right now, I'd say I'm public enemy number one in this country. I wouldn't rule anyone out, strangely enough, not even Alexa."

"Damn sure got me scared," Manny said.

"Look, Manny, I can tell you that my dad is using his speeches like I'm using my columns. We're trying to generate attention, build public opinion. We're not into violence."

"Tell that to those young Maroons," Manny said. "At least I have a gun now. Will gave me that Sig he took from the guy in the tunnel."

Will looked at Manny. "You keep quiet about it. If you get caught carrying, you go to gun court. A judge can put you away for years just for possession."

"You don't have to worry. It stays in my back pocket with my shirt untucked and covering it. I'll only take it out if it's a matter of life or death. If that happens, I'll take my chances with the gun judge."

They were about to make the turn up to the mansion when Will's phone chimed. He glanced at the caller ID and said, "It's her majesty." He pushed the button to accept the call. "Taylor."

"Yes, ma'am."

"Yes, ma'am."

135

"Yes, ma'am."

He disconnected the call and dropped the phone into the center console. "Damn command performance. She wants me in Kingston in three hours. Is that enough time to get there?"

"Yeah, just barely," Vertise replied. "We're on the northwestern end of the island. Kingston is on the south coast and up toward the east end. You'll have to wind through the mountains to the south coast highway and then into Kingston. You know the address?"

"Yeah, I was actually there once. I think I'll remember the way once we get to Kingston."

"Hell," Manny said. "I'm going with you. I want to tell her personally what her mine is going to do to the rainforest. And I might as well tender my resignation today."

"You two are not going to leave me behind. It's about time I met Ms. Pritchard."

Will looked at Vertise and shook his head. "Expect to be thrown out of her office about five minutes after we get there."

CHAPTER 35

The receptionist led them into Pritchard's office. Global's president no longer looked like an executive with an international corporation. She was wearing no make-up. There were dark circles around her eyes. Her blouse had stains on the front from almost constant coughing. Her skin was pale. Her hands were shaking. She stared at Will and his two companions, but before she could speak, a series of coughs rumbled from deep in her chest. She reached for cough syrup on her desk and downed about a third of the bottle. Then she took a deep breath.

"I don't recall inviting three people for this meeting. Will, you're the one on the carpet."

"Mrs. Pritchard, you probably don't even remember me. We only met once," Manny said. "I'm Manuel Rodriquez, one of the company's mining engineers. I've been up to the Cockpit Country and have seen what our mine is going to do to the rainforest."

Pritchard turned her back on the visitors and pushed a button on her phone.

"Please, Mrs. Pritchard, there must be other places in the world we can get bauxite without destroying the ecosystem."

Pritchard whirled around and pointed her finger at Manny. "You're fired."

Manny straightened his back. "That's just fine, ma'am. I intended to resign if I couldn't get you to change your mind. I've failed, so I'm happy to be off the payroll."

Pritchard lit a cigarette, broke into another coughing spell, and turned to face Vertise. "And you, I know who you are. I see your headshot beside your column. You're Vertise Broderick, the woman who is trying to torpedo my mine. How dare you set foot in my office?"

Vertise looked her in the eye. "I thought it was time that I heard your side of the story."

Before she could say anything more, the door flew open and two guards burst through. They grabbed Manny and Vertise and forcefully escorted them from the office. Vertise broke away momentarily and turned to Pritchard. "Your coughing is lung disease. It's part of the curse that is on you. The only way you can end the coughing is to get off the island." Before she could say more, the guards seized her again and shoved her to the door.

Once they were gone and the door was closed, Pritchard said, "Taylor, I'm about ready to fire you, too. I don't really give a good goddam any more that your dad plays golf with the CEO."

"Look, Alexa, you need to go back to those Tootsie Pops. You heard Vertise. Maybe you should listen and just get the hell off the island."

"Shut up, Taylor. I'm doing the talking. And I damn sure hope that you're not buying into all this Jamaican voodoo crap."

Will started to say something. She interrupted. "I'm about to lose my mine, all because of a few lousy plants and some blacks who want to live in the Stone Age. You have a week to get this mess cleaned up. Understood? Also, I want even more security at our other facilities. Get it done."

Will stood, put his hands on Pritchard's desk, and leaned in. "I'll clean up your frigging mess. Just stay the hell out of my way." When Pritchard said nothing, he turned and walked out of the office, slamming the door behind him. As he left, he heard her begin to cough again.

CHAPTER 36

Richard Snyder finished his last martini at the bar of the Kingfish restaurant in Kingston and asked the bartender for his check. While he waited, he glanced around the room. He was the last customer. He paid the bill and walked to the front door. A valet met him and hurried around the building to retrieve his Lincoln. Snyder stood at the curb as the valet stopped his car and opened the door. He reached in his pocket for money to tip the valet. When he looked up, he saw the valet had a knife in his hand. He may have noticed that it was a snake dagger, maybe not. It all happened so fast. The valet plunged the knife into his chest and watched as Snyder slid to the ground. Once he was satisfied that Snyder was dead, the man peeled off the valet jacket, dropped it on the ground and ran down the dark street. The two ruby snake eyes blinked in the light of passing cars.

***

Miles Harper spotted Will having breakfast by the pool at the Ritz. When he approached the table, Will rose to shake his hand. "I'm having breakfast. You want a menu?"

"No. I had breakfast at home. It's a tradition with my wife. I often don't get home until long after the dinner hour. So, once we get the kids off to school, we have a leisurely breakfast. Coffee will be fine."

Will motioned to the waiter who brought a cup with the Ritz logo on it and a silver-plated carafe of coffee.

"First question," Will said. "Why are we meeting here instead of in your office?"

Harper smiled. "I could say the view is a helluva lot better and that would be the truth. Real reason is I didn't want my staff and cops to know I am conferring with you."

The waiter returned with Will's breakfast: bacon, scrambled eggs, and two English muffins. "You mind if I eat while we talk?"

"Of course not."

"I understand that Vertise told you about some men trying to kill us up at Rose Hall two nights ago."

Harper nodded. "Damn good thing she knew about that tunnel. What the hell were you doing up there in the middle of the night?"

"Not really important, but we were trying to understand more about snake daggers. I presume that you didn't find a body in the tunnel at the cave-in."

"No. Some signs of them dragging it back to the entrance, nothing else. Any idea who wants you killed?"

"No idea. Short list would include some Maroons, maybe a competitor, maybe even Pritchard. I think they were after me and, maybe, Manny. I suspect they wouldn't have harmed Vertise."

"My problem is this. I have a crime wave in my parish. Now the Minister of Mines is killed with a snake knife in Kingston. All I've got is a bunch of dead ends. The commissioner is on my ass. And would you believe that some of my cops are buying into the belief that the White Witch has returned?"

"Not a surprise. Still, I think we have to assume it's some of the young Maroons. They would have a reason to kill Kaven, that guard up at the mine site, and even Snyder. As for trying to kill Rodney, I have a different idea that may not involve them. Vertise says that her father is not involved. I have no reason to disbelieve her."

"If it's the Maroons, why kill Snyder with a knife? I know that those Maroons have a small arsenal up in Accompong. A gun would be swift and easy."

Will shook his head. "Damned if I know. Someone wants to perpetuate the myth of the White Witch. Like you say, even some of your cops are believing it."

Harper stared off across the water as a sailboat glided by. "You want to tell me your theory about Rodney?"

"Not yet. I need to have more facts. I can tell you it may have something to do with his computer being taken."

Harper took a deep breath and exhaled. "Okay, you can forget about

140

what I said about staying out of my way. I'll take whatever help you can give."
Harper lowered his voice. "This is not on the street yet, but you should know
that we got an anonymous tip a couple of days ago that Snyder took a half a
million bribe from your company to license the mine."

"Rodney figured that out. He may be the one who sent that note. That's
part of what I'm trying to sort out."

"How's he doing?"

"I just called the hospital. He's breathing on his own now, so they moved
him out of ICU. Still not awake. I'll probably drop by the hospital later today.
You uncover anything about the death of that guard up at the mine?"
Harper grimaced. "Just another damn unsolved murder. You still have that
Glock you bought from the old man?"

Will hesitated, not sure what to say.

"Forget what I said before. I know you have it. Keep it handy. I'll cover for
you if you have to use it."

CHAPTER 37

It was a moonless night. An old fishing boat motored into a small, dark bay on the coast between Montego Bay and Negril. As it approached the beach, a man waded into the water and caught the bow line that was tossed to him by a friend in the boat. He pulled it to shore until the bow was several feet onto the beach. Two other men were in the boat and two were behind the man on shore. They said little. They wanted to maintain silence, and besides, they had done this many times before. The men on shore started hauling bundles of ganja down the beach and passing them off to the ones on the boat. Within a half hour the boat was full. The three men on shore pushed the boat back into the water and watched as the engine was started and the boat disappeared around a point, headed for the open ocean. Once away from land, one of the men on the boat pulled out a cigarette and was about to light it.

"No. No light, not even the glow of a cigarette. I know this is your first job, but show a little common sense," the driver said.

"If they don't have any lights and we don't, how will we find them?" the man with the cigarette asked.

"I'm on a compass heading they gave us. They will hear our engine and will flash a light. We will flash twice in return."

The boat picked up speed as it left the island behind. When the boat was about three miles offshore they saw a flash in the distance. The third Maroon moved to the front of the boat and retrieved a large flashlight he used to provide the acknowledgment signal.

The driver looked to his back and to each side. "No sign of any patrols. We're okay." He eased the boat up beside a dark blue cigarette boat. The

Maroon on the bow and an American lashed the two boats together.

"How much you have?" the American asked.

"Hundred kilos, just like we promised," the Maroon said.

The Maroons and two Americans started moving the marijuana into the big boat. When they finished, the Americans handed over pistols, AK-47s, and C-4 plastic explosive. The lead Maroon carefully counted the weapons as they were passed onto his boat. When they finished, the first American released the lines.

"Nice doing business with you. When will you have another shipment?" the American asked.

"Probably a week," was the reply. "I'll call when we're ready. We'll need more AK-47s and plastic explosive next time."

"No problem," said the American. "You get us the ganja. We'll supply whatever you need."

***

Manny left the hotel the next morning and crossed over to the Rose Hall entrance. He hiked up the road and circled around the mansion until he was at the edge of the forest. To his left was the White Witch Golf Club. He walked along the tree line and back again three times until he spotted what he thought was an abandoned trail, overgrown with vines and brush. He was glad he was wearing long sleeves and long pants. On his back was a pack with a knife and clippers, two bottles of water, and baggies. The knife had a six-inch blade that he had sharpened that morning until he could shave the hair on his arm. Once he saw the thickness of the brush and vines, he dropped his pack and strapped the knife's sheath on his waist before re-shouldering the pack. Then he moved forward slowly, hacking at the brush and vines. The knife was not as good as a machete, but with a razor-sharp blade, he made slow progress. He was not even sure he was on the Maroon Trail until he broke through into a clearing. He walked to the other side to discover that only recently someone had notched trees up ahead. Must be some modern Maroons who decided to mark the trail that now appeared to have been used recently. He put his knife in the sheath and followed the trail up the mountain. Every hundred yards or so he stopped to listen. Nothing. He saw only a few birds and squirrels that scurried up trees as he passed. After two hours he reached his destination, the Global mine that was now closed, awaiting a new bulldozer.

Manny brought his cell phone, not for communication, but for its camera. He took pictures of the devastation left by only a few days of dozing the forest.

It was only two or three acres, but he could extrapolate the scene to show a thousand acres of destruction before Global was finished. He was not going to let it happen.

Satisfied that he had enough pictures to portray the mine, he wandered into the forest looking for some of the leaves and roots that Vertise had shown them. After studying bushes, trees, roots, and vines, he realized he couldn't identify anything. He had no idea whether a particular root or leaf had medicinal value. So, he randomly chose plants. He would take a photo of the bush or tree and cut a sprig of leaves or a root, taking a picture of the specimen before placing it in a baggie and then into his pack. After two hours, he figured he had close to forty. Time to head back down the hill. He would ask Vertise to take a look to see if he had identified any that might help cure sickness.

He made his way down the Maroon Trail, occasionally stopping to cut other specimens, and was soon back to the mansion. He crossed the street to the hotel and walked by the guardhouse.

"Afternoon, sir." a voice from within said. "You have a nice hike?"

"Excellent. Thanks for asking."

When Manny got to his room, he opened the door slowly and peeked inside. Seeing no one, he checked the bathroom, the closet, and the balcony before locking the door. He retrieved a Red Stripe from the small refrigerator and sat down in front of his laptop. Before doing anything else, he wiped the computer clean of anything to do with Global or the mine. Then he emailed Pritchard to advise her about what he had done and to tell her that he would put his company ID in the mail to her in Kingston. Once he was finished, he downed the Red Stripe and paused a second to celebrate his freedom from Pritchard. He would worry about another job later. Next, he went to the internet and typed in: "SaveJamaicasRainForest.com," the site that he had started the day he left Pritchard's office. While not yet ready to go live, he uploaded the photos of the mine and each one of the plants, trees, and specimens. Once done, he emailed the photos to Vertise and asked her to identify any that might have medicinal value. He explained that he would be using the site to publicize what was about to happen in the Cockpit Country. He suggested that once the site was ready she might contact some of her friends in the media in the United States. He would make himself available for interviews. As a former Global mining engineer, they could hardly find a better source. And he was ready to talk.

CHAPTER 38

The young Maroons came in groups of two and three and entered Lawrence's house. Guns and explosives lined the walls of the small living room. The first groups sat at a small table and on a sagging brown sofa that had seen better days, maybe thirty or so years ago. Lawrence stood in front of the fireplace. When he counted fifteen men, he asked, "We missing anyone?"

The others shook their heads.

"Okay, then I declare this Maroon war council open for business." He received nods from several of the men. "We are going to have to adopt the tactics of our ancestors when they fought the British. We will swoop down from our mountains, attack, and hightail it back up here. There's only one road to Accompong, and we can defend it."

"What about the trails?" Aaron asked.

Lawrence shook his head. "Shouldn't be a problem. I don't think anyone, white man or Jamaican, will risk getting ambushed on our mountain trails."

"Yeah," Aaron said. "Global will learn why the British fought for nearly a hundred years and finally gave up."

Several of the others joined in. "That's right, mon," "This is our country and nobody's going to take it from us," "Let's make them pay."

The voices in the house grew louder until Lawrence raised his hand. "I agree with all you're saying, but we need to keep it down. Colonel Broderick doesn't know what we're planning. If he learns, he'll try to stop us. We don't need him to get in our way."

When the room was quiet, Lawrence continued. "Aaron, James and I have appointed ourselves as leaders of this new Maroon uprising. I will be captain with Aaron and James my lieutenants. Any objection?" He surveyed the room and saw no disagreement. "Okay. Here's the plan for the first attack. We know that Global brings bauxite down from their mines in the interior to be loaded on one of their ships docked at Discovery Bay once a week, usually on Wednesday. We now have enough explosives to blow the train. Once the locomotive is out of commission, it will be months before they can get another one shipped. That will give us plenty of time to plan more attacks. Aaron will tell you how we are going to do it."

CHAPTER 39

The sun had set. The bauxite port about forty miles east of Montego Bay was quiet. The Global ship was docked with lights twinkling on spars above the deck, waiting on one last trainload of bauxite before weighing anchor and heading to the Gulf Coast of the United States. The train would be coming down from the mountains on tracks that extended to the end of the dock. It would stop next to the ship where giant cranes with shovels mounted on the ends would scoop one car empty of bauxite and drop the red dirt into the hold of the ship. As each car was emptied, the engineer would move the train forward enough to allow access to the next car. With twenty cars to be unloaded, it would be morning before the ship left, and the engineer would put the locomotive in reverse and push the empty cars back up the mountain.

Shacks dotted the mountain above the facility. They were occupied by Global workers and their families. People were walking the dirt streets. Some gathered to talk in groups. Most of the adults either had a spliff or a Red Stripe. A Jeep made its way up the hill and through the town. It was occupied by five Maroons dressed in the uniforms of Global guards. The people watched as they drove by, wondering why guards were here in the town instead of watching over the bauxite loading operation. The Jeep stopped at the railroad track on the edge of the village. Aaron and Lawrence stepped out carrying plastic explosives. The other three formed a perimeter, watching for signs of the real Global guards or anyone else looking to cause trouble. AK-47s hung from their shoulders. Aaron walked the track until he found a depression in the dirt below it. Lawrence shined his flashlight at the place Aaron had selected. Aaron had already rolled the explosive into tubes. He placed them under the track, affixed a detonator to the plastic, and backed slowly away leaving a trail of wire running to the explosive.

Lawrence could make out the light on the front of the locomotive approaching. "Hurry up, mon. The train is almost here."

"We're good, Lawrence." He glanced at the distance between the Jeep and the track. "Should be just fine. Get in the Jeep and we'll watch the fireworks. Should put this operation out of business for a couple of months, maybe more."

A long whistle came from the locomotive, a signal from the engineer to alert people in the town of its arrival. He intended to emit two long whistles, followed by a short one. Only half way through the second, long whistle, Aaron detonated the explosive just as the locomotive was crossing the street. The locomotive was lifted into the air and slammed down twenty feet from the track, as if thrown aside by a giant hand. Fire engulfed it and even rained on the Jeep. Behind the locomotive, at least half of the bauxite cars tumbled on their sides and rolled off the track. Lawrence could hear the cries of the engineer that came from inside the flaming engine.

"Help me. Help me, please. I'm on fire."

Lawrence shook off his feelings of sympathy for a man dying a gruesome death. "We better get out of here. Guards and cops will be here in no time."

Lawrence gunned the engine and raced down the mountain. They were almost to the highway when they saw a Land Rover loaded with guards, real ones, with weapons in hand and around their necks. When the driver of the Rover saw the Jeep hightailing it away from the train, he flipped the steering wheel so that the vehicle blocked the road. Guards jumped from the Rover and started firing at the occupants of the Jeep. They returned the fire and one of the guards was hit in the chest.

"Now what?" Aaron screamed.

"Keep firing at them. I'm turning around, and we're going back up the hill. There's an old Maroon Trail up there. Hasn't been used in years. Probably overgrown with bushes and vines, but we can use it. We'll leave the Jeep there. We can steal another one later." Lawrence wheeled the Jeep around and roared back up the mountain through a hail of bullets.

"I'm hit, Lawrence," a Maroon in the back seat shouted.

"Hang on, John. I can help you when we get on the trail."

With the Land Rover not far behind and gaining on them, Lawrence turned onto a little used dirt road that dead ended at the forest. The five Maroons piled from the Jeep with Aaron helping John and disappeared into the forest as the Land Rover rounded the corner.

The guards jumped from their vehicle and ran into the forest but soon lost the trail in the darkness.

"Lost them, boss," the first guard said as he stopped to listen. "I don't hear a sound."

"They had to be Maroons. Let's head back down the mountain. We'll start looking for them in the morning. Alan, check the Jeep. If they left the key in it, follow us back to the guard station. I'll call the parish police."

The Maroons had been no more than fifty yards up the trail where they froze like statues when they heard the guards enter the forest. Aaron had to put his hand over John's mouth to muffle his cries of pain. Finally, when the guards were gone, Lawrence said, "Let me look at that wound."

He carefully tore what remained of John's shirt from the area of the wound to his abdomen. He studied it carefully with a small flashlight, then walked up the trail flashing the light to both sides. He returned in less than two minutes with big green leaves. "It would be better if we could heat these leaves, but we can't. Still, I can make a poultice. It will serve to stop most of the bleeding and help to ease the pain. Aaron, take off your shirt. We can use it to bind the leaves to the wound. John, tough it out until we get back to Accompong. Colonel Broderick can take it from there."

"But," John winced through his pain, "I thought you said that we couldn't tell the colonel."

Lawrence shook his head. "You're right. I can do almost as good a job as the colonel. Let's get going."

He turned and started up the trail. Aaron and a second Maroon lifted John to his feet and braced him as they followed Lawrence. If there had been any doubt before, now there would be none. The Maroon War had started.

CHAPTER 40

Will only had to circle the police station parking lot once before he spotted another car backing out of a space. He parked his Rover and hurried into the building, a grim look on his face. He bounded the stairs to the second floor and made his way to a door with a sign that identified the office as that of Chief of Detectives Miles Harper. He opened the door to find a large, middle aged woman behind a desk working on an old Dell computer. She didn't look up until Will spoke.

"I'm here to see Chief Harper."

Still looking at the computer screen, she asked, "And you are?"

"Will Taylor."

She turned to look at a paper desktop calendar. "I don't see that you have an appointment."

Will took a step to stand over her. "Look, ma'am. He'll want to see me."

She let out a sigh. "He's very busy, but I'll check." She picked up the phone and pushed a button. "Chief Harper, there's a Will Taylor here. Says you want to see him. Yes sir." She looked up at Will. "You can go in."

Will walked around the secretary's desk and opened the door behind her. Harper was walking around his own desk to meet Will. "Taylor, have a seat."

The office was small with room enough for a desk, a chair behind it, and two chairs in front. The walls were like the outside of the building, made of cinder block but painted beige. Harper's diploma hung on the wall behind his desk. There was a small window on the wall to his right where one could see the bay off in the distance.

"Thanks, but I'll stand," Will replied as Harper returned to his chair. "Look,

Miles, what do you get paid for? My company's facility at Discovery Bay is down for at least two months. It'll take at least that long to get a new locomotive shipped here. We've got a dead engineer and a seriously wounded guard in intensive care. Alexa Pritchard is on my ass."

Harper stood and walked to the window and gazed out at the bay before turning to speak. "I know all you're telling me. I haven't had this many murders under investigation since I became Chief Detective."

"You know damn well it's the Maroons. You need to get some men up to Accompong and search the houses. You're bound to find an arsenal of weapons along with a stash of C-4."

"Can't. You know about the treaty. A judge here is not going to give me a search warrant. It would take an act of parliament, and they're not even in session right now. I'm calling in the Jamaican army. They'll be patrolling the streets every night. We'll eventually catch the killers."

"You need to do one more thing."

Harper looked at Will. "What's that?"

"Call Alexa Pritchard and tell her that you're doing everything you can. One of my men told me that she's thinking about importing some mercenaries from the States, former Iraq contractors. I'm out of the loop on that plan, but she's not about to lose the Cockpit mine. I don't think that she's pulled the trigger on it yet, but I can't be positive. You need to convince her that you have the situation under control. Otherwise, you'll be facing trained killers."

Harper shook a Marlboro from a pack and lit it with an ornate, gold lighter from his desk. After he inhaled and blew the smoke from his mouth, he said, "I'll arrest them as soon as they arrive at the airport."

"You'll never recognize them. They'll be dressed in Hawaiian shirts and shorts. Their weapons will be shipped separately."

"They'll never get up to Accompong. There's only one road."

Will shook his head. "You forget that Pritchard has at least two, maybe three helicopters on the island."

Harper thought while he took another puff on his Marlboro. "Has she gone mad?"

"Not mad. Just ruthless. She's never lost a fight in her life. She's always believed that when anyone gets in her way, it's her right to crush him like a cockroach. That means the Maroons, you, hell, even me. I've worked for her for nearly six years now, but if she ever though that I was an obstacle to her plans,

I'd be out on the street."

"I'll do the best I can. We don't need another Maroon war."

When Will was entering his car, his cell chimed. "Mr. Taylor, this is Nurse Burrow. Rodney is starting to awaken."

"That's good news. I'm at the police station. I'll be there in ten minutes."

Will exited the parking lot into another one that was supposed to be a street. Traffic in Montego Bay was always bad. Now it was bumper to bumper, moving at maybe five miles an hour. Will wanted to catch Rodney while he was still awake, but he was stuck. He joined with others in honking his horn, knowing it would do no good. Twenty minutes later he turned into the hospital. He hurried inside and pushed the elevator button. When the door didn't open immediately, he spotted the stairs and took them to the third floor. He stopped at the nurse's station. "I'm Will Taylor. Is Rodney still awake?"

"Should be," the nurse said. "I just took him some chicken broth."

Will turned and walked down the hall to Rodney's room. He entered without knocking. Rodney's bed was elevated, and he was sipping the broth though a straw. He tried to smile as Will stepped in. He took the straw from his mouth and said in a weak voice, almost a whisper, "Good to see a familiar face."

"Good to see you coming around," Will said. "You had us worried. I called your parents. As soon as you're up to it, you need to call them and let them know you're going to be all right."

Rodney nodded.

Will filled Rodney in on the events since he was attacked at the hotel. When he finished, he asked, "Do you remember anything about that night?"

Rodney thought before he spoke. "I've been lying here trying to dredge up something useful. I remember he was a big guy, picked me up like I was a sack of flour. He was black. Didn't say much. When he did, he spoke like you and me, like he was born in the United States, not Jamaica, southern drawl, kind of."

"Shit, I wonder if Alexa already has her mercenaries on the island."

CHAPTER 41

When Will returned to the hotel, he called Vertise. "We need to talk. Can you meet me for dinner this evening about seven?"

"Sure, where?" Vertise asked.

"How about the hotel restaurant by the pool."

"I'll be there. You want to tell me what this is about?"

"Not on the phone."

Will got to the restaurant early and picked a table with no tables occupied around it. He didn't want anyone close enough to hear what he was going to say. When the waiter spotted him, he walked to the table. "Can I get you something to drink?"

"A double 10th Mountain bourbon on the rocks. I'll be joined by a lady. She'll have your best Chardonnay."

As the waiter went to the bar, Vertise approached. Will rose and hugged her before pulling out her chair. "I ordered you Chardonnay. Hope that's okay."

"You must have been reading my mind."

When the waiter returned with their drinks and two menus, they sipped silently as they perused the options. Vertise closed hers, and Will motioned to the waiter, who took their orders.

"Okay, I enjoy having dinner with you," Vertise said. "But, I have been wondering ever since you called what you need to talk about."

"First, Rodney started waking up today."

"That's terrific. Is he going to be okay in the long run?"

"Looks like it. He'll still be in the hospital for a while recovering and then put on a rehab program."

"Thank God. Does he remember anything about that night?"

"Not much. It was a black guy, which doesn't narrow down the suspects on this island."

"Does he think it was one of the Maroons? I don't want to get my people in trouble, but it sounds like something Lawrence or Aaron might try."

Will shook his head. "Those two are short and probably strong, but Rodney is at least six feet and two hundred pounds. He said this guy was big, picked him up like a sack of flour. And he could be remembering this wrong, but he said the attacker had a southern United States accent."

"That's at least a small relief. Besides, my father has been preaching non-violence."

"Hasn't done much good. Kaven is dead, Rodney nearly died. A guard up at the mine site and the engineer on that bauxite train, same fate. Another guard at Discovery Bay wounded. Snyder killed."

Vertise rose. "Look, I'm not hungry any more. I need a walk on the beach to clear my head."

"I'm coming with you." He waved the waiter over. "We're not ready to eat right now. Put those orders on hold and put the tab on my room. Add twenty percent for your tip."

"Did I do anything wrong?" the waiter asked.

"Not a thing. We just need to take a little walk."

They walked in silence down the beach, each lost in thought. Then Will spoke.

"That little girl was killed at the Cudjoe Day celebration, and Kaven was killed that night. It wasn't a coincidence. He didn't cause her death, but they might have killed him up there if the cops hadn't pulled him out. Seems to me like your father is no longer in charge."

"He's still the colonel, but some of the young ones got pissed when your company started clearing trees. I suspect they're led by Lawrence and Aaron, but I have no proof. The only weapon I have is the written word. I have an idea for an editorial. I suggest you come by the paper tomorrow afternoon and I'll give you a preview."

Will saw a shadow step from behind a tree ahead. He shoved Vertise to the ground and fell on top of her just as a shot was fired. "Stay here," he said as he got to one knee, pulled his Glock from his waistband, and returned the fire. "I'm going after him."

Will was closing the distance and fired off another round. When he got to the edge of the hotel property, he was confronted with a group of storage buildings. He warily circled a couple of them but saw nothing. He stopped and listened but heard nothing. He turned and walked back to Vertise. "I lost him."

Vertise's voice cracked when she spoke. "Now, I'm scared. That's the first time anyone has tried to kill me."

Will pulled her to him in a long hug. "He wasn't trying to kill you. It was me."

CHAPTER 42

It was late afternoon when Will entered *The Montego Bay Monitor* building. Vertise was at her computer. She looked up and motioned him to take one of the chairs near the front window. Will picked up the latest edition of the paper and thumbed idly through it, hoping to find some sports scores from the United States. After about fifteen minutes, Vertise walked to a printer where she retrieved her editorial. Will rose as she approached him.

"Keep your seat. I haven't written the headline yet, but it's intended to focus on the Maroons, Global, and what has been happening. I did some research on the destruction of the rainforests around the world and am trying to attract international attention by tying our Cockpit Country to what's going on elsewhere. It will appear in tomorrow's *Monitor*. I also have a friend with the *New York Times* who thinks she can get her editors to run it."

Will settled back into his chair and began to read.

Why should we care about rainforests? When most people hear that word, they think of the Amazon, Borneo, or maybe the Congo. Aren't they far away? Aren't they just occupied by indigenous tribes that wear loin cloths and paddle around in canoes like they did a thousand years ago? They have never even tried to advance their culture. So, why should we care?

Not only should we care, but we must care. Consider the benefits we derive from rainforests. Their ecosystems comprise only about three percent of our planet, but they are critical to sustaining life throughout the world. They are critical to our efforts to stop global warming. They are home to more species of plants and animals than any other ecosystem. They serve as watersheds for some of the earth's major rivers. Bush doctors have tapped their resources for hundreds of years to cure diseases, but they have only scratched the surface.

According to satellite data, about twenty million acres of the earth's rainforests are being destroyed each year. Besides increasing greenhouse gases and warming the earth, who knows what plants are being wiped out that might have cured cancer, HIV, malaria, or hundreds of other diseases?

Fortunately, leaders in some parts of the world are beginning to pay attention to the devastation caused by so-called civilized man. The destruction is slowing ever so slightly each year.

Here in Jamaica we have our own rainforest. Oh, it's minuscule when compared to the Amazon. Still it provides tremendous benefits to our relatively small island. It's the Cockpit Country. Most Jamaicans have never been there. You would have to climb way up in the mountains above Montego Bay to find several hundred thousand acres, much of which is owned by the Maroons who have fought to preserve it and their way of life for three hundred years now. The Maroons signed a treaty with the British in 1739 guaranteeing them their land in return for laying down their arms. Until recently, both sides have honored the treaty, and the Maroons have lived quietly and simply up in their mountains. Only now a change is under way, and a sad change it is. Global American Metals is a giant conglomerate based in the United States. It already has bauxite mines in other parts of our country. Now, though, they claim they have the right to strip mine the Maroons' rainforest. They do not! They must be stopped. Right now, the Maroon rainforest is the watershed for five rivers that provide water for nearly everyone in western Jamaica. If they strip the forest, the rivers will be delivering pollution to the towns and villages downstream. With no forest, floods will become commonplace.

And it gets worse. The bush doctors that live among the Maroons have identified many plants that are found nowhere else on earth and may be critical in man's efforts to cure diseases. If the forest is gone, those potential cures will vanish with the smoke from the burning trees.

Last, open warfare is about to break out. There have been several deaths that appear to be directly related to the battle over the Maroons' rainforest. Jamaicans must rise up and tell Global American Metals that they cannot have the Cockpit Country. It belongs to the Maroons and it must remain in their hands, not just for them, but for all Jamaicans and for all of mankind.

Will handed the story back to Vertise. "Terrific. I wouldn't change a word. When Alexa sees it, her blood pressure will go through the roof. Now, let me tell you why I'm here."

"I'm listening."

"My mind has been in overdrive since last night. I want to go to Accompong in the morning and visit your father. I have an idea about how to put an end to this fighting."

"You want to tell me?"

"No, but you're invited to our meeting. Besides, I need you to call him and set it up. The earlier in the morning the better."

CHAPTER 43

Will parked the Land Rover in front of the Cudjoe Monument. When he and Vertise exited the car, they saw Colonel Broderick walking from the community hall. He hugged Vertise and took Will's outstretched hand.

"I hear you saved my daughter's life last night."

Will shook his head. "I ran him off. I think he was after me, not Vertise."

Broderick motioned. "Follow me." He led them to the edge of the village and started up the trail to the Peace Cave. "I think you are safe with me, but just for good measure we should get away from the village."

When they moved deeper into the forest, Broderick picked up the pace.

"You sure your father is eighty? He moves like he's half that age."

"Knowing we're going to visit the Peace Cave invigorates him."

When they arrived at the cave, Will was breathing hard. Broderick appeared to have merely been on a stroll across a mountain meadow. Broderick seated himself on a rock and invited Will and Vertise to join him. "First, let's clear the air as much as possible. I must assume that some of my young men are taking things into their own hands. While I have tried to resist their efforts, that tradition among the Maroons goes back hundreds of years. I'm deeply sorry for the death of Mr. Tillman and your bauxite engineer and the guard at your site up here. Vertise says your other man in the hospital is going to live. I will continue my efforts to control the young men. Now, Vertise tells me you have an idea."

"First, I thank you for the apology. Here's my idea. You have a treaty with the British who were in control of the island when it was signed. I've read the copy on the wall in your community hall. I think you should enforce your treaty."

"I don't understand," Vertise said.

"I suggest that you hire a lawyer and take Global to court. You can establish that the treaty is valid and seek an injunction against Global moving forward with the bauxite mine. Once you have an order, I doubt if Global or any other mining company will try anything up here."

The Colonel looked out across the valley. The sun was peaking over the tops of the mountains to the east, filling it with light and shadows. "Do you think we have a chance?"

"Sir, I'm a lawyer and actually tried several cases in years past. I'm not licensed in Jamaica, but I can assist some local lawyer. No guarantees, but you have a good chance of winning."

Broderick lowered his head and put his hands between his legs, almost as if he were in prayer. When he looked back at Will, he said, "I think we should try. And it may be that I can persuade my young Maroons that we have a chance of winning without bloodshed. I have a little money put away so that we can at least make a down payment for a lawyer. But what about you? You're a Global employee."

"I'm resigning from Global."

Vertise's eyes shone with delight and then tears formed. Quickly, she wiped them away.

"Vertise has convinced me that this land is much more valuable as it is. I'll drive to Kingston to submit my resignation in the next couple of days, and before we see a lawyer."

Then, the unexpected happened. Colonel Broderick grunted, and the sound of a shot echoed across the valley.

"Dad, are you all right?"

"Got me in the arm. I'll be okay. Will, did you see where it came from?"

Will studied the mountain across the small valley. "Get down behind these rocks. I saw the glint of metal over there close to where our bulldozer was working." He sized up the wound in Broderick's arm. "Vertise will take care of you. I'm going to try to catch the sniper."

He took off down the trail at a run and within five minutes was on a trail that climbed the other side of the valley. The sniper had been waiting, hoping to get another shot, when he heard Will breaking through the brush moving rapidly toward him. He pulled a Sig Sauer and fired in the direction of the noise.

160

Will returned fire. The sniper grabbed his rifle and ran for his truck. He opened the door, tossed the rifle in the back seat, and fired several shots in Will's direction. Will ducked behind a tree, then heard the pickup engine start. He ran up the hill just in time to see a white pickup disappear into the forest on the other side of the clearing.

Realizing he had no way to catch the pickup, he searched the area until he found what he was looking for: a rifle casing that was still slightly warm to the touch. He pocketed it and jogged back down the mountain, across the valley, and up to the Peace Cave where he found Vertise and her father with several of the young Maroons.

When they saw him, they surrounded Will. Two of them pinned his arms behind his back while one rammed a fist deep into his gut, doubling Will at the waist. "You bastard," Lawrence said. "You led Colonel Broderick into an ambush."

Vertise had shredded the hem of her shirt and wrapped it around her father's wounded arm. With her help, he got to his feet, shouting, "Stop this right now. I was only nicked in the arm. I'm your colonel and you *will* listen to me."

The group of young men turned to him as Will doubled over, trying to get his breath.

"We have come up with a plan to defeat the American company that doesn't involve any more killing. Listen to me. When you hear me out, I demand you give us a chance to get it done."

CHAPTER 44

The woman parked her white, gleaming Cadillac Escalade right in front of a sign that read: *NO PARKING, Violators Will Be Towed,* outside of the St. James Parish Courthouse. The woman climbed from the driver's side and stretched with a smile on her face. She stood nearly six feet tall and weighed close to three hundred pounds. Her ebony face was topped with a mass of curly black hair. Others were not sure that she ever ran a brush through it but were not about to ask. She wore a brightly colored shirt with splotches of red, green, yellow, and purple appearing against a light blue background. Her skirt was black. Gold loop earrings hung from ears that were somewhere under that mop of black hair. A gold necklace was draped over her ample bosom. Her shoes were black pumps with three-inch heels. After she finished her stretch, she shut the driver's door and opened the rear door to extract a large black briefcase on wheels. She locked the Escalade and walked around the back of the vehicle. She wasn't worried about her car being towed. All the cops in the area knew it was hers. They also knew that many years before, her car was towed from that spot on two occasions. Both times she made life miserable for the cops. She filed an injunction against the police department. She dug through the municipal records until she found that the sign had never been approved, merely installed by the city. When she threatened to sue for theft of her precious car, the police called a truce. If she would tell no one else the sign was illegal, they would leave her alone.

When she stepped onto the curb in front of the pink courthouse that filled the block, she announced in a loud voice to no one in particular, "I'm here. Matilda Massengale is ready to fight for justice this very day in this very courthouse. Any of you folks that want to see a great lawyer at work, now's your chance."

She marched up the steps that fronted the courthouse, her briefcase bouncing along behind her. When she got to the top, a deputy opened the double doors and ushered her in.

"Morning, Ms. Massengale. Whose court are you in today?" Behind him was a metal detector that he motioned her around. "Can I help you with your briefcase?"

"No, thanks, Henry. I've got it," she said as she walked around the security station. "I'm appearing before Judge Lancaster this morning. Have a bail hearing to tend to. Shouldn't take long."

As was usual, the hallways were packed with people milling around and talking among themselves. When they saw her, they parted like she was Moses about to cross the Red Sea. She hadn't made it ten feet before an elderly black man put his hand on her arm.

"Ms. Massengale, can I talk to you about my grandson? He's been charged with assault. He didn't do it."

Her demeanor changed. "Sir, I'm sorry about your grandson. I can't talk in the hallway." She dug into a pocket. "Here's my card. Call my office to schedule an appointment."

Two more times she was stopped and each time she shook her head and handed over her business card. When she arrived at the door to Judge Lancaster's courtroom, she threw it open with a flourish and marched in like she was Patton invading Germany. The courtroom was packed with no space in the audience. The judge was seated at his bench. He had a mane of white hair that flowed down to his shoulders and a white bushy mustache. Gold rimmed glasses framed his eyes. Two lawyers were standing before him. Matilda continued her march through the gate in the low wall that separated the lawyers and court from the audience. Judge Lancaster looked up when she entered.

"Well, I suspect this will be an interesting morning. Please find a seat, Ms. Massengale."

There was one vacant in the row of wooden chairs that were reserved for lawyers and parties. She slumped into it with a loud moan, loud enough that the judge started to say something but then thought better of it. Just as soon as she took her seat, she was up again and looking over a row of inmates in orange jump suits until she made eye contact with her client. She smiled and nodded at him before returning to her seat. Next, she made a show of opening the briefcase on the floor at her feet. She began pulling out manila file folders, one at a time, bringing the file folder up to eye level as she read the label. Then she replaced it and did the same with another. After five, nearly everyone in the courtroom was watching her. Finally, Judge Lancaster said, "All right. Let's pause just a moment while Ms. Massengale finds her file."

Almost as quickly as he spoke. Matilda held up one more. "Got it, Judge. Now I'll be ready when it's my turn."

Once the courtroom had overcome the entrance of Hurricane Matilda, the judge moved the prisoners along on their bail hearings. Lancaster was somewhat lenient in the bails he set for lesser offenses, those that did not involve charges of murder or violent assault. He knew everyone here was confined to the island. If the accused agreed to surrender his passport, bail was usually reasonable. Matilda and her client were the next to last to be heard.

The judge looked at Matilda. "Ms. Massengale, are you and Mr. Sanchez ready?"

Matilda pushed to her feet and motioned to her client. The bailiff escorted him in handcuffs and ankle chains to where Matilda stood in front of the judge with the prosecutor, who looked around the nearly empty courtroom and breathed a sigh of relief that his busy morning was coming to an end.

"How's Mrs. Lancaster getting along these days, Judge?" Matilda inquired.

"Very well. Thank you for asking." The judge looked at the prisoner. "Mr. Sanchez, you are charged with burglary of drugs from a pharmacy. How do you plead?"

Sanchez stared at his feet and murmured, "Not guilty, Your Honor."

"Mr. Prosecutor, do you have a recommendation for bail?"

"Judge, I think $10,000 would be appropriate. I concede this is his first offense."

"Ms. Massengale, do you wish to be heard before I rule?"

"I certainly do, Your Honor. This young man is only guilty of being in the wrong place at the wrong time. He was walking by the pharmacy after it closed when the alarm went off. Next thing he knew, the cops arrived, and he's handcuffed on the sidewalk. It's true that several bottles of hydrocodone were found in the drain near there, but his fingerprints were not on them. He's willing to be put under oath right now to say he knows nothing about them. Besides, Judge, he's an honor student and captain of his football team where he's all district goalkeeper. And, I might add, he plans to become a lawyer, maybe even a judge, when he completes his education."

The judge gazed at the clock on the back wall while he thought. "Bail is $1,000. Ms. Massengale, you know our courts are clogged, but I'm moving this one up toward the front. Trial is in ninety days. You are excused."

Matilda motioned her client over to the side. "I'll call your mother. All she has to do is scrape up a hundred bucks, ten percent of the bail. I'm sure she can call on some of your relatives. Once you get out, call me and we'll schedule a meeting."

She turned, grasped the handle of her briefcase, and after nodding to the judge, she strolled from the courtroom, her briefcase trailing behind her.

CHAPTER 45

Will and Vertise left Colonel Broderick and several other Maroons at the Cudjoe Monument and started the drive down the mountain.

"You think Lawrence and his buddies will play ball for a while?" Will asked.

Vertise hesitated, and then replied. "I think so. At least as long as we can convince them we're making progress. I've covered the courts. I know that there's a huge backlog. We need a lawyer who can figure out a way to move us from the back up toward the front. Lawrence is damn sure not going to wait a year or two."

"I know a little about courts. If Jamaica has an injunction procedure, maybe we can stop them in their tracks while we wait for our trial."

"That could work," Vertise mused. "Might also get Global to join with us to push the case to the front of the line. I must tell you that your idea about proving the treaty was brilliant. When did you come up with that idea?"

"Just popped into my head. The more I thought about it, the better I liked it. I'm going to drop you off at the newspaper and then go by the hotel to send Manny back to Maryland. Next stop will be with Jamaica's twenty-first century White Witch in Kingston. It's getting a little late to go to Kingston tonight, so probably first thing in the morning."

"What are you going to tell her?"

"First, that I'm quitting. Second, I might as well tell her about the treaty lawsuit that will be coming down on her like one of those bauxite trains out of control. You have an idea for a lawyer?"

"Actually, I do. If you're available, I'll get us an appointment for day after tomorrow. Let me warn you she carries a big stick, but speaking softly is not in her nature."

After Will dropped Vertise at the paper, he returned to his room where he called Manny. When he got no answer, he tried Manny's cell. "Hey, Will, what's going on?"

"Where are you?"

"Coming down the Maroon Trail above the plantation. Been taking photos and gathering plants and roots. I'll get on line and identify them when I get back to my room."

"Can you interrupt your botany career long enough to have dinner with me?"

"What time?"

"Seven in the main restaurant downstairs."

"I'll be there. Even have time to take a shower."

Will and Manny arrived at the hostess stand at the same time and were escorted to a table in the far corner of the room. After they ordered, Manny took a sip from his Red Stripe and said, "So, what's up?"

"I want you on the first plane out of here in the morning. Things are getting too hot. Kaven is dead, Rodney's lying in a hospital bed. You're not needed here. So, I want you to get safely back to Maryland."

"But I've got a bunch more plants to catalog and photograph. I can't take them back into the country with me. They'll be going up on my website."

"Then you better pull an all-nighter. Maybe you can come back later when things have settled down."

Manny downed his Red Stripe and ordered a second. "What are you going to be doing?"

"First, I'm going to Kingston to resign. Then I'm going to help Colonel Broderick and Vertise prove that their treaty is valid."

"Whooee," Manny said. "I'd like to be a fly on the wall when you tell Pritchard. You're going to represent the Maroons?"

"Can't. They don't allow outside lawyers to act as advocates. I'll be advising, though. Take a taxi to the airport since I'll be leaving early. We'll stay in touch."

Will was in Kingston by ten the next morning and at Pritchard's door fifteen minutes later. When he entered, he saw a receptionist he didn't recognize. "Is Alexa in this morning?"

The young woman looked at her calendar. "I don't see that she has any appointments this morning. Can I have your name?"

"Will Taylor. I'm head of security for Global. I'm sure Alexa will want to see me."

The receptionist picked up her phone and punched in a number. "She'll be with you in a few minutes."

Will nodded and moved to the sitting area where he started rummaging through old magazines. After an hour, he looked at his watch for the third time. He expected that Alexa was going to let him cool his heels, but not this long. Finally, her receptionist said, "Mr. Taylor, you can go in now."

Will walked through the door to find Alexa glaring at him. An ash tray was overflowing with cigarette butts on the corner of her desk.

"Gave up on the Tootsie Pops, I see."

"Cut the crap. Tell me why you're here."

Will smiled as he remained standing. She had not invited him to take a seat. "I'm resigning from Global, effective today."

"Then get your ass out of here," she snarled. "Leave your Range Rover in the garage and give me your identification."

"You can have my ID; I'm going to drive the Rover back to Montego Bay. I'll leave it at the airport where I can rent a car. You can have someone pick it up this afternoon or tomorrow. And there's one thing more you should know."

"I'm listening."

"Broderick and his daughter, Vertise, have convinced the Maroons to sue Global to establish the authenticity of their treaty. If they succeed, you'll have to find another bauxite mine."

"That's bullshit. I'll bring my legal team down from the States. They won't stand a chance."

"You can bring your team down here, but they can't appear in court."

Alexa grinned. "I don't really care about some trial court, I have dinner with the Chief Justice here in Kingston regularly. I suspect he'll do as I ask. In fact, I know he will. So, you tell them to take their best shot."

Will started to leave but stopped and said, "One more thing. I'll be helping the Maroon team. I haven't been proud of my work since I joined Global. It's about time I got back to doing something that makes me feel good about myself."

"You son of a bitch, get the hell out of here."

CHAPTER 47

After he left Pritchard's office, Will drove to Montego Bay. When he saw Scochie's, he gave in to the growling in his stomach and turned into the gravel lot. He ordered a full jerk chicken and went to the outdoor bar, where he ordered a Red Stripe and talked to the bartender. "You hear much about the Maroons and their dispute with Global American?"

The bartender leaned his elbows on the bar. "I keep up with it by reading that woman's column in the paper. What's her name, Vertise? And occasionally I'll hear people talking about it."

Will saw a chance to gather a little information on a future jury panel. "What do most people think?"

The bartender straightened up and rubbed his bald head before he replied. "Most folks around here think that the Cockpit Country is owned by the Maroons. I hear they even have a treaty. If people read the *Monitor*, they probably read that woman's column. She claims that Global will destroy the Maroons' land and pollute the rivers that we all need. Hey, there's your chicken in the window."

Will retrieved his chicken and returned to the bar to order a second beer. He mentioned Usain Bolt and the bartender took over the conversation, describing Bolt's history from high school through the 2016 Olympics. Clearly if Bolt wanted to run for Prime Minister of Jamaica when he retired from the track, he would win in a landslide.

Will tipped the bartender and drove to the Hertz lot at the airport, rented a Suburban, and arranged to leave his company Range Rover with the attendant, saying that someone from Global would be picking it up no later than tomorrow.

The next morning, Vertise was waiting in her Beetle in front of the hotel when Will came out. He doubled over and squeezed into the passenger seat. "Great reliable car, just not quite the right size for me." He smiled.

"Gets me where I need to go without draining my pocketbook." Vertise patted the dashboard like it was a faithful horse. "Thirty-five miles to the gallon."

As they drove from the hotel, Will asked, "Tell me again who we're seeing this morning?"

"Matilda Massengale."

"And she's a lawyer?"

"One of the best on the island and a real force of nature. Her nickname is Hurricane Matilda. She lives up the hill above the Hip Strip."

"How is it you know her?"

"I was her secretary, clerk, Jill-of-all-trades. Worked in her office all through high school. Thought about becoming a lawyer."

"You would have been a good one. Still could."

"Nope. I decided to do my fighting with my column."

Vertise wound up the hill and stopped in front of a bungalow painted bright yellow with brown trim. The yard was well manicured. The bushes in front of the house had flowers blooming. Will did a double-take when he saw a basin in the middle of the front yard with bottles hanging from it.

"Is she a voodoo muda, too?"

Vertise laughed. "No. She bought that at a yard sale years ago. She planted it in her front yard just in case a prospective client believed in the occult. This is her house. The front is her office, and she lives in some very nicely appointed quarters in the back."

They walked up four steps to an expansive veranda with a breathtaking view of the ocean in the distance. Vertise rang the doorbell.

"Come on in, Vertise. I'm making some tea. Make yourself at home." Matilda's voice boomed from somewhere beyond the door.

Upon entering the living room, to the left was a large desk with shelves full of books behind it. A computer and legal pad were on the desk. There were two guest chairs. To the right was a sitting area with a flowered blue couch, a coffee table, and four small chairs surrounding it. The window to the back yard opened onto a fountain that spilled water into a pond that Will guessed held a variety of tropical fish. The wall at the end was filled with diplomas, licenses, and letters of thanks from clients.

Vertise directed Will to take one of the small chairs at the coffee table. She took one beside him. Then the hurricane burst through a door from the back carrying a tray with a teapot and three porcelain cups with saucers, along with cream and sugar. Matilda was dressed in a giant red muumuu. Her feet were bare, revealing brightly painted toenails, also red. Vertise got to her feet to assist with placing the tray on the table, then hugged Matilda. "Maddie, this is my friend, Will Taylor."

Will stood to shake her hand. Matilda stepped back to size up Will. "Well, I expect he'll do just fine. You going to marry my Vertise?"

Will smiled. "Well, the thought of some kind of romantic involvement had crossed my mind."

Vertise looked at Will and blushed.

"You be good to her or you'll have me to deal with." Then she stuck out her hand and shook Will's before slumping down into one of the chairs. Will wondered briefly if it would support her bulk. It did. Vertise poured tea into the three cups. "Maddie, you still like yours with two heaping teaspoons of sugar and heavy on the cream."

"You got it, honey."

"Will?"

"Just tea for me."

Matilda stirred her tea and sipped it, returning it to the saucer in front of her. "Vertise, I'm always glad to see you, but something tells me this is not a social call. I follow your column. If I had to guess, we're about to talk about the Cockpit Country and Global Metals."

"Right as always, Maddie," Vertise said. She nodded toward Will. "Will just resigned yesterday as worldwide vice president of security for Global. It took us a while, but my father and I finally convinced him that the Cockpit Country can better serve mankind in its natural state."

Matilda sat back in her chair, which squeaked as she shifted her weight. "I certainly agree with what you're saying. And welcome aboard, Will. What can I do?"

Will leaned forward. "Alexa Pritchard is president of Global. She was my boss until yesterday. She is ruthless and will spend any amount of money to accomplish her goals. And she doesn't mind bashing a few heads, maybe doing something worse."

"You mean like killing?" Matilda asked.

"I don't rule that out. The Maroons can't afford to get into a war with her. They think that they could engage in guerrilla warfare and run back up to their rain forest, but it just won't work. This is not the eighteenth century. Alexa can hire former Green Berets and SEALs with modern weapons, including helicopter gunships if need be. The Maroons can no longer hide up on their mountains."

Matilda nodded. Will continued. "Are you familiar with the treaty that Cudjoe signed with the British back in 1739?"

"Heard about it since I was a little girl. I think we even spent a little time on it in history class in high school. Are you telling me it still exists?"

"It does. I've seen it," Vertise said. "A copy is on the wall of the community hall in Accompong. My father has shown me the original, which is carefully hidden, but well preserved," she added.

"So, what do you want me to do?"

"This is my idea," Will said. "Let me explain. The original of the treaty on the wall was signed by Cudjoe and a British general. The British wanted to end the fighting with the Maroons. They knew they could never win and didn't want the damn mountain tops anyway. The treaty deeded to the Maroons all the land as far as the eye could see from a cave up there. It was never surveyed, but it's probably in the range of 150,000 acres."

"Were the Maroons a sovereign nation back then?"

"That's debatable, but the only other country that laid claim to the Cockpit Country was Great Britain. They were willing to give up their claim in return for a cease fire. Whether they're a country or not, the Maroons have a right to the land."

"Who do you want me to sue?"

"My former company, Global, is the one claiming the land and wants to strip mine up there. Alexa says she has a permit from the Minister of Mines, who I should add was recently killed outside a restaurant in Kingston. If we're right, he couldn't issue a mining permit up in the Maroon country. Knowing Alexa, I suspect he took a substantial bribe. So, to get to the bottom line, I'm a licensed lawyer in the United States, but that won't get me into court here. We want you to represent the Maroons and sue Global American Metals to establish that The Treaty of 1739 is valid and enforceable. In short, the Maroons own the land and Global needs to get the hell out of there."

Matilda gazed up at the ceiling for a while and dropped her eyes to focus on Will. "Since you've been a lawyer in the past. You know my first question. How am I getting paid? I've sued multi-national companies a few times over the years. Each time I won, but each case nearly bankrupted me before we got to the finish line."

"My dad says he has set aside $10,000. I can mortgage my car for another couple of thousand," Vertise said. "And some of the young Maroons have been selling marijuana offshore. I think they've been trading for weapons. I'll talk to them about selling the ganja for cash. Bottom line, Maddie, is I'll make sure you get paid. And I'll be your legal assistant."

"While I can't open my mouth in a Jamaican court, if you can arrange for me to sit at counsel table, I can assist," Will added. "I was even pretty good at legal research back when I practiced. And I always enjoyed plotting trial strategy."

Matilda pushed out of her chair again and paced around the room, finally stopping to stare out the window, obviously deep in thought. When she turned, she said, "I'm inclined to do it, but I don't want to commit until I see the real treaty. Can that be done?"

"I'll call my dad. My guess is that we can meet him in the morning at the Community Hall."

CHAPTER 48

Colonel Broderick rose before dawn the next morning, and with the aid of a flashlight, walked along the trail to the Peace Cave. When he arrived dawn was breaking, but he still needed the flashlight to make his way to the back of the cavern. The cave floor was wet, the water coming from the small stream that ran through it. The water barely covered the soles of his work boots, but at his age, he didn't need to slip and break a hip; so, he took it slowly when he waded the stream and climbed over small boulders until he could go no farther. He flashed the light on the ground until he spotted the group of rocks he sought. Propping the light between two rocks, he kneeled and carefully began removing rocks from a hole in the ground. After removing a few, he retrieved his light and shined it into the hole. The light revealed a piece of plywood about three feet by two feet that covered the case containing the treaty. When he lifted the plywood, the glass front of the case gleamed. Broderick smiled and continued to pull the rocks away until he could grasp the case and retrieve the treaty. As he looked at it, he remembered back to when he was a young man. At that time, he talked the custodian into letting him take the treaty to Kingston where he waited three days for a cabinet maker to make the case. When the woodworker was finished, he carefully placed the treaty face up in the glass enclosure and made the trip back to Accompong and to the cave where he and the custodian hid the treaty. Cudjoe would have approved.

Now he pulled the case from its hiding place and placed it under his arm. Using the other hand to hold the flashlight, he returned to the mouth of the cave to be greeted by a bright, sunny day, a good omen he thought. When he broke from the forest into Accompong, he saw a Suburban parked in front of

Cudjoe's monument. Vertise, Will, and a large black woman were reading the tribute to Cudjoe. He joined them.

"Hi, Dad. I see you have it. You know Will. This is Matilda Massengale. She's considering representing us against Global. She wants to talk with you and have a look at the original of the treaty. Matilda, this is my dad, Colonel Broderick."

Matilda extended her hand. "Pleased to meet you, Colonel. Is there a place where we can sit a spell?"

Broderick smiled and motioned for them to follow him across the gravel road to the community hall. Once inside, he pointed to the wall at the entrance. "This is an exact duplicate of what I have in my hand, only enlarged three times so that it can be read more easily. Let's go to the front where there's a table."

The colonel gently laid the treaty on the table. Will pulled four chairs up. Broderick excused himself momentarily and went to a wall where he turned on overhead lights. "Now, you can see it better."

There was silence while Matilda slowly read the treaty from top to bottom. Then she started at the top again and worked her way down once more. "How do we know this is authentic?"

"I have been the custodian for the past thirty-five years. Before I moved to Canada many years ago, the custodian and I hid it in a safe place. It was still there when I returned. Within a year or so later, I was designated custodian and have been ever since. If you'll excuse me for a few moments." He left the community hall and returned five minutes later. "I keep these in a metal box under my bed. Maybe not the safest place, but it has worked so far." He opened the box and retrieved several documents. "We Maroons knew the importance of this treaty. One of us has been designated as custodian of the treaty for his or her life. As one custodian approached death, he or she would pass it on to the next. Each custodian signed a letter attesting that this was the original and was authentic. Only once did a custodian die before he executed his authentication. When that happened, the next wrote that he knew the previous custodian and that the treaty he received from the former custodian's widow was authentic. We even had her sign a document to that effect. Sorry, but we didn't have notaries back in those days. I hope these will be sufficient."

Matilda's gaze dropped to the bottom of the treaty. "I see that Cudjoe signed with his mark. I presume that he could not read and write."

"That's correct," the colonel replied.

"Do you have any other documents with his mark on them?"

"There are several. I can get them if you want," Broderick said. "There's one that could be important. It's a memo from Cudjoe, confirming his understanding of the terms of the treaty."

Matilda abruptly rose and walked out the door, saying, "I don't need to see them right now. I'm not the one to testify that one X is the same as another. We'll need an expert for that. I'll be back in a few minutes."

After twenty minutes, Will began to worry and walked to the door. He saw her walking slowly around the parking area, head down, hands grasped behind her back, obviously in deep thought. He turned and went back to the front of the hall. He told the others what she was doing.

When she returned, she stood at the head of the table.

"Before you say anything, Matilda, let me interject something," Will said. "I think I know what is worrying you. It's proving the authenticity of the treaty, right?"

She reached forward and rested her hands on the table. "I've got a lot of worries about taking on a company the size of Global, but that one is up near the top of the list."

"I thought so," Will replied. "Let me suggest this. I'll track down the best forensic documents examiner in the United States and fly him here at my expense. He should be able to opine on its authenticity, when it was signed, and that the X on it and the other documents came from the same hand."

"Will, you shouldn't have to pay for him out of your pocket," Vertise protested.

"That's the least I can do. It'll ease my conscience just a little for what my company has done. Hopefully, an expert can conclude it was signed sometime in the early 1700s. And, if we can produce other examples of Cudjoe's mark, we can determine if they were from the same hand. Will that be enough?"

"That plus these letters from the custodians of the treaty," Matilda said. "It's the best that we can do. I can probably persuade the judge to let us go to the jury. Here's my other big worry. Our trial courts in this country are a mess. Takes forever to get to the top of the docket. Frankly, it's those damn gun courts. You know about them?"

Will nodded. "Detective Harper told me that's where I would end up if I was caught carrying a gun. Of course, a few days later he realized he needed my help and told me to forget about the gun courts."

176

Matilda shook her head. "We waste too damn much time and energy trying to enforce the gun prohibition on this damn island. And, what good does it do? People can still buy guns, particularly lawbreakers. Judges ought to be putting away real criminals and resolving civil disputes. Now let me get off my soap box to explain how it impacts us. If we were to file our lawsuit tomorrow, it might be two, three years before we go to trial. By that time the mine would be running at full capacity, and destroying the forest that's right out our door."

Will ran his hand over his chin realizing he forgot to shave that day, and then spoke. "Do you have an injunction practice in this country?"

"Hell, yes." Matilda smiled as she said it. "You talking about us presenting some evidence to temporarily stop the mine until a trial?"

"Exactly," Will said. "Vertise tells me you carry a pretty big stick at the courthouse in Montego Bay. If you draft the petition and we win an injunction, we stop the mine in its tracks. With the original of the treaty and Colonel Broderick's testimony about the custodian letters, would that be enough for starters?"

Matilda again remained silent. "You're saying that we use that to get the injunction and then get your questioned documents expert in here to study all we can get together? I think it might stop the mine and buy us some time. Maybe with it shut down by a judge, Global will agree with us to seek an expedited trial, maybe in two or three months."

"And there's one more thing. When I went to Alexa's office to quit, she said that she wasn't worried about what any trial court did. Said she had dinner with the Chief Justice of your Supreme Court about once a week when she's on the island."

"You mean Wilber Cunningham? That bitch. I know him pretty well myself."

"What I'm thinking is that you can whisper in the ear of the Global lawyers that if Cunningham said the word, we can go to the head of the line."

Matilda grinned. "I like the way you think. You and I are going to make a damn fine team."

Vertise had been quiet as the lawyers strategized. Now she spoke. "We need to make this a media event. The story needs to be big enough that it gets picked up by the wire services. Maybe we can attract a few reporters from the States. I want to start with a procession of Maroons coming down the mountain on the day of trial, escorting our treaty as an honor guard or something of the sort."

"Happy to have you on our team, too, Vertise."

"Actually," Colonel Broderick said, "I'm concerned about taking the treaty into Accompong. Ms. Pritchard might hire some thugs to try to overwhelm my Maroons and steal it. No treaty, no rainforest."

"Let me give it some thought," Will said. "I'll talk it over with Harper. Maybe he can figure out a way to have them armed. Worth a talk anyway. Matilda, how soon do you think you can prepare that petition?"

"Give me a week. I want you to look it over when it's done."

They shook hands all around. Colonel Broderick was smiling as he waved goodbye to them. Next, he returned to the table and picked up the treaty to return it to its hiding place in the Peace Cave. He made it to the door, then stopped and returned to retrieve the other documents. Perhaps it was time to hide them somewhere besides under his bed.

CHAPTER 49

Matilda bubbled over with conversation as they returned to Montego Bay.

"There's nothing I love better than a good fight. How about you, Will?"

"I've had my share of fights. I view a fight only as a last resort, when all else has failed."

"Well, just let me add that I really like a good fight when I know my client is right. No doubt in my mind that we're on the right side of this one."

They stopped in front of Matilda's bungalow. She patted Will on the shoulder as she exited the car and shouted, "Matilda Massengale is on the case. Justice will be done."

Vertise exited the back door and hugged Matilda before taking the front passenger seat. Will shook his head when they drove away, but he was smiling. "Force of nature is right. I'm glad she's on our side. Just her personality may sway a couple of jurors. You have time for a drink at the pool bar."

"You're on," Vertise responded with a twinkle in her eye.

When they left the Suburban with the valet, he commented, "New ride."

"The Range Rover is a thing of the past," Will replied.

Once they arrived at the poolside bar, they chose a table close to the beach. It was a sunny day that brought a flotilla of brightly colored sailboats out into the water just off shore. The waiter approached. By now Will knew his name. "Peter, have the bartender make the lady one of those trademark old fashions of his, and I'll have a double bourbon on the rocks, 10th Mountain bourbon, of course."

"Of course, Mr. Taylor."

They sat beside each other so that they could watch the parade of boats.

Vertise reached over and put her hand on Will's. "A penny for your thoughts."

Will enjoyed the warmth of her hand on his before he spoke. "For you, my lady, you don't even have to pay me a penny. I was just thinking about the change in my life that has taken place since I hit this island. A week ago, I was a company man doing the bidding of my president. Almost overnight, I changed to the other side, quit my job, and am preparing to launch an attack against the hand that fed me. You're the biggest reason for that, you know."

"I know. Can I ask you a couple of questions?"

"Sure."

"Are you married?"

"Nope. Had a couple of long term relationships, but for different reasons they didn't work out."

"No children?"

"None that I know of."

"Interested in having children some day?"

Will shook his head, not sure how to reply. "I suppose so. I'd like to raise a pitcher, or maybe a shortstop. A quarterback wouldn't be bad."

Vertise leaned over and kissed him. "Well, when you're ready to make another change, so am I." She blushed. "Oh, I don't mean marriage, at least not yet."

Will kissed her back. "I understand. I may just take you up on that proposal; only, I think it's best we get through this first round in court. If we get that injunction, I may have nothing but time on my hands for a couple of months until the trial. Maybe you can fill some of that time."

CHAPTER 50

Lawrence pushed through a beaded doorway into a dimly lit local bar, one not usually frequented by tourists, and found the table where Aaron, James, and two young Maroon women, Patrice and Jackie, were finishing their second round.

"Sorry I'm late." He motioned to the bartender for a beer. The bartender set a Red Stripe in front of him. Lawrence drained half the bottle, then belched. "I'm the one that called this meeting. I'm not liking what Colonel Broderick and Vertise are doing. All they're going to do is waste time with this damn lawsuit, time we don't have. I know Matilda Massengale's reputation. She's good, but she can't stand up to a multi-billion-dollar company."

"Vertise says that Will Taylor is a lawyer and is now on our side," Aaron said. "Won't that help some?"

"Just how the hell do you know that he's on our side?" Lawrence asked. "He could be playing the Colonel, Vertise, and the rest of us. Just getting us to stop our guerilla warfare until they get a couple more bulldozers and a locomotive to replace the one we blew up at Discovery Bay."

"Shit," James said, "I hadn't thought of that. You have any ideas?"

"Been thinking hard. We need to kidnap someone important and hold him for ransom."

"Why bother with that? Let's just go back to our guerilla raids. They were working pretty damn good. Global has stuff all over this island. Few more raids and we can shut them down."

Lawrence shook his head. "We made a promise to Colonel Broderick. He may be old, but they don't make them any tougher. First thing that we blow up, he'll have us all lined up in front of a firing squad. Treason is what he'll call it. He still has the backing of enough elders that we'd be dead meat."

"Then forget the ransom. I've got another plan," James said. When he finished describing his plan, glasses and beer bottles were raised in a silent toast to the truth.

Will had just stepped out of a shower and was in his bathrobe when he heard a knock at his door. He walked to the front of the room and peered through the eyehole to see a very attractive young woman, dressed in a waitress outfit. Now wary of anything out of the ordinary, he asked through the door, "Why are you here?"

"Compliments of the hotel. A little brandy, some warm milk, and two fine chocolate chip cookies to make you sleep better."

Will opened the door a crack but kept the chain on. He saw no one with her.

"Just put the tray on the floor."

Before he could shut the door, a foot showed itself and kicked it in. The safety chain was ripped from the wall. Two men burst through. Will lunged for his Glock on the nightstand but never got to it. One of them cold-cocked him with a sucker punch. The other took a cloth that smelled of chloroform from his pocket and put it over Will's nose and mouth.

When Will woke, he was in a dark room with his hands duct taped behind his back and ankles bound together, also with duct tape. He tried to holler but found that the only sound he could make was muffled by more tape. He considered his options. He was not at sea level because the dark room was cold, not just cool. He had to be in the mountains that meant some of the Maroons must have kidnapped him. Why? Colonel Broderick promised to talk to them and was sure that they would buy into the lawsuit. He must have been wrong. As his eyes became accustomed to the dark, he saw a sliver of light coming through a crack in the wall. The moon was rising. He scooted around the room like a caterpillar. As he did so, he realized he was still wearing the hotel bathrobe. The only thing it had going for it was that it was warm. At least his eyes were not taped. Still, he found nothing to aid in his escape. He had pushed himself up against a wall to a sitting position and was searching his mind for a solution, when he heard voices and the door opened.

Five Maroons, led by Lawrence, entered with a flashlight. "Well, Mr. Taylor, you like your new accommodations? Not quite the Ritz, but the best we

182

have for guests up here in the Cockpit Country." He ripped the tape from Will's mouth.

"What do you want?"

Lawrence smiled, and his teeth gleamed behind the flashlight. "Only the truth. You and your Ms. Pritchard are running a scam on us. You think we Maroons are stupid? You convinced Colonel Broderick to go along with this lawsuit idea. Nice try. All it's going to do is buy Global more time."

"No! You're wrong. I quit Global to help you. I've even agreed to pay for a document expert with my own money. I believe in your cause, but not in violence as a way to solve it."

"Enough, Mr. Taylor. We will not waste time with torture. Aaron?"

Aaron stepped into the glare of the flashlight. He held the head of a snake in one hand. The body of the snake curved up his arm. Will's eyes were wide. He tried to scoot away from the snake, but was stopped by Lawrence and another man.

"One bite from Aaron's snake will not kill you, but you will wish you were dead."

"No, wait, I am telling you the truth," Will pleaded, trying to hide his fear of snakes. Was Vertise in on this? Did she tell them about him and snakes? Too late. Aaron approached. Lawrence pushed Will's head to the side, exposing his neck. Aaron lowered the snake until Will felt the fangs sink into his skin.

"We'll be back later. If you do not tell us the truth, we have a second snake that will provide you with a slow painful death."

"Why don't you just shoot me and be done with it?"

"We Maroons have our own ways of executing our prisoners of war."

The Maroons left Will in the dark. The reaction started in Will's gut. His intestines began to heave. His bowels let loose. The pain advanced throughout his body. He feared his head was going to explode. There was nothing he could do. After an eternity, the door opened again. He expected to see Lawrence and his buddies. Instead it was Vertise behind a flashlight. She had a bag in one hand and a machete in the other. She studied Will. "It was one of Aaron's snakes, wasn't it?"

Will nodded. "They said it wouldn't kill me." He gasped as his abdomen spasmed. "Only, I would wish I were dead. They got that right."

Vertise pulled a large bottle of water from the bag.

"Here, drink this. It's just water, but it will help you get over that venom.

You'll start feeling better in ten minutes. Only it'll take at least thirty minutes before you will be thinking clearly. And I've got clothes for you."

Will hesitated and then took several gulps of the water that she poured into his mouth. "How the hell did you find me?"

"I was calling your room until about one in the morning. I finally gave up and went to the hotel. You weren't there, and the door was kicked in. I talked them into giving me your jeans, a sweater, and some sneakers. When they weren't looking, I stuck your Glock and cell in my back pocket.

"But, that doesn't tell me how you found me."

"I'm getting there. I figured it had to be some of the Maroons. They had to bring you up into the Cockpit Country where they're the law. This building is an abandoned roadside store. The old woman that ran it died. No one has claimed it. She may not have had any relatives. I was driving up to Accompong when I saw a sliver of light on the trail that leads back up to the village. I stopped and stayed in my car until I was sure it was clear. Aaron raises snakes. One look at you and I knew what they did. Here, put on these clothes. Then, I'll tell you how to get out of here."

She cut the duct tape with the machete and helped Will to his feet. "The venom will wear off in about thirty minutes. Only you can't wait that long."

Will used the robe to clean himself and scrambled as best he could to get into the clothes. Vertise put his shoes on and tied them. "Now, I want you to follow a trail to the east about three hundred yards. You'll have this machete, and your Glock, and my flashlight. Oh, and your cell. You'll run into a bigger trail. That's a Maroon Trail that will take you down the mountain above Rose Hall. From there you can get to the hotel. I'll try to divert Lawrence and the others. I'll be talking to my dad in the morning about all of this crap. He'll deal with them."

Will hugged Vertise and staggered through the door. Vertise left the door open and took a seat with her back to the far wall. Within fifteen minutes she heard male voices on the trail. "Shit, the door's open," Lawrence said. He and Aaron were the first ones inside. Vertise rose when Lawrence shined his light on her.

"What the hell have you done, woman?"

"I was looking for him and I found him. That's all you need to know. Aaron, you can turn around and take your pet back home."

"I ought to turn this snake loose on you."

"Big talk. I know you're not about to do it. My dad would have every damn one of you killed."

"Which way did he go?"

"Don't know, and if I did, I wouldn't be telling you."

Lawrence turned to his men. "Aaron, take your snake back home, then drive down the road. He's probably on foot. I'll take three men and head over to the Maroon Trail. He's going to be groggy for a while. We can catch him."

Will followed the trail that circled around the bottom of the village. He tripped over a root but managed to brace himself with his hands as he fell. He crawled to a sitting position. "Shit," he said to himself. "I feel like I just drank a fifth of bourbon. I've got to move slowly for a while." Then he said, "Yeah, but if you move slowly, they may find you, so, what are you going to do?" "I suppose I'll haul ass and pray for the best." He climbed to his feet, picked up the machete, checked his back pocket to make sure he still had the Glock, and pointed the flashlight down the trail. In ten minutes he came to what he figured must be the Maroon Trail Vertise described. Fortunately, it was wider and a little smoother.

When he turned onto the bigger trail, he decided that he could not keep the flashlight on continuously; so, he started blinking it on momentarily to get a visual picture of the trail and any obstacles. Then he would flick it off and rely on the moonlight that filtered through the canopy. He was making good progress when he stopped and was about to turn on the light, but heard voices in the distance above him. Will turned on the light and spotted a vine winding around a tree to his right. With the machete he cut a piece long enough to stretch across the trail. He picked two trees on either side, wrapped the vine around one about eighteen inches above the ground, and secured the vine to the tree on the opposite side of the trail. Muttering to himself, Will said, "I'll show those damn Maroons," as he continued down the mountain.

Lawrence and his three companions were jogging down the trail. Lawrence figured that if Taylor came this way, he couldn't be more than five minutes or so ahead of them. One Maroon had gotten slightly ahead of the other three. He tripped on the vine and tumbled to the ground. The other three toppled over him. Lawrence and the two other men got to their feet. The first stayed on the ground, holding his ankle.

"Michael, you okay?" Lawrence asked.

"It's broke or hurt bad. You guys go on. Pick me up on the way back."

185

Lawrence nodded, and the three Maroons continued their jog. Up ahead, Will spotted a boulder looming beside the trail. It looked to be about eight feet tall. Will walked around it and saw a tree with low hanging branches. He grabbed the first branch, and then the second, and was able to boost himself to the top of the boulder. He lay on his belly until he heard voices getting closer. Two Maroons passed, then the third. As the last man passed, Will dropped behind him, covered his mouth with one hand, and pinched a nerve in his neck with the other. The Maroon fell to the ground. Will had now become the one in pursuit. He closed in on Lawrence and his friend. When they all were on a straight part of the trail, he pulled his Glock and shot the trailing Maroon in the leg. Lawrence twirled around to face Will and started to reach for a weapon.

"Easy there, Lawrence. I haven't killed any of your friends. I don't want you to be the first to die." Lawrence dropped both of his hands to his side and started back up the trail toward Will. "If you want it here, that's fine. Tell you what, you drop your gun and that machete. I'll drop my gun. My machete is somewhere back up the trail. We'll go at it. Best man wins. You up to that, Lawrence?"

"Let me by. There'll be another day." Lawrence stuck the machete in his belt. Will stood aside to let him pass. When Lawrence was even with Will, he pulled his gun from his waistband. Before he could raise it, Will slammed his Glock down on the back of Lawrence's head. Lawrence slumped to the ground.

"Sorry I had to do it that way. Other than a headache when you wake up, you ought to be fine." Will holstered his Glock and continued the walk down the trail. Now he kept the flashlight on since he no longer had to worry about anyone seeing the beam. He passed Rose Hall and was soon on the street across from the hotel when his cell rang. *Damn, I forgot I even still had it on me.* He reached into his pocket and answered.

"You get down okay?" Vertise asked.

"Yeah, just crossing the highway in front of the hotel."

"Good. Get a shower and some sleep. Can we meet at the hotel about ten in the morning? I have something that needs your approval."

CHAPTER 51

When Will woke the next morning, it seemed as if every muscle and joint in his body was crying in unison: "What did you do to us last night?" He started with his neck and gently rotated it. Then he flexed his shoulders and stretched his arms and so on until he was flexing his toes. Once that was accomplished, he thought he could make it to the bathroom, which he did, only stooped over like an old man. Rather than his usual shower, he filled the tub with water as hot as he could handle. When the tub was near full, he eased into the water and punched the button for the water jets. He soaked for fifteen minutes, thinking that he needed a hot bath more often. After scrubbing himself he stood, reached for a towel, and found he could step out of the bath almost like a normal man. He glanced at his watch and realized he must hurry. After shaving and brushing his teeth, he checked the mirror. Everything looked pretty good. He was glad that he had a short brush cut that didn't require a comb. Walking to the elevator, he reminded himself that he needed to stop by the desk to change his room from Global to his own credit card.

When he arrived at the dining room, he saw Vertise, already at a table and sipping coffee. "Sorry I'm a little late. Had a hard time getting all of my body parts moving after last night." He bent over and kissed her on the cheek, then took a chair to her right.

"Let's finish that subject." She glanced at her watch. "My dad has ordered those young Maroons to meet with him right about now in the Community Hall. You've seen my dad as a kind, older man. He also has a different personality. When someone breaks his rules, or breaks a promise to him, he'll come down on them like a hawk on a rat. As long as he's colonel of the

Maroons, they will have only one more chance to follow his orders. I think they'll get the message."

Will took a sip of his coffee. "I suppose that makes me feel just a little better, but I'll still be looking over my shoulder. Let's order breakfast."

The waiter took their orders and excused himself. Vertise took a document out of her purse and handed it to Will. It was styled, *Colonel Rafael Broderick, Individually and In His Capacity as Leader of The Maroon Nation v. Global American Metals.*

"Matilda finished this more quickly than she expected."

"Yeah, she emailed it to me last night. She didn't have your email address and said in her email to me that she didn't want your email involved, anyway, for fear that Global may still be monitoring your laptop."

Will nodded. "Good point. If you'll direct me to the right store, I'll buy a new laptop today. Give me a couple of minutes to look through this. Then we'll talk."

Will read carefully and put it on the table. "Let me summarize. This is a suit for a declaration that the Maroons' treaty is valid, and they own the land described in the treaty. Then she asks the court for a hearing on an injunction, stopping Global from doing anything in the Cockpit Country until the case goes to trial. It's ten pages, but I just summed up all the legalese. It's well thought-out and well written. I don't see one sentence I would change. By the way, I like her calling it *The Maroon Nation.*"

"Good. I'll call Matilda and tell her to expect us in about an hour."

When they finished breakfast, Will said, "Leave your car here. After last night, I like having that big old Suburban protecting me on the streets of Jamaica." As they walked to the front of the hotel, Will took Vertise's hand. They drove up the hill to Matilda's house in silence, each wrapped in thought. Vertise was thinking that she was delighted to have Will and Matilda championing the cause she had been fighting for. Maybe they could win without any more bloodshed. Will, on the other hand, was wondering exactly how a business trip to Jamaica could result in multiple attempts on his life, and now he was joining a legal battle against his former employer. Fate deals most unusual hands, ones that could not be anticipated, he concluded.

When they parked on the street, they saw Matilda sitting on her front porch in one of her lawyer outfits—assuming a floral shirt, black skirt, black jacket, and black pumps qualified as a lawyer outfit. She rose to greet them. "I like working with people who are on time. Will, you like my petition?"

Will took her outstretched hand at the top of the steps. "I couldn't have done it half as well. I'd just like to be there when Pritchard sees it."

"Come on in and let's talk about where we go from here." Will and Vertise followed Matilda and once again took seats around the table. "Can I get you coffee, tea?" Matilda asked.

"I'm fine, thanks," Will said.

"Same for me," Vertise agreed.

"So, Matilda, what's our next step?"

"I'm taking this down to the Parish Clerk this afternoon. I'll hand file it. They will serve Global in Kingston by certified mail. That will take two or three days. But in the meantime, I can email a copy to Pritchard if you have her email address. No reason to postpone upsetting her."

"Alexa.Pritchard@GlobalAmericanMetals.com. Can I give you the money to pay the filing fee?"

Matilda shook her head. "No need. It'll be an expense item on my first bill."

"Okay, you guys know this stuff," Vertise said, "but educate me a little more."

"Hold on. I'm getting there. While I'm in the clerk's office, I'll ask for a date for the hearing on the injunction. Best guess is that it'll be ten days to two weeks from now. Once that date is set, we need to start planning for that procession, escorting the treaty down from the mountain to the courthouse. Vertise, I figure you can write a couple of articles that you can put out on the wires. Stir up as much publicity as you can."

"And I'll have a talk with Harper about the need for some of the Maroons to be armed," Will said. "Don't know what he'll say, but I'll give it my best shot."

189

CHAPTER 52

Angela Stephens, Pritchard's long time Jamaican secretary, threw open the door to her office and rushed to her desk.

She glanced up with irritation obvious on her face. "Did you forget to knock?"

"I'm sorry, Ms. Pritchard, but I knew you would want to see this. It came by email ten minutes ago. I printed a copy." She handed the petition to Pritchard and stood in front of her desk, awaiting further orders. As Pritchard read the document, she could literally feel her blood pressure rising. Stephens eyed her carefully, worried that she might be having a heart attack.

"Call Thomas and Henderson. I want them here in one hour. Make sure it's the two named partners, nobody else. I pay their law firm enough money that I expect them to drop everything when I insist."

"Yes, ma'am. Right away, ma'am." Angela turned and quietly closed the door behind her. Pritchard walked to the bar and poured a large glass of bourbon, dropped two cubes of ice in it, and returned to the desk where she sipped the bourbon quietly and thought. *First, you need to remain calm. You're not going to make the right decisions if you're angry. Then you've got to recognize that it's a smart move on someone's part. The petition was filed by a Matilda Massengale. Is this her idea? And this Colonel Broderick, I've been told that he is uneducated, but that doesn't mean he's not smart. Wait a minute. This has the fingerprints of Will Taylor all over it. He must have come up with the plan, but he's not a lawyer in Jamaica; so, he got Massengale involved. Should I call Judge Cunningham? No, too soon. He won't get involved until the trial is over and the case is on appeal. I can ask him for a favor or I can wire money to a Swiss Bank account in his name. And despite what I said, I don't really know if he will do what I ask. That will have to be a later day.*

Her intercom dinged. "Ms. Pritchard, Mr. Thomas and Mr. Henderson are here."

"Send them in."

Thomas and Henderson could have passed for Laurel and Hardy, the old comedians, albeit with darker skin. Paul Thomas was tall and rotund with a fringe of white hair. Michael Henderson was short and angular. His hair was black and beginning to thin. Dark horn rim glasses covered his eyes. A gold chain was clipped to each earpiece and circled his neck so that he could drop them to his chest when he chose. Each of the men was dressed in a dark suit, white shirt, and a blue patterned tie. They carried what appeared to be a copy of the Maroon petition.

"We came as quickly as we could, Ms. Pritchard," Thomas said.

"Have a seat. I see Angela gave you a copy of the petition. Have you read it?"

"No, ma'am. She just handed it to us," Henderson said.

Pritchard sighed. "Read it quickly. I want to start plotting strategy immediately. We have less than two weeks until the hearing."

When both men completed their reading, Pritchard asked, "Who is this woman, Matilda Massengale?"

"I've dealt with her a time or two over the years," Henderson said. "The best way I can think of to describe her is that she's half lawyer and half P.T. Barnum. When the word gets out that she's going to trial, the courtroom is filled. She well represents her client but expects to put on a show for the jury and the audience. She rarely fails."

"And what about Judge Lancaster?"

"We don't get over to Montego Bay that much, but I think he's a decent judge. We'll check him out more and let you know."

"My former head of security, Will Taylor, has defected and is helping out the Maroons and this Massengale woman. He's a lawyer in the United States. Can we muzzle him some way?"

"No problem there. He's not permitted to practice in Jamaica. He can assist Massengale, but he can't address the court or jury or cross-examine witnesses."

"Thank God for that. He's a devious bastard. So where do we go from here?"

"I see the treaty is attached as an exhibit to the petition," Henderson said. "We need to put some lawyers to work on it. Damn thing is nearly three hundred years old. I suspect it's been interpreted a few times over the years. I remember we studied it briefly in high school. There was a debate about its continued validity. Can we meet again in three days and give you our game plan?"

"I suppose that's okay. Meantime, I'm going to call a couple of our lawyers in Maryland. Maybe they'll have some bright ideas."

Three days later Thomas and Henderson walked into Pritchard's office with smiles on their faces. Pritchard motioned to chairs in front of her desk. "So, what do you have for me?"

Thomas pulled a thick brief from his case. "We've had several lawyers working around the clock to look at issues surrounding the treaty. This is what they have found."

Pritchard looked at the brief and tossed it on her desk. "I don't want to read it. Give me the summary."

"Delighted to, ma'am," Henderson replied. "The Colonial Government first passed the Maroon Lands Allotment Act in 1842. It was an attempt to abrogate the 1739 treaty by splitting up the Maroon lands and deeding them to individual Maroons. The Maroons thumbed their collective noses and the colonial rulers did not force the issue. Finally, we became our own nation in 1962, but the new Constitution did not address the Maroon Treaty. We have an expert, a lawyer and historian, name of Archibald Branbury, who has studied the issue of Maroon autonomy extensively. He's prepared to testify that with nothing mentioned about the treaty in the new Constitution, it must be assumed that the Maroon Treaty is now null and void. Thus, the minister of mines was within his rights to lease the land to Global."

Alexa pondered what she had just heard. "So how do you propose we use this Mr. Branbury?"

"Paul and I have debated this. We must assume that we may lose the injunction and there will be a trial. We save this witness and put him on in rebuttal. He's a powerful witness who will impress a jury. He'll be the last word from the witness stand. Hopefully, he'll carry the day."

CHAPTER 53

Will smiled at his good fortune when he found a space right in front of the police station. As he exited his car, he realized just how hot the afternoon was, probably in the nineties. He glanced out toward the ocean and could see storm clouds forming. He hoped he could get in and out of the station before a thunderstorm hit. He entered and nodded to the woman at the desk just inside the door and acted like he knew where he was going. He climbed the stairs two at a time, reminding himself that he needed to get back to a regular exercise program. He knocked on Harper's door and pulled it open.

"Afternoon, ma'am. I'm Will Taylor. Can the Chief spare a few minutes for me?"

"I know who you are, Mr. Taylor. Hold on." She picked up the phone. "He said he'll be right out." Harper opened his door, dressed in a pale blue shirt and bright yellow tie. He shook Will's hand. "Come on. I'll buy you a drink down in the cafeteria." Will nodded his agreement and followed Harper out the door and back down the stairs to the end of the hall. The cafeteria was deserted. Harper went behind the bar. "What can I get you?"

"Bourbon on the rocks works for me."

"Then, I'll make two." He handed one to Will and motioned him to a table. "So, what's up?"

Will took a sip of his drink. "Couple of things to talk about. I know you saw Vertise's column about the lawsuit the Maroons filed against Global. By the way, did I tell you that I left Global?"

"You didn't, but I heard it from somewhere. You have your fill of Pritchard?"

"That pretty well sums it up. I had been thinking about leaving for two or three years. It just seemed like this was the right time."

"Was it your idea to try to prove the treaty is binding and that the Maroons own the Cockpit Country?"

"I'll take a little of the credit. I figured that might be a better way to resolve this and avoid more violence."

Harper nodded. "Damn smart idea. I hope it works. As I told you before, I've had too many murders on my plate lately."

Harper walked back to the bar and re-filled both of their drinks. When he returned to the table, Will said, "There's something else that you should know. A few nights ago, the Maroons kidnapped me from the hotel and took me up to an abandoned house near Accompong. They tortured me for a while, even had a snake bite me on the neck." Will rotated his head. "Scared the shit out of me. Damn thing still hurts, but I'm okay."

Harper's face clouded. "How'd you escape?"

"Vertise came to the rescue. Directed me to the Maroon Trail back to Rose Hall. I was chased, but it wasn't much of a fight."

"Strange, the hotel didn't report it to me."

"It's over and I think that Colonel Broderick read the riot act to the young Maroons. He's old and speaks softly, but there's an authority in his voice. I'm not worried."

Harper shook his head. "I'm going to have a talk with that guy who is head of security for the hotel. I don't like guests being kidnapped and no report is filed with my office."

"Last thing, Chief. Broderick has the original of the treaty in a glass case. It's hidden in some place only he knows. Well, there may be another elder or two who are aware of its whereabouts, probably Vertise, too. Here's the thing. Matilda Massengale..."

Harper interrupted. "You couldn't have gotten a better lawyer. Hell, if I was charged with something, she'd be my first choice."

"That's what I hear. I've been working with her. She's got a sharp mind. I wish I could take an active part in the trial, but Jamaica has done a good job of keeping lawyers from the United States out of the courts. To get back to what I was about to say, Matilda says that she wants to introduce the original of the treaty at the injunction hearing next week. Broderick won't let her take it out of Accompong without armed guards. I need permission from you to have some armed Maroons escort their most valuable document to the court."

Harper rose and poured two more drinks while he thought. "You just told me that some of these Maroons kidnapped you and tried to kill you, and now you're asking me to let them come into Montego Bay with weapons displayed. Taylor, it ain't going to happen, no way, no time, no sir. You'll have to figure out some other plan. I'm not about to let those guys carry guns into Montego Bay and have them armed in the courthouse. Forget it," he said as he downed his last drink in one gulp. "I hope you enjoyed your drinks. Thanks for bringing me up to date. Now I need to get back to work."

Harper abruptly rose from the table and walked out the door. Will watched him go and finished his drink, thinking that they would have to go to Plan B. The problem was, they didn't have a Plan B. It's time to pay a call on Matilda, he thought. No time like now.

CHAPTER 54

Will took a seat across the desk from Matilda, but turned down her offer of another drink. "Thanks, but I just came from a meeting with Chief Harper. We had three drinks in the police cafeteria. You know about that place, don't you?"

Matilda smiled. "Yeah, sure do. Even had a couple of drinks in there with him in years past. He's about as good a cop as you'll find in Jamaica."

Will leaned forward, his hands clasped between his knees. "He may be just a little too much of a stickler for the rules. He says that we will not have any armed Maroons guarding the treaty when we bring it from Accompong. Any ideas?"

Matilda leaned back in her leather executive chair and stared at the ceiling. "Yeah, I've got at least one. Our courts have a rule like yours in the United States. If someone can authenticate a copy, it can be used. Maybe we can go up to Accompong and take a photo of the treaty. I always carry a good camera in my car. Better to use it than a cell phone. Colonel Broderick is due to meet me right about now to discuss the trial and what testimony we need from him. We'll talk it over when he arrives."

Will glanced out the window. There was an old Lincoln Continental in gleaming, mint condition parking behind his Suburban at the curb. Momentarily, Colonel Broderick exited, locked the Lincoln, and walked up the sidewalk and the steps, a small briefcase in his left hand.

Matilda went to the door and opened it before Broderick could knock. She stuck out her hand. "Colonel, thanks for meeting with us. Come in." Will rose to shake the Colonel's hand. Before he said anything, Broderick reached in his hip pocket and pulled out a wallet. From it he extracted a check which he handed to Matilda. "I hear lawyers work better when they're getting paid. Here's my personal check for $10,000. I hope that will serve as a retainer. I'm working with my young Maroons to raise more."

"Thanks. That's a good start. And you should know that I'm cutting my hourly rate in half on this case. We need to win it not just for the Maroons, but for all of us on this side of the island. Now, Colonel, I tried to talk Mr. Taylor into a drink. He declined. Can I offer you one before we go back and sit beside the fishpond?"

Broderick broke out in a grin. "Ms. Massengale, at my age I don't have many vices left, but one I still have is I like a good shot of whiskey at the end of the day. While the day's not yet over, I'd be delighted to share a drink with you."

"Well, hell," Will said. "I might as well have one, too. If I get stopped, I'm going to blame it on Harper."

"You gentlemen go out the back door and have a seat at that table with the umbrella in the middle. I'll bring the drinks. Will, you might as well tell Colonel Broderick about your meeting with Harper today."

Will had just finished bringing Broderick up to speed, when Matilda joined them, carrying a tray with three glasses of bourbon. They each took one and Matilda proposed a toast. "Here's to our success against Global."

"One more thing, Colonel," Will said. "You know that some of your young Maroons kidnapped me and threatened to kill me before Vertise got me out of that house. Vertise says you have them under control. I need your assurance."

Broderick lowered his eyes and then looked back at Will. "I am very sorry that happened. I have told each of the ones involved that if you are harmed in any way, they will be executed by firing squad. I believe they got the message. In fact, they may now become your best security."

"You satisfied, Will?" Matilda asked.

Will nodded his agreement.

"Then, let's talk about a plan B. I propose that we go up to Accompong and take a photo of the treaty. We will not use a flash since the treaty is behind glass. I will have the photo blown up to the same size as the treaty. Colonel Broderick, we will need you to testify that it is an exact replica of the treaty. I think we can get by at the injunction hearing with that. However, assuming we win, I still want to explore ways to get the real treaty in front of the jury, maybe just for an hour or less. I'll want you to testify as to its importance to the Maroons and people of this island. They will be more impressed with the real document."

"I understand, but I have been entrusted with the original of the treaty, and I owe it to my people to preserve it. Now, you asked for some other examples of Cudjoe's mark. I found a few." He opened his briefcase and placed several documents enclosed in plastic sleeves on the table. "The first four are orders that were written for him, promoting various officers. This last one may become very important. It's self-explanatory. I invite you to read it.

March 1, 1739

I am Cudjoe, Captain of the Maroon Army. On this date, in my capacity as leader of the Maroons in the war against the British I signed a treaty. While I am the leader of the Maroons, I cannot read or write. I had to sign the treaty with my mark. I am dictating this to Nanny of the Windward Maroons who can read and write. She visited on the day after the British had returned to their camp. Both sides agreed to lay down their arms and never engage in warfare against the other again. In return for the Maroons making that agreement, we are to be a free state within the state of Jamaica. We agreed to accept land to be governed solely by us as far as the eye could see from the Peace Cave in all directions up to 150,000 acres. Since I could not read the treaty and had it read to me, I wanted to document the understanding of the Maroons and the British.

X

Cudjoe

His Mark

"I have read the treaty and know that it talks about 1500 acres," Colonel Broderick said. "It's an error, a typo it would be called today. This should aid us in securing all that is rightly ours."

"What do you think, Matilda?" Will asked.

"If it was an error, we will ask the judge to correct it. If it was intentional deception, we will ask the judge to rule against the British who committed the fraud. It'll be a battle since we're claiming that it's a binding treaty. We'll figure it out. Colonel, can we meet you at about nine in the morning in Accompong. If you can retrieve the treaty from its hiding place by then, I'll take some photos and take them to a sign shop in Montego Bay. I'll have the best one blown up to the same size as the original. First step in our plan."

CHAPTER 55

Will left Matilda's house and drove into Montego Bay, knowing that he had seen the computer store that Vertise recommended somewhere. After meandering through the traffic, he finally spotted it and parked in a lot reserved for its customers. He purchased a new laptop and walked out the door, when a big man brushed by him.

"Taylor, Will Taylor, is that you?"

Will turned to recognize Buzz Arnold, a SEAL he had served alongside in a former life "Damn sure is. How you doing, Buzz? Must have been ten or twelve years."

"At least," Buzz replied as they shook hands. "What are you doing in Jamaica? Last I heard you were a lawyer with some fancy firm."

"I've got some friends that live here. I take a few days in the sun to visit them now and then. You?"

"Just got back from Iraq. Worked security over there. Made more in a year than ten as a SEAL. Couple of my buddies and I decided to see the sights here, maybe do some diving. Where you staying?"

"At the Ritz, east of town."

"That's too rich for our blood. We're staying in a motel a little farther down the beach. Let's get a beer one of these days."

"You got it. Good to see you."

Will returned to his car and immediately called Vertise. "Can you talk for a couple of minutes?"

"You bet. I'm home, sitting out on the front deck. What's up?"

"They're here."

"Who's here?"

"The mercenaries I warned you that Pritchard was going to bring in. Just ran into one of them. Served with him in the SEALs. Says he does private security now. That's shorthand for hired muscle, maybe hired killer. Said he was down here on vacation, but I don't believe him. Alexa's up to something. Nothing for us to do now; just wanted to give you a heads up."

***

Miles Harper walked back to his car that was parked in front of Rose Hall mansion and placed a call to Will. "Taylor, get your ass out of bed. Come to the mansion. The gate's open."

Will moved from a prone position to one sitting on the edge of the bed. "Come on, Miles, I've had a long day. Can't this wait until tomorrow?"

"Hell, no."

"You setting me up? The last time a Global employee was lured up there at night, he didn't come back alive."

"I'm here alone. I'll be waiting for you at my car. You remember I told you there was one security guard that drove around the plantation and the golf course at night. I told him to call me if he saw anything strange. He just did."

He clicked off the phone and reached in his pocket for a cigarette. He was on his second when he saw lights coming up the drive. Will parked beside him and climbed out of his Suburban.

"Just so it's clear, I'm packing my Glock."

Harper ground his cigarette out under his heel. "I told you that was no longer an issue."

"What's so important that it couldn't wait until morning?"

"Follow me," Harper said as he led the way around the mansion using his Maglite to illuminate the trail. Will began to feel apprehensive in the shadow of the mansion and finally pulled the Glock from his waistband.

"That's okay with me, but there's no one alive around here."

Harper shined the light on what Taylor knew to be Annie Palmer's tomb. He didn't believe in voodoo. Still, he felt a shiver go up his spine when he saw that the concrete top of the tomb had been twisted open.

Harper stepped aside and flashed his light into the tomb. "Take a look."

What he could make out after nearly two hundred years were a skeleton, or pieces and parts of one sufficient to identify it as a human skeleton, a few tufts of hair, and pieces of dingy gray cloth that was probably once a white dressing gown. "Is that really her, Annie Palmer?"

"You're face to face with the White Witch."

Will stepped back. "Who broke into the crypt, and why?"

Harper lit another cigarette. "Can't tell you who did it, but I can tell you what's missing. You remember I told you there was a snake dagger buried with her?"

Will nodded his head and glanced around, not sure what might be coming out of the shadows.

"According to legend, the one buried with her was the most powerful. Annie could will it to fly through the air. Supposedly that's how the overseer was killed. It's gone."

"Wait a minute. This is the twenty-first century. We fight with guns and bombs. Who would do this just to get to that dagger?"

Harper ignored the comment. "They had guns back in Annie Palmer's time, too. She was a tiny woman. She ruled her plantation with cruelty and voodoo. Anyone could fire a gun or swing a machete. Voodoo struck fear into the hearts and minds of her slaves. Nothing's changed much since then. Most of us don't believe in the occult, but the ones that do will avoid it at all costs. And, who's to say, maybe the occult arts really do exist. I can't prove that they don't."

Will stared at Harper's face that was reflected from the flashlight to see if he was bullshitting. He wasn't. "So, you think someone on this island has strong enough voodoo powers to control the White Witch's dagger?"

Harper shrugged his shoulders. "Can't say. Remember I told you that only another priest or priestess would dare to desecrate Annie's tomb."

CHAPTER 56

On the morning of the hearing, the crowd began assembling early. Some arrived at the courthouse before dawn even though they knew the doors would not open until eight. Once the doors were open, they would have to make a decision: wait on the steps to see Matilda's arrival or rush in to get a seat in the courtroom. Most were hoping that Matilda would arrive before eight, so they would not have to make the choice.

They were in luck. At about ten minutes before eight, the white Escalade, polished the day before to make the paint almost glow in the morning sun, parked in the no parking zone.

"There she is."

"I wonder what she'll be wearing today."

"Is it true she's the best lawyer on the island, maybe in the Caribbean?"

"Is she really as good as everyone says she is?"

"Better, mon, better."

Matilda climbed from the driver's side as Vertise, acting as her paralegal, closed the passenger door and pulled her rolling briefcase from the back. The briefcase had a round cardboard container affixed to it. Matilda's attire was slightly more subdued. She wore a light blue blouse with dark blue pants. A yellow scarf was draped around her neck and tucked into the front of the blouse. She still wore the gold hoop earrings, a gold bracelet on her right hand, and a Rolex watch on her left.

Matilda shouted, "Matilda Massengale is here. Justice will be done."

The crowd cheered. When she walked toward the steps, Colonel Broderick, dressed in a brown suit and tan striped tie, stepped from the crowd and met her.

He shook her hand and hugged Vertise. As they talked, Will hurried down the sidewalk to join them.

Matilda turned to the crowd. "We have about ten minutes before the doors open. I'm always on the look-out for clients. If you want a business card, stop me, but I can't talk today."

The crowd parted as she, her clients, and associates passed. People stuck out their hands for cards. Matilda shook each hand with a smile and then put a card in it. At the top of the steps, the doors magically opened. Matilda and her party were escorted around the metal detectors. The crowd streamed behind them. She flung open the courtroom door and announced, "Home, sweet home." She walked down the middle aisle and through the gate, pointing to the table closest to the jury box. She winked at Colonel Broderick. "I want to establish this as our table for the upcoming trial. I always want to be as close to the jury as I can. I'd take the middle chair on the first row in the box if I could." She walked over to the bailiff, Joshua Gamboa. "Mr. Bailiff, is there justice available in this court today?"

The bailiff grinned as he stood. "Yes, ma'am."

"Then I would like a full helping for my client."

She walked to the small desk in front of the witness stand where a chair was occupied by an attractive court reporter. "And a good morning to you, Ms. Rogers. Are your nimble fingers ready to fly when I talk?"

Ms. Rogers nodded. "I certainly never have to ask you to raise your voice to be heard."

Out on the street, Pritchard and her lawyers had watched the show. She turned to Thomas and Henderson and said, "Is there any way you can put a muzzle   on   her?"

"Afraid not, Ms. Pritchard," Henderson said. "Judge Lancaster will give her a great deal of latitude. I hear he gets a little bored with his job, but with Matilda in his courtroom, it's like a three-ring circus and he's the ringmaster."

"Let's go in," Pritchard said. "At least there's no jury today. Maybe he'll be persuaded by the power of our logic." They entered the courtroom. All eyes in the audience glanced back at them as they quietly took their seats. Thomas and Henderson, always professionals, walked over to shake Matilda's hand. She introduced them to Colonel Broderick, Will Taylor, and Vertise.

The bailiff rose and asked, "Are all parties ready to proceed?" When the lawyers agreed, he called Judge Lancaster's chambers. Within a minute, the judge stepped into the courtroom as the bailiff said, "All rise." He stood beside the bench while the bailiff intoned, "This Honorable Court, Judge William Lancaster presiding, is now in session." He bowed his head and continued. "God save Queen Elizabeth and this Honorable Court." The lawyers and parties, as well as most in the audience, took their cue from him and bowed their heads.

"Be seated, please," Judge Lancaster said as he took his bench. He had been a judge for twenty-five years. Handling both criminal and civil matters; there was very little that he hadn't seen. He was generally a kindly man, well thought of by most of the advocates that appeared before him. He had seen Matilda dozens of times, maybe hundreds, and, like the audience, looked forward to what she might do. However, he also knew that he would have to rein her in from time to time and was more than prepared to do so. As to Thomas and Henderson, their firm was known as one of the best on the island. He had met them at bar association meetings and seemed to recall that he had served on a continuing education panel with Paul Thomas. He also had read the pleadings and knew that this was a case that could have ramifications throughout the island. A friend had even called to say that the New York Times and Washington Post had reporters in the audience.

"This is the case of Colonel Rafael Broderick, individually and as representative of The Maroon Nation, against Global American Metals. We're hearing the plaintiff's injunction motion this morning. What say the Plaintiff?"

Matilda rose, "We are ready, willing, and able to proceed, Your Honor. Also, may I introduce Colonel Broderick, the leader of The Maroon Nation and Will Taylor, a distinguished lawyer from the Commonwealth of Virginia? He will not be taking an active role in the hearing, but I request that he be permitted to sit at counsel table."

"Ms. Massengale, I presume that you are always willing and able, just an announcement of ready will suffice. As to Mr. Taylor, we welcome you to my court, but you must understand that you are not a member of our bar and may not have a speaking role in this or any other proceeding." Will rose and nodded his head. "What say the Defendant?"

Paul Thomas rose and in a strong voice announced, "Global American Metals is also ready to proceed, Judge Lancaster."

"Very good. I have read the pleadings, and I believe that I understand why we are here today. With that understanding, does either side wish to make an opening statement?" The judge was trying to discourage oratory from the lawyers, and it worked.

"Your Honor, if the Defendant agrees to waive opening argument, Plaintiff will do likewise," Matilda said.

"We agree, Judge," Thomas said.

Judge Lancaster smiled and directed Matilda to call her first witness.

"Your Honor, Plaintiff calls Colonel Rafael Broderick."

"Colonel Broderick, please take the stand," Judge Lancaster said.

Broderick unfolded his six-foot, five-inch frame from the chair at counsel table and walked briskly to the witness stand, where he was given the oath by the court reporter. The bailiff brought him a cup of water. He nodded his thanks.

"Colonel Broderick, please tell the judge a little about yourself."

The rich voice that came from the witness stand was not that of a man of eighty. "I was born and raised in the Cockpit Country. My father had a few acres where he grew crops and tended to a few goats and chickens. My mother was a bush doctor. I followed her around when I could and learned about the medicinal properties of the roots, leaves, and flowers that grew in our forest. I dropped out of school in the tenth grade and moved to Canada, where I worked as a conductor on the railroad. After thirty years, I qualified for a pension and moved back to Jamaica.

"Do you still receive that pension?"

"Yes, ma'am. It comes in the mail every month."

"What did you do when you came back to Jamaica?"

"Wasn't back long before I married a woman quite a bit younger than myself. She lived over in Trelawny Town. We had one child. That's Vertise, the young woman sitting beside you. Unfortunately, her mother died in childbirth. I raised her." He smiled. "And I must say, I did a pretty good job. She went to college in the United States on scholarship and returned here when there were rumors that Global was going to destroy our rainforest."

Broderick stopped to take a sip of water. That gave the judge the opportunity to say, "Ms. Massengale, can you move this along more quickly?"

Matilda rose to respond to the judge. "Certainly, Judge. He is our only witness and I thought it important that you have some of his background. "Sir, you carry the title of Colonel. How did that come about?"

"The leader of the Maroons several hundred years ago was called chief. When we started fighting with the Spanish, and then the British, those old

Maroons wanted him to have equal status with those leading the troops we were fighting. Cudjoe and several others were Captains. Somewhere along the way, the leader started being called Colonel. When I returned from Canada, the leader of the Maroons had recently died. I ran for the office and won. We Maroons have a democracy. I must run every five years. So far I have never had an opponent."

"Are you familiar with the treaty that Captain Cudjoe signed with the British?"

Will rose from the table and walked to Matilda's briefcase where he retrieved the cardboard cylinder and removed the top before placing it on the table.

"I certainly am." The Colonel turned to Judge Lancaster. "Your Honor, I am the current custodian of the original of the treaty. I was designated as custodian by my predecessor after I returned from Canada and shortly before he died. I can trace the custodial care of the treaty all the way back to Cudjoe."

Matilda pulled several copies of the treaty out of the cylinder. "I'm marking one as Plaintiff's Exhibit 1 and providing duplicate copies to the court as well as counsel for Global." She handed one up to the judge and marched over to the opposing counsel table, where she handed one to Henderson.

"Is this the original of the treaty?" Matilda asked.

Broderick shook his head. "No, ma'am. We wanted to bring the original to court, but we were concerned about its security. So, you arranged to have copies made."

Will pulled a cork board on rollers to a place beside the witness stand. Matilda took one of the copies and pinned it to the board. "Can you tell the judge whether this is an exact duplicate of the one that you have in Accompong? By the way, who knows the location of the original?"

Broderick scratched his chin. "It is an exact copy. As to who knows the location of the original, that would be myself, two of the other elders of the Maroons, and Vertise has a pretty good idea about where it is."

"Your Honor, having established that the copy here on the board and the ones I have provided to you and counsel are exact duplicates, I now offer Plaintiff's Exhibit No. 1 in evidence." Matilda knew what was coming next.

Henderson rose from his chair. "Your Honor, Defendant objects most vigorously to this exhibit. This is not the original. In fact, we were not advised that it was to be an exhibit at all," he sputtered.

206

The judge looked over his glasses at Henderson. "Mr. Henderson, did you not go to high school in Jamaica?"

"Yes, sir."

"Surely, you must have studied the wars between the Maroons and the Spanish and British."

"I did, Judge, but how can you let Colonel Broderick testify about something that occurred three hundred years ago? He wasn't there."

"Come now, Mr. Henderson, if the American Revolution was potentially relevant to some issue, or maybe the War Between the States, wouldn't you agree that historians could discuss it in this court?"

"Your Honor, this is just Colonel Broderick, not a historian."

That brought some rumblings from the audience. Judge Lancaster turned to them. "We will have none of that in my courtroom. The audience must be seen but not heard. Any more outbursts and I have the authority to clear the courtroom. Understood?"

Silence from the audience was the response.

"As to your objection, Mr. Henderson, I'm going to overrule it. This is not a jury trial but a hearing. You can cross Colonel Broderick. Frankly, this is most interesting to me. If we get to a trial, maybe we can figure out a way to safely get the original in front of the jury. Proceed, Ms. Massengale."

"Colonel Broderick, are you sufficiently familiar with the history of the treaty that you can tell the judge how it came about?"

"Certainly. In fact, the treaty itself fairly well tells the story. In the preface, the treaty states that Captain Cudjoe and others have been in a state of war and hostility against the King of England. The British wanted to end the hostilities, and his Majesty George the Second granted full power to John Guthrie and Francis Sadler to negotiate this peace treaty with Captain Cudjoe."

"Was it clear from the treaty that the Maroons were being treated as a separate state by the British?"

"Certainly. As part of the agreement, the Maroons were given ownership of the Cockpit Country as far as the eye could see, up to 150,000 acres. Further, the Maroons were entitled to make their own laws on land deeded to them with one exception. If the Maroons determined that someone must have the death penalty, they had to involve a British judge. That was the only limitation. I should add as a matter of long standing tradition, if there is a killing in the Cockpit Country, the Maroons have always interpreted that section as meaning that Jamaican authorities can investigate."

Taylor handed Matilda her next exhibit. "Sir, can you identify this?"

Colonel Broderick studied it for a moment and then turned it upside down. "There, now I can explain. This is taken from Google Maps. It shows the western end of Jamaica, including the Cockpit Country."

"Your Honor, we offer Plaintiff's Exhibit 2 for the limited purpose of showing the Cockpit Country. I don't mean to suggest this is to scale, but it will be helpful to understand Colonel Broderick's testimony."

Henderson rose to object, but the judge directed him to return to his seat.

"This is a bench hearing, no jury yet. I'll let it in and I'll determine what part of it to consider."

Matilda tacked it up beside the treaty. "Can you identify the town of Accompong on this map?"

"Yes, ma'am. It's right there." He pointed to a small clearing in the forest with a road leading to it.

"Is the Peace Cave relevant to this discussion about the treaty?"

"Absolutely. That is where the treaty was signed."

She handed him two small flags. "Can you use these to mark Accompong and the Peace Cave?" Broderick did as he was directed.

"Now, what was the intent of the treaty?"

"It granted the Maroons 150,000 acres in the Cockpit Country. Well, I believe that it was as far as the eye could see from the cave up to 150,000 acres. That is our land and has been for nearly three hundred years."

Matilda looked at Will who nodded his head and motioned her to him. "You need to wind this up. The judge has heard enough," he whispered.

Matilda turned back to the podium. "When did you learn that Global was trespassing on Maroon land?"

"Must have been about six weeks ago. I stepped out of my front door and heard the rumbling of a bulldozer just beyond the hill. I walked over there to see what was happening and ran into two armed guards who told me to turn around or expect big trouble. I didn't know what to do. I went back to my house, got the keys to my car, and drove into Montego Bay to talk to Vertise. To make a long story short, that led to this lawsuit and this hearing."

"Was Global bulldozing Maroon land?"

"Yes, ma'am."

"Did you give them permission to be on your land?"

"Of course not."

Matilda handed Colonel Broderick one more small flag. "Can you place this flag where Global is attempting to mine."

Broderick studied the map and then placed the flag immediately adjacent to the Peace Cave. Matilda studied the proximity of the flags and asked, "How far away from the Peace Cave is that?"

Broderick rubbed his chin while he thought. "Probably five hundred yards or so."

"Pass the witness, Your Honor."

Michael Henderson rose from his chair and walked to the cork board. He took his glasses from his chest and perched them on his nose. That left the gold chains dangling along his cheeks. He peered at the treaty and then at the map before he turned to confront Broderick. "Colonel Broderick, by the way, did you serve in any branch of any military to earn that title?"

"No, sir. It's a title that the Maroon people chose to give their leader. I could be called governor, or president, or in the old days, chief. My people settled on Colonel before I was born. I might also add that the treaty refers to Cudjoe and several others with the title of Captain."

Henderson moved to the podium. "I see. Far be it from me to disrespect your title.

In looking at that treaty, I don't see any paragraph that deeds you Maroons 150,000 acres. All I see is 1,500. Can you explain?"

"I can. As I am sure that you and Judge Lancaster learned in school, Captain Cudjoe was a fierce warrior and a true leader of men. Only, he never learned to read and write." Judge Lancaster was leaning over his bench to catch every word and nodded his understanding at the witness's comments about Cudjoe. "There are several typos and mistakes in the treaty that don't really change its meaning. As I stated, the treaty was carefully preserved and handed down from custodian to custodian. It was probably a hundred years before there was a custodian who could read the treaty. By then, everyone, Maroons and British, accepted that the 150,000 acres belonged to the Maroons. In fact, no one has challenged that right until Ms. Pritchard here decided to invade our country."

"But, Colonel, you do agree that this document says you have the right to only 1500 acres, doesn't it?"

Broderick nodded. "It also doesn't say where the land is except northwest of Trelawney Town. The treaty was signed at the Peace Cave just outside of

Accompong. Even if it was merely 1500 acres, your client's bulldozers were just across the valley from the Peace Cave. And we have more documents to establish our ownership of the 150,000 acres."

Henderson left the podium and walked to face Broderick. He took a position just outside of the witness box. "So, Colonel, if you have such documents, where are they?"

"There's really just one that makes it clear, but that should be enough."

"Where is it, Colonel Broderick?"

Matilda rose and in a booming voice said, "Your Honor, when we have a trial, we will produce more proof. Right now, the issue is whether we have produced some evidence that the treaty is valid and enforceable. If you so find, then I say the burden would shift to the defendant to prove that it was *not* trespassing on my client's land when it started strip mining just over the hill from Accompong and a stone's throw from the Peace Cave."

The judge leaned back, put his hands behind his head and stared at the ceiling. There was silence in the courtroom for at least a minute. Finally, he tilted his chair forward and looked at the lawyers, the parties, and the audience. "Ah ha, Ms. Massengale, I think that you're right." Like judges in every country in the world, he wanted to rule in the narrowest way possible. If he could postpone a hard decision for another day, that was exactly what he would do, and Matilda had just given him a reason to postpone it. "Mr. Henderson, do you have any document that says where that 1500 acres you claim is in the treaty is, any metes and bounds description? Anything?"

"May I have a moment, Judge?"

"Certainly."

Henderson conferred in whispers with his partner and with Ms. Pritchard. Then he looked back at the judge. "Your Honor, frankly, we did not anticipate that this would be an issue today. We do not have any such document."

"Very well, then I am going to grant the injunction."

"Counsel and Ms. Pritchard, I direct Global to stop any activity anywhere in the Cockpit Country. Further, you are to remove any equipment from that land until we try this matter to a jury. I can set this in about a year."

Pritchard exploded. She leaped to her feet, yelling, "You can't do that, Judge. We

can't wait that long to get the mine in operation."

Lancaster banged his gavel. "Mr. Henderson, would you please control your client. Otherwise, I'll have my bailiff escort her from the courtroom."

Henderson glared at Pritchard and told her to take her seat. Next, he turned to the judge. "My client and I apologize to the court. I happened to look at the court's docket just yesterday. As I understand it, you had a case that was set for next month that recently settled. May I suggest that we try this one at that time? I can assure the court that it will take less than a week."

Lancaster pondered the request and turned toward Matilda. "Ms. Massengale, do you wish to respond?"

Matilda looked like the cat that just swallowed the canary and tried to hide the delight she was feeling. She had laid a trap and the defendant walked right into it. They would get their trial—and sooner rather than later. "Well, Your Honor, I've been coming to your court for years and have never seen a case moved so rapidly, but if it will assist opposing counsel, and you choose to do it, we agree."

The judge again glanced up at the ceiling as if looking for divine guidance. "Let's do it. I'll be taking some flak from other attorneys who will think they have a greater right to that week than you." He smiled and shrugged his shoulders. "But, what can they do? I'm the judge and they're not. I presume that with this shortened time, neither party will be requesting any discovery."

Matilda and Henderson nodded their agreement.

"Then we'll do it the old-fashioned way, trial by ambush. That's how it was when I was a young lawyer. Each party will exchange witness lists a week before trial. I'll see you next month." The judge banged his gavel and left the bench almost before his bailiff could say, "All rise."

Matilda turned to those at her counsel table. "Don't say anything. The walls in here have ears. We'll let the audience leave ahead of us and meet at my office."

Matilda and Vertise were the first to return to her house. Close behind came Will followed by Colonel Broderick. Will noticed he had a personalized license, *Maroon I.*

When Will and the Colonel walked through the front door, Matilda had already poured a glass of Chardonnay for Vertise and two bourbons for her and Will. "Colonel, what can I get you? Remember this is a celebration."

"I'll be happy to share one of those bourbons over rocks."

She poured one more and directed everyone to follow her out to the patio where they took seats beside the fish pond.

"I propose a toast," Matilda said. "Here's to the first of our wins with more to come."

"And I add to that toast a second toast to Will Taylor, who came up with this strategy." Vertise smiled.

They all clinked glasses and sipped their drinks in silence for several minutes, basking in their victory. Colonel Broderick spoke first. "I know we won today, and that stops Global in its tracks for now. Only, I don't understand why we agreed to such an early trial."

"Colonel, we're on a roll," Matilda said. "When the dice are hot, you want to keep hitting your number. I want to try this case while it is fresh in the judge's mind. Today we got away with putting on just enough evidence to get what we wanted. No reason we can't be ready in a month. And I really didn't want to give Global's lawyers any time to do discovery." She turned to Will. "You need to get on the phone and line up that forensic documents examiner. We've all looked at the documents, and I am certain they are authentic, right, Colonel?"

"Yes, ma'am. I'd stake my life on it."

"Then just have him down here a week before trial, and tell him to bring any instruments, chemicals, you name it, to authenticate the documents and date the treaty as close as he can." She laughed. "I can just see Thomas and Henderson now. They'll be screaming bloody murder, but they're boxed in. They will want to bring their own document examiner, but the deadline will have passed, and there's no way that Pritchard is going to let them ask for a continuance. Our plan is coming together. Now, let me re-fill your drinks. Then, I've got four steaks for the grill. I can cook almost as well as I can try lawsuits." She patted her large belly for emphasis.

CHAPTER 57

Will walked down the hallway to Rodney's room. The door was open, and he was seated in a wheelchair, dressed in a yellow T-shirt with Montego Bay splashed across the front, and jeans. He had a cast on his right leg and a computer in his lap.

"About time you got here. I told them that I could walk out on my own two feet." He pointed to two crutches that were leaning against the bed. "I'm getting pretty damn good with those things."

Will smiled. "I'll bet. Let me round up a nurse or somebody."

He left the room and was back in less than a minute with an orderly who had a name tag identifying him as Al. "So, you're ready, huh, Rodney. I hate to lose my gin rummy buddy."

"Same here, Al, but I'm ready to get the hell out of this place."

Al directed Will to pick up a small bag of clothes and books along with the crutches, as he pushed Rodney down the hall. When they arrived at the front entrance, Rodney and Al waited while Will retrieved his Suburban. He stopped at the front and went around to the passenger side to assist.

"No, I've been practicing," Rodney said. "Just steady me while I get the crutches in place." Once he was up, he crutched the few feet to the Suburban, turned, and pulled himself into the seat. "See there," Rodney said with a smile. "Nothing to it." He shook Al's hand and Will shut the door. When they pulled away from the hospital, Rodney asked, "Now where to?"

"We're going by the hotel. I took the liberty of packing your stuff. We can grab a bite to eat. Then, you're on a four o'clock flight back to Maryland. I'll fill you in on all that's been going on over lunch. Now that I think about it, you probably still have a job with Global."

Rodney shook his head. "I'm done with Global. I've got three weeks' vacation coming. I'll take that, starting tomorrow. I should be able to land another job during that time. Had enough of Pritchard's scorched earth policy. My preference would be to stick around here and watch the trial. Any chance of that?"

"No way. You almost died once. Kaven's gone. Someone has been trying to kill me. I've already sent Manny home. I think it best that you just get off the island."

***

Pritchard sat in the back of Henderson's black Lincoln Navigator, arms folded and refusing to talk until they were on the outskirts of Kingston. Henderson and Thomas took their cue and rode in silence. At last, Pritchard leaned forward to speak to the two men in the front seat. "I don't know how you got the reputations you have. One woman in one morning stopped my project dead in its tracks. I should have hired her."

Thomas turned in his seat. "Now just a damn minute, Ms. Pritchard," he said, trying to keep his voice under control and avoid doing more damage to the already frayed attorney-client relationship. "You had us talk to your lawyers in the United States who couldn't make the time to attend the hearing. We warned you that the judge was going to accept much less proof in the injunction hearing than at trial."

"You call that proof? Some old man getting on the witness stand to say that he knows that a copy is the real treaty. You even told me that the treaty probably didn't exist, that it was just a folk legend."

"Maybe there was a treaty, maybe not. No one could prove it since the treaty hadn't been seen in nearly three hundred years. And you forgot our game plan. We chose not to fire our best shot at this hearing. We're saving it for trial. Our expert will testify that the treaty hasn't been enforceable in probably two hundred years, or at least not since Jamaica became a sovereign nation. Just bear with us." Thomas took a deep breath. "Besides, we talked the judge into a trial just a month away. And as I understand it, you still don't have a bulldozer to replace the one that was destroyed or a new locomotive. So, you may end up losing a week, maybe two."

214

"And, what about Judge Lancaster? He seems to let Massengale do whatever she damn well pleases. Can we move the case to another court?"

"No, ma'am. Our rules don't permit it. Besides, he's the one that has an opening in a month. Some other judge could very well put us at the end of his docket, likely a trial two years from now."

"I don't like this, not one damn bit. I'm accustomed to being in charge. I just may have to take matters into my own hands."

"I don't know what you're thinking, but I think it's best that we are left in the dark," Henderson said.

"You don't have to worry. You won't know what I have done until you read it in the paper. Besides, I'm going to Baltimore for a few weeks. I'll be back the week before trial, if there is still one by that time."

215

CHAPTER 58

Will discovered that he had assigned himself a task that looked to be impossible. He tried three experts in the United States, all with very good credentials and plenty of testifying experience. He heard the same from each of them. They could not date the ink on a three-hundred-year-old treaty. While they might be able to do carbon dating on the paper, they would need the treaty in their labs for such testing. Further, none of the three were willing to say they could date the paper to the early 1700s. Last, the quotes he received for the project were way beyond anything he was willing to pay. And, of course, he knew that Vertise and Broderick were not going to allow the treaty to be flown to the United States.

On his last call, he talked to Randolph Bailey, PhD., a scientist at the University of Colorado who specialized in handwriting analysis. When told that Cudjoe's X was on the treaty as well as several other documents, he said that he could compare them all and offer an opinion as to whether they were made by the same man. He laid down a caveat that he really needed more than just the X, but if that was all he had to work with, he was willing to give it a shot. Will called Matilda to discuss his efforts and the use of Bailey.

She paced around her office, the cell phone to her ear as she listened. "Let's use him. If nothing else, jurors here will be impressed that we brought a scientist all the way from Colorado. Hopefully, they will be willing to accept his opinions. And we have to assume that Global will not have anyone to counter his testimony."

After calling Dr. Bailey back and arranging for him to fly to Montego Bay on the Monday, a week before trial, Will realized that he was out of a job, could not do much but support Matilda in her trial preparation, and had time to kill. He began by changing into shorts, T-shirt, and Nikes for a long, slow run on the beach. Averaging what he figured were about nine-minute miles in the sand, he ran east for forty-five minutes before turning back to the west. After an hour and a half, he reached the hotel pool, where he stripped off his shirt and shoes, dived into the water, and floated on his back, gazing up at the azure sky. Before he drifted off to sleep and risked waking with a nose full of water, he swam to the pool bar and slid onto a stool. The bartender walked over to him.

"What can I get you, Mr. Taylor?"

"You guys are really good with names."

The bartender smiled. "Not hard. You've been here over a week, and I rotate among the bars. Besides, I've been knowing Vertise for a long time. I've seen you hanging with her."

"Okay, if you know so much about me, figure out what I want to drink."

He turned to pull a Red Stripe from the cooler. "I figure this is just what you need."

Will took it from his hand. "No need for a glass. I like these straight from the bottle."

"You mind if I ask about your scars. Looks like you've seen battle."

Will glanced down at his chest and stomach. "You know, they're just a part of me. I hardly even notice them, even when I'm shaving." He pointed to one in his right shoulder. "These are all from tours in the middle east. I tried to dodge a bullet and didn't move quite fast enough. The ugly scar on my abdomen is from shrapnel. IED blew under our Humvee and a piece hit there. Spent six weeks in the hospital. Lost my spleen, but I learned that I get along without it quite well." He smiled. "Fortunately, I killed more of them than they did me."

The bartender thought about that for a moment and then burst out laughing. He reached for another beer. "Thanks for your service. Compliments of the hotel."

The bartender moved off to take care of other customers, leaving Will to finish his second beer. When he finished, he hollered, "Put whatever I owe on my room."

Back in the room he took his cell phone out to the balcony and called Vertise. He told her about the expert, then changed the subject. "I'm in the mood to play tourist tomorrow. I was thinking about heading toward Dunn's River Falls, followed by lunch somewhere in Ocho Rios. Can I talk you into taking a day off?"

"You don't have to say that twice. You know my condo is in that direction. Pick me up at nine."

Will pushed the "off" button on the phone, thinking that he and Vertise just might make a fine twosome.

Will pulled up to the front of Vertise's condo promptly at nine. After waiting a couple of minutes, he honked his horn. When she didn't come out, he shrugged his shoulders and walked to the front door and knocked. Vertise opened it almost before he finished. She was wearing a pink sun dress and matching sandals. Her breasts bulged gently above the front of the dress. A large beach bag hung from her left shoulder. She smiled and kissed him full on the lips.

"As I understand it, we're going on a date. My protocol for dates is that the man comes to my front door and escorts me to his car." She took his hand and led him down the sidewalk.

"Yes, ma'am. I won't forget that," Will said. "Oh, and do you have some other shoes. I read a brochure about the falls. They recommend running shoes."

Vertise patted her bag. "I've been there before. I also have a couple of towels in here."

The road to Ocho Rios hugged the northern coast of Jamaica, providing a constantly changing panorama of white beaches and clear blue water. They passed Discovery Bay and the Global bauxite facility, now idle as the company waited for another locomotive.

"I wouldn't have approved what was done here, particularly since the engineer lost his life," Vertise said. "Still, what the Maroons did here, assuming it was them, and up at the Cockpit mine slowed Ms. Pritchard down enough for you and Matilda to stop their operation completely. You think you can make that happen?"

"No guarantees, but we have a good chance." Will then told her about his efforts to find a document examiner. "His testimony doesn't go quite as far as I wanted, but Matilda thinks a jury will be impressed."

Vertise nodded her agreement and they drove in silence for the next thirty minutes, each lost in thought and enjoying the view. "Just around this next bend we should see the falls. We'll cross over the river and then turn right into the park."

They slowed to admire the falls to their right and a beach of pristine white sand to their left. Will turned into the park. "I read they have guides that take you up the falls. Do you recommend one?"

Vertise laughed. "I'll be your guide. I started climbing these falls when I was five. And I won't be asking for a big tip at the top, only lunch at a really good restaurant in Ocho Rios."

They drove up the hill to the parking lot adjacent to the river. Will stripped off his shorts and shirt and folded them in the driver's seat. He watched as Vertise opened the passenger door and pulled her sun dress over her head to reveal a flesh-pink bikini. Will found himself staring at her bronze body, only slightly hidden by the bikini top and bottom. When she pulled her sneakers from her bag and turned to sit on the passenger seat to put them on, Will couldn't believe what he saw.

"Vertise, is that a tattoo of a snake dagger, peeking above your bikini on your right cheek?"

"First, you're only seeing the top of the handle, which, I might add is all you'll see today. And, yes, it's a snake dagger."

Will let her words sink in and then replied, "Can I ask why you have one of those as a tattoo?"

Vertise turned her head to look at him, mystery in her eyes. "You can ask, but you won't get an answer any time soon, maybe not at all." She finished tying her shoes and changed the subject. "Now, you want to tell me about those scars?"

Will grinned. "Let's just say that they were earned in a prior life. I'll tell you more when you decide to tell me about that tattoo."

Vertise folded her dress and put it on the seat along with her sandals. "These falls can be pretty rough. Don't carry anything you don't want to have washed away. Just some cash for the entry fee, nothing else."

Will pulled two twenties from his wallet and placed the wallet back in his pants as Vertise shut her door. He walked around to her side of the car, again admiring her beauty, only now confused about who she was and why she had a snake dagger on her butt.

They paid the entry fee and made their way down a series of wooden steps and platforms to the bottom of the falls. The water roared and splashed over rocks and cliffs on its way to the sea. "The water is not deep, but it's swift and can knock you off your feet if you make a wrong step," Vertise said. "If you land on your butt, you may get bounced along the rocks for twenty or thirty feet before you can stand again. Just stay behind me and step where I step and we'll both make it. It's a lot of fun."

They arrived at the bottom landing. A muscular young guide walked up to them. "Hey, Vertise, long time, no see. You want any help today?"

"It's been a while, Denzil. This is my friend, Will. Thanks for the offer, but I've done this at least fifty times over the years. We'll be okay. Nice to see you."

Vertise took Will's hand and guided him into a pool of water at the bottom of the falls. She walked him to the right side and started the first climb up the rocks. Will watched carefully where she placed her feet. When she reached the next level, she turned and directed Will, having to yell to make herself heard over the roar of the falls. Behind them, Denzil had assembled a group and led them to the other side of the falls to start their trek. When Will joined her, Vertise said, "You're doing great. This next climb will take a little longer."

"I'm watching you," Will replied. He was enjoying watching the serpent's head on Vertise's butt, since it almost seemed to have a life of its own, twisting and contracting as Vertise climbed ahead of him. This time, they had to use their hands as well as their feet to get to a place where they could stop and catch their breath. While they rested, two young boys, probably about ten, scampered by them and climbed up the next level like they were monkeys climbing a tree. "I bet I could have done that when I was their age," Will said. "I'm ready. Let's make a final assault to the top."

Twenty minutes later they arrived at the top of the falls, where the two boys were horse playing while they waited for their parents to catch up. Vertise led the way down a path back to the parking lot, passing through an area of shops where vendors tried to talk them into buying T-shirts, caps, sandals, bags, and assorted other items to remind them of their journey up the falls. At the car, Vertise grabbed her bag. "There are restrooms over there." She pointed to the edge of the parking lot. "I want to get out of this wet bathing suit."

"I'll do the same. Meet you back here in fifteen."

When they were back in the Suburban, Vertise asked, "You up for the bobsled run?"

Will looked puzzled.

"It's like one of those alpine sleds that I hear are springing up in the ski resorts to attract tourists in the summer, except this one is going through the jungle at the top of a mountain. You'll feel like a kid again."

"Then let's do it."

220

They drove a couple of miles and turned into the park. After paying for the ride, they walked along a paved trail past a crystal-clear pond to the base of a ski lift. When their turn came, they seated themselves in the lift, pulled down the safety bar, and soon found themselves gliding above the treetops with another spectacular view of the ocean to their left. Twenty minutes later they exited into another tourist area with a restaurant, gift shop, and a group of acrobats and gymnasts contorting their bodies like pretzels in hopes of tips at the end of their performance. Will and Vertise passed them and found the line for the bobsled run. When they made it to the front, Vertise was strapped into a single seat car that was designed to look like a bobsled. Once she was secure, Will took the one behind her and was pulled by a chain imbedded in the track to the edge of the run where gravity took over. Will had been shown how to brake his sled, but elected to free fall as it twisted and turned like a roller coaster. Will figured that he might have reached two or *three Gs'* on a couple of the turns. He enjoyed the one-minute ride before his sled slowed and was pulled back to the top. Vertise was waiting when he climbed from his sled. "Again?" she asked.

Will looked at the line, now longer. "I think I'm ready for some lunch. It's nearly two o'clock. Are we eating here?"

Vertise shook her head. "This is just for the tourists coming from the cruise ships. Let's head back to the chairlift. I'm taking you to one of my favorite restaurants in Ocho Rios."

Once seated on the chairlift, Vertise crooked her arm through Will's. Will accepted the invitation and turned to kiss her—this time a longer, lingering kiss. "Something about bobsleds must be romantic."

Vertise hit him on the arm. "Hey, works for me."

When they approached Ocho Rios, Vertise directed him to Bamboo Blu, an upscale restaurant on the beach. It was mid-afternoon, and the place was sparsely occupied; so, they chose a table close to the water. A waiter seated them and introduced himself as Lionel. Vertise ordered Chardonnay and Will settled for a Red Stripe. After studying the menu, Will said, "You pick."

He signaled for Lionel to return. Vertise ordered jerk pork and rice for two. They ate quietly, both wondering exactly where this was going to lead. Vertise knew that Will would be in Jamaica until the trial was over. That was several weeks away—enough time that they would better know one another. Will had not had a serious romance in probably three years. Maybe it's about time, he thought. They finished their meal with coconut ice cream. Vertise led Will

221

down the steps to the beach, where she kicked off her sandals. Will did the same. They walked hand in hand on the water's edge for close to an hour, until Will said, "I suppose we ought to start heading back to Montego Bay. I'm getting pretty darn good at driving on the left side of the road, but I'm just not as comfortable with it at night."

When they stopped at Vertise's condo, Will exited his side and went around to open Vertise's door. "See, I'm a quick study."

Vertise took his hand as she stepped from the Suburban. Will opened the back door to retrieve her beach bag, and they walked slowly up the sidewalk to her door. Vertise turned to kiss Will. "I had a great time. Your tourist day could not have been more perfect." She lowered her eyes and looked back up at Will. "Would you like to come in for a nightcap?"

Will fumbled the keys she handed him to open her door, anticipating what he hoped would be more than just a drink once inside.

CHAPTER 59

Colonel Broderick sat the front porch of his cottage, drinking coffee and watching the sun rise over the mountains. He was content for the first time in many months, ever since he first learned what Global and Ms. Pritchard were trying to do. He was surprised—no, shocked that Will Taylor had come over to their side. He could see the look in Vertise's eyes when she talked about him. He seemed to be a good man. Certainly, Vertise could do far worse, but any discussion with her about Will would wait until after the trial. If she still had that look, he would suggest that Will should have a talk with him before they went much farther down that road. He rose, stretched, and stepped into his house to put the coffee cup in the sink. When he came out, he had a cap and was ready for a walk to the Peace Cave. Walking through the village he heard a voice. "Morning, Colonel."

He turned to see Lawrence beside his house, feeding the chickens he kept in a pen. "Morning, Lawrence. It's going to be a fine day, don't you think?"

Lawrence closed the gate to the pen and walked over to him. "Couldn't agree more. Colonel, do you really think this lawsuit against Global is going to do any good?"

Broderick pondered the question he had asked himself so often in the past few weeks. "I believe it will work. I have confidence in Ms. Massengale. We don't need any more lives lost in this fight with Global." He shrugged his shoulders. "We'll know in a couple of weeks. I'm taking a walk over to the Peace Cave. Want to join me?"

"No, thanks, Colonel. I'm heading into Montego Bay. Trying to get a job with a restaurant on the Hip Strip. Have a good walk."

Broderick continued down the trail and arrived at the Peace Cave in thirty minutes. He sat on a rock at the entrance and marveled at the beauty of the mountains and green foliage of the jungle that rolled before him for miles. He hoped that the effort they were undertaking would preserve it for generations to come. He pushed to his feet, stretched once more, and started the walk back to Accompong. He took his time but still arrived at his house by nine o'clock. He was meeting Vertise at the newspaper at noon; so, he had time to kill. He made another pot of coffee and filled his cup to again sit on his porch. Now, the village was coming to life. Various neighbors walked by, visited for a few minutes, and drifted off. When it was close to ten, he re-entered the house, took his keys from the kitchen table, locked the door, and walked to his Lincoln. He patted her fender like she was an old and cherished horse. "Let's go down the mountain to town," he said to the car as he entered, turned the key, and backed it out onto the one street that bisected the village. He lowered the front windows and was enjoying the crisp, morning air. He waved to a couple of farmers who were tending their crops. These days, he knew that while they might have banana trees along the road, behind them would be marijuana, since it had been confirmed that under the terms of the treaty the Maroons could legally grow ganja in the Cockpit Country as long as the Maroon Council did not object.

He was half way down the mountain when a sniper's bullet struck his brain. He died instantly—so quickly that he never heard the sound of the rifle that trailed behind the bullet. The Lincoln veered into an embankment. His body slumped forward into the steering wheel, setting off the horn that echoed down the road.

Four hundred yards away the sniper climbed from a tree, dismantled his rifle, and put it in a case which he placed into the trunk of a rental car. He didn't need to check on Broderick's body. He knew it had been a clean kill, like so many he had done over the years since Iraq. He was more interested in getting back to Montego Bay before anyone discovered Broderick's car.

He got away, but within a few minutes another car came up behind Broderick's Lincoln. The driver, a Maroon elder, jumped from the car and ran to the open window. His first thought was that the car must have had a blowout. "Colonel, Colonel, are you all right?"

When there was no movement, he pulled Broderick's body away from the steering wheel and noticed a hole in the windshield. It matched the hole in the Colonel's forehead. He knew that Broderick was dead, but he put his hand along his neck, hoping that he might feel a pulse. Nothing.

He considered what to do and glanced up and down at the road. No one was in sight; so, he called the St. James Parish Police Department. When the dispatcher learned that Colonel Broderick had been killed, she immediately called Miles Harper. He dropped what he was doing and called Vertise. "Your father has been in a wreck on the road from Accompong. It's serious. You want me to pick you up?"

"No. I'll call Will. You get on up there. We won't be far behind."

As soon as Will got the word, he called the valet service and said that it was urgent that his car be brought up immediately. He threw on a shirt and shorts and tied on his Nikes, then practically ran to the elevator. The Suburban was waiting at the front. He jumped in, fastened his seat belt, and drove as fast as he could down the highway to the newspaper office. Vertise was standing in front when he arrived. She opened the passenger door and fastened her seat belt.

"What happened?" Will asked.

"I don't know. Miles only said that my dad had been in a bad accident." She teared up and through sobs she said, "I think he may be dead."

Will reached across the center console and took her hand. "I'm so sorry, Vertise. We'll get there as quickly as we can." He opened the console and pulled a box of tissues from it. Vertise took several and began to wipe her eyes. Will didn't know what to say and chose to remain silent as they left Montego Bay and started up the mountain.

The first thing they saw was Harper's vehicle, red and blue lights flashing, with two other patrol cars behind his. Then a civilian car. Then Broderick's Lincoln smashed into the mountain. Vertise jumped from the car before Will could come to a stop. She stumbled once, then righted herself and ran to her dad's car. Harper stopped her. "Vertise, I don't think you want to see this. He's dead."

Vertise shoved by the detective and went to the car where she opened the door, glanced at her dad's body and threw herself over him, wailing. Will walked up to Harper, nodded and put his hand on Vertise's back. When she could compose herself, she pulled away and fell into Will's arms, her chest still heaving with the sobs that wracked her body.

"Vertise, I've got an ambulance on the way up here," Harper said. "We'll transport your dad's body down to the morgue. It seems clear that his death was caused by the one shot, but we'll still check a little further."

"Miles, stay here with Vertise. I want to walk down the road a way," Will said. "The killer must have left in a hurry." He looked at the road, looked at the hole in the windshield, and started walking down the mountain looking more to the right than the left. He had walked several hundred yards when he spotted what he thought were impressions in the dirt left by tires. He turned off the road and walked into the forest, where he found footprints and several limbs of bushes broken by someone trying to make a hasty exit. He came to a tall tree and saw evidence of crampons used to climb to the first big limb. He glanced up to where Harper and Vertise stood and satisfied himself that he had located where the killer waited. He considered the distance and the probable speed of the Lincoln. The killer had to be someone trained as a military sniper. His mind went back to seeing Buzz. He didn't recall that Buzz had trained as a sniper. Still, he almost surely knew someone who did. That person had to be on the island.

Will walked back to where Vertise and Harper stood. "Vertise, do you want to wait for the ambulance?"

Vertise wiped her eyes again. "Not really. Nothing I can do. I'd rather get back to the newspaper and write a story about my dad."

"After you're done, I'm not going to leave you alone. We can go back to your condo or to the hotel. We'll decide after you tell your dad's story."

CHAPTER 60

Will sat at the front of the newspaper office and pretended to be reading a magazine when, in fact, he was carefully watching Vertise at her computer. She wrote about her father's death, and his life, occasionally stopping to dry her eyes. When she finished, she printed a copy and walked over to her editor's desk. He read it and then hugged her, saying it would be on the front page tomorrow with a black border around the story.

When they returned to Will's car, Vertise said, "I could use a drink, maybe two."

Will nodded and drove to the hotel where they found the lobby bar nearly deserted in the middle of the afternoon. "What can I order for you?"

"Vodka on the rocks—a double."

When the waiter came, Will ordered their drinks. The waiter had just put the drink down in front of Vertise when she picked it up and drank half before returning it to the table. Seeing and feeling her grief, Will sipped at his. They drank in silence until Vertise finished her second drink.

Will cleared his throat. "Vertise, I need to say something. I know this is not a good time, but I don't think it can wait. You think that Alexa Pritchard had something to do with your father's death. That's a statement, not a question." He turned his hands palms up. "Look, I don't know whether she did or not, but you must not seek revenge on her, at least not now. And that goes for Lawrence, and Aaron, and their friends. We go to trial in less than two weeks. We need to stay focused on winning. If we establish that the treaty is valid, we will deal a crippling blow to Alexa."

Vertise stared at Will as if she could not believe he would make such a statement. He saw the anger in her eyes, the clinching of her jaw. Abruptly the face changed. "I am now the custodian of the treaty," she said.

"You're what?"

"You heard me. A couple of weeks ago, my dad wrote a letter naming me as custodian of the treaty if something happened to him. Premonition or not, he did it. He also showed me exactly where the treaty is. Whatever he was going to testify about, I can now do the same."

"Your father was a remarkable man."

"If we win this lawsuit, I'm going to ask the Maroons to re-name the Cockpit Country. I want it to be known as Broderick Forest."

Will nodded his agreement. "Now, let me take you back to your condo. I'll arrange to get your Volkswagen back to you by this evening. I know it's parked in that lot behind the newspaper. I need to see Matilda. She'll need to amend the pleadings in the lawsuit to name you as plaintiff."

Will walked Vertise to her door and gave her a long, tender hug. "You going to be okay? I can stay."

Vertise cast her eyes to the ground. "I'll be fine. Go see Matilda."

"Then, lock your door and don't open it for anyone. Call me if you even suspect a problem."

Will knocked on Matilda's door. She threw it open with a smile. "How about this, I've got a handsome man standing on my front porch." Her smile disappeared when she saw the look on Will's face. "Something's happened. Is Vertise okay?"

"She's fine, only her father was killed by a sniper on the road from Accompong this morning."

"Shit," she said. "How's Vertise?"

"I just took her back to her condo. She comes from strong stock. She'll be all right."

Matilda motioned for Will to step into her office. She walked behind her desk and plopped her three hundred pounds into the chair with a grunt. Will sat opposite her. "What the hell does this do to our lawsuit? He was our main witness."

"The Colonel took care of that. He wrote a letter just a week or two ago, designating Vertise as custodian of the treaty if anything happened to him. He even showed her where the original is."

Matilda turned to her computer. "I need to amend our pleading to name

Vertise as the lead party. She okay with that?"

"She is. That's one of the reasons I'm here."

While her computer went through its warmup cycle, Matilda asked, "When's the funeral?"

Will shook his head. "I don't think that Vertise has thought that far ahead. I'll let you know."

CHAPTER 61

Will left the hotel at ten for the two o'clock funeral. Vertise had stayed the night in her father's house; so, he was alone. He drove the winding mountain road slowly as he thought about Colonel Broderick and his life. By all accounts he was a good man. He could be tough if the situation called for it, but at heart, he was a gentle, peace-loving soul. It was sad that he could not be there for round two of their trial. The higher up the mountain Will drove, the heavier the traffic became. When he was close to Accompong, a young man dressed in a long sleeve white shirt, white pants, and white shoes directed him to park along the road nearly a quarter mile from the town. Vertise had told him that the funeral was planned for two o'clock because Maroons from throughout the island were expected to attend.

He joined with others who were walking slowly toward the gate. A few of the walkers looked at him, obviously wondering why a white man was attending the funeral. When Will walked through the gate, he saw that not only had every seat in the community hall been lined up in front of the Cudjoe Monument, but every chair from every house had also been placed there. The casket was in the front, closed because of the bullet wound to the head. On either side of a pulpit were two flags, one the Jamaican flag with four intersecting triangles. The top and bottom were green with the two side triangles black. The other flag was maroon with one gold star in the middle. It took Will a moment to realize it must be the Maroons' flag. Then he realized a similar flag was draped over the casket. Will was surprised to see that most of the Maroon men, young and old, were dressed like the young man who directed him to park, white shirt, white pants, and white shoes. In contrast, the women wore black dresses with black veils. Will recognized a number of the Maroon men who remained silent when they passed him. Uncertain what to do, Will decided not to take a seat. Instead, he stood at the back. A few minutes before two o'clock, a man who was obviously a preacher rose from a chair on the front row and stepped behind a podium. Realizing that people were still coming through the gate, he clasped his hands behind his back and observed.

Will felt someone standing beside him and turned to see Matilda, also dressed in black with a black veil. She squeezed Will's arm. He smiled in return.

Will heard a door open and shut. Vertise left her father's house, dressed as the rest of the mourners. On either side of her were Lawrence and Aaron, dressed in white. They escorted her to the back of the mourners and then down the middle aisle to a seat on the front row. Her head was bowed the entire way, and it did not appear that she even noticed Will and Matilda. Once she was seated, the preacher was about to start the service when a large black limo drove slowly through the gate. On either front fender were Jamaican flags. The limo stopped, and two guards stepped out. After scanning the crowd, one opened the back door and Henry Rawlins, the Prime Minister of Jamaica, exited. Rawlins was a tall man with white hair and beard, both neatly trimmed. He sized up the situation and walked slowly to the middle aisle and down it. He paused to say something to the preacher, and then turned to take Vertise's hands in his as he murmured a few words to her. When he took the seat beside her, the preacher began with a prayer. Will hadn't noticed an old upright piano at the front until the pianist began to play *The Old Rugged Cross*. When the song was finished, the preacher began to talk about Colonel Broderick and what a great man he was. Will listened, noting that there was no humor in the message, just sadness that such a fine man should meet such an untimely and brutal death. When he finished, a young woman stood beside the piano and sang a beautiful rendition of *The Lord's Prayer*.

At the conclusion Lawrence and Aaron rose and walked to the casket and removed the Maroons' flag. They folded it like they were soldiers at the Arlington National Cemetery. Aaron walked to face Vertise, kneeled in front of her, and then handed her the flag. The crowd was quiet. The only sound was Vertise sobbing.

The preacher nodded to the Prime Minister, who walked to the podium. He looked over the mourners and spoke. "I will be brief. I drove from Kingston today for one reason. That is to pay my respects to a long and trusted friend,

Colonel Rafael Broderick. I have known him for thirty years. We must have met publicly and privately at least fifty times during those years. Never have I met a more honest and trustworthy head of state. Vertise, we will all miss your father. Your loss is our loss, too. I can only hope that the Maroons can find a new leader that is half the man as he."

The Prime Minister returned to his seat. Vertise rose to shake his hand and whispered something to him. Next, she walked to a bouquet of mountain roses, mounted on a stand. She removed them from the stand and placed them on her father's casket. Last, she bent over, whispered something to her father, and kissed the casket.

The preacher said a final prayer and reminded the mourners that Vertise would be standing at the back to speak to anyone who wished to say a few words. Thereafter, Vertise, accompanied by Lawrence and Aaron, walked to the back. The mourners rose and stood in line to speak to her. While they waited, the Prime Minister walked around the side and left in his limo. It took nearly an hour for the mourners to pay their respects. Matilda whispered to Will that she needed to get off her feet and would talk to him the next day. When the last of the mourners left, Vertise walked to Will and fell into his arms, her body shaking with emotion.

CHAPTER 62

Will and Vertise were outside luggage claim at Sangster International Airport, along with others awaiting passengers arriving on a flight from Denver. A small, dapper man with gray hair and a matching mustache, wearing a brown suit, light blue shirt, and yellow bow tie, left baggage claim. He was pulling a very large trunk. He blinked at the brightness of the sun and then heard Will calling his name. "Dr. Bailey?"

When Bailey looked in his direction, Will walked up to him. "I'm Will Taylor. Here, let me take care of that case."

Bailey nodded his thanks. "And this is Vertise Broderick, the representative of the Maroons in the lawsuit."

Vertise extended her hand and it was taken by Bailey. "Delighted to meet such a charming lady. Where are we headed?"

"My Suburban is just over here in the visitor lot. It's a little late in the day to make the drive up to Accompong. I have a room for you at the Ritz. I suggest we head over there. After you have had a chance to unpack and rest a little, we can meet for dinner. Let me take that trunk."

At six-thirty, Will and Vertise were seated at a table in the restaurant. Will saw Dr. Bailey, now dressed in white slacks and a green polo shirt, looking around the room. Will stood and waived. Bailey nodded and made his way to the table. "I hope I didn't keep you waiting."

"Not at all, Doctor. We got here a little early. We've already ordered drinks. What would you like?"'

"I hear that Jamaica is famous for its rum. I suppose I'd be content with a rum and Coke."

Will waved their waiter over to the tableand placed the order, then asked for menus.

"Is your room satisfactory?"

"Mr. Taylor…"

"Let's make it first names: Will, Vertise and…?"

"Randy."

"Will, I live in the mountains and love them, but I have never felt more relaxed than sitting out on the balcony outside my room, watching the boats and listening to the waves lap up onto the beach. Delightful, just delightful." He turned to Vertise. "I heard about your father. You have my deepest condolences. I always say that it's the natural order of things that our parents pre-decease us, but that doesn't make it any easier when it happens. And so suddenly. I'm sorry, my dear."

Vertise blinked back tears. "Thank you, Dr. Bailey, I mean, Randy."

The waiter brought their drinks. Bailey proposed a toast. "To the ancient craft of calligraphy and how it can help us win your lawsuit and preserve your forest."

The three clinked glasses, sipped their drinks, and Randy continued. "You sent me copies of the documents. Obviously, I'm not going to rely on them for my testimony. I want to see the originals. But, I can tell you some things I am sure of."

Will nodded expectantly.

"You say that the treaty was signed in 1739. I can't establish that with certainty, but I can say that it was signed before 1800. You see, the writing is with a quill. Quills were used as writing instruments until the 19th Century. In fact, the Declaration of Independence was written with a quill. Metal pens were not developed until the early eighteen hundreds in England. Quills were crafted from the flight feathers discarded by birds during their annual molt. Goose feathers were most favored. The first feather is the one liked by the expert calligraphers in that time. However, the second and third feathers were also deemed quite satisfactory."

Bailey paused to take a sip of his rum and coke. "Jamaican rum is certainly all it's touted to be."

"Please continue," Vertise said.

"Of course. In studying the documents, I found the body of the treaty is written almost certainly written with a quill from the first feather of a goose.

Cudjoe's marks and the writing on the other documents appear to be from a different quill, perhaps not the finest—probably a second or third quill. I can do better tomorrow when we see the originals. Is this going to be useful to you?"

Will smiled. "Certainly will be helpful. Hopefully, you can determine that Cudjoe's marks on all of the documents came from the same quill and same person."

"That is my wish, also. I look forward to tomorrow. Now, perhaps we should order. The airplane food was not very tasteful, nor plentiful. I would hope that we can get some excellent seafood tonight."

Vertise's eyes sparkled at the expert's wish. "That's one thing that I can guarantee. Let's hear the specials from the waiter, and I'll make a recommendation."

CHAPTER 63

Will met Dr. Bailey at the valet. He was carrying a small briefcase. Once they were belted in, he said, "We're going to pick up the Maroons' lawyer. You'll like her. Vertise is ahead of us. She's going to retrieve the treaty and the other documents. She should be in the community hall when we get there."

"Tell me the lawyer's name again."

"Matilda Massengale. You might offer her the passenger seat when we get to her house. She's a large woman and needs the extra room."

Matilda was sitting on her front porch when they drove up. Will stepped from the driver's seat. Bailey exited his side. Matilda came down the sidewalk to greet them and reached her hand out to Randy. "I'm Matilda Massengale, and you must be Dr. Bailey."

"My pleasure, Ms. Massengale."

She turned to Will. "Honey, I'm so glad you rented this Suburban. I had to go to Miami a while back and reserved what they said was a standard sized car. I went to the space where it was and took a look. I could barely have put one leg behind that steering wheel. I marched back up to the counter and demanded an SUV." She winked at Will. "And you know when I demand something, I usually get my way. They didn't even charge me for the upgrade."

"Ms. Massengale…"

\"Sweetie, you just call me Matilda."

"Matilda, you take the passenger seat and I'll sit behind you."

Matilda climbed into the vehicle and draped the seat belt over her shoulder without fastening it. "Learned long ago that these seat belts won't stretch over my belly. At least this way, if a policeman sees me, he can see the seat belt through the window. Will, don't go having any accidents, you hear?"

"Loud and clear, Matilda. Here we go."

Vertise's Volkswagen was parked in front of the Cudjoe Monument when they arrived in Accompong. A couple of the Maroons hollered at Matilda when she got out and stretched. She hollered back. "I've represented some of these folks from time to time when they need a lawyer in Montego Bay. For the most part, they're good, hard working people who just want to be left alone."

Will waved them over to the Community Hall where Vertise was standing in the doorway. "You get everything?"

"All inside. Morning, Randy. Morning, Matilda. I even brought the coffee pot from my dad's house."

Bailey nodded his thanks. "Be glad to have some good Jamaican coffee when we're finished. But, while I'm looking at documents, I don't permit any liquid or food on the table. I don't want to risk a spill on an ancient document. Please lead the way."

They walked to the front of the hall where the glass case containing the treaty was placed alongside a metal box. Bailey walked around the table twice. "Very nice; very, very nice. You say this was done more than sixty years ago?"

Vertise, Will, and Matilda took metal chairs close to the table. "It was my father who had the case built," Vertise said. "Shortly before he moved to Canada; he came up with the design."

Bailey nodded and said, "The glass top is hinged. It may take a little WD40 to get the hinges to budge after sixty years. There are two clasps on the side opposite the hinges. Then, it looks like the woodworker used putty to seal the edges. Very smart of him. What I want to do is chip off the putty, then oil the hinges and try to gently open the glass lid."

Vertise nodded her understanding.

"I'm not going to take it out of the box, but I've got a variety of magnifying glasses in my case along with a light with certain filters that will not damage the treaty. Everybody okay with my plan?"

"I have a question," Will said. "Once you get it open, can you seal it later?"

"Of course. Back in that big trunk in my room at the hotel I have some silicone gel. We'll seal it after the trial. Also, I have an apparatus that will suck the air out of the case to better preserve it."

He reached for his briefcase and opened it next to the treaty, then pulled what looked to be something like a putty knife from it along with a small hammer. "This is going to take a while. I will try not to scratch or scar this beautiful case."

After an hour, he announced that he had removed the putty. Using a small brush to clean the area around the case, he used the small hammer and an equally small screwdriver to open the clasps. He tried once to open the case and failed. He looked up and smiled. "Time for the WD40." He sprayed small amounts on both hinges, waited a few moments, and tried once more to lift the glass. This time it responded. He stepped back and wiped his glasses. "Gazing on such an ancient and important document is like a religious experience for me. Let me sit for just a minute. Maybe I'll have a little of that coffee, Vertise, black please." He took a metal chair away from the table beside Vertise, who ran to the coffee pot and returned with a mug. He took a sip.

"I was told about how great Jamaican rum is. I didn't know your coffee was so rich." After resting ten minutes and drinking half of the mug, he returned to the task at hand. "Let me get a couple of magnifying glasses and that light I was talking about."

Although primarily interested in Cudjoe's mark, the scientist started at the top and read very carefully down the page, studying each word with one or both magnifying glasses. He had picked up the light several times and finally said, "Vertise, would you mind holding this light and just follow where my glass is going. Hold it up about two feet from the treaty."

Vertise did as she was told. Twice he stopped and moved back up several lines until he got to Cudjoe's mark. After studying it for at least a minute, he put the magnifying glasses down and told Vertise to turn out the light. "Just what I thought. The treaty itself is written with a very fine quill, one of those first goose feathers I told you about last night. The X that is Cudjoe's mark is from a different quill, a second or third feather I would say. Any questions?"

The other three in attendance shook their heads.

"Then, Vertise, I'm ready to see what is in the metal box."

He could open the box without difficulty. Once it was open, he took gloves from his briefcase and put them on. "I'll have to take these out of the box, and I don't want any oil from my hand left on them." He gently removed the memo dictated by Cudjoe to Nanny and four other documents from the box. "I'm surprised," he said. "These are in very good condition, too." He started with the memo from Cudjoe and went through the same process, getting to Cudjoe's mark at the end. "This letter is clearly around the same time as the treaty.

Looking at both marks, you can see that Cudjoe pressed down hard at the top of each line on the X and let up slightly at the bottom. Certainly, the same hand made the mark. Just out of curiosity, who is this Nanny that is mentioned in the letter?"

"She was the leader of the Windward Maroons," Vertise replied. "They lived on the east side of the island. Nanny was their military strategist. While she didn't engage in the fighting, she planned the attacks on the British over there. Legend has it that she was also an *Obeah* woman, skilled in magic. She may have even cast spells on the British. She heard Cudjoe was signing the treaty and tried to get over here to witness it; only she was a day late. She was an important enough figure in Jamaican history that our five-hundred-dollar bill has her picture on it."

"Interesting. That's one of the great things about my job. When I'm asked to authenticate an ancient document, I always learn some history. You said she was also an *obeah* woman. Is that the same as voodoo?"

"That's a slang term, commonly used," Vertise said.

"Are there still people on this island that cast spells, put hexes on people, that kind of thing?"

Vertise looked away, as if unsure how to answer. "If you asked around enough, you could probably find someone who claims those powers."

Bailey nodded. "Back to the task at hand. What are these other documents?"

"As leader of the Maroons, Cudjoe would appoint or promote other officers. Each of these is documenting those events."

Bailey laid the four documents side by side, read them carefully, and studied each of Cudjoe's marks with a magnifying glass. He looked up with a sense of satisfaction. "I can say with absolute certainty that all of Cudjoe's marks were made by the same man."

Matilda pushed out of her chair and bear hugged the little man until he had to push away to get a breath. "Let's get ready for trial."

"Now, there is one very important thing," Bailey said. "I need the originals of these in court."

Vertise sighed, and her smile turned into a frown. "We have a problem there. We can't just drive this treaty down the mountain. Our men have guns, but the Chief of Detectives in St. James Parish won't let them escort the treaty with weapons."

Matilda walked over and gazed out the window, then turned. "I have an idea. It may or may not work, but it's worth a try."

CHAPTER 64

It was late the same afternoon when Matilda parked in her usual spot in front of the courthouse—so late that the area was virtually deserted. With no one to hear her, she saw no reason to announce her arrival. She locked her car and walked up the steps to the entrance. The security guards were still manning their post. She stopped to visit and asked about their spouses and kids before walking around the metal detector and down the hall toward Judge Lancaster's courtroom. She continued past it to a door that was marked as the judge's chambers. She entered to find Alyssa Allison, Lancaster's secretary, hunched over her computer. Alyssa was sixty-seven, gray hair in a bun, no make-up. She didn't like idle chitchat, except when it was with Matilda. Matilda made a point of befriending everyone in the courthouse who might be able to do her a favor, and that included Alyssa.

"Hey, girl, 'bout time for you to be heading home. They don't pay any overtime in this place."

When Alyssa heard Matilda's voice, her countenance softened. "Matilda, what brings you around here so late in the day? Judge has already gone home. He's probably kicked back watching a Premier League football match."

"Wasn't looking for him. I need to pick your brain about something."

"Don't have much brain left at this time of day, but pick away."

"You know about our case involving the Maroon Treaty?"

"Of course. Everyone does. It's set next week."

"Here's my problem. The original of that treaty is safely hidden up in Accompong. We must have it for trial, but the Maroons can't bring it down here without some security. We talked to Harper about letting some of the

Maroons escort it, serving as armed guards. I guess you know that they can have guns up there?"

Alyssa nodded.

"Harper said they couldn't bring their guns into town. I don't know what to do. So, I was wondering if you might talk to the judge about alternative ways we can protect the treaty."

Alyssa leaned back and scratched the top of her head. "Let me think about it, and I'll let you know."

The next morning Harper was having his second cup of coffee at home before heading to work when his phone rang.

"Miles, Judge Lancaster here."

"Morning, Judge."

"About this Maroon Treaty trial, the Maroons can't make a case without it in court. I understand your decision not to allow the Maroons to bring their guns down from the mountains."

"Yes, sir."

"So, here's what I want. Trial starts next Monday morning. I want you to send four police cars and eight officers up to Accompong at the crack of dawn. They will be tasked with the responsibility of securing that treaty on its way down the mountain and taking it back up at the end of the trial."

"Wait a minute, Your Honor. That's a big chunk of our force."

"I understand. They'll only be out of the area for a few hours. Once the treaty gets to the courthouse, the guards here will take over. One more thing. I want your police cars with lights flashing and sirens blasting."

Harper gulped the last of his coffee and said, "Is that an order, Judge?"

"Damn right. I just said it, didn't I?"

***

Back in Kingston, Thomas and Henderson had again been summoned to Pritchard's office. As was her habit, she kept them cooling their heels in the reception area for nearly an hour before her secretary said they could go in. Pissed that they had been kept waiting, they still maintained their composure. After all, Global was one of their biggest clients. "Good afternoon, Ms. Pritchard," Henderson said. "How were things in the United States?"

"We're not here to talk about the United States. I understand that while I was gone Colonel Broderick met with a most unfortunate accident."

Thomas and Henderson looked at each other and back at Pritchard. "I don't think anyone could characterize it as an accident," Thomas said. "Broderick was killed by a sniper. One shot through the windshield to the head."

Pritchard lit a cigarette and exhaled smoke across the desk. "Well, maybe my choice of words was not the best. Where I'm going is this. How can they have a case anymore? Their key witness, the custodian of the treaty, is dead."

Henderson held up his hand like he was a traffic cop, signaling a stop. "Not that simple, I'm afraid. They have substituted Vertise Broderick as named party in the case. They say that she is now the custodian."

"She's the bitch that writes for the newspaper. I don't guess I ever paid any attention her last name. Can they just keep coming up with custodians?"

Henderson grimaced. "That's what they've been doing for three hundred years. We'll argue that doesn't authenticate the treaty, but the way Lancaster has ruled so far, we must presume he's going to let the treaty in evidence. And there's one more thing; they have a forensic documents examiner from the United States. From their designation, they must have some other papers that will assist him in validating the treaty."

"Shit. Do we have one of these experts?" Pritchard asked.

Henderson tried to control his voice. "No, ma'am. They only had to designate witnesses on this shortened trial schedule two days ago. We didn't see him coming. Now it's too late for us to add to our witness list."

Pritchard rose, her face a thunderstorm of anger. "I certainly can't depend on you to get the job done. We have a few days before trial. I think it's time I invite Chief Justice Cunningham to dinner."

"Beg your pardon, Ms. Pritchard. I would strongly urge you not to discuss this trial with him."

"Don't worry, Mr. Henderson. I just want him to know I'm in Jamaica, working on getting our new mine up and running. I won't even mention the trial."

***

On the Sunday afternoon before trial, Will, Vertise, and Matilda were sitting beside the pond behind her house. "Matilda, I still don't know how you managed to get a police escort for the treaty," Will said.

Matilda laughed. "I've been building friendships at that courthouse for about thirty years. Occasionally I ask for a favor and hardly ever get turned down."

"Vertise and I will drive up to Accompong early in the morning in my

243

Suburban. It will be the official treaty and associated documents vehicle."

"And every vehicle in Accompong that runs will be filled with Maroons, trailing us down the mountain and to the courthouse," Vertise added. "We want everyone around there to get the impression this is a really big deal. I've already written a story about the trial and the Maroons battle with Global. It'll run in tomorrow's paper."

"No harm in trying to brainwash a couple of prospective jurors in advance, is there Mr. Taylor?"

"Not where I come from, anyway, and I don't recall the judge issuing any gag orders."

CHAPTER 65

Will had found a men's shop and was fitted for a new suit just for this occasion. He donned it in his hotel room along with a blue military striped tie. He used a towel to dust off the one pair of dress shoes he brought to Jamaica. After checking himself out in the full-length mirror in the bathroom, he called the valet.

Fifteen minutes later he was pulling to a stop in front of Vertise's condo. Before he could even turn off the engine, she was walking down the sidewalk. "This isn't a date, so those rules don't apply."

"Nice looking black dress," Will said as she buckled her seat belt. "And that string of pearls around your neck adds just the right touch. You'll make a formidable witness."

At six o'clock they approached Accompong. Someone had already opened the town gate. Will backed into the space in front of the Cudjoe Monument and kept his lights on. Maroons started drifting out of their houses, some with coffee mugs. A friend of Vertise's brought two black coffees for her and Will. All of them were dressed in their finest Sunday clothes. The excitement in the air was palpable. Maybe, at last, their claim to the Cockpit Country would be validated. Vertise turned to Will. "Come on, we have to go to the Peace Cave. It's time." She turned on a flashlight. Will followed her along the trail to the cave. He held the flashlight while she removed stones until the treaty case and the metal box were revealed. She handed them to Will, and she took the flashlight. "Stick close to me. I don't want you tripping and dropping the case."

At seven, a boy standing by the gate said, "I see headlights of three—no, four cars coming up the mountain. A minute later, the four cop cars turned through the gate and stopped in front of Will's Suburban. Vertise knew the driver of the first car and walked to him. "Watson, you in charge of this detail today?"

"I guess so. That's why I'm in the lead."

"Look, I don't expect trouble, but we've seen our share ever since Global came onto the scene."

"I'm sorry about the loss of your father, Vertise. I think he spent his life just trying to do what was right."

"I appreciate that. This is Will Taylor. Going down the mountain, we'd like two of your cars in front of the Suburban and two behind it. The rest of the Maroons will be following in their vehicles. Were you told that you are to have your lights flashing and siren blasting?"

"Vertise, you really think that's necessary?"

"Yeah, I do. But, tell you what, don't turn them on until we make that last turn off this road and are on the North Highway. That should wake everyone up within five miles. And don't turn them off until we stop in front of the courthouse. Clear?"

Watson turned to talk to his men, and they headed back to their cars. Two drove out the gate and two waited for Will's Suburban, then followed. The Maroons piled into old pickups and sedans. While they had been washed and polished for the occasion, their clean exteriors didn't hide the fact that they were all at least ten years old. Well, except for Lawrence's. Apparently, the ganja business was good enough that he had a two-year-old Camaro.

The procession was quite the event. Counting the cop cars, there were at least twenty-five vehicles winding down the mountain with headlights on. When they reached the bottom of the mountain, dawn was breaking.

"Right around this next bend is where the cops are to turn on their lights and sirens," Vertise said. And it happened. Blue and red lights started flashing, and sirens sounded to their front and back. When the Maroons saw the cop cars, they started laying on their horns. Hearing the noise, people began to step out their doors to watch as the parade went by. Most had never seen anything like it and talked among themselves about what was happening. Children ran to the edge of the street and waved. Watson slowed at red lights and stop signs, but once satisfied there was no cross traffic, the signals were ignored. When the Maroons saw what was happening, they followed suit, laughing and cheering as they went.

A crowd was already beginning to assemble at the courthouse. The trial was big news, and with Matilda representing the plaintiffs, everyone wanted a front row seat. When Judge Lancaster heard about the size of the crowd, he asked Joshua to set up speakers in front of the courthouse so the overflow could at least hear how the trial was going. The crowd began to hear sirens several blocks away that grew louder quickly. Two blocks up the street, Watson's car turned the corner, followed by the rest of the cop cars, Will's Suburban—now with his safety flashers activated—and the Maroons. The cops and Will stopped in front of the courthouse where Matilda awaited them. The cops jumped out and faced away from the Suburban, looking for any sign of trouble. On Watson's signal, Vertise and Will stepped out with the treaty and the box. A courthouse guard unlocked the door and locked it behind them. Watson and one other officer escorted them through the front door of the courthouse and down the hall to Judge Lancaster's courtroom. Once there, Watson said, "I understand this is as far as we are to go. Good luck, Vertise."

"Thanks. You guys were perfect. Yeah, we'll take it from here."

Joshua approached their table. "My job is to make sure that nothing happens to your documents. I suppose everything will be all right while court is in session. I brought a cot from home and will be spending the nights in the courtroom with the door locked. My wife will bring my dinner and the judge is letting me use his bathroom to shower. If you're ready, I'll go to the room next door and see if jury panel is there. If they are, I'll bring them in. They'll occupy the first two rows."

"Josh, maybe you ought to wait for the Global lawyers before you do that," Matilda said. Josh grinned sheepishly and nodded his agreement.

"And I'll go out front and look for Dr. Bailey. Maybe I can get him in here ahead of the crowd," Will said. He walked to the security point and found Bailey, chatting with the guards. He was dressed in the same outfit that he wore on the plane, only freshly cleaned at the hotel. "Deputies, this is Dr. Randolph Bailey. He's with Ms. Massengale. Can I take him on back to the courtroom?"

Massengale was obviously the magic word. The guard motioned Bailey around the metal detector. "Interesting. They were just telling me that the treaty was brought down from the mountain with a police escort, lights flashing, sirens on. You have anything to do with that?"

"Not me," Will said. "Only I have it from a reliable source that someone on our team arranged it."

Bailey nodded. "Remarkable woman, that Ms. Massengale."

As they walked down the corridor, they heard a loud voice behind them. "Damn you, Will Taylor, I'll have your ass disbarred when you get back to the States."

Will glanced back. "And a cheery good morning to you, too, Alexa. Oh, and enjoy the day. It may be the last one you can enjoy for quite a while."

Will opened the courtroom door and stepped back with a flourish of his hand. "After you, Alexa."

She glared at him as she rushed past, trailed by Thomas and Henderson and a paralegal. Once the lawyers had unpacked their briefcases, Henderson walked over to Matilda. "Good morning, Counselor."

"Morning, Michael."

Henderson was gazing at the treaty in its case. "Can I have a look? Is this really the original?"

"Look, but don't touch. And we'll prove it's the original."

Hearing the conversation, Thomas walked over. Henderson took his glasses from his chest and positioned them on his nose. He studied the treaty. "If you prove it's the original, it's very remarkable that the Maroons have been able to preserve it in such good condition for all these years."

They were interrupted by the bailiff, who entered from the hallway. "All rise for the jury panel."

Thomas and Henderson scurried back to their table so as not to be seen fraternizing with the enemy. The bailiff directed twenty-four people of all ages, genders, shapes, and sizes to certain seats on the first two rows. Nearly all were black with two Anglos and one possibly Hispanic. Matilda thought they were a reasonable cross-section of the population of the island. Joshua then handed the lawyers copies of juror information cards that gave basic information on each: name, address, marital status, occupation, age, etc.

Next, Gamboa opened the door and allowed the audience to enter. The Maroons were scattered throughout the audience. Several reporters stood in the back and along the side walls. Both *The New York Times* and *The Washington Post* sent representatives to Jamaica for the trial.

Will whispered to Matilda. "How are juries selected here?"

Matilda turned to face him and in a low voice answered. "Here's the *Cliff Notes* version. Lancaster graduated from law school in Florida and was a trial lawyer there for several years before he returned to Jamaica. He liked how the

American judicial system worked and has adopted much of it. He has his own method that you won't find in our rules of procedure. Still it's fair and no one has ever complained to the Supreme Court about it. In a civil trial, we'll have a jury of eight. Each side gets four peremptory challenges. That leaves eight that can be challenged for cause. The judge will be lenient on challenges for cause at first, but if he sees we're close to busting the panel, he'll toughen up and not let any more off. I don't think he's ever permitted enough challenges that he had to get a second panel. Waste of time and taxpayer money, he says at seminars."

She took a yellow marker from her briefcase and started skimming through the cards. She paused a few times to highlight something that a panelist had written. When she finished, she whispered to Will, "Not a bad panel. I know a couple of them, but they won't say we're friends. There are a couple of businessmen and one Global employee that works over at Discovery Bay. He'll be gone early."

The bailiff looked at the jury and then the lawyers. "Everyone ready?"

Getting nods from the lawyers, he knocked on the door to the judge's chambers. Momentarily, Lancaster threw open the door and walked to his bench. "All rise," Gamboa said. When the judge took the bench, he stood while the bailiff announced, "This court is now in session, the Honorable William Lancaster presiding. God save Queen Elizabeth and this Honorable Court."

"Be seated, ladies and gentlemen," he said and then read the style of the case. "I'll call for announcements from the lawyers.

"Plaintiff is ready," Matilda boomed.

"Defendant Global is ready," Henderson replied.

The judge looked at the jury. "Thank you for coming this morning. Your service to our judicial system is very much appreciated by me and by the parties to this lawsuit and their lawyers. You will be pleased to know that I move my cases along quite rapidly. You can rest assured that this case will be over by the end of the week. I'm going to give each side thirty minutes to ask you some questions, a process known as voir dire."

Matilda rose, "Excuse me, Your Honor, I think thirty minutes will not be enough for me to do a thorough questioning of the panel. Could we make if forty-five?"

Lancaster looked over his glasses at Matilda and with sternness in his voice said, "Ms. Massengale, you've been in my court many times. You are fortunate that I'm not limiting you to twenty minutes."

Matilda nodded and returned to her seat.

Lancaster shifted his gaze back to the jury panel. "And one more thing. Most of you have read or heard about this case. It's going to involve the validity or invalidity of the Maroon Treaty of nearly three hundred years ago. You probably learned something about it in a history class. I want you to forget anything you may have heard outside of this courtroom and decide the questions asked based on what you hear and see in this room. Is there anyone that cannot do that?"

Silence from the panel. Several nodded their heads in agreement.

"Ms. Massengale, you may begin."

Matilda walked to the small podium that Joshua had placed in front of the jury, smiled, and began. "I'm Matilda Massengale, a lawyer practicing here in Montego Bay for longer than I care to say. I'm proud to be representing the Maroon Nation."

"Objection, Judge. The Maroon tribe is not a nation," Henderson said.

"Overruled. I understand the evidence will be that the British signed a treaty with them three hundred years ago. I think that will create a fact question as to whether they have nation status or not. For purposes of this trial, Ms. Massengale, you may refer to the Maroons as a nation."

Matilda smiled as she turned back to the jury, particularly pleased that she did not even have to say anything to obtain the judge's very favorable ruling so early in the case. Little things like whether to call the Maroons a nation or tribe could weigh heavily when deliberations began.

"Like most of us in this courtroom and on this island, the Maroons were descendants of slaves that were brought here to work on the sugar plantations."

Nearly every member of the jury panel nodded their agreement, causing Pritchard to whisper to her lawyers. "Do we have a prayer of getting a fair trial on this island?"

Thomas shook his head and motioned that he would discuss her question later.

"Only the Maroons refused to remain slaves. One by one, over many years, they escaped up into the mountains. On this end of the island, we know it as the Cockpit Country. Once they had a sufficient number, they started fighting for their freedom, first with the Spaniards and later with the British."

Thomas rose. "Objection, Your Honor. This is not the time to be making closing argument."

"Sustained. Move on, Ms. Massengale."

"Thank you, Your Honor," Matilda said, pretending that the judge had just made another great ruling in her favor. "Then, I'll jump to 1739, nearly three hundred years ago when the treaty in question was signed, ending the fighting and declaring the Maroon Nation's right to the Cockpit Country. Your Honor, I expect to prove the authenticity of the treaty. May I display it briefly to the jury panel?"

Henderson started to object, but the judge motioned him to sit down. "Briefly, Ms. Massengale."

Will handed the treaty to Matilda. She turned and slowly walked up and down in front of the panel. Several on the second row, stood to get a better look at the document.

"The judge is not going to let me tell you about the reason we're suing Global American Metals during voir dire, only that it involves this treaty. Before I go any farther, let me introduce Vertise Broderick. Vertise, stand up, please." Vertise stood and smiled at the jury. "Ms. Broderick is the current custodian of the treaty and will testify. Beside her at counsel table is Dr. Randolph Bailey, a forensic document examiner from Colorado. Last, I'd like to introduce Mr. William Taylor. He's a lawyer, licensed in Virginia. Our rules don't permit him to take an active role in the trial, but he's here to assist me as needed."

Matilda next began asking individual questions to each of the panel members. She was able to challenge for cause the man who worked for Global and two men who were in the banking business and believed that Global was a good corporate citizen, important to the economic development of the country and one woman who had been broadsided by Lawrence as he sped through an intersection, ignoring a stop sign. She looked once more through her notes and jury cards and said, "Thank you, ladies and gentlemen. That's all from the plaintiff, Your Honor."

Henderson moved to the podium. He gazed over the jury panel in silence for at least a minute. As a seasoned trial lawyer himself, he wanted the jury to be wondering how he would respond. He began. "I also am a descendant of slaves that worked on a sugar plantation. Those slave years were a dark time for this island and for all of the islands in the Caribbean as well as the United States. Fortunately, those times are in the past. Was there a treaty signed by the Maroons and some British officer? That's for Ms. Massengale to prove.

"What we will establish is this: Jamaica separated from the British

Commonwealth in 1962 and became, for the first time, a nation state. From that date until now, if there was a treaty with the Maroons, it has never been ratified by our government."

The statement caused puzzled looks to appear on several of the jurors.

Vertise elbowed Matilda and whispered, "Is that going to be a problem?"

Henderson noted the jurors and continued. "I represent Global American Metals, the defendant. Most of you probably know about Global. It's been on this island for many years, almost back to the beginning of our country. Alexa Pritchard is Global's president. Ms. Pritchard, would you stand?"

Pritchard stood and smiled at the jury.

"Global mines and exports bauxite from locations around the island. Bauxite is one of our most common metals. Estimates are that we will be able to mine it for at least another one hundred years. Global has created thousands of jobs for our citizens and paid more taxes than probably any other corporation in our country."

"Now, Judge," Matilda rose and said, "It's my turn to request that Mr. Henderson save argument for a later time and ask the jury some questions."

"Agree, Ms. Massengale. Move on, Mr. Henderson."

Henderson methodically talked to each juror and after his thirty minutes, he had disqualified two who had been represented by Matilda in other matters, one who had an uncle who was a Maroon, and one woman who was a dedicated environmentalist and said she would do anything to save the rainforest.

"Ladies and gentlemen, you can take a break, stretch your legs, stand outside and enjoy this beautiful sunshine we have been blessed with today," Judge Lancaster said. "The lawyers will have fifteen minutes to make their strikes. Ms. Massengale, you may use the jury room. Mr. Henderson and Mr. Thomas, you may use the reception area outside of my chambers. I'll ask Joshua to have Alyssa step out for a cup of coffee. You are excused."

In the reception area, Henderson had barely closed the door when Pritchard exclaimed, "Do we really have a chance on that failure to ratify argument?"

Both lawyers nodded. "It's untested, but a viable argument. We also have Dr. Branbury. Doesn't matter what Judge Lancaster does, the Supreme Court will make the final decision."

"Hell, that shouldn't be a problem. The Chief Justice owns stock in Global. I always try to tip him off when there's something big that's going to affect the price."

"I didn't hear that, Alexa," Henderson said. "If that got out, he would have to disqualify himself."

"Then, I'll just have a little chat with him and suggest that there are some good reasons for him to put his Global stock in a blind trust for a while. Let's get this trial over and go on appeal."

"Not so fast, Alexa," Thomas said. "They still have to prove that the treaty is real. I'll have plenty of opportunities to knock some holes in that argument. Appeal is only if we lose."

In the jury room Vertise had a frown on her face. "That's the first time I've heard about that ratification argument. Why didn't we see it coming?"

"Darling, I knew it was out there," Matilda said. "We'll deal with it on another day. We have a jury trial to win."

"But, Alexa says Cunningham is her friend."

"Honey, Cunningham has lots of friends. I've been appearing with him on legal education panels for twenty years, even before he became a justice on the Supreme Court. He and I also serve on the Jamaican Olympic Committee. We're on a first name basis with Usain. I'll find a way to take his pulse in due time."

Vertise folded her arms. "I'm still going to be worried until this son of a bitch is finally over."

While they were talking, Matilda struck four jurors. "I don't need any advice on these. I probably just could have taken the first eight and saved time. Let's get back out there so the judge knows he's not waiting on us."

CHAPTER 66

"Ms. Massengale, you may give your opening statement. Please make it brief."

Matilda turned, walked to the jury, and paced up and down in front of them three times, her head down, her arms clasped behind her back. She paused in the middle and looked each one in the eye. "This is an important case, probably one of the very most important tried in this courthouse. We will prove that the Maroons own 150,000 acres in the Cockpit Country and have for nearly three hundred years. They have lived quietly and peacefully all that time. They have never been rich, but they have something more. They have been happy, blessed with long, healthy lives because their bush doctors knew that their forest had plants with medicinal properties. That changed when Global and this woman trespassed on the Maroons' land." She paused to point at Pritchard. "They took core samples and began stripping the trees from the land just over the hill from the monument to Cudjoe. They never asked permission of the Maroons. They ignored the treaty. Mr. Henderson wants us to prove the treaty is legitimate. We will do so, and once you so find, we will ask for an order barring anyone from using the Maroons' land for any commercial purpose without their express permission." Matilda nodded to the jury and returned to her seat.

Thomas rose to face the jury. "Like it has done with mines in Jamaica several times over the years, Global went through the proper channels. It completed the necessary paperwork, a lot of red tape I might add, and requested a permit for the mine in the Cockpit Country. It even published notice in the *Kingston Gleaner*. No one objected and the minister of mines at the time approved it, never once suggesting that Ms. Pritchard had to have the permission of the Maroon tribe."

"Objection, it is the Maroon Nation, not a tribe."

"That's correct, Mr. Thomas, please follow my ruling."

"Regardless of whether they are a tribe or a nation, they claim ownership of the land by way of that so-called treaty. I invite them to try to establish it has existed without alteration for three hundred years. If they do, we will contest that it is currently enforceable. I should also point out that our permit is only for the minerals. We have, and accept, the duty to restore the forest when the mining is complete. In the interim, we will provide hundreds of jobs and pay taxes to build new schools and hospitals, just as we have done with our mines in other places around our country. You see, my partner and I love our country. Like you, we do not want it harmed in any way. You have my word that will not happen."

"Call your first witness, Ms. Massengale."

"Plaintiff calls Vertise Broderick."

"Ms. Broderick, please approach the bench to be sworn and then take a seat in the witness box."

"You are Vertise Broderick."

"Yes, ma'am."

"You write for the newspaper here?"

"I do."

"Are you a Maroon?"

"I was born in the Cockpit Country and will always be a Maroon, although I was educated in the states and spent several years there as a writer. Now I live in Montego Bay."

"That brings up an interesting question. Are Maroons different from other Jamaicans? I mean, are you different from these jurors or from Judge Lancaster or, for that matter, from me?"

Vertise straightened in her chair and turned to face the jury. "Our flesh and bones are the same. It is our heritage and culture that makes us different. We are descended from people who yearned for freedom so fiercely that they were willing to fight and die for it. We continue in that belief today."

Several jurors nodded their understanding.

"Do you have some official capacity with the Maroon Nation?"

"I recently became the custodian of the treaty and related documents. My father, Colonel Rafael Broderick, had been the custodian for many years. Sadly, he was killed just a couple of weeks ago when he was on his way from Accompong to have lunch with me. As was our custom, some time ago he had drafted a letter, appointing me as custodian in the event of his death."

"Do you have any other official capacity with the Maroons?"

"Our nation is a democracy. After this trial, there will be an election for a new leader to take my father's place. I intend to run for that position."

Matilda rose and walked to the witness box and carefully placed the treaty in its case on the shelf in front of Vertise. "Can you identify this for the jury?"

"Of course. This is the original treaty signed by Cudjoe."

Thomas rose. "Your Honor, we object to any testimony about this treaty until it is properly authenticated."

"No need for the objection, Judge. We will do exactly that. Ms. Broderick, do you know the history of the Maroons and the treaty?"

Vertise turned to face the jury. "Certainly. As you alluded to in your voir dire, the Maroons were brought here as slaves to work on sugar plantations. They had been free in Africa and wanted freedom once more. Over time, groups of them disappeared into the mountain jungles. They formed villages, hunted, fished, and raised crops. They also harvested wild berries, nuts, bananas, and other fruit from the forest. I'm not sure who started the fighting. I suspect that the Spaniards chased some of the escaped slaves up into the mountains where they were ambushed by the Maroons. Soon the Maroons were mounting guerilla attacks against Spanish troops. They would swoop down from the mountains, strike suddenly, and just as suddenly would be back up to the safety of the Cockpit Country. They fought the Spaniards for about a hundred and fifty years until the Brits took over the island. The British forces continued to try to destroy the Maroons. After about eighty years they gave up and proposed a treaty that would give them the flat lands close to the ocean, which is all they really wanted, and deeded the Cockpit Country to the Maroons. That treaty was signed and has never been violated, until Ms. Pritchard came along."

The jury was captivated. Vertise was telling them the story, under oath, that they had heard about most of their lives.

"Ms. Broderick, how do we know this is the original of the treaty?"

Vertise glanced at the counsel table. "Can you hand me that metal box?"

Will took the box and walked the few steps to the witness. "This box has a memo from Cudjoe and letters from each of the custodians from the time of his death up to when I was so designated by my father. It also has four documents, signed by Cudjoe, that are promoting Maroons to higher rank. His X is on each of them."

Vertise opened the box and carefully retrieved Cudjoe's memo, the eight letters, and four memos of promotion.

"This is Cudjoe's memo, dictated to Nanny the day after the treaty was signed."

One of the men on the front row reached for his wallet and pulled out a $500 bill, confirmed that Nanny was the portrait on it, nodded, smiled and put his wallet away.

"Then we have eight letters from eight custodians confirming that they received the documents in good order from the previous custodian and kept them in a secure place until the next custodian assumed the responsibility. The last is a letter from my father to me, appointing me as custodian in the event something happened to him. Perhaps he had a premonition. Next are the four memos of promotion."

Matilda took exhibit stickers and said, "With the permission of the court, I'm going to place the exhibit stickers on the back of these documents so as not to do any unnecessary harm to them."

"That's acceptable, Ms. Massengale."

"Then, Your Honor, Exhibit One is the Maroon Treaty, Exhibit Two is the Cudjoe memo, and Exhibits Three through Ten are the custodial letters. Exhibit eleven is the letter from Colonel Broderick. Exhibits twelve through fifteen are the promotion memos. We offer them into evidence, subject to some additional proof to come from Dr. Bailey."

Thomas rose quickly, his voice raised. "Objection, my most strenuous objection, Judge Lancaster. These are nothing more than rank hearsay and should not be considered for any purpose."

"Judge," Matilda said in a very calm but forceful voice, "perhaps Mr. Thomas should read up on his hearsay exceptions. These are admissible as ancient documents under Rule 16 and under Rule 20 as evidence concerning boundaries or general history."

The judge raised his hand. "Hold on. Let me read my rules of evidence." He flipped through a book on his bench until he came to the appropriate section and read very slowly, trying to absorb every word. He closed the book and looked at Matilda. "Mr. Thomas, your objections are noted but overruled.

Plaintiff's Exhibits One through Fifteen are admitted. Of course, I want to hear what Dr. Bailey has to say."

"Your Honor, while I proceed, may I have Mr. Taylor pass the treaty along with the Cudjoe memo, which I have put in a plastic sleeve, among the jury for their inspection."

"You may."

Will walked to the jury box and handed the documents one at a time to the eight jurors, each studied them and handed them back to Will before he repeated the process with the next juror.

"Ms. Broderick," Matilda continued, "Why are you bringing this lawsuit?"

Vertise composed herself and again turned to the jury. "Several reasons. First, Global has trespassed on our land. Next, they are going to destroy a substantial part of our rainforest. Then, their pollution will run into the five rivers whose watersheds are in the Cockpit Country, endangering the water supply to everyone on the western end of our island." Her eyes turned hard as she looked at Alexa Pritchard. "Last, it's just wrong. Might does not make right. Someone must stand up to these giant multi-national corporations who are destroying rainforests around the world. We Maroons have fought for our country once before. We are doing it again."

As she finished, Will retrieved the exhibits from the last juror and returned them to counsel table.

"Pass the witness, Judge."

"Mr. Thomas, you may cross-examine."

Thomas rose, buttoned his coat, and took a sip of water from a small cup in front of him. Clearing his voice with a slight cough, he walked to the table where the exhibits were. "Ms. Broderick, I only see eight custodial letters. Are you telling this jury that in three hundred years none are missing? Each custodian must average about thirty-five or forty years. That just can't be, can it?"

Vertise smiled. "You just don't understand, Mr. Thomas. Our people live long lives. We eat lean meat, fish, vegetables and fruits and nuts from the forest. Then we have bush doctors that know which herbs and roots and such will help us fend off illnesses. It's nothing to see our people reach a hundred. My father was eighty and probably would have lived to be a hundred if he had not been killed by a sniper. So, forty years or so is about right. You can read each of the letters and see that there is no break in the custodial care."

Thomas saw Henderson motioning to him and he returned to a whispered conference with his partner before walking back to the podium. "Ms. Broderick, you've been talking about history. I'm sure you know that Jamaica became an independent country in 1962."

"Objection, Judge, relevance," Matilda said.

"I'll give him a little leeway to see where he goes. Proceed, Mr. Thomas."

"Yes, sir. I studied about our independence in school."

"Here's the important question. Since that time has anyone, on behalf of the Maroons, petitioned the Jamaican government to ratify this so-called treaty you claim gave you the rights to all of this land?"

Vertise frowned only slightly. "No, sir. Not to my knowledge. No one thought it was necessary."

"Then, last thing, Ms. Broderick. Let me hand you the treaty. You see where it says that the Maroons have the right to 1,500 acres. Do you see anywhere that you have title to 150,000 acres?"

Vertise regained her composure. "Sir, I think that is resolved by Captain Cudjoe's memo, dictated to Nanny, where he explains that he could not read the document but was told it said the Maroons would have title to and dominion over the Cockpit Country as far as the eye could see from the Peace Cave up to 150,000 acres. Now, I don't know that anyone has ever surveyed that land. It would be hard to do because it is a land of mountains and valleys and overgrown with rainforest and jungle, but it's certainly far more than a mere 1,500 acres. I might add that Cudjoe's reputation was that of a fearless warrior and a totally honest man. He would not have dictated that memo the day after signing the treaty if he did not believe it to be the truth."

"Objection to the last statement about Cudjoe, Judge, as being non-responsive."

"Sustained. The jury will be instructed to disregard."

That brought a smile from Will who knew that the jury would no more disregard the comment than they would look to the west for the sun to rise tomorrow.

The judge glanced at his watch and at the jury. "Ms. Massengale, what do you have, one or two more witnesses?"

"Yes, sir. No more than two."

"Mr. Thomas, anyone besides Ms. Pritchard?"

"Not right now, judge." He glanced at Henderson who slightly shook his head at his partner. Thomas got the message not to disclose Branbury yet. "Maybe a rebuttal witness. We'll confer tonight."

259

"Excellent. Then, we'll quit a little early today. Please do not discuss this case with anyone, even your family. If you are watching the news tonight and this case is mentioned, you must turn the television off. Understood?"

The jurors nodded.

"Have a nice evening. Bailiff, please take charge of the exhibits."

Matilda, Will, Vertise, and Dr. Bailey waited for the jury and audience to clear the courthouse and walked to Matilda's car with Will's Suburban conveniently parked behind it in the NO PARKING zone. Dr. Bailey joined Matilda while Will and Vertise followed them up the hill to her house. Once inside, Will served drinks before they adjourned out to the table by the pond.

"Okay," Matilda said, "Assessment of the first day. Will, you go first."

"Good day. The jury paid attention. They were fascinated by the exhibits, particularly the treaty. It's a little like a jury in my country getting to see the Declaration of Independence up close and personal. By the way, Randy, you might look for an excuse to point out that the Declaration was drafted with a quill and is close to the same age as the treaty and is still in good shape."

Bailey nodded.

"Vertise, I thought you did quite well as a witness."

"Let me add," Dr. Bailey said, "I find this fascinating. I never thought my career would lead me to Jamaica to authenticate a three-hundred-year-old treaty. I'm having so much fun I may cut my fee."

"I have an idea," Will said. "Let's call Miles Harper as a witness."

Matilda didn't try to hide a confused look that popped onto her face. "And for what, may I ask?"

"He told me once a while back that he could not allow his department to set foot in the Cockpit Country because of the treaty. The only time he has jurisdiction is if there has been a murder."

"I don't guess I knew that," Matilda replied. "You sure?"

"I am. Do we need to subpoena him?"

"I left my cell inside. Let me step into the house and give him a call. He'll talk to me if he's there. If he confirms what you just said, I'll ask him to be the first witness in the morning."

Matilda excused herself and returned in fifteen minutes. "He's coming. He'll go on first, followed by Dr. Bailey." She raised her glass to Will. "Good idea, co-counsel."

CHAPTER 67

When Matilda and her team entered the courtroom the next morning, they found Miles Harper seated alone on the back row, dressed in a brown suit, yellow shirt, and green checked tie. He had freshly shaved his bald head. He stood when they entered. "Morning, everyone. I don't know this gentleman."

"Thanks for coming without a subpoena, Miles," Matilda said. "This is Dr. Bailey. He'll testify after you. I intend to make your time on the stand very brief. You might as well take a seat on the other side of the bar. This space for the audience will be packed in about ten minutes."

Not being from Montego Bay or St. James Parish, Thomas and Henderson did not know the man seated behind the plaintiff table. Henderson walked over to Matilda. "May I inquire as to who this gentleman behind you is?"

"He's Chief of Detectives Miles Harper of St. James Parish. He'll be our first witness. Shouldn't take very long."

"I don't recall that he's on your witness list."

Matilda shook her head. "He's there. Let me show you." She pulled her witness list from a stack of papers. "Right here. Miles Harper. Expected to testify about matters pertaining to Parish procedures."

Henderson nodded and realized that he had no objection. That was one of the risks of agreeing to an early trial with no discovery. He nodded and walked back to his table where he engaged in a whispered conversation with Thomas and his client.

"Introduce yourself to the jury, please," Matilda said.

"My name is Miles Harper."

Several of the jurors recognized either him or his name.

"How are you employed?"

"I'm Chief of Detectives of St. James Parish and have been for fifteen years. I'm the head of law enforcement in this area."

"Chief, does that parish extend into the mountains, the Cockpit Country, and even to Accompong?"

"It does."

"Chief, I'm going to make this brief. Does your department investigate crimes in the Maroon Nation?"

Harper turned in his swivel chair to the jury. "We are only authorized to investigate the crime of murder. All other potentially criminal acts are handled by the Maroon Council and their designees."

Matilda could tell that the jury was puzzled. She was about to enlighten them. "Can you explain?"

"I've been a cop in this parish for thirty years. We were taught as rookies that Jamaica has a treaty with the Maroons that has been in force since sometime in the 1700s. Under the terms of that treaty, the Maroons are a sovereign nation, as designated by King George, I believe it was the second. We were told to respect that treaty and we do to this day."

Matilda looked at Will who nodded. "Pass the witness, Judge."

Thomas walked to the podium to address the witness. "Chief Harper, I'm Paul Thomas. I represent Global American Metals."

"Yes, sir."

"Have you ever had dealings with Global in your professional capacity?"

Harper searched his memory. "I think I've approved some permits for their guards to carry guns at their facilities. Oh, and we were called in to lend assistance with the investigation of that locomotive that was bombed over at Discovery Bay. The chief over there was shorthanded; so, we helped."

"Anything else?"

"Nothing that comes to mind."

"Chief Harper, would it be fair to say that Global has been a good corporate citizen during your time on the force?"

Harper raised his eyebrows. "I suppose that's fair."

"As to the Cockpit Country, where did you get the idea that you could not investigate crimes up there?"

Harper crossed his legs. "I'm not sure. It's just what we were taught."

"Have you ever read the treaty in question?"

"No reason to, Mr. Thomas. We've got enough crime down here. I don't need to be going up there, looking for more to do which, I might add, would only make my already over-worked officers put in more hours. I'm okay with the arrangement."

Thomas looked at Henderson who indicated he should cut it off. "That's all, Judge."

"Tell the jury your name and where you're from, please, sir," Matilda said.

Dressed in the same suit and bow tie as before, only now with a clean white shirt, the witness said, "I'm Dr. Randolph Bailey. I'm a scientist and forensic document examiner. I live in Colorado."

Thomas glanced at his witness list and noted that Bailey was there as an expert in ancient documents. He knew he should expect some harsh criticism from Alexa Pritchard since he and Henderson did not have anyone to rebut Bailey's testimony. He could only hope that Archibald Branbury would carry the day.

"Tell the jury a little about your training to be a forensic document examiner," Matilda said.

Bailey had been on the witness stand many times over the past thirty years and knew how to captivate a jury, whether in the United States, Jamaica, or many other countries where he had been called to examine and explain documents. He understood the importance of body language; so, he put both feet flat on the floor and rested his arms on the arms of the chair. His message was that he was an open book with nothing to hide.

"I have an undergraduate degree from the University of Colorado and a doctorate in Forensic Science from George Washington University. I worked in the FBI lab for ten years as a document examiner. I'm accredited by the Forensic Specialties Board and have been Chairman of that board. I have been in private practice for the past thirty years. I've examined documents in, I believe, thirty-eight states and fourteen countries. This is the first time I have been called to Jamaica, and I'm honored to be in your country."

The last statement brought smiles and nods from several of the jurors.

"With your expertise, can you assist the jury in deciding if this Maroon Treaty is the original?"

"I believe I can. May I take the treaty and the other documents to that little table we set up in front of the jury box?"

The judge nodded his approval. Bailey very carefully lifted the case with the treaty and placed it on the table, then did the same with the other exhibits. Next, he placed the treaty on one end of the jury rail so that it could be seen by the jurors, taking care to make sure it did not fall.

"First, I can tell you that this document was written and signed with a quill. That helps us on its age. Pens were not developed until the early 1800s. You might find it interesting to learn that the United States Declaration of Independence was written with a quill. Goose feathers were the ones primarily turned into quills. If you can see the treaty, you'll note that the body of the document is written with a quill with a slightly finer point. Then if we go to the bottom and look at Cudjoe's mark, it's done with a different quill."

"What can you tell us about Cudjoe's mark?"

Bailey held up the case so the jurors on the back row could see the bottom. "His mark is an X. Both legs of the X start at the top with a broader stroke and become narrower as he reached the bottom. I then compared that X with the other document in the sleeve that was purportedly written by a woman named Nanny the next day. The two marks are identical. Last, I was given several orders signed by Cudjoe, promoting officers in the Maroon army. Once again, the X is the same."

Matilda stepped from her table and went to stand by her expert. "Then, what conclusions did you draw as to the treaty?"

Bailey turned to face Matilda. "Ms. Massengale, there is no doubt in my mind that the treaty is authentic and signed by Cudjoe around the time it was dated. The Maroon people have done an outstanding job in preserving these documents as part of their very important heritage."

Matilda nodded. "If you would return to your seat, Dr. Bailey, we'll pass the witness, Judge."

Henderson stared at the witness and asked one question. "Sir, you are not able to say whether this treaty is enforceable in this day and time, are you?"

Bailey shook his head. "Not my expertise. I can only tell you that it is the authentic original document."

"With that, Your Honor, Plaintiff rests," Matilda said.

After a morning break, Thomas called Pritchard to the stand. He suspected she might not be well received; so, he moved rapidly. He established that she had spent her entire career with Global, that Global had been mining bauxite on the island for more than forty years, that it had paid tens of millions of dollars in fees and taxes. As to the Cockpit Country mine, it went through all the permitting with the ministry of mines just like it had always done and was shocked to find that the Maroons claimed to own the land. Last, she was happy to be here in court just to clear up the title to her company's mine. She tried to be a pleasant person on the stand, but Matilda could tell that the jury was not buying what she was selling and chose to ask her no questions.

After lunch Henderson said, "Your Honor, the Defendant calls Professor Archibald Branbury, Esquire, as its last witness."

Matilda stormed to her feet. "Your Honor, Your Honor, we must object. I know this person is not on the Global's witness list."

Henderson shook his finger at Matilda. "Madam, you very well know that we do not have to list rebuttal witnesses. May I suggest, Your Honor, that you instruct Ms. Massengale to take her seat?"

Lancaster stood at his bench to castigate both lawyers. "Ms. Massengale, you will not shout in my court. Mr. Henderson, I will not permit finger-wagging. You may both take your seats, and Mr. Henderson is correct. He does not have to list a rebuttal witness."

One of the jurors on the back row turned to his companion and whispered, "It's about damn time we had a few fireworks. I was about to take an afternoon nap."

"Your Honor, I believe that Professor Branbury is waiting in the hall."

"Bailiff," Judge Lancaster said, "Please ask Professor Branbury to join us."

When Joshua walked out, Matilda saw that Vertise's eyes were large and sweat had popped out on her upper lip. "Who is this guy?" she asked.

Matilda shook her head. "I have no idea. You don't need to worry. This isn't the first time I've had to cross a witness with no notice. I'll listen to the direct and will figure out how best to attack him when Henderson finishes."

Branbury followed Joshua down the middle aisle as every head turned in his direction. What they saw was a tall, distinguished gentleman, his skin a light shade of brown, dressed in a three-piece, vested suit. His white mustache helped to disguise a rather prominent nose. His white hair was carefully combed. He carried a small attaché case. His black shoes were shined to perfection. All in all, he was an imposing figure. He approached the bench, and without waiting to be instructed, raised his right hand to be sworn. When he took the stand, he poured a cup of water from the pitcher beside him, turned, and smiled at the jury. He received eight smiles in return.

Henderson walked to the podium. "You are Professor Archibald Branbury?"

"Yes, sir."

"Where do you live?"

"I was actually born and raised in Ocho Rios just down the road a piece, but I've lived my adult life in Kingston."

"You have an esquire after your name. Are you a lawyer?"

"I am, sir, but I haven't practiced since I was a young man. I also have a PhD. in history and have taught at the university in Kingston for nearly 30 years."

"Sir, are you familiar with the Maroon Treaty with the British?"

The witness laughed. "That, Mr. Henderson is like asking if the beach is familiar with the sea. I first read about it in high school. I found the story fascinating. I've studied the treaty, its history and impact on our country off and on for most of my career. I've even written a couple of journal articles about it, particularly as to its relevance today."

Matilda looked at the jury and was dismayed to find that they were sitting on the edge of their chairs, taking in every word from the man seated before them. She nudged Will, who could only shake his head.

Henderson walked to the table and picked up the treaty. He decided to now concede the obvious. "Professor, does this appear to be the Maroon Treaty with the British, signed in 1739?"

Branbury pulled a pair of cheaters from his coat pocket, put them on his nose and over his ears, and studied the treaty. "Appears to have the exact language that I have studied."

Henderson then took a daring tactic. "Then, we have nothing to talk about, do we? The Maroons own that land up in the Cockpit Country."

Branbury took off his glasses, held them in his hand and said, "No, sir. I disagree. They have no more right to that land than you or I. Would you like for me to explain?"

Henderson allowed a small grin to creep onto his face. "Please do."

"First, there's no doubt that in return for laying down their arms in 1739, the British deeded them some amount of land up in the Cockpit Country. Maybe it was 1,500 acres. I hear that they claim it could be 150,000 acres. Doesn't really matter, though."

"I must admit I'm confused," Henderson pretended.

"Look, there's no doubt that they owned something up there for about a hundred years. Only in 1842 the colonial government passed the Maroon Lands

Allotment Act that broke up the treaty land and gave it to individual Maroons."

"And, Professor, did that end the Maroons' claims in the Cockpit Country?'

Branbury shook his head. "Not exactly. The Maroons chose to ignore the act and the colonial government decided not to push the issue. So, the Maroons continued to treat themselves like a sovereign nation with no one claiming the right to any certain parcel of land."

Several of the jurors had puzzled looks on their faces.

"So, does that continue to this day?"

"Well, yes and no," the witness said. "As we all know, in 1962 Jamaica broke away from the Commonwealth with the permission of Queen Elizabeth and Parliament. We became a country. Wrote our own Constitution. There was no mention of the Maroons or the Maroon Treaty in the Constitution. Since the Maroon Lands Allotment Act had never been repealed, the only conclusion to be drawn is that the framers of our Constitution concluded that the treaty of 1739 would automatically be rendered null and void by the creation of the new nation of Jamaica."

Henderson's voice rose. "So, tell us your opinion as a lawyer and historian. Do the Maroons in 2017 have any right whatsoever to the original Maroon lands up in the Cockpit Country?"

Matilda pushed to her feet. "Objection, Your Honor. That's a matter for the court to decide, not the jury."

Lancaster gazed at the clock on the wall at the back of the courtroom and watched a minute tick by before he spoke. "I'll let him answer."

Bradbury's voice raised to express confidence in his opinion. "They have no such right."

The woman who was the first juror chosen on the front row shook her head. Clearly, she found satisfaction in how the Maroons had fought for and won their freedom. She clearly did not like anyone suggesting that after all these years, it was for nothing.

"Pass the witness, Judge."

Matilda marched to the podium. "Let me think about where I want to begin," she said to no-one in particular. "How about here." The jury moved another inch forward in their seats, determined to not miss a word of this exchange. "You know, do you not, that the Maroon Nation Treaty was made with the British crown, not some local government?"

"That is correct, Counselor."

"That was a solemn charter between the Maroon Nation and King George the second, agreed?"

"No doubt it was authorized by the king himself, according to the language of the treaty."

"And that Maroon Lands Allotment Act was not promulgated by the King, but some local colonial governing body. Not surprising that the Maroon Nation would not accept it?"

Branbury glanced at Henderson.

"Don't you be looking at Global's lawyers for the answer."

"Then, I don't have an answer to your question."

"Of course, you don't. And you know that the Maroons have never paid one dollar in taxes on their land to the British before 1962 or the Jamaican government after that date?"

"I understand that attempts to tax the Maroons have been made, but without success."

"That's for nearly three hundred years."

"Yes, ma'am."

The jury could see that the witness was shifting nervously from one hip to the other and starting to cross and uncross his legs, uncertain of how to now find a comfortable position in the increasingly hot seat.

"Isn't it true that up until colonial rule ended in 1962, when a new British governor was appointed, he always received a delegation from the Maroon Nation early in his administration?"

"I'm sure most did. Can't speak with certainty for every governor, going back to 1739."

"And, in turn, Professor, the colonial governors and their entourages paid ceremonial visits to the Maroon leaders for all of those years."

Branbury bit his lip. "I suppose, if you say so."

"Even after Jamaican independence, our Prime Ministers have continued to give the Maroon Nation the recognition they expect. And even to this day they make a point to be accessible to the Maroon leaders."

The witness shrunk into his seat and lowered his head. "Yes, ma'am."

"You heard from this witness stand that Colonel Broderick was shot and killed just a few weeks ago?"

"Yes, ma'am. I also read about it in the paper."

"Did you also know that the Prime Minister made a special trip from

Kingston to Accompong to attend Colonel Broderick's funeral."

"No, Ms. Massengale, I didn't hear about that."

"Were you aware that the Prime Minister stood in front of the mourners and lauded Colonel Broderick in his capacity as a head of state?"

"I was not aware of that."

"But you would agree that when he used those words, he must have been referring to Colonel Broderick as the leader of a nation?"

Branbury looked at the floor and then to the ceiling before answering. "I suppose that would be correct, Ms. Massengale."

Matilda looked at the jury and saw several of them smiling at her.

"Last question, Mr. Branbury. If we took a poll of citizens in Jamaica, don't you know that it would be heavily in favor of the Maroons keeping the land they fought and died for?"

Branbury remained silent, knowing what he thought would be the correct answer but also knowing that he was being paid by Global. The judge saw several of the jurors nodding their agreement.

Lancaster broke the silence. "Ladies and gentlemen, please take a break and stretch your legs. Be back in the jury room in thirty minutes, and we'll do closing arguments at that time. You are excused."

When the jury filed out, Will grabbed Matilda's hand and shook it. "Brilliant, Matilda. Couldn't have gone better if you had prepared for a week. I've been watching the jury. I think we're going to be okay."

At the other table, Alexa Pritchard was proud of their scholar at first and thought they had the case in the bag. Only, once Matilda began her cross-exam, a scowl etched itself on her face that only grew worse as the jury left the room.

The arguments were almost anticlimactic. The judge only allowed fifteen minutes per side. Matilda thought she could have stated their case in about five minutes, but like most lawyers, managed to fill the allotted time. Thomas addressed the jury for Global. Clearly, the wind was out of his sails. He focused on the direct exam of Professor Branbury. When he finished, he returned to his table, shoulders slumped. The jury was out only a half hour before returning with a finding that the treaty was valid and still enforceable.

The courtroom erupted in cheers. Judge Lancaster pounded his gavel until Joshua could restore order. The judge then looked at the jury. "Thank you for your service, ladies and gentlemen. I suspect people will be talking about this trial for a long time. You are now excused."

Once the jury was gone, Gamboa released the audience, who poured out onto the steps of the courthouse. Pritchard followed. Matilda asked Thomas and Henderson to remain behind, since she had a matter to take up with the judge.

"Your Honor, I'm now concerned about what to do with the exhibits. I would ask that we substitute copies to be made a part of the record and permit Ms. Broderick to return the originals to Accompong for safe-keeping, with, of course, the understanding, that they will be available to the court or counsel on reasonable notice."

The judge looked at Thomas and Henderson. "What do you think, gentlemen? We don't have the manpower to watch over these documents while the expected appeal goes forward."

Thomas and Henderson conferred. "With the agreement that Ms. Massengale has just expressed, we agree. And, we do hereby give notice of appeal."

"Then, Judge, I'll bring my camera tomorrow. After that, Joshua can sleep in his own bed."

Matilda and her group walked down the steps of the courthouse and were almost to their cars when they were confronted by Alexa Pritchard. She walked up to Vertise and yelled in her face. "You just remember this is only the first round. I'll see you in Kingston in the Supreme Court."

Vertise maintained her composure, although Will saw her clinch her fists. She replied, "No, Ms. Pritchard, I think you and I will be meeting before that."

Pritchard turned and stomped down the street to where her lawyers were waiting, wondering just what the hell the Maroon bitch was talking about.

CHAPTER 68

Will watched her go. "Typical Alexa. Once the trial's over, she reverts to her old self." He turned to his colleagues. "Come on. Dinner's on me at the Ritz. Join me in an hour."

They helped load Matilda's trial briefcase and another box into her car. Vertise rode with her, back to the house where she left her Volkswagen. Will and Randy Bailey returned to the hotel and parted ways at the elevator. Will was ready to get out of a suit and tie. He changed in a hurry and returned to the first floor, where he ordered a drink at the bar and waited for the others. Bailey was the first to arrive, now dressed in white pants and a golf shirt with the White Witch logo on it.

After he ordered a drink, he said, "I figure this shirt will be the souvenir of one of my most memorable trials. I saw this in the gift shop and started reading about Annie Palmer on the internet. Do you believe all of that stuff, or is it just a convenient legend?"

Will took a sip of his bourbon. "That's one of those stories that has original truth, embellished by legend over time. Do I think she existed? I do. Did she have voodoo powers? There are plenty of people around here who say she did. I wasn't there, so I can't agree or disagree."

They were on their second drink when Matilda and Vertise joined them. Will hugged Matilda and gave Vertise a kiss on the cheek. Randy reached out to shake each of their hands, but Matilda stopped him. "Sorry, we're past the hand-shaking stage. I'll take a hug from you, too."

She wrapped her arms around the little man. He tried to do the same but could only reach to each side of her waist. When she finally released him, he took a deep breath and smiled.

They were escorted to a table, where the ladies ordered drinks—bourbon for Matilda and a Cabernet for Vertise. After they placed their dinner orders, Vertise said, "Look, I know this is a celebration, and I thank all of you for what you've done for my people, but I'm worried. Pritchard claims she sees Chief Justice Cunningham regularly. I've now heard a rumor that he even owns Global stock. Is our jury verdict worth anything in the Supreme Court?"

Matilda reached over and put her large hand over Vertise's. "Now, look here girl, we got our verdict and Lancaster is going to enter the judgment. I'll file it tomorrow. As to Cunningham, I'll start putting out some feelers to see if I can get a sense of what he's thinking."

Vertise sighed and sipped her wine. "That's not very comforting, Matilda. We know that bribes are common in this country. I can get out of a speeding ticket just by slipping the officer a twenty. People in high places aren't paid much money. They figure that they're entitled to money under the table to live the lifestyle they expect. Hell, I've been reading that the United States is now looking the other way when corporations are bribing officials in other countries. Just a cost of doing business. Global could easily wire a million dollars or more to a Cayman bank account in Cunningham's name, and we would never know it. As long as Pritchard is in charge of Global, I'm not going to sleep very well."

After the celebratory dinner, Will walked Matilda and Vertise to the valet stand. Will shook Matilda's hand. "You did a great job. It's certainly a trial I'll always remember." Matilda thanked Will for his help as her car arrived, and said, "I'll take care of getting the judgment entered. Vertise, I'll get copies of the exhibits made and take the originals to my house. I've got a sturdy safe there. You can pick them up or send someone."

Vertise nodded her understanding.

Once Matilda was gone, Will and Vertise had a few minutes alone.

"What are your plans, now?" Vertise asked.

"I'm taking Randy to the airport tomorrow. Then I think I'll lie on the beach for a couple of days, maybe finish that round at the White Witch that was interrupted by the hurricane. Can we have dinner tomorrow, just the two of us?"

Vertise looked away. "I've got some things to do. I'll call you when I have some time."

Will didn't hear from Vertise the next day, nor the next. He spent the morning on the beach and scheduled a tee time for the afternoon, where he was matched with three businessmen from Toledo who were in Jamaica for a conference. After a round of golf where Will was pleased to have shot a seventy-eight, he started down the hill and called Vertise. No answer. It was almost closing at Rose Hall. He parked in front and entered the dungeon bar to find the bartender and two tourists. When he asked about Vertise, the bartender said he hadn't seen her in several days. For some reason, Will found himself drawn outside and around the corner to the tomb of the White Witch. Someone had restored the top of the crypt to its rightful position. He sat on the tomb, hoping the White Witch would not be upset, and wondered about where Vertise had disappeared. The sun was low on the western horizon, casting shadows with its beams breaking through in several places before all was dark. Will was watching the day fade away when he saw something sparkle in one of the last rays of the setting sun. He walked toward what he saw, bent over, and retrieved the object. He immediately recognized it. Vertise had earrings with a small pearl in each. The object was Vertise's earring. What the hell? Why is Vertise's earring here? What was she doing wandering around the White Witch's tomb? Surely, she didn't break into the crypt and steal the dagger. But maybe she did. If so, why? He reached for his cell again and touched her name in the recent list of calls. Again, no answer. He put the earring in his pocket and walked slowly back to his car, trying to make sense of what appeared unexplainable.

CHAPTER 69

Alexa Pritchard was on the phone in her Kingston office. Nothing had gone right since she first arrived over a month ago. It was late at night. She had given up any attempt to look like the president of an international company. She was dressed in jeans, a Global golf shirt, and thongs. The shirt was streaked with sputum from her coughing spells, which she accepted because she needed her cigarettes. The ash tray was overflowing with butts. A bottle of vodka, two-thirds gone, sat beside an empty rocks glass on her desk. "Dammit, don't tell me we can't get another locomotive down here for three months. I don't care about a backlog at the factory. I'll pay a premium. Buy a used one, but I want it down here next week." She slammed the phone into its cradle and fired up another cigarette.

Pritchard glanced at the clock, took one last puff on her cigarette, snubbed it out in the overflowing ash tray, and left her office. She rode the elevator down to the ground level and walked to the front door of the building where she saw her driver, leaning against the fender of her limo, arms folded. His eyes were shut. She pushed the red button beside the door that would permit her to exit late at night. The driver snapped to attention when he heard her approach and moved quickly to open the back door.

Without warning, a black pickup careened around the corner and slammed to a stop behind the limo. Two men leaped out with guns drawn. The driver tried to pull his weapon but was too late. One of the attackers shot him in the chest. As he fell to the ground, Pritchard yelled, "You bastards. Do you know who I am?"

"Shut up, bitch, or you'll have a bullet in you like your driver." The man walked closer and in one motion, threw her to the ground. The other man rolled her over and produced a roll of duct tape that he wrapped around her wrists and ankles. When she continued to scream, he taped her mouth, leaving just enough room for her to breathe through her nose. He went to the driver's side of the limo and popped the trunk. The other man lifted her and tossed her inside. Once the trunk was closed, he checked the limo driver who was alive—barely. He looked at his friend.

"Leave him. Let's get out of here. You drive the limo. I'll follow in the truck."

CHAPTER 70

The sun was setting the next afternoon when Will and a guide returned from a deep-sea fishing trip. They docked the boat. Will tipped the guide well. "Thanks for a great trip. I had no idea we would catch that many."

"My pleasure, Mr. Will. Just sorry we couldn't land that big one you hooked. Maybe another day."

"Yeah, another day. Keep those fish. Your wife and kids will have some good eating tonight."

The guide smiled his thanks.

As Will walked up the dock to the parking lot, he pulled his cell from his pocket now that he once again had service. Miles Harper had tried to call him several times. Without checking messages, he returned the call.

"Taylor, where the hell have you been?"

"Out fishing for the day. What's going on?"

"Pritchard's missing. Her driver was found last night, shot in front of the Global building in Kingston. Her limo is gone. I've had cops looking for her all day. We don't have a clue where she is or even if she's still alive."

Will thought about Vertise's comment about seeing her long before the case got to the Supreme Court. Fingering the pearl earring he still had in his pocket, he said, "I have an idea. I'll let you know if it's right."

Will clicked off the cell with Harper still yelling from the other end. He hurried to his car, climbed in, and reached for the glove compartment where he retrieved his Glock and silencer and put them in the passenger seat. After fastening his seat belt, he burned rubber when he raced from the parking lot.

He pushed the big Suburban as hard as he could on the dark, winding road up to Accompong. He thought about what he would do if he got there and found Pritchard alive, but nothing came to him. He didn't know the situation or her circumstances. He wondered if Vertise was the one that had taken matters into her own hands. He knew that she was worried about Alexa's influence with the Chief Justice. She had gone along with his plan and, so far, it was working. Could she be so worried that she would resort to violence? No way to know until he arrived in the village. Just be prepared for anything.

He rounded a curve and his lights picked up something. "Shit, it's that damn yellow boa again." He swerved to the other side of the road and pushed the vehicle even harder until he felt his rear tires losing traction on a curve. He dropped his speed by ten miles an hour. When he was nearly to Accompong, he saw the road blocked with an old black pickup and two guards pointing guns at him. He screeched to a stop, barely missing one of the guards. He took a few seconds to reach for his gun and fit the silencer to it, then jumped from the Suburban as he stuck the pistol in his waistband.

One of the guards said, "This road is closed. Get your ass back in that truck and haul it back to Montego Bay."

Will said nothing and there was momentary silence, broken only by the sound of night birds.

The second guard moved closer to Will. "Look you bastard, what's going on up there is none of your business. It's a Maroon tribal meeting."

Will shook his head. "And all this time I thought you guys were a nation. Okay, I get the message." He stepped toward the first guard. The guards didn't expect what happened next. He pulled his pistol and, before the guard could react, he saw the pistol six inches from his nose.

"Drop your gun and tell your friend to do the same unless you want to die right here." The guard hesitated. Will pushed his Glock into the guard's face. He dropped his gun and nodded to his friend to do the same. "Let's see what's in the back of this truck," Will said as he kept his gun pointed at the two guards. "Well, I'll be damned. Here's a roll of duct tape. I think I even recognize it."

He walked back to the first guard. "I want you to wrap this tape around the wrists and hands of your friend, then tape his ankles. Tight, you understand?"

The guard nodded and did as he was told.

"Now, I'm going to put this gun on the hood of my truck while I do the same to you. If you resist, I'll promise I'll break your neck before you know what is happening."

The guard chose not to resist while Will taped his hands and feet. "Now, I'm going to tape each of you to the bumper of your truck, one in the front and one in the back so that you can't expect help from the other."

Will dragged each of them to a bumper and wound the tape securely. Satisfied that they could not escape, he took their guns and tossed them over the cliff, smiling as he heard them bounce to the bottom of the ravine.

"Now it's my business."

Will climbed into his Suburban and drove around the truck and went the last hundred yards to Accompong. His lights shone on a locked gates with a sign, VILLAGE CLOSED UNTIL FURTHER NOTICE. Stopping in front of the gates, he checked his weapon, then climbed the gates and dropped to the other side. Before he advanced beyond the gates, he checked carefully for more guards but found none. In the distance, Will heard the sound of drums and saw the glow of a massive fire that had to be in the parking lot close to the Cudjoe Monument. He crept toward the Maroons who were focused on the monument, not concerned about the possible approach of strangers.

The sound of the drums grew louder. The Maroons, both men and women, were no longer dressed in street clothes, but in loin cloths. The women also wore a maroon T-shirt. Someone must have taken the children to another village. The center of attention was Alexa Pritchard, tied to the monument with vines. The Maroons seemed high on something, maybe marijuana, maybe moonshine. They danced around Pritchard. Periodically, one would reach into an urn to take a handful of red bauxite, spit on it, and throw it into Pritchard's face. Alexa was helpless and coughing.

The drums reached a crescendo and stopped. Vertise stepped from the darkness behind the monument, dressed in a red gown with a gold cross hanging from her neck. Will studied her carefully. She appeared to be in a trance. She moved slowly. Her unblinking eyes stared straight ahead to a giant black man whose face was painted white. She kneeled in front of him.

In a loud bass voice, he said, "We are here to celebrate the consecration of our *Obeah* Priestess. Her name among the tribe from this night forward is Makayla, one with God." He picked a small earthen cup from the ground. "Rise to your feet, Makayla. This is the blood from a freshly slaughtered goat. Drink," he commanded.

Vertise took the cup, raised it over her head, then tilted it to her mouth and turned it over for all to see that it was empty before she handed it back to the elder. She spoke.

"My name is Makayla. I was trained by my father to be an *Obeah*. I can trace my *Obeah* lineage from him all the way back to the overseer who killed the White Witch of Rose Hall two hundred years ago. I can hug the sun. I can kiss the moon. I can bring down the stars. I can bring forth lightning with my fingers." She raised her hands into the air and pointed toward the distant mountains. Suddenly lightening crackled above the mountains and a star shot across the sky.

The crowd shouted, "Makayla, Makayla, *Obeah* Princess, our leader!"

Vertise raised her hands for silence as the man beside her offered another cup of goat's blood. "My father served as your colonel and priest for forty years, and now he is gone. I learned at his feet. I am young and expect to be your priestess and leader for much longer than my father. For three hundred years we have lived in peace. That peaceful existence may be coming to an end because of this woman."

Pritchard's look of defiance had faded and been replaced by one of fear.

"Let me go," she mumbled. "I promise to leave the island and never return. The Cockpit Country is yours."

"No, no. You do not speak the truth. You are the reincarnation of Jamaica's White Witch. Your deeds in our country can lead to no other conclusion." Vertise threw the cup of goat's blood into her face. Pritchard could do nothing but let it drip into her eyes and down her cheeks.

"We all know," Vertise continued, "the White Witch was never buried in the *Obeah* manner. That has permitted her to come back to our country in the form of this woman to destroy our land and our people. This wasn't her land in 1800. It is not her land now. With her own dagger I, an *Obeah* Priestess, will finally send her back to her grave."

The third dagger with its gleaming ruby eyes, mysteriously appeared from the folds of the red gown. Vertise took two steps toward Pritchard and raised the dagger over her head. Before she could bring it down to drive it into Pritchard's heart, a metal on metal ping was heard and the dagger flew from her hand to the ground.

The Maroons started backing up, astonished, frightened, and mumbling among themselves.

"This woman must really be the reincarnation of the White Witch."

"She just used her power to make the dagger fly out of Makayla's hand."

Vertise snapped from her trance and walked over to pick up the dagger.

"Stop!" Will yelled as he made his way down the hill, holding his Glock in his right hand. Uncertain what to do, the Maroons scattered and let him approach Vertise. He had just shot the dagger from her hand. No magic, just good training.

"Will, what are you doing here? I can handle this," Vertise said, shocked that Will was standing in Accompong before her, interrupting a sacred Maroon ceremony.

"I saw how you were trying to handle it. Whatever Alexa may have done, it's a matter for law enforcement, not you."

"No. She's a murderer. You know that. She's going to destroy Jamaica and my people."

Will took a machete from one of the Maroons and cut the vines binding Pritchard. She leaned against the monument for a few moments, and then stood upright with a scowl on her face, her confidence restored when Will came on the scene. She looked at Will. "Get me off this goddamn mountain. I'm willing to face a judge in Montego Bay like you just said, not this pack of savages. She turned to Vertise and the Maroons and said, "You are all going to pay for this. Am I a murderer? This is war. I have mercenaries on this island right now. Forget about what I said about leaving the island. I've just changed my mind. Global is going full speed ahead with an appeal and will open the mine as soon as Chief Justice Cunningham and his court rule in our favor."

Vertise shoved her back against the boulder. "You're not going anywhere. Lawrence, you and Jorell hold her against the monument."

Will looked as Jorell stepped from the crowd. So, now the puzzle was starting to fit together. Jorell must have been at the mansion the night Kaven was killed. He must have known a way to get inside without being detected. Maybe he knew where the key was hidden, just as Vertise did. So, maybe one of the murders is solved.

While Will was trying to understand what happened at the mansion, Robert, a Maroon who played for a semi-professional cricket team in Montego Bay, was in the back of the crowd, his eyes studying the ground. When he saw what he was looking for, he reached for a rock about the size of a baseball. When he saw an opening between him and Taylor, he threw the rock at Will, striking him in the forehead. Will slumped to the ground.

Jorell and Lawrence forced Pritchard against the monument. "Admit it,"

Vertise demanded. "You had Kaven killed, and Snyder, and my father."

"I'm not admitting a damn thing to you, bitch."

"Then, we'll do it the hard way. Aaron, step forward."

Aaron moved from the shadows with one of his snakes wrapped around his right arm, its head in his hand, fangs bared and hissing. As he approached Pritchard with the snake, her screams pierced the air, echoing among the houses the closer Aaron came.

"Get that snake away from me, please," she whimpered. "Then, I'll talk."

Vertise nodded at Aaron who backed away a few feet. "Wise decision, Ms. Pritchard. One bite from that snake and you would have experienced a very painful death."

Alexa took a deep breath. "I don't know anything about Kaven's death."

Through the fog that was temporarily clouding his brain, Will heard the screams and pushed to a sitting position, found his gun beside him, and tried to get to his feet, only to feel his legs buckling under him. He sized up the situation, realizing he needed another minute or two to clear his brain and get control of his arms and legs.

"I figured that some of your Maroons did that," she continued. "I had to have Snyder killed. I paid him $500,000 and got nothing but a worthless piece of paper. He knew too much." She paused to take another breath. "Rodney hacked into our servers and learned information he had no business knowing. I knew he had to be eliminated. Too bad he lived. There, are you satisfied?"

"Not quite," Vertise said. "Aaron, maybe you better step closer." Vertise turned back to Pritchard. "What about my father?"

Pritchard slumped, and her shoulders sagged. "Yes," she murmured. "Please keep that snake away from me."

"Louder," Vertise demanded.

"Yes, I arranged for the sniper. Is that enough?"

"Not quite. How did you get the second snake dagger used on Snyder, and why?"

A slight smile actually crossed Pritchard's face. "

"I wanted to make it look like it was the Maroons getting revenge for what Snyder did. I learned that your people were trading ganja for guns. I had someone track down the head gunrunner. Paid that guy $20,000 to have one of your Maroons locate and steal the knife." She nodded toward Lawrence. "I suspected it was somewhere up here. I'll bet he could tell us. Of course, he might have just taken his share of the money and used the knife on Snyder himself. Made no difference to me, as long as it happened. Life is cheap on this island. It was a good plan, but I obviously made a mistake in having Colonel Broderick killed. Otherwise, I probably would have gotten away with it."

Pritchard had been eyeing the dagger on the ground as she talked. When she saw that Jorell was distracted by the discussion about the murder at the mansion, she pulled away from the monument and seized the snake dagger. She lunged for Vertise, but tripped on the uneven ground and could only stab Vertise in the side. Vertise collapsed. Will saw that Alexa had pulled the dagger from Vertise's side and was standing over Vertise, intending to finish her off. The Maroons were paralyzed, uncertain as to whether Pritchard was really the White Witch. Will had to do something. He forced himself to his feet and saw that Alexa had kicked Vertise onto her back. Will was trying to aim his gun, but his hand was shaking. Alexa brought the dagger into the air when a bullet hit her in the shoulder. The dagger hit the ground and bounced several feet away. The sound of the shot reverberated through the mountains as Miles Harper broke through the Maroons. "Okay, this is now over. Everybody settle down."

"How the hell did you get here?" Will asked.

"Same as you. Pritchard had to be either six fathoms deep in the ocean or up here."

"Harper, you told me yourself that you don't have any authority in this town."

"I do now. I just heard Pritchard's confession. That makes this a murder investigation."

"Wait just a damn minute, Harper," Pritchard said. "I didn't confess to anything. I was under duress. I had a poisonous snake at my neck, for God's sake. I was willing to say anything. No jury will ever convict me if that is all you have."

"Come on, Ms. Pritchard," Harper sneered. "We may not be as sophisticated as your F.B.I., but we haven't just been sitting on our hands. With a little help from our friends in London, we have traced that $500,000 from Global to Snyder's bank account. And we talked to Gore the afternoon before he left. He'll testify about all of those other public officials you've bribed." He looked around at the Maroons. "I figure I've got about a hundred witnesses to your confession. Ought to be enough evidence to send you to the gallows. Matter of fact, just for good measure, I'm going to appoint Matilda Massengale as special prosecutor."

Vertise had gotten to her feet and listened to what was being said. In a seeming moment of compassion, Vertise helped Pritchard up and assisted her to sit on one of the rocks that served as the border around the monument. Will watched, wondering what had come over her, when she whirled and walked three feet to the dagger where she extended her hand. Will blinked his eyes. The dagger appeared to rise to her hand. Surely, it was his imagination. Vertise started to grasp the dagger, then hesitated. The dagger went beyond her hand and seemed to float in the air.

"Vertise; don't do it." Will shouted as he lunged for her and knocked her to the ground. The dagger fell harmlessly beside her.

Will helped Vertise to her feet and took the dagger from the ground. Harper pulled Pritchard to her feet and handcuffed her before holding a hand out to Will. "Give it to me."

Will handed him the dagger.

The drums and chanting started again. They grew louder until Harper fired three shots into the air. "I told you this was over. Go back to your homes and don't come out until daylight. Go on now. Get the hell out of here."

The crowd slowly dispersed. Harper turned to Vertise. "Is that wound serious?"

Vertise shook her head. "No, she was too weak to do any real harm. It's not much more than a scratch. I'll put a poultice on it. I'll be fine."

"Then get it done. And get out of that red gown. I need you back here in five minutes."

Will and Harper watched her walk away. "Miles, a Maroon named Jorell probably killed Kaven. He works at the mansion. He's not likely to confess, but you might take his fingerprints and compare them to the knife that was in Kaven's chest."

Harper nodded his understanding.

"And there's one more loose end. I think I know where those mercenaries are staying. We need to neutralize them." Will explained that they were in the motel east of the Ritz. Just as he finished, Vertise returned dressed in jeans, Nikes, and a green T-shirt with *MARROON WARRIORS* across the front.

"Vertise, Will and I are going to arrest those mercenaries," Harper said. "I need you to stay here to make sure that none of your Maroons interfere. Use some of those magic powers, if you have to."

"No, Vertise said. "If one of them killed my dad, I want to be there."

Will stepped between them. "Look, I understand what you're saying, but we can't risk Lawrence and Aaron and the others interfering with our operation. Give us about three hours. We'll take them dead or alive. Hopefully alive, since they may want to testify against Pritchard to save themselves. You'll be more useful right here."

Vertise dropped her gaze to the ground and slowly looked up until her eyes were locked on Will's. "All right. I'll do it. Just don't fail me."

Will smiled his agreement as he pulled Vertise to him. "You have my solemn word." He turned to Harper, who was checking Pritchard's shoulder wound.

"Flesh only. She'll live," he said as he put his hands on Pritchard's cuffs and began pushing her to his car. Then he stopped and looked back at Vertise. "I need someone to unlock the gates."

Vertise pulled a key from her pocket and caught up to them. "I figured you would need this," As Will and Harper led Pritchard away, Vertise yelled, "You are cursed, Alexa Prichard. You are going to hang from a gallows like so many of my ancestors did on the White Witch's plantation!"

When they got to the cars, Harper forced Pritchard into the back seat and turned to Will. "I'll call ahead and have two jailers in front of the police station waiting for me. I'll also have six officers armed with AK-47s. Go on to the motel, but stay in the parking lot until we get there. Shouldn't be more than ten minutes behind you. We'll be coming without lights and sirens. If you see anyone trying to leave, follow them and call me. Don't try anything else. Understood?"

"It's your operation, Chief. I can follow orders."

***

Will turned his lights off as he approached the motel and pulled to the side of the road. He watched his rearview mirror until he saw four cars approach. They also darkened their lights as they fell in behind him. Harper walked up to his window. "You and I will drive up to the front of the motel to get their room numbers. Then, I'll direct my men. I have an extra AK-47. You want it?"

"Thanks, Miles, but I'm comfortable with my Glock at close range."

The two men entered a shabby reception area. A night clerk came from a room behind the desk. "Help you gentlemen?"

"Looking for some men—big guys, tattoos, probably three or four of them,"

Harper said.

"One of them has his black hair in a flattop," Will added.

"Sorry, but I can't help you," the clerk said.

Harper pulled his credentials at the same time as Will seized the clerk's tie and dragged him halfway across the counter.

"Young man, I am Miles Harper, chief of detectives in this parish. Do I need to ask that question again?"

"Sir, you're choking me. Please let me stand up and I'll tell you anything you want." Will released the tie and the clerk was able to stand. "They are in rooms 114 to 117."

"The guy with the flattop, which one is he in?"

"117, sir."

"These men are wanted for murder," Harper said. "You go back to your office and shut the door. If I learn you have tried to contact them, you'll be doing ten to twenty. Got it?"

"Yes. Yes, sir."

They walked back to the cars. "I've got you a mic and an earbud. We can all hear and talk to each other.

"Miles, I want Buzz."

"Okay with me, but we have seven officers along with you. I'll have one of my guys up against the wall by his door, just for good measure."

Will and the officer walked to Room 117. Will glanced down the row of rooms to make sure that two officers were at the other three doors. Harper positioned himself in the parking lot with an AK-47, ready to assist where needed.

Will knocked loudly on the door. Buzz, dressed in jeans, no shirt and no shoes opened it, a beer in his hand. "Will, what are you doing here this time of night? You want a beer?"

"It's over, Buzz. Alexa's in custody. She's ready to sing like a bird if it'll save her life."

Buzz blinked his eyes. "Sorry, let me get a cigarette." He turned. Will forced his Glock in Buzz's back. "You're not going anywhere. Miles, tell the others to bust down the doors. The next thing he heard were large boots splintering hollow, plywood doors. Shouts followed and two or three shots.

"Report," Harper ordered. Each of his men said they had their room occupant in custody. One of the mercenaries had a wound in his shoulder. Then the officers in room 114 stepped out, pushing a mercenary in front of them. "Chief, we found a sniper rifle in there."

"Secure it and bag it. We'll probably find a match to the round that killed Colonel Broderick. Lock him in the back of your car. We'll question him first. Buzz is second. My guess is they'll roll over on Pritchard pretty damn quick if they know they will live."

Harper turned to Will, his hand extended. "Couldn't have done it without you. You have my thanks and the thanks of my country. Are you heading back to the states? If so, I'd like to get a statement first."

"I'll call you tomorrow."

"And Will," Harper said, "Now that this is over, ditch that Glock. I don't want the airport police finding it."

Will reached into his waistband and handed the Glock to Harper. "With my compliments."

CHAPTER 71

Will was folding his clothes and placing them in his suitcase. The door to the hallway was open and the television was tuned to CNN. The newscaster was discussing the events in Jamaica and the arrest of Alexa Pritchard for murder. The screen shifted to Alfred St. John, Global's CEO, who was speaking. "Yes, Mary, we are shutting down any mining efforts in the Cockpit Country. Today, I have instructed our Jamaican lawyers to advise Judge Lancaster that we are accepting the decision of the jury and his judgment that the treaty is valid. We will not be appealing that judgment to the Supreme Court."

"Two more questions, Mr. St. John. First, we know that you have been fighting cancer for two years. How are you doing? Second, can you comment about Alexa Pritchard?"

St. John smiled. "I can answer the first one. I'm feeling much better. I am going to resume full time duties with Global and will be interim president as well as continuing to act as CEO. As to Ms. Pritchard, we have had no contact with her. I presume she will have a lawyer who can speak for her in due time."

"What, were you just going to go off and leave me without even a goodbye?" Vertise said. Will turned to find her leaning against the doorway, dressed in a green blouse and white skirt. She stepped into the room, closing the door behind her. "You now know I'm an *Obeah* woman and have magic powers. For example, I have a cure for that goose egg on your forehead."

Vertise walked to Will and stood on her tiptoes to kiss the goose egg. "Tomorrow it will be gone."

Will took her in his arms and kissed her gently and slowly. Then, he stepped back. "Now, if you'll just let me get in a word edgewise, I wasn't going anywhere without finding you first. You weren't answering your phone. If you hadn't showed up here, I would have been on my way up to Accompong,"

Vertise reached into her pocket and retrieved her phone. "Hmm, battery's dead. You're forgiven."

"Now, I have a question. Last night, I'm almost positive that I saw you levitate that snake knife, but it went past your hand and floated above it. Did you do that, and if so, why?"

Vertise smiled coyly. "Well, it could be that what you saw occurred. Maybe I started for the knife and changed my mind. If I had killed Alexa, I would have been no better than her. Maybe I had a premonition that there would be enough evidence to see her hang." She smiled again. "Or maybe I don't have any magic powers and you just imagined all of that. Believe what you choose."

Will shook his head. "As to Alexa, Harper called me this morning. After our raid at the motel, those guys are climbing over each other to blame everything on Alexa. No doubt she will get the death penalty. As to magical powers, I don't think I need to believe a thing. I told you from the beginning that all this occult stuff, including *Obeah,* was just a bunch of bull."

Vertise stepped to Will and wrapped her arms around his waist. "Why are you packing?"

"The CEO wants me back in Maryland for a couple of days for debriefing. I figure I owe him that much. Then I'll be back here. You're looking at the President and owner of Caribbean Investigations, home office in Montego Bay. At your service, ma'am."

Vertise kissed him. "Then, if you can postpone leaving until tomorrow, I'm in need of some services."

"I suppose I can tell the CEO that I still need to talk with Harper. Besides, I've never been under the spell of a voodoo priestess."

"I'm only Makayla once a year for the tribal meeting. Standing here in front of you is Vertise."

Will turned off the television and walked to the balcony doors to pull the curtains. When he turned back, he found Vertise doing a slow, sexual striptease, reminiscent of Annie Palmer two hundred years before. She twirled to step out of her panties and Will got his second look at the snake dagger tattoo. He pulled her to him and put both hands on her butt.

"So, let's just see what magic you can conjure up with that dagger."

AUTHOR'S NOTE

First, based on my research, Annie Palmer, the *White Witch,* did live in the 1800s. As Vertise said, the stories that swirl around her today are partly real and much legend. It was not my goal to separate out the two parts.

Second, there is no doubt that the Maroons continue to live up in the mountains. They did actually fight the Spaniards and the British for about two hundred years. No one questions the treaty or that it exists. It can be read on line and I have read the one on the wall in the Community Hall in Accompong. Some scholars do question its validity, and academics have studied it, some saying it is no longer valid and some saying it continues to be binding. I choose to believe the latter. Frankly, the Maroons fought and died for that land and they should have dominion over it.

Then, I must add a word of thanks to Johnny Cash. I used a few lyrics from his *Ballad of Annie Palmer* at the beginning. I tried every way I could think of to get permission from his estate, but never received a response. So, I hope his estate will sell a few more copies of the ballad.

Special thanks go to my son, Kel Thompson, a really great movie director and photographer. He came back from a job in Montego Bay several years ago and told me about the the *White Witch.* Shortly thereafter, he and I spent five days in Montego Bay, digging into the story. We stayed at the Ritz, played the White Witch Golf course, and against advice of several people, drove to Accompong and talked to the Colonel and a number of his associates. And, of course, we toured the Rose Hall Mansion.

Now, a request for a favor from you, the reader. We writers spend much time researching and writing stories like this. We always hope to sell many copies. Even though we write a good story, if readers don't talk about it and stir up interest, we won't succeed. For that reason, I ask that if you like my tale, please go on Amazon or any other site that accepts reviews and say a few kind words. I will appreciate it and promise to keep turning out more stories that will be equally as good, maybe even better.

LARRY D. THOMPSON

ABOUT LARRY D. THOMPSON

After graduating from the University of Texas School of Law, Larry spent the first half of his professional life as a trial lawyer. He tried well over 300 cases and won more than 95% of them. Although he had not taken a writing class since freshman English (back when they wrote on stone tablets), he figured that he had read enough novels and knew enough about trials, lawyers, judges, and courtrooms that he could do it. Besides, his late, older brother, Thomas Thompson, was one of the best true crime writers to ever set a pen to paper; so, just maybe, there was something in the Thompson gene pool that would be guide him into this new career. He started writing his first novel about a dozen years ago and published it a couple of years thereafter. He has now written five highly acclaimed legal thrillers. *White Witch* is number six with many more to come.

Larry is married to his wife, Vicki. He has three children scattered from Colorado to Austin to Boca Raton, and four grandchildren. He has been trying to retire from the law practice to devote full time to writing. Hopefully, that will occur by the end of 2018. He still lives in Houston, but spends his summers in Vail CO, high on a mountain where he is inspired by the beauty of the Rocky Mountains.